where *the* light gets in

where *the* light gets in

ZOË COYLE

ultimo press

Published in 2022 by Ultimo Press,
an imprint of Hardie Grant Publishing

Ultimo Press
Gadigal Country
7, 45 Jones Street
Ultimo, NSW 2007
ultimopress.com.au

Ultimo Press (London)
5th & 6th Floors
52–54 Southwark Street
London SE1 1UN

A catalogue record for this work is available from the National Library of Australia

Where the Light Gets In
ISBN 978 1 76115 001 2 (paperback)

10 9 8 7 6 5 4 3 2 1

Cover design Amy Daoud
Cover photograph Jacob Mejicanos/Unsplash
Typesetting Kirby Jones | Typeset in 12/15 pt Adobe Garamond Pro
Copyeditor Jody Lee

Printed in Australia by Griffin Press, part of Ovato, an Accredited ISO AS/NZS 14001 Environmental Management System printer.

MIX Paper from responsible sources FSC® C009448

The paper this book is printed on is certified against the Forest Stewardship Council® Standards. Griffin Press holds FSC® chain of custody certification SGSHK-COC-005088. FSC® promotes environmentally responsible, socially beneficial and economically viable management of the world's forests.

Ultimo Press acknowledges the Traditional Owners of the country on which we work, the Gadigal people of the Eora nation and the Wurundjeri people of the Kulin nation, and recognises their continuing connection to the land, waters and culture. We pay our respects to their Elders past and present.

For my mother, whom I loved first.
And for Martin, whom I will love forever.

There's a crack in everything.
That's how the light gets in.
– Leonard Cohen

Kintsugi is the 'golden repair' or 'the art of precious scars'. The Japanese practice of mending broken ceramics with gold. Rendering the repaired object, with its golden fractures, more beautiful than the original.

Metanoia
Meh-ta-noy-ah (from the Greek)
1. (n.) the journey of changing one's mind, heart, self or way of life.
2. (v.) the act of reforming; becoming new.

2019

CHAPTER 1

Delphi flushes with feeling looking at her mother's handwriting. Once it was beautiful and elegant, but now it's wobbly and deranged. As if done in a child's hand with the innocence swapped out for desperation. Vivian has a terminal degenerative disease. It's killing her. Incrementally destroying her capacity to move, to swallow, to hold her eyes open and to write. The words slop around the page and fall off the lines.

Darling girl,
Hurry to me.
Things fall apart.
The centre cannot hold.
All my love,
Mummy.

William Butler Yeats. Vivian used to read poetry to Delphi and her brothers instead of bedtime stories. Other children were offered *The Very Hungry Caterpillar*, but in her household it was 'Desiderata' or 'The Second Coming'. Delphi thinks of the poem's final lines.

And what rough beast, its hour come round at last, slouches towards Bethlehem to be born?

She lifts her mother's letter to study the printed page behind it. A flight reservation in Delphi's name. London to Australia for the following week.

*

Delphi pulls off her clothes and hunts about in her bedroom cupboard for a nightie. The one she wants belonged to her mother when Delphi was a child. It's made of flannel, old-fashioned and falls loosely to the ankle. It's the softest shade of blue with bunches of flowers all over it. Delphi finds it within the tangled mess and holds it to her face and inhales. Impossible for it to smell of her mother all these years later but Delphi finds the attempt, however futile, comforting and has done it countless times. She pulls it on, clicks off the lamp and folds down into her bed in the blackness. As her body stills, Delphi's internal organs settle. She blinks unseeing. She is making space, paying attention, and her emotional cartography evolves to map the deep valley of dread. She doesn't want to face it. She doesn't want to go, to make it all real. Paradoxically she holds a second truth too. She craves her mother. She wants to be brave for her. She wants to be a good daughter. She wants to help.

Delphi finds the hard edge and she softens. She decides that she will go. Of course, she will go. The rules of love are clear. You turn up whatever the cost.

*

Having given up on sleep, Delphi inhales deeply on the joint and holds the smoke as long as she can before slowly releasing it into the night. She loves sitting up here. She has to climb out of the kitchen window, along the ledge, then pull herself up to this little patch of roof. Her oasis. No stars but she knows they're up there, way above the pollution, clouds and city lights. She still believes they're up there, even though she can't see them and that makes Delphi think about faith and love. She smooths the nightie down over her freezing legs and shivers.

*

Outside her bedroom window, London in the morning sparkles with precious winter sunshine. The curtain rail hangs sideways down the wall as if it has given up. Delphi has asked her landlord to have it fixed to no avail. She loves this room in her funny little Camden apartment.

Delphi opens her laptop and watches it fire up. She takes a sip of tea as she scrolls through her emails. She's punching delete judiciously and will swoop back to open the survivors. She takes another sip from her favourite cup, avoiding the chip in its rim. Delphi stops scrolling and pauses, reading and then re-reading. *Horizon Art Studio.*

Since she left art school Delphi has applied for countless jobs in nearly every art gallery and studio in the city. Her applications have been ignored or refused. She's never been granted entrance to the citadel. She seldom paints as she can't afford the canvases nor the self-hatred. Also, despite her efforts to budget each week she blows her meagre waitressing salary going out on the lash with her friends and buying second-hand books.

Delphi once read about an experiment where rats were put in a bucket of water and had to swim for their lives. They didn't last long before they gave up and drowned. But if a rat was taken out of the water, close to exhaustion, then put back in, it would swim on, renewed, revitalised. Sometimes those poor rodents would swim for days. Hope. The rats would swim longer because they had been given hope.

Delphi clicks the email open and controls her exhalation.

Hello Delphi,

Thanks so much for your application regarding the advertised job to be Orlo's assistant. Sorry we've been slow coming back to you. Your references check out really well, and Orlo would love you to pop in tomorrow to see if you're a good fit.

Please let me know ASAP.

Kind regards,
Emma Moorfield
Horizon Art

Delphi's smile radiates gold throughout her body and she emails back that she would love the opportunity to meet. She shuts her laptop and falls back on her bed. Doors opening are much more fun than them closing. She fizzes with excitement.

CHAPTER 2

DELPHI DOUBLE CHECKS THE address and pushes the big steel door open and goes in. Navigation is not one of her skills and she spends an inordinate amount of time lost. Inside the space is large, a converted warehouse, whitewashed walls, empty of people, and canvases of all sizes are propped against the walls. BBC4 is playing somewhere.

'Hello?' Delphi calls. An old dog totters forward on bandy legs to welcome her. Delphi squats down to give him a pat. He's a cocktail of breeds with a sweet face and broad head. Delphi rubs between his ears. When he trusts her she shepherds him into her arms and cuddles him. He smells like corn chips.

'It says good things about you if Jeremiah lets you do that to him.' Delphi looks up and sees a man descending the stairs to her left. He's wearing denim overalls, splattered in paint. She can't see his face properly as he's backlit.

Delphi stands and introduces herself. 'Hello, I'm Delphi Hoffman, I'm here to meet Orlo.'

The man is cleaning a paintbrush with a rag. He nods his head. 'Hello, yes, that's me.' He steps down the last two risers, crosses the space and shakes her hand.

He resembles a lion. Aslan. He has a beard and straw-coloured hair pulled back at the nape of his neck.

'Hello,' she says again, repeating herself.

'Come up and talk to me?' He turns back towards the stairs. 'Tell me about yourself.'

Delphi takes a moment to press her hand against her heart to encourage it to stay put within her ribs. The action is so adolescent that she has to suppress a laugh. Physical beauty is just winning the genetic lottery, she reminds herself. As her mother would say, *It's not an achievement, nor an indicator of virtue.*

'Well, I graduated from the University of Arts two years ago, before that I read Art History for a bit at Bristol. You trained at Slade, right, and also Paris College of Art?'

'Uh mmm,' he responds, looking back to her as he rounds the top of the stairs.

Delphi skips lightly on, filling the silence. 'I waitress to survive. I don't have any family left in London. I have a grandfather in Berkshire whom I see as often as I can. My mama moved to Australia a decade ago, my big brother is in Paris, so pretty much everyone important has scattered into the wind.'

'And your father?'

'Ah, he's remarried and I'm pretty sure he lives in Berkshire too.'

'You're pretty sure?' he asks wryly.

She nods.

The silence falls between them like leaves.

He smiles. He's playful.

Delphi flushes with a red-tinctured ache. She moves through with more words. 'I read. I love films. I try to meditate every day. My friends are really important to me. I probably go out too much. I'm not good at saving money. I live in a tiny apartment in Camden. Um, what else… I think that's pretty much it.'

'Where were you born?'

'Berkshire, well, technically Reading. This feels oddly formal, doesn't it? And rudely one sided.'

'Oh, I'm sorry,' he says.

'No, not you being rude, me,' she stammers. 'Where were you born?'

He is looking at Delphi, studying the fall of the light on her.

'Me? I was born in India. My parents were diplomats.'

'I watched a documentary about the hospital system there just the other day and it looked frightening.'

'It's better now, if you're lucky enough to be able to pay. My birth was pretty traumatic so they chose to have my little sister back in the UK, but we lived in Delhi until I was eight, then we moved to France for a few years before we came here for me to have a British education and all that guff. Tell me about your art.'

'I'm not really painting at the moment, which is weird, maybe I'm stagnating, but I've wanted to be an artist for as long as I can remember.'

He is so present with her that she's derailed by the intimacy of his attention.

She gestures to the huge canvas that he's working on. A rugged coastal landscape in greens and blues.

'That's very beautiful,' Delphi says truthfully. Together they stare at the painting.

'Thank you,' he answers. 'It's for a show in Germany. It's not quite home yet, but maybe it's close. I find it hard to know where the end lives.'

'Where the end lives? That's an interesting way to phrase it.' She steps closer to the painting. 'I think the end is where we are when we're without love. Home is the opposite.'

Orlo considers what she's said and smiles broadly. The quality of the air changes. It begins to dance.

*

He looks at the clock on the wall, which only has one hand yet he deciphers the time from its denuded face.

'Hey, you've been here for hours,' he says. 'It's been lovely talking to you. Do please take the job if you'd like to. It won't be very interesting, I'm afraid, but God knows I could use the help.'

Delphi thinks how disappointed her mother will be, but surely she can't say no to this. This job makes sense of her life. This changes

London from a lock she's trying to crack to an open doorway. And Orlo is a brilliant artist. Just to be in his proximity, to learn from him, to be around him. He is her conduit back into a truly creative world. With this job she will have the bandwidth to paint again. There may even be a space for her in the studio. An artist's assistant isn't like getting her own agent, but it's in the right neck of the woods. She senses she's metaphorically and literally in the correct room.

'Oh amazing, thank you. When would you need me to start?'

'As soon as possible, tomorrow? When would work for you?'

Sod's law.

'Can I have a night to think about it? I want the job, but I have a thing… with my mother.' Delphi is agitated that this precious opportunity is infused with a possibly fatal complication.

'Sure, sure,' he says lightly as he goes to a paint-streaked sink to wash his hands in methylated spirits and then soap and water. She wants to step towards him and run her hand down his spine.

'Thank you for your time, Delphi. Let me know soon. I have another interview tomorrow afternoon.' He turns around and dries his hands on his overalls.

'Yes, of course.' She bends to pick up her bag.

'Hey, when you're painting what's your work like?' he asks.

Straightening up she doesn't quite hear him. 'Sorry, what did you say?'

'Your painting? What style is it?'

'Oh,' she is embarrassed, as if she's being asked about a lover she's irrationally neglected. 'Figurative.'

He nods; this confirms something for him. 'And the predominant subject matter?'

She takes a moment. 'What interests me is the human form. It's all about people for me. About how they interrelate and connect. Who they love and how they love.'

'And for me it's all about place. I wonder what that means was missing from our childhoods?'

They regard each other and Delphi listens to the tin of the roof ticking as it contracts. When she can no longer hold her half of what is alive between them, she starts to laugh. Orlo laughs too. She rights herself and they make eye contact; both of them peel off in arcs of more laughter.

It dissipates and they stand in front of each other, sparkling.

'Well...' she says.

'Well...' he responds.

She turns to leave and walks into the arm of a dilapidated sofa and nearly falls. It makes a screeching sound as it shifts. She shoves it back into place and forces herself to look at Orlo to say goodbye. He looks at her, amused.

'I seem to have forgotten how to walk,' she blusters, setting off towards the stairs.

'I'll show you out.'

'No, thank you.' She waves her arm. 'It's always important for a woman to know where the way out is.'

'Why?' he calls as he picks up Jeramiah and cuddles him.

She pauses at the top of the stairs, looking back at him. 'Umm, it's hard to explain. I guess the answer to that can be found in my childhood too.'

She sets off down the stairs and at the bottom she clasps her hands over her mouth and spins around, exhilarated. She struggles a little with the heavy door out to the street and looks back to see Orlo watching her from the top of the stairs, smiling, the dog still in his arms.

CHAPTER 3

VIVIAN ANSWERS DELPHI'S SKYPE call in a flurry of 'I'm here, yes, I'm answering' but is holding the iPad to her head so all Delphi can see on the screen is the side of her mother's face.

'Mama, this is Skype. I'm looking at your ear.'

'What, darling girl? I can hear you,' Vivian responds as if talking to someone on the moon or at the bottom of the ocean.

'Mama, take the screen away from your face and look at me.'

Vivian fumbles as she follows the instructions. When she focuses on her daughter her harried face blossoms with ebullience and love.

Vivian is sixty-one and she's a force, at least she was before she was ravaged by the disease. Now she looks soft, diluted, her blue eyes milky, her once beautiful face strangely fuzzy as if she's defused, floating atom by atom from her mortal body.

Delphi is shocked to see her mother. The deterioration is evident.

'Delphi, my flower, how are you, darling? Are you eating enough?' Vivian is wearing a pink dressing-gown, no make-up. She pushes a lock of lank hair back from her face. Delphi notices she isn't wearing any of her jewellery. As a child Delphi loved hearing her mother's bangles clink as she moved about the house. Always glamorous, always bejewelled and made up. Delphi would lie on the floor and watch her mother sitting at her dressing table. A row of lights surrounding the mirror, like a 1950s film star. Her mother would begin by saying, 'Okay, it's time to put my face on,' and when she applied mascara to one eye, she would turn to Delphi twinkling and declare, 'One big eye and one small eye,' and they would guffaw together.

'Where is your jewellery, Mama?'

'Oh love, it got too much for me.'

Delphi is marbled with anguish. Her mother looks denuded, diminished as if parts of her have been erased. Maybe this is how death comes, bit by bit. Taking one chunk and then coming back for another.

'Are those prayer beads you're wearing, my flower?'

Delphi loops her fingers through them. 'Yep. Tiger's eye. They're pretty, aren't they?'

'They are. Very Eastern.' Vivian rolls her eyes and Delphi laughs.

'My flower, I can't wait to see you.' Vivian has called Delphi this nickname since she was tiny, sometimes she uses it in the French, *ma petite fleur*, and Delphi longs to put her head in her mother's lap.

'Mama, about that… I know it's been too long, thank you, thank you for the ticket, it's so generous of you, but, Mama, I've just landed the most amazing job as an art assistant at Horizon for Orlo Corwin, do you know his work? Orlando Corwin. You'd love it.' Delphi races on. 'And I will come to see you, I so want to come, but now the timing…'

Delphi pauses to focus on her mother's response, but there is none. Vivian is passive, waiting, detached.

'What about I come in a few months? Would that work for you? Then I can lock the job in and negotiate a long holiday down the track to be with you. This is the break I've been waiting for, Mama.'

Vivian puts a hand to her mouth and looks steadily out of the screen. Delphi nervously picks some dead skin off her thumbnail. She can't get it free so tries using her teeth.

Vivian, blinking, floating, watches.

'Mama? Are you thinking? Are you mad? Do you understand?'

Vivian drops her hand and responds steadily. 'Delphi, darling girl, I am unwell. I'm worn out. I'm done. I am asking you to come to me now. It has to be now, my flower, *do you* understand?'

And Delphi does.

'It is time, *ma petite fleur*.'

When Vivian was diagnosed she told the family she had no intention of letting the disease kill her in its own perverse time. She would euthanise before all dignity was stripped from her. Delphi, in theory, stands in solidarity, but dark foreboding begins to settle on her head and shoulders like volcanic ash. With each breath it becomes heavier, pressing its way down through Delphi's body, colonising her heart, her belly and turning her insides black.

'Delphi, I've decided and I might need your help. So please just get on the plane and I shall see you next week.'

Then an explosion of a dog barking, Pilot, her mother's ancient dachshund, raging at the doorbell.

'I have to go, Delphi. It takes me an age to get to the door now and Pilot has declared that the postman is here or some unfortunate trying to sell me Christ. Too late for that! Actually, it's far too late for the post or evangelists. Oh, I can see it's Lillian. Drat, I forgot she was coming over for a drink. I look a fright! Can't be helped. Goodbye, my flower, love love.'

And with that, more fumbling, the call ends. Delphi is left looking at her blank computer screen.

*

Romy is dressed in a David Bowie t-shirt, men's trousers and bright green high-top Dr Martens. She's a singer and guitarist in a punk band that just can't seem to catch a break, so by day she works in a kebab shop. Romy's parents tried to have children for well over a decade and had all but given up when the miracle of Romy's conception changed and refocused their lives. All of their attention and pent up parental aspirations were poured into and onto their one most precious bairn. They'd kept her tightly safe to the point of suffocation. And as much as Romy complains about their rules and conservativeness, she's never left home, on the surface complying with their curfews and no boyfriend policy in exchange for the security and love. Her grandmother was born in Nigeria and Romy's flesh is deep golden brown. She is a quintessentially modern London girl, with an accent to match, sometimes teasing Delphi for her middle class voice and roaring with laughter whenever Delphi says something like 'goodness me'.

The young women both recognised their easy connection from the moment they met at a waitressing gig years before, but their sisterhood was truly forged when Romy had her heart broken for the first time. A boy with a studded leather necklace, who promised emotional banquets, but instead ransacked Romy's heart. Night after night, Delphi had ridden her scooter across the city and scaled into her friend's first floor window, careful to remain undetected by Romy's parents who were at a loss as to why their child was so depressed. Delphi would bring Romy small gifts and hold her tightly as she wept. She would kiss her friend's forehead and tell her that huge love was coming her way soon. Romy, comforted, would eventually fall asleep. Delphi would tuck her in, and then climb back out the window, and ride to her flat as dawn was breaking. Delphi stayed the course, weeks of this, until Romy found her feet again, and then they used them for dancing. Their night-time meet-ups now happened at gigs and clubs all over London. They danced until their feet ached, drank cheap beer, kissed lots of strangers. Romy, mesmerised by the musicians, confessed her desire to have her own band, and Delphi had clapped her hands and championed her friend's dream.

When the clubs and bars closed the two of them would spill out blinking onto the grimy streets. Not yet ready to be separated, they would aimlessly walk around holding each other's hands with endless conversations surging between them.

And now shoulder to shoulder once more they stroll through Hampstead Heath. Romy, with oversized white sunglasses obscuring most of her face, says, 'Holy shit, Delph, I didn't know your mother was that sick already.'

Delphi looks out across the tumbling field of grass and then down at the rocks and pebbles passing beneath their feet.

'She looked terrible on Skype. And it's always been her plan to euthanise, to stay in control. She said she's ready. That's why she wants me to get on that plane.'

Romy stops and turns to face her friend. Delphi sees a bird taking flight from a nearby tree. She wishes she was able to name the species. One day she'll buy a book on ornithology. Bird watchers are called twitchers, Delphi remembers, and the name pleases her.

'What, Delph? Seriously?' Romy is on high alert. 'You can't help her with this, you can't even be in the room. That would be, well, that would be a crime.'

Delphi is far away, still in flight with the bird.

'Delph, are the laws different in Australia?' Romy shakes her friend gently by the forearm.

'I'm sorry. I feel weird. Disassociated or something.' Delphi looks at Romy's tender face full of concern.

'Yes, you can be charged with murder if you help someone die.' Delphi rubs her nose hard with her hand. 'But she's got it all sorted, I'm just going to be in the house.'

Delphi can't bear to look at her friend, so she drops her gaze back to the path and starts slowly walking onwards.

'Suicide, man that's so full on, Del.'

Delphi stops walking. 'Suicide and euthanasia are two different things.'

'Are they? How?'

'Suicidal people want to die. People that euthanise want to end their suffering.'

'Okay, but still… wow, what a thing for her to ask of you. So shitty.'

'Oh please don't say that. Who else does she have to ask?' Delphi's insides twist with defensiveness and fear. 'My father is entirely selfish and they hate each other. Jack is, for all intents and purposes, missing in action. I know he's in sporadic contact with Mama, but he never emails or calls me back. So it's just me.' Delphi takes a deep breath.

'You seem resolved about this,' Romy threads an arm through Delphi's.

Delphi shrugs. 'Oh God, I'm not. But what other option do I have? I love her, she needs me. She was there at my birth. It seems, I don't know, fitting somehow that I'm there at her death. What would you do?'

'Oh Minx, I don't know. Should I try harder to talk you out of this?'

'No, because the last time I saw her I tried to talk her round, tried to talk about a whole lot of things and it just went totally pear-shaped.' Delphi lifts her hands up and cups her head as if stopping it exploding. 'I think I'm going to shatter like glass.'

Romy, her hair in two crazy antenna-like topknots, throws her arms around her friend and says, 'I love you. You're seriously the strongest and most loyal person I know, but I don't want you to do this. I think you'll regret it. The Buddhists wouldn't be down with this shit one bit. Aren't you frightened that this is some kind of dance with the devil? It goes against everything in us to kill our parents. Even if they're fuckers. And I don't mean your mum. She has always been cool with me. Your dad, he's a fucker, though. I guess I could see how you could kill him.'

Delphi laughs a little. 'I hear you, but what if she tries to do it alone? And I know her, she will.'

'Try again to change her mind.'

'I'm not sure I have the right? When I tried she pushed me away. Looking back, I think, maybe I was making her choice about me, which is unforgivable, right? This is excruciating; I feel poisoned, but in my core, I believe this is her decision. She's an adult, it's her life, her terrifying illness, her death, and the best I can do is not judge her and turn up. I don't know... I truly don't know.'

Romy kisses Delphi's cheek. 'You want me to come with you?'

'To Australia?'

'Yes.'

'I adore you, and because of that there's no way I'm pulling you into this.'

The fat, soft afternoon light makes them luminous. The bird Delphi was watching carries on circling above their heads, oblivious to the women holding each other tightly below.

*

The gates to Highgate Cemetery are still open, but she won't have long before it's locked for the night. Delphi walks beneath the massive sandstone entranceway, with its turrets and arches.

Delphi loves this cemetery. The pathways dug into the hill are sheltered by ancient trees, ivy dappling the weak English light. Moss-covered headstones and guardian angels, proud tombstones and grand family vaults, humble graves overtaken by wildflowers and the delicious recolonising of tree roots. One site has a white marble grand piano, another a life-sized stone lion, another an ornate crown for each family member below. Colossal Celtic crosses and higgledy-piggledy headstones sit like rows of teeth. Karl Marx is buried here. As is George Eliot. And lonely Catherine Dickens, her Charles all the way over in Westminster Abbey. Squirrels dart about, birds sit in formation on branches, and more than once Delphi's seen foxes here. Vibrant, resilient nature. A verdant counterpoint to all this death.

The air is cool and Delphi imagines herself like Alice tumbling through to a gothic wonderland. She is struck anew by how dramatic the Victorian attitude to death was. Her mother has joked that she wants a funeral in keeping with that period; a black carriage drawn through the streets by eight black horses wearing feathers on their heads. And in true Vivian style, her mother wants a Viking bent on the proceedings, with her body laid onto a barge for it to be set alight and pushed out to sea. The flames licking the sky in outrage.

Delphi wends her way up Egyptian Avenue into the Circle of Lebanon, with its huge cedar tree. She finds a mossy bench and sits down amongst the stillness. It's sober here, this sacred, reverential place.

In front of her is a gravestone with an open book carved in marble. On the left page, the name of a man and on the right the name of his wife. One plot along, an exquisite angel lies slumbering, a tear on her cheek. Inscribed below: 'Our Beloved Mary Lost'. Delphi looks at the angel for a long time and she is keenly moved.

A doorway low down within her is opening, the breach between that world and this is unsettling.

Further along another angel stands with a sword held aloft, but the peculiarity is that she's encased in plastic; a huge bag keeping her dry, duct tape lashed around her legs.

We are here for but an instant and then gone. Our ashes scattered to the winds. Our bones eaten up by the earth.

Delphi doesn't want her mother to die. What will the world look like then? She once read someone describe the death of the mother as 'the ultimate and final tearing of the fabric'. Delphi is not sure she understands that idea but shudders to think she soon will understand it intimately.

*

On her way through Hampstead village Delphi decides to go into the Holly Bush for a drink. A sharp edge running through her body needs taking off.

Delphi orders a double whisky and a glass of wine and then moves from room to room to find somewhere to sit. Eight hundred years ago, this place housed horses. The ceiling is low, and the thick stucco walls crammed with paintings. This evening it is filled with people talking and laughing.

Finding nowhere to rest she walks back to the small room that overlooks the cobbled lane. Every seat is taken except one. It's opposite an old man, who is reading with a half pint by his elbow. Delphi hesitates but her fatigue encourages her forward.

'Excuse me,' she asks, trying to look innocuous, 'If this is free, may I sit here?'

The old man looks up, nods and waves his hand in assent. He stands a little as she sits. Old school chivalry, then he goes back to his book.

Delphi settles down, readjusting her limbs. She takes a gulp of whisky and sighs. She lets herself unobtrusively study her companion. He is wearing faded grey suit pants, folded a little at the ankle, no socks, and expensive brogues bought a generation or two before. A white shirt, not entirely clean, and a cravat knotted at his throat. He is crumpled debonair, she thinks. Not a bad name for a song. She marks it to tell Romy later.

He senses her attention and looks up. Their eye contact makes a small flash.

'Have you read this book?' he asks, holding up Oliver Sacks' memoir, *On the Move*. The man's voice is strikingly beautiful.

'Yes, I have,' answers Delphi, 'and not only that…' she bends down to rummage in her bag and retrieves a copy of Sacks' slim volume *Gratitude*. She presents it to the old man and it takes him a moment to calibrate the coincidence. He laughs warmly and picks up the book to inspect it.

'How simply marvellous,' he says, brimming with wonder.

'So sad about Oliver's death. Years ago now, but to think of him, I still reel.' The man continues. 'He was born just near here, did you know?'

Delphi lifts her chin and the corners of her mouth in accordance.

'I never met him, but I feel as if my dear friend died. Quite, quite wonderful that one can feel that for someone one has never met.'

Delphi nods and the weight of the topic abruptly crushes her. The old man notices.

'Are you quite well, child?' he asks so kindly that Delphi has to resist the urge to move the table aside and meld into the safe harbour of his arms.

'I don't know if I am.'

He takes a sip of his half pint and turns to face her fully. 'I'm listening if you fancy entrusting me with your woes.'

Delphi does trust him and it's fascinating to her that kindness is such a powerful conduit.

'My mother is dying,' she says quietly. 'She has a disease that's eating her brain.'

The old man's blue eyes widen slightly to make room for his empathy.

'She's going to end her life and I feel so sad that I don't really know what to do with myself.' Delphi flips her coaster over but finding the back sodden she flips it back again.

'You love her deeply?' the old man asks.

'I love her deeply,' Delphi echoes.

The man blinks through the abhorrent memories of his parents' protracted deaths, and raises his glass, 'Let us drink to your mother and her spectacular bravery.'

Delphi lifts her glass and the man speaks on. 'Let us drink to dignity and the wisdom to know when enough is enough.'

Delphi clinks her glass to his and they drink. A silence. Companionable, shimmering, whole.

'Child,' he says gently, 'you will survive this as millions have done before you. Bereavement is undiluted agony but do you know what I have witnessed in my long years? I have witnessed that grief can build a cathedral inside us. A place of immense wisdom and empathy, of perspective and gratitude.'

Delphi lets these words of hope filter into her. They take effect and she leans forward and picks up the old man's hand. She looks to him to see if she's overstepped but his warmth is untrammelled. She brings his hand to her face and rests her burning cheek to it. 'Thank you for being so kind. It's odd for me to tell you all of this, I'm sorry if I've burdened you.'

'Not at all. I love to swim in the deep end.'

With his free hand he pats her head and she's not sure, but she thinks he says, 'Don't be afraid. Death is inevitable. It's the "Great Return". *We are all just walking each other home.*'

*

The top of Primrose Hill is especially magical at night with London glittering like a magic carpet below. Delphi pauses to let the beauty in. She is buoyed by meeting the old man in the pub. *We are all just walking each other home.*

Delphi already knows loss; it has travelled as her brutal wing mate since she was six years old. Since the death of her little brother Arthur. *Grief can build a cathedral inside us.*

Delphi perceives clarity arrive like breaking dawn. She will turn down the job at the studio. She must. There will be other jobs. She thinks of Orlo and has a mad moment of seeing them in love, painting side by side, but she dismantles the fantasy. It's not possible. She will go to her mother. Delphi senses the woman she wants to evolve into, her future self, looking back at her through time. And that Delphi, her face sanguine with compassion, calls Delphi to bravery. She is charged to walk into the arena and go to war for love but also for her sense of self. She stretches her arms wide and leans forward down the hill, her body weight tipping her. Delphi flies down the hill, arms spread wide like a bird.

*

The next day, Delphi is sitting on the floor of Orlo's studio peeling the label off her bottle of Heineken. Orlo's boots don't have laces and she notices that his socks are striped, like a child's or a clown's, but she's sure he is neither.

'I'm really so grateful for the job offer, Orlo, but my mother needs me. The timing is shitty. If you're still looking for someone in a few months when I'm back, you know where to find me.'

'I hope everything is okay with your mum,' Orlo offers gently, but Delphi has no intention of unpacking all of that with him and she drops her head to focus on the removal of the label.

She senses Orlo withdraw and she takes it as her cue.

'I should leave you. I'm sorry to interrupt when you're working. And I know you have another interview this afternoon so I will skedaddle.'

'Not at all. They've rescheduled to tomorrow, so no intrusion.'

Orlo gets up and changes the music. Someone French starts singing. Looking at Delphi's face just now he was reminded of Sally Mann's work. Where innocence and wisdom are folded together.

Eyes that have seen everything and yet glisten with defiance and hope. He searches for a book of Mann's photographs and, finding it, he holds it up to Delphi and asks, 'Do you love her too?'

'Yes, of course, particularly the family series of her children.'

'I have that book too, *Immediate Family*.' And he turns back to his bookshelf to dig it out.

Grabbing it, he settles beside Delphi and starts flipping through the pages. The proximity of their bodies alters the lucidity of everything around them.

'The intimacy is extraordinary, isn't it? As if her camera sees truth and fear, not just in her children, but in all of us,' he says.

'And love, she captures the rawness and transience of love. The tenderness of that is what fascinates me most. And frightens me.'

'Yep I agree, and the majesty, almost regality, but there's also humour and something a bit feral.' He laughs and turns another page.

'And grace,' Delphi adds. 'Every image, for me anyway, emanates sublime grace.' He swallows.

'This one,' Delphi says, putting her fingers on the page below the image. 'This one of little Virginia. I think I love this one most of all.'

'Oh yeah,' Orlo agrees. 'She'd be what, four or five in this?'

'Sweet little girl. Her cherub's face covered in tears… that bite mark on her arm… but you can see she's loved, you can see she's safe, she's right at the beginning, brimming with hope and possibilities. Do you know her brother Emmett, he gave her that bite? He's dead now. Pain, so much pain is waiting for her just in the wings.'

'I didn't know Emmett died. Looking at the power in his face it's hard to reconcile, isn't it? Where did that force go? Why didn't he get a full life? The arbitrariness of it is brain bending. I like that adage – *ageing is a privilege denied to many*. I hope I grow to be old. I hope that for you too. For everyone. And these photos capture all of that. The preciousness of time. As if Mann is savouring what she knows will dissolve in the blink of an eye. This is why I make art, to wrestle with mortality, to try to capture beauty, to touch something of the divine. I fail all the time but the attempt, it's valiant don't you think? I make, therefore I am.'

Delphi doesn't notice that a tear has streaked down her face and dropped onto the page. Orlo does though and he holds his breath.

'I understand you,' she says. 'But I make art to keep a record. Not in the sense of legacy, I hate that word, that's an old school man word, but I paint and draw and photograph to try to hold time still, maybe like Sally Mann, but I also do it as a form of penance.'

'Penance?'

'Yes, and reparation.'

'Reparation?'

'I'm bearing witness.'

'For whom?'

She shakes her head. 'For my… I don't want, to um… I'm sorry…'

'Don't be sorry.' He moves slowly and blots a falling tear from Delphi's cheek with the backs of his fingers. He rubs another away from her jawline with his thumb. She can feel the warmth of him and she lifts her face. He squints slightly as if turning over a problem in his mind's eye.

'I'm actually happy you didn't accept the job,' he says, tucking her hair behind her ear and away from her face.

'Why?' she asks.

'Because if you had I wouldn't have been able to kiss you.'

*

They're naked on the floor in each other's arms and Jeremiah waddles over and gives Delphi's head a lick.

'Hey, don't do that.' Orlo prods the dog gently back and Delphi giggles.

'No, I like it. Come here, Jeremiah.' She stretches her arms out to the dog.

'Are you cold?' Orlo rubs his hand across Delphi's belly.

'No,' she smiles. 'I'm happy.'

Brushing the hair from her eyes he says between kisses, 'You walked through my front door and I didn't even need to go out to find you. I'm already sad that you're leaving. When'll you be back?'

'Don't talk about it.' Delphi covers his mouth with her hand. 'I don't want to think about anything else.'

He shifts his bodyweight to roll on top of her, scrunching up the blanket beneath them.

'What would you like to do for the rest of the day?' He looks up through the dormer windows and sees that it's dark. 'Oh man, doesn't look like there's much of this day left, but we could probably make it to a gallery. I would love to have a go at drawing you. I could order us some food? What time do you have to go?'

She holds his face and thinks of the Balzac quote. *A woman knows the face of the man she loves as a sailor knows the open sea.* 'I'm due at work at eight tomorrow morning so we have time.'

'Not enough time,' he says and kisses her neck and throat. 'An outing is definitely off the table. And so is food.'

Delphi folds her legs around Orlo's waist and Jeremiah takes his cue and shuffles away.

*

Dawn means London is unfurling in a cool almost green celestial light. Humming, Delphi looks both ways on the street before she crosses the road. She beams openly, catches herself, and bursts out laughing. A woman in a cheap red coat arches an eyebrow at Delphi as they pass each other.

Delphi can still feel Orlo's hands all over her body, the weight of him, the smell of him, and a fierce life force charges through her. The city looks so gorgeous. The vibrancy of the red bin, the curve of the cobbles beneath her feet, the window box tumbling verdant winter plants. She is elated, high. She stops at the traffic lights as a taxi passes and sees a tattered quote tapped to the pole.

Maturity is the ability to hold the tension of opposites within us.

She runs her eyes several times along the typed line. In a mystical way it seems left here just for her as it's a way of understanding the cross-torsion alive within her. It's confusing, such happiness bursting through such misery. A newborn love affair and a dying mother. It is as if her heart is simultaneously inflating and deflating. She is being called to her mother and yet Orlo tastes like home.

Delphi has a crystalline memory of Orlo's jaw as she kissed it, of running her fingers over the curves of his hips. The shape of his brow and cheekbones as he tilted his head between her legs. The power of the images make her stumble. Her internal buttressing collapses and explodes. Delphi can't help but skip. A delivery man walks past her with a trolley and says, 'Good mornin', love?'

'Yes!' she answers. The man twinkles at her, remembering love that alive.

She takes the carefully folded drawing out of her pocket and looks at it again. Orlo has drawn her bathed in light. The way she looks through his eyes makes her feel ablaze. She hopes he feels the same about the drawing she did of him. She'd wanted to keep it as it captured something of his magic, but he had refused and insisted that wasn't the deal. He asked her to sign it, then he carefully tore her signature off and ate it. She had roared with laughter and copied him by eating his signature from the corner of his drawing. 'Perfect!' He'd been delighted and handed her the half full glass of water to wash it down.

CHAPTER 4

Delphi convulses with panic, madly kicking off her blankets to sit up. Disorientated, she makes grabbing motions with her hands and stares wildly into the blackness. Delphi grapples for the light and feels intense relief as the room bursts into recognition.

The nightmare was awful and the horror is still slick on her flesh. She heard the doorbell ring, she was happy, the light of her apartment, dappled sunshine. She opened the door smiling and there before her was her dead mother, standing, covered in soil and leaves. Her skin streaked with mud, her hair twisted and crazed. She'd clawed her way out of her grave. Her eyes burrowed into Delphi. A bird flapped through the doorway. Its wing clipped Delphi's cheek. The smell of rotten meat. The light began to strobe. Her mother holding up an axe. No words are spoken but Delphi understands. 'You failed to kill me. Try again. Do it right this time.'

She woke up terrified.

Delphi takes the glass of water from her bedside table and gulps. She stands up, but her legs are wobbly so she puts herself back to bed. Curled up she turns towards the lamplight. The fear is so palpable that Delphi can taste it, like metal in her mouth. Now grief comes at her from every point of the compass. She wishes Orlo were here and wraps her arms around herself to combat her shivering.

*

Delphi read once that falling in love activates the same receptors in the brain that are fired up by MDMA. Makes sense then that love is addictive. She needs to see Orlo. She hopes he will lay his hands on her and take away the chill she can't shake.

Delphi tries not to run as she makes her way towards his street. She ducks across the road and rounds the corner. Suddenly, unexpectedly, he comes into view. He's standing outside the front of his studio with his arms draped around a woman. They are talking with an intensity and intimacy that makes Delphi want to scream. She instinctively recoils, claiming a less conspicuous position against the buildings. Orlo is stroking the woman's face and she is turned up towards him. Delphi is lit with outrage and its brutalising slower-moving twin, shame. Of course, a man like Orlo would have many lovers. She was a fool. Always such a fool for love.

Delphi turns and as she does she trips and hits the pavement hard. She lies still for a moment. Her hands hurt and her left knee too. Delphi sits up to pick bitumen from her knee and stems the bleeding with her sleeve. Rage subsides and all that is left is a great big wound, right where her self-worth should be.

*

Heathrow Airport is cavernous and illuminated like an interrogation room. She ignores another text from Orlo. 'Where have you gone? Please call back?'

In front of Delphi, standing in the long line waiting to check in, a family of three queues happily. The grandmother is besotted with the baby, a chunky little pudding strapped in a stroller. They are playing peekaboo and the baby girl is giggling, the joke a fresh miracle every time. When the baby laughs, this sets off a chain reaction of rejoicing. The grandmother peals with laughter and the mother watches on delighted. Three generations of women vivified by their togetherness, safe in their belonging. A wholehearted tribe, a clan, a proper family.

Pain radiates from Delphi's centre, and her eyes sting with tears that force their way out to drop down her cheeks. She will never have what these women have. Never will her mother see her pregnant. Never will her mother play a game with Delphi's future children. Never will Delphi have that sacred safety net. Her mother is to die and Delphi will be left alone, and the great sadness of this blows bitter winds. Tears continue to stream and Delphi lets them track uninterrupted until she can bear it no longer and forcefully wipes her cheeks.

*

On the plane she's drinking hard and blinking down films on the tiny screen with the distorted pixels. I'm the personification of that, she thinks, pixelated. She takes another sip of scotch.

Is it the booze or the altitude that makes one more emotional on planes? An inane romantic comedy compels Delphi's heart to throb and throat to constrict. Yesterday Delphi felt resolved, sure that she had the grit to be able to help her mother die, but now she thinks it is inconceivable. How on earth can Delphi kill the woman who gave her life? The person she loves more than all others?

She rubs her hands, they're sore from cleaning out her apartment. She'd been unable to get anyone to sublet it so had reluctantly handed the key back to the real estate agent and stored the stuff she wasn't taking at Romy's parents' house. She thinks of Romy hugging her goodbye at the tube station, and how much she wishes her friend was with her now. That yearning makes way for another and she has a vivid image of Orlo making love to her, of him kissing the length of her naked spine. The memory scorches and she grimaces against it.

The man in the seat beside Delphi has taken ownership of the armrest and his leg has flopped out to impinge into her space. Delphi has been trying to talk herself out of being irritated but she is unclipped by fatigue, sadness and booze. And the heat of him is starting to feel like a burn.

This man's encroachment balloons to encompass all the men on all the flights, trains, buses and cinemas that have done this before.

Delphi turns to look at the man. He is eating nuts and laughing at a kid's cartoon. She taps him gently on the arm, aware of the wiry texture of his hair against the pads of her fingers. She takes a stabilising breath and offers a smile.

'Excuse me, sir.'

He looks at her blankly.

'Could you please move over a little?'

A beat of nothing. He looks down at her hand gesturing towards his splayed leg. He turns his eyes back to the screen and moves his leg into alignment as if under duress. His arm stays where it is. Delphi looks at it, transfixed. She plunges back in.

'Umm, sorry but…'

Christ she's done it again! Sorry? I'm sorry for having needs, sorry for being alive, sorry for asking for equality, fairness, the destruction of the patriarchy.

'I wonder… Can we share the armrest?' She asks.

He lifts off the right side of his headphones, irritated. 'What?'

'You're probably not aware,' she continues, 'but you've taken the armrest this whole flight?' Her voice is louder than she'd like but receding emotional control has jacked up her volume.

'Are you for real?' he asks disdainfully. He replaces his headphones and moves half his arm off the rest. She almost misses the word over the pulsing in her ears. 'Bitch.' That is the match to the fire.

'Did you just call me a bitch?'

He looks at her impassively. 'Imagine someone speaking to your mother like that, or your sister or daughter? Imagine them moving through their life with men like you telling them they deserve to feel less comfortable, deserve less space and less respect just because of their gender and your misogyny. And when women ask for what they're entitled to, nothing more than you, just the same please, and politely I might add, they get abuse. Can you tell me how all of that is okay to you?'

Delphi is clutching the seat in front. People are staring. She twists to see the man on the other side of her looking on, riveted. A steward arrives and speaks to her in strict schoolmarm tones. Embarrassed,

Delphi evades eye contact, her righteousness spent. She stands up and moves past the passenger beside her, avoiding the steward and into the aisle. She makes a break for the back of the plane and stumbles past a woman who reaches up and takes hold of Delphi's hand. 'That was awesome,' she beams. Delphi keeps her eyes down and walks on, but the solidarity has given her a small bolster against the shame and she takes a titanic breath. She raises her fingers to her mouth; she has to keep it together. Her lips are trembling. She gets to the back of the plane and turns her face to the wall. She counts her breaths, but her chin is wobbling, her throat constricts painfully and tears fall as if her soul has been punctured. Alone, way above the earth, as silently as she can manage, Delphi sobs.

*

The much smaller plane is circling over southern Tasmania towards Hobart. Delphi looks out of the window at the tawny, sunburnt fields. Her mother is too unwell to come to the airport so Delphi will make her own way to Vivian's little white weatherboard house.

It's well over thirty hours since Delphi left her flat in London. She's almost on the other side of the planet. She rubs her fingers on the bridge of her nose. Her head aches and her eyes feel like smouldering lumps of coal.

She wonders what her father would think of all of this, allowing herself a moment of indulgence; the fantasy of a supportive and present father. One who would be waiting to scoop her up. One who would take the reins and see that everyone is defended and secure. A proper parent. She remembers a doll she'd become acutely attached to when she was little. Her father had taken it away and told her it was weak to be dependent.

Delphi presses her fingers harder into eye sockets. Who will I be when I get off this flight?

Delphi strategises to strictly not think about herself, to keep her attention on her mother. She will try to rise, try to be strong enough. Surely love and respect are the robes one needs to wear to be a good death attendant? Delphi is longing to tuck her face in her mother's shoulder, to lie down on her bed and rest with her. After her parent's divorce, when Delphi came home for holidays from boarding school, she moved into her mother's bedroom. They would read and sleep together companionably. Sometimes Vivian would spoon Delphi and say, 'Tell me if my arm is too heavy on your waist, my flower.' And Delphi would respond, 'Never, it's never too heavy, Mama.' And they would drift off to sleep in almost matching flannel nighties. The same one Delphi still wears when she's homesick for her mother, and has packed into her suitcase in the cargo hold below.

The wheels of the plane are lowered with an electric whine and Delphi takes a moment to say a prayer. She doesn't know to whom, but she sends it to the heavens with a tremulous heart. Be kind to us please. She lets her mind go blank. She focuses on her breath, the simple in and out of it. She is crushed to think her mother's breath will stop soon. A lifetime of breath ending. Bizarre in its finality. Delphi bunches up her fist and pushes it against her mouth to stop herself from crying out.

CHAPTER 5

In the taxi Delphi sits silently, conserving her energy, watching this low-rise, clean city unspool beside her window. 'Yes, just let me out at the bottom of that steep driveway there, number forty-five. Thank you very much.' The yellow letterbox that Delphi painted during her last visit leans off-centre as if it is braving a storm.

Delphi pulls her overstuffed suitcase from the boot. Weeping willows cascade on either side of the driveway. It's nearly blissful, but there is something parched, something slightly off. Delphi walks over the inscription Vivian wrote in the wet concrete; *la maison est ton ancre,* home is your anchor. This place has never been Delphi's home, but it has been for Vivian. Her mother moved here to make a fresh start after Delphi finished school. England was too painful for her to find her breath she had said. 'But it's so very far away,' Delphi begged her mother to stay. 'And that's the point,' Vivian had answered. 'As far away as I can be from Arthur's death and Edward's women, but I'm not abandoning you, my darling. You must come to visit me often. Tasmania has a gentle climate like England and I can begin again, in preparation for my old age, to wipe the slate clean.'

Delphi had been devastated but the spiritual umbilical cord that attached them stretched to accommodate the distance.

She hears her mother call before she sees her. 'Delphi, darling, my girl, is that you?' Delphi cranes her neck up to see Vivian standing at the top of the stairs, holding the railing with both hands. Thick hydrangeas tumble between them. Her mother is smiling, wearing a pink dressing-gown, an exotic scarf wrapped around her head. It calls to mind a magical fairy-tale turban, constructed from a nestled peacock.

'Yes, Mama, it's me. I'm here.'

'Well, I thank the gods, every single one of them!' Her mother's face is luminescent with emotion and Delphi rushes to close the gap between them. They enfold in each other's arms and press their hearts as close as possible. Delphi is taller than Vivian, but she finds a way to tuck down into the crook of her mother's neck, and there it is, that smell of love. The women laugh, they pull apart to study their changed but ever beloved faces. The equation is being rebalanced. Distance, time and illness equals tyranny.

Vivian is weak and aged with disease, yet still glamorous and straight-backed. Arms entwined they make their way inside, the Derwent River holding the space quietly behind them.

'Tea or gin, my flower?'

'Both, Mama, both. Let's have everything.'

Vivian stops to speak, 'When the storytelling goes bad in a society the result is decadence.'

'Who said that, Oscar Wilde?'

'Plato.' Delphi sees the tiny zigzag of lightning as her mother congratulates herself for outwitting her audience.

Vivian cups her daughter's face with both hands. 'My beautiful, beautiful girl, you came.'

Delphi places her own hands over her mother's. 'Of course, Mama, you call and I come.'

The two marvel at each other. Pilot, Vivian's dachshund, has awoken to discover the interloper and is bouncing around yapping furiously, taking his Chief of Security status seriously. Delphi drops down and lies on the carpet. Pilot is rabid with excitement, he twirls and jumps, he makes whinnying noises of joy, he repeatedly lunges to stamp Delphi with his wet nose. Delphi rolls around in delight, trying and failing to protect her face from the furry kisses and the more she laughs, the wilder the dog becomes. Two puppies playing together. Vivian, unsteady, holding the doorframe for support, looks on delighted.

*

Dr Edens, in green corduroy skirt and a navy short sleeved shirt, sits opposite Delphi. She's slight and has an intelligent, weathered face. Her grey hair shines silver in the morning sunlight. The waitress delivers the coffee and drifts off to be impassive elsewhere.

'Thank you for meeting me,' Delphi says to the doctor again. She nods and sips from her cup.

'I saw your mother a few months ago, how is she?'

'Ah…' Delphi doesn't know where to start so she dives into the deep. 'She's ready to die.'

Dr Edens nods again holding steady eye contact.

'Thank you for all the advice you've given her about euthanasia. I read about you and I think your work, your campaigning to get the laws changed, it is important…' Delphi loses her train of thought and her voice fades away. She is self-conscious, her skin is itching; this is surreal. Delphi clenches her teeth hard and her mouth fills with the taste of salt.

Dr Edens' energy is calm and efficient, professional. She asks, 'So what can I do for you?'

'Well, I'm here, in Hobart to help her… to help her die. Can you tell me what the rules are? I don't mean the rules, I mean the laws.'

The doctor hems gently, 'The law as it currently stands, but we are petitioning hard to get it changed, is that euthanasia is illegal. While suicide itself is now decriminalised, helping someone else to commit suicide is still treated very seriously by the law and is still punishable by imprisonment of up to ten years. Anyone who incites or even counsels another to commit suicide is liable for five years in prison if the other person commits or attempts to commit suicide.'

'If the legislation passes how long will it take to be enacted, if that's the correct term?' Delphi asks.

'We are hoping to hear next year and if it succeeds it would take a good 18 months for the new laws to come into play.'

Dr Edens continues. 'While you have what I presume to be the most compassionate of motives for helping your mother to end her life, if you do so your actions are illegal.' Percolating terror makes Delphi's skin broil. She can feel herself become a skittering mess.

'Have you heard of Andrew Quinn? Did you read about his case in the papers?' Dr Edens asks.

'No,' answers Delphi. She coughs to loosen the tension in her throat. 'I live in the UK.'

'Right, right, your mother told me that. Mr Quinn was an old man, who, after being diagnosed with Alzheimer's, on frequent occasions had expressed a wish to die. He had attempted suicide several times. His partner, Susan Salter and a long-time friend, Elizabeth Clarke, knew of his desire to end his life and decided to place the means to do so within his control.

Elizabeth purchased and illegally imported a fatal veterinary drug, Nembutal, from Mexico to Australia. Elizabeth placed some of the drug next to a glass within Mr Quinn's reach. He poured the drug into his glass and drank it knowing that it would kill him. Both women faced charges. Elizabeth was charged with murder. She had no prior criminal history but the case centred around the state of Mr Quinn's mental capacity at the time he took the drug. There was considerable concern over the likelihood that Quinn was no longer mentally capable as a consequence of his increasingly debilitating Alzheimer's. Elizabeth ended up with twenty-two months of weekend detention and Susan killed herself following the trial.'

'My God.' Delphi is horrified. 'Those poor women.'

Dr Edens finishes her coffee. 'Of course, your mother doesn't have Alzheimer's but she does have a degenerative disease of the brain. These women, Elizabeth and Susan, facilitated Quinn's death. And because of the draconian laws it was a disaster for them.'

Delphi finds the manner of Edens' speech unusual. 'So, anything I do must be a secret or I will go to prison?' Delphi asks slowly.

'Yes. Of course, I cannot and am not counselling you but if you were to make a choice to help your mother you would need to be exceedingly careful.'

Delphi hears a toddler demanding 'park park park!' and sees his bedraggled mother chasing after him as they clatter past the sad island of her table.

'Can I be in the house while she dies? What if I'm not actually in the room with her?'

'Yes, you can be in the house, but you would need to claim that you did not know she was taking her life at that time.'

Salamanca Market bustles around them. Delphi looks at the people surrounding her, living an ordinary day. Dr Edens shifts about in her chair indicating that she's getting ready to leave.

'This is a truly awful situation you and your mother are in.' On a napkin she writes down two websites and passes them to Delphi. 'You'll find all the information you need here.' She smiles politely, stands, they shake hands, Delphi thanks her again. Dr Edens walks away, free of this nightmare, to join all the other liberated people. Delphi is pulled back down by ghouls. There is no escape for her and she holds onto the table to stop her world swaying.

*

'Thank you for this, darling girl. Will you come in or do you want to wait in the car with Pilot?'

Delphi turns off the ignition. 'No, Mama, I will come with you.' She cracks the window so that the dog has air while they're in seeing Vivian's GP. Delphi goes around the front of the car and waits to take her mother's arm as Vivian faffs with her handbag. Everything takes so long now. A lone seagull minces about watching Delphi archly, an idiot's attention. The women walk across the quiet road, up the wheelchair ramp and into the nearly empty waiting room. It has cheap decorative prints on the walls, and a massive hand sanitiser pump standing righteously on the counter. Delphi decides to use it while she waits for the secretary to check her mother in. She smells the alcohol and thinks about morgues.

The receptionist finishes her phone call and looks up. She has a spherical head and body as round as a ball. Her parrot earrings swing wildly from her stretched lobes as if they are trying to fly away. Delphi swallows and reminds herself to soften her face and find her manners even though she's compelled to put her head down on the counter and never stand up straight again.

'Hello, Vivian Heath here for 11 o'clock.' She indicates her mother and cracks a lopsided smile. Her face feels like a sloppy mask resting on the slipshod scaffolding of her facial bones.

'Alright. The doctor won't be a moment, your mother is next.'

'Thank you.'

Delphi sits down beside her mother in a plastic chair and reaches out for her hand. They are here to get more pills. Vivian has been doing this for months, several different doctors, stockpiling sleeping tablets.

'Mama, do they know why you want the pills?'

'Oh yes, darling, I presume so. I'm not really interested as long as they give me the prescription. And if they don't I see someone else.'

Delphi rubs her mother's hand tenderly. 'How many pills do you have?'

'More than enough, sweetheart, one doesn't want to scrimp on these things.' She twinkles looking out through the window to the quiet street beyond.

Delphi places her mother's palm against her own, measuring for size and similarities. Identical. She has a flush of love so intense that the coal of her grief is compressed into a diamond.

*

Delphi likes this pub. It's across from the docks and the wood panelling makes you feel like you're inside a ship. Her elbows are supported by the table and she leans forward, holding the weight of her head in both hands. Her hair falls like a curtain over her face and around her resting pens and pencils. She breathes in the warmth and privacy of her miniature ecosystem. For a peaceful interval she's been drawing. Eyes, mouths, hands. The creativity sets her free of her relentless fear.

'Hiya. Hello there.' Delphi looks up to see an Asian woman leaning down towards her. Black hair in two long plaits, a nose ring. 'Why do you have "Mama" written all over your arm?' Delphi pulls her sleeve down to cover the smudged biro lettering. She's found the word radiates warmth and has taken to writing it onto her body. If she's calm enough she can travel deep within herself and feel the letters pulsing comfort.

The stranger is waiting for an answer.

Delphi doesn't want to speak so she just smiles.

'Well, either your mother has done something very, very bad or very, very good.' Without being invited the woman sits down beside Delphi in the booth, forcing Delphi to jostle backwards.

'Don't move away. I want to see you up close.'

Delphi is addled by the unexpectedness of her.

'This is for my father.' The woman says, rotating her bicep to expose an ornate seahorse tattoo. 'Did you know male seahorses are the ones who get pregnant and give birth?'

Sea dragons do that too, Delphi thinks, keeping her voice tucked up safely inside.

'My mother was MIA so it was just me and my dad, that's why the tattoo.' She runs a bitten fingernail over it affectionately, sending a bracelet of bells tinkling. Watching, Delphi gets a pleasant buzzing sensation where the back of her skull meets the top of her spine.

'I'm Sabrina.' This woman is all fire and play. Delphi offers her hand to shake. Sabrina takes it, turns it over, interlaces their fingers and looks at Delphi. A pebble is thrown into the pond within Delphi, desire radiates out, concentric circles of electricity. She suddenly misses Orlo so keenly she winces. His deceit has left a wound in her middle as if she's been lanced through. Sabrina places Delphi's hand flat on her chest and sways in close. 'Hey, do you want to come with me?' She smells like coconut oil and almonds. Delphi looks into Sabrina's dancing eyes and wonders if this is a good idea or if this is ushering chaos right in through the front door. At this point Delphi doesn't care. She is tired of trying to think of the right way of doing things. Anything to not feel like this for a moment. She wants to desecrate the promises her body made to Orlo. She often dreams about him, wakes desolate and again listens to his voice message asking where she's gone. She repeatedly writes him texts and then edits them into oblivion. Self-preservation makes her scream torrents in her head but hold her steady silence towards him.

Delphi looks down at the drawings she was doing and is disturbed to recognise every feature belongs to him. Orlo has taken ownership of her subconscious and creative self. She gave herself to him so completely that reclaiming her autonomy is like waging war against the ocean with a gun.

Sabrina is an attuned huntress. 'I think you want to come with me. How about I make that decision for you?'

Delphi can feel Sabrina's heartbeat through the palm of her hand. 'Yes please.'

Sabrina nods. Delphi downs her wine, gathers her things and lets herself be led away from the bar, and herself.

*

Sitting close together in the park Sabrina encourages Delphi to finish the bottle of vodka. They kiss and Delphi fights against an upwell of despair.

Sabrina guides Delphi back on the grass, climbs on top of her and starts to undo her belt.

'What can I do for you, sad white British lady?'

Delphi's head is spinning. The booze has converted the earth into a slanting merry-go-round.

'I… I don't know.'

Sabrina giggles. 'Okay, we'll just work it out as we go along.'

Delphi is passive. Weighed down by nausea and all that is insurmountable. Sabrina runs her hands over her breasts. Looking down at her in the gloom she asks, 'Are you crying?'

'No.' Delphi lies as a tear finds the shell of her inner ear.

'Jesus. What's that?' Sabrina is squinting at Delphi's exposed belly. Every inch covered in pen. She tilts closer and deciphers the same incantation as before. *Mama Mama Mama.*

'Yikes, girl, that's intense.'

Delphi covers her face with her hands. 'I'm sorry. You can stop. I'm a mess.' She wants to twist out from underneath Sabrina but can't find the strength.

Sabrina takes Delphi's hands away from her face and leans in close. 'Hey, I like stuff-ups. Makes me feel like I've got my shit together.' She places her mouth over Delphi's. Sadness is burnt away in the fire of sex as Delphi gulps for life.

*

The birds are issuing their dawn chorus as Delphi rummages through her bag for the keys to her mother's house. Cursing, she realises she must have lost them. Probably when she was rolling around in the park with Sabrina. Delphi still feels drunk as she moves around the house looking for an open window. There's no way her mother would have left a door unlocked. There it is. Her entry point and she hoists herself up to the sill of the bathroom window. Jemmying herself through, she has a body memory of how she used to do this all the time. In her own childhood house in England, the boarding house, Romy's parents' place, and anyone else's that took her fancy.

Unfolding inside, Delphi is struck by her dishevelled reflection in the mirror. She looks like an animal or some poor soul who's been to war. She wipes at the mascara that's escaped downwards over her cheekbones. Delphi takes off her boots as quietly as possible and tiptoes into the corridor as she's loathe to wake her mother. Yet once she's outside Vivian's bedroom she is compelled to go in. The gravitational force of love. She turns the handle and the room is as quiet as a church. Delphi sees her mother sleeping and watches the gentle rise and fall of her chest. She looks at her profile. From this angle Vivian still looks like the woman Delphi idolises from childhood. The bedside table is covered with books, photos of Delphi, her brothers, and a plaster cast of a toddler's handprint. Arthur's. The curtains are half open, and Delphi looks at the river snaking past, silver and eerie in the dawn light. *You'll keep flowing long after we're all dead.* That thought comforts and horrifies in equal measure.

Delphi goes around to the far side of the bed, lifts the covers and gently gets in. Vivian stirs, she's medicated to sleep so she won't surface entirely.

'It's just me, Mama, go back under.' Delphi moves over to snuggle in behind. Spooning, reverentially holding this woman who gave birth to her. This is her mother, the sacred She, and the tenderness is so whole that a state of grace emanates from the bed and shimmers glittering particles into the room.

The baton has been passed, the roles switched, the wheel turned. Delphi surrenders gratefully to sleep and its kind oblivion.

*

'Can I get you anything else to eat, Mama?'

Delphi and Vivian sit at the dining table together. It is dark out-of-doors and Pilot is asleep at her mother's feet.

Vivian starts hacking. This happens when she eats as her throat control is going. All her bodily functions are unraveling; Vivian slurs her speech, can hardly control a pen to write and is unsteady on her feet. Her eyelids are thickening so it's hard to hold them open and she has a continuous band of searing pain around the circumference of her head. Earlier in the day Vivian told Delphi that some mornings she wakes and for a moment thinks the disease an awful dream. What heart-shattering cruelty that is.

Once the coughing has subsided Vivian rests her head in her hand. She looks terminally worn out.

'Are you okay? Is there anything I can do for you?'

'No, Delphi, there is nothing anyone can do for me anymore.'

They sit in silence for a minute and Delphi marshals her courage. 'I read your copy of *Final Exit.* Did you find it helpful?' Christ 'helpful?' Delphi resents her impoverished vocabulary. An entirely new language is required to talk meaningfully at this altitude.

Vivian nods. 'Yes, I did. I'm just sorry I didn't get my act together when I was still able to go to Mexico and buy some Nembutal and a sombrero.'

'I wish you'd let me buy it for you.'

'Which, the drug or the hat?'

'Both.' They smile.

'Too dangerous, my flower. They'd have surely traced it back to you and you'd have been locked up. That would be too terrible.'

'Mama, if you'd had cancer would you have wanted to fly to Switzerland to go to Dignitas to die?'

'Of course, I would. Euthanasia clinics are a civilised if not an overly sanitised way to do it, but as you know I don't qualify, with my old brain turning to mush, and then I do so like my room, I want to die there. I love the proportions. It's a perfect cube.'

They say *perfect cube* in unison. Delphi has heard her mother relish this cube factor many times and she finds it endearing. Fascinating what gives other people pleasure.

'Mama, if the voluntary assisted dying laws are passed next year you'd only have to wait eighteen months after that.'

'Delphi, I can't live like this for another eighteen months. I haven't even got eighteen days left in me.'

Delphi drags air into her lungs and it scrapes its way past her clenched throat.

'So, you have all the pills you need now, and you have a special bag for your head?'

Vivian talks calmly, slowly. 'Yes, I thought it would be funny to use a Glad bag. That's a brand of kitchen bag here, but apparently, that doesn't work nearly as well as a death bag. I bought a proper one designed for the job.'

Delphi had seen the details of the suicide bag circled when she'd been reading *Final Exit.* Durable plastic with Velcro fastening at the neck because when people suffocate the survival instinct is so high they struggle and panic as they run out of air. It's called the hypercapnic alarm response. They grasp at the bag and if they get their thumbs under the seal then air rushes in, and they survive. A big fat suicide fail. Delphi's neck muscles are turning to stone; she rolls her head to and fro.

Vivian looks at her child. 'Darling, this is what I want so please let's not unpack it all again, I'm too tired. I made my decision as soon as I was diagnosed. You can't possibly want me to live my final years in a high dependency ward unable to walk, stand or sit, unable to eat, nor read, unable to breathe unassisted but kept alive by tubes, trapped under the bell jar. Locked into the lower realms of hell.'

'No, Mama, of course not. I think your choice is brave, but my opinion is beside the point. It is your choice and I respect that, I support you. It's just that… I don't want you to go. I don't want you to leave me.'

Vivian leans back. 'And I don't want to leave you, my love. I wish the ending of my story was going to be different, but I'm not bitter. Having you and your brothers was a miracle three times over. Being your mother has been my greatest gift. Life can be very hard… but you, Delphi, you're pure magic.

The women look at each other. Tears slip down Delphi's face.

'Will you do one thing for me, my flower?'

'Anything.'

'Please start to paint again. You have a gift. You always did and if we don't take care of our gifts we lose our way in the world, we lose our purpose.'

'And what has your purpose been?'

Delphi wipes the tears from Vivian's cheeks.

'Oh, that's easy, darling, being a mother.'

*

Pilot is in Delphi's lap and the bottle of wine beside them is nearly drunk. One of Vivian's cigarettes is clamped between Delphi's teeth, the smoke is making her squint. The garden is softening with the close of another very long day. The alcohol is performing the same rite on Delphi's body.

She has been sifting through a box of old family photos. Her parents so young, charismatic and full of hope. Some of the images are early enough that they actually look happy. Jack, her big brother, in a brown and red eighties jacket and blue Carrera ski sunglasses. Vivian looking glamorous, long-legged, with black eyeliner and big hair. Her father, Edward, intense, almond-eyed, white-toothed, handsome.

The photograph that Delphi has been clutching in her hand for half an hour is of baby Arthur. Her little brother. She adored him. She'd begged her parents to have a baby for her and when they actually did, an accidental rather than generous act, Delphi knew why she was on this earth, to love that baby boy with all of her heart. Arthur with his tiny milk teeth, his waddle, his few words; *bird, more, no, bye-bye, truck.* She still remembers holding the pudgy starfish of his hand. And he had drowned just before he turned two. Delphi was meant to be looking after him but somehow he'd ended up in the pool. So many of the details lost but Delphi's grief is always present, solidifying to be the foundational slab of her identity. She let him die, and there can never be reparations, no matter how hard she tries.

Pilot has had enough, and he slops off her lap to mosey around the grass. Delphi stubs out the cigarette and takes a sip of wine. Rolling the liquid around in her mouth she looks at the dappling sky. It's so stunning against the green of the trees and the blue of the river. She looks out at her body from way back in her head until she is distracted by Pilot darting about. The dog is frolicking for the hell of it. Delphi lifts herself up and joins him.

CHAPTER 6

'Hugh Harrison! Godfather o'mine!' Delphi wraps her arms around him, grateful he has come.

'Ah, no-longer-so-little Delphi. It is terrific to see you even under these awful circumstances.'

They sit down out on the back deck and sip potent gin and tonics. Vivian is sleeping again so they have some time alone. Hugh is wearing a Panama hat and waistcoat. Delphi relishes the eccentricity of him always being in some variant of a suit. As if at any moment a gramophone might start playing John Coltrane and a game of croquet with martinis will begin. Hugh met Edward and Vivian at university and had chosen to stay close to both of Delphi's parents for all these years. She can't for the life of her see what he draws from his relationship with her father. But Hugh was the only friend of her parents who survived their bitter divorce without taking sides, remaining loyal to both. Unlike June, Hugh's wife, who very much took Vivian's side. The two women had stayed close until June's death from a heart attack a few years preceding. June was Australian by birth and had agitated for Hugh to emigrate to Melbourne as soon as their younger child went off to university. She longed for the sunshine, the vibrancy of the Australian skies and an escape from Hugh's ever disapproving upper-class family. With their disinterested children's blessing they did move to Victoria and cultivated a life of productivity and happiness. Hugh growing to love his job as Professor of English at the University of Melbourne and quickly gathering together a small circle of interesting friends.

Hugh often returned to Europe to get his fix but June never felt the need. She returned seldom, and only to see her two grown children whom never asked her any questions, but she forgave them their stunning lack of interest and drank up their news and pallid faces like nectar. Hugh would have loved to be closer to his children geographically and intellectually, and unlike his wife he found their self-centredness a personal rebuke which pained him like the throbbing ache of a rotten tooth. Delphi's brother Jack had once said he found it interesting that Hugh was closer to them than his own children. Delphi wasn't sure how to square it but she suspected it an easier job being Hugh's godchild than his flesh-and-blood child, as their relationship blossomed around shared interests and never had to heft the deathly weight of expectation, nor the strictures of discipline.

And so in Australia June grew brown as a berry and was never happier than beetling about in her extraordinary antipodean garden. She was cutting hydrangeas one day, chatting to her neighbour about her magnolia tree and keeled over stone dead. Delphi had been so shocked when she heard the news. She'd always loved June. A quiet, gentle woman ever kindly moving in Hugh's effervescent wake. As time passed Delphi began to think that the nature of June's death was actually tremendous, and she admired how Hugh had worked through his grief by writing a memoir all about his late wife. 'The longest love letter in history' he called it, and Delphi looked forwards to holding it in her hands and pressing it to her heart whenever it was to be published.

'Delphi, I'm sorry I can only stay another hour before I have to head back to the airport, but I understood from talking to your mother on the phone last week that if I were to make it in time I should do it fast. I came as soon as I could, Fem.' As long as she can remember he has used this nickname for her. It wasn't until she was nearly a teen that she asked him why, and he'd answered it was in celebration of her quintessential femaleness. She'd not entirely understood but felt the warmth that infused it every time it passed his lips.

'I'm going to cut to it and say with great love that I'm worried you're in the country to help your mother on her final journey.'

Delphi looks into his soft brown eyes and a memory surfaces of when he introduced her to whisky, explaining that it helped digestion and staved off dementia. She was eight or nine at the time.

He carries on. 'Delphi, you must promise me you will proceed with caution and care.'

Delphi retorts as playfully as she can. 'I always choose caution, Hugh.'

'Good Lord, Fem, you are a wildling, you've never chosen caution in your life. As a three-year-old I saw you stride into the sea at Cornwall, completely unable to swim but without a jot of fear. Bravery to a fault. Always so curious, taking care of everyone, drawing all the time, your wide eyes not missing a single trick. Old before your time, Fem.'

Hugh had been an attentive godfather. Coming to her school art shows, and each year on her birthday, Delphi would receive a hardback classic accompanied with a long letter sharing all the reasons it was correct to worship that particular book. To Delphi's delight there were also newspaper clippings either directly or sometimes tenuously connected to the author or subject matter tucked inside the dust jacket. In response Delphi read the novels studiously and used their inspiration to draw or paint a response. She wasn't aware, as she'd never visited his home in Melbourne, that he had every one of those artworks framed, going back to when she unintentionally started this ritual at the age of four, by using crayons to scratch out a funny-looking Peter Rabbit.

Delphi moves closer to Hugh. The sides of their bodies touch companionably and she's saved from the intensity of his imploring gaze.

They talk on, around and over their lives, updating, communing and back inevitably to the only topic between them. Hugh starts. 'Fem, did you know in the Middle Ages, suicide would result in a person being excommunicated from the Church, no Christian burial and the confiscation of all property belonging to the person who killed themselves?'

'Bloody hell, Hugh, isn't it lucky Mama and I are heathens – an atheist and an agnostic-slash-wannabe-Buddhist.' She takes a sip of her drink. 'And anyway, historically I wouldn't be able to be buried in a churchyard as I have a tattoo so Mama can be out in the unconsecrated soil with me.'

Huge waves a fly away from his face. 'Have you been in touch with your father or your brother?'

Delphi shakes her head. 'I've still not spoken to my father and I gave up chasing Jack a while ago. He never returns my calls or emails. He knows how to find me if and when he's ready. I miss him of course. Every day.'

'A family estranged is a thoroughly sad business.' Hugh shakes his head. Delphi agrees with him right to the nucleus of her being, and drops her head onto his shoulder. She doesn't want him to leave. Hugh always brings with him the sense of anchorage, of belonging.

They are interrupted by Vivian calling out from indoors. 'Hugh Harrison!' Always his name in full. 'Hugh Harrison, I demand to bathe in your most excellent company!'

They rise and Hugh takes Delphi by the shoulders. 'I suspect I'm a lapsed atheist,' he smiles a little, 'so I'm praying for your mother and I'm praying for you. If you need me for anything at all, you have my number. And Melbourne is only an hour away from here.' Delphi smiles gratefully and thinks, there is God right there, in the kindness and interconnection. They walk inside arm in arm so that Hugh can say a final goodbye to his old and dear friend.

*

The next morning, Vivian shuffles out of her bedroom a little after eight, looking like a crumpled piece of cloth. Delphi hears her and goes to her taking her arm. 'Can I make you a cup of tea, Mama?'

'Yes, please, I'd like that.' The pair of them list like a dilapidated vessel into the sitting room. Vivian says, 'It's today.'

Delphi absorbs the information as if she's forcibly swallowing cyanide. Once her mother is safely seated in her armchair, Vivian speaks firmly, almost aggressively as if addressing a subordinate in the army or an unruly kindergartener: 'Delphi. Today.'

Delphi pulls a blanket over her mother's knees and says, 'Okay, Mama, okay.' An uncanny peace is swelling in the room. Vivian looks out of the huge square window at a bird looping in the sky. 'This evening after dinner, does that suit you?'

'Whenever you want, Mama.' Delphi squats down and reaches her hands onto her mother's lap. 'Do you want to call Jack to tell him what's happening? I think we should.'

'Oh lord no, Delphi. Your brother can't do anything from Paris. I don't want any drama. And I don't want anyone else involved.'

'Okay, okay.' Delphi soothes and abandons the fledgling thought to negotiate with her mother, the embodiment of stubbornness. Delphi let's her ideas splinter and discards them.

'Delphi, promise me you won't call him? Not until afterwards, until tomorrow? Legally you know it would be foolish and emotionally messy for all of us.'

Delphi relents and gives her word. 'What do you want to do today?' she asks.

'Let's just stay at home, let's potter and I want to watch *The Bill* this evening, it's an episode I think I may not have seen.'

Delphi's brain is unable to straighten out the buckle these words afflict. She breathes consciously. She must be lionhearted. She will not allow hysteria to swamp this last, this most precious day. Vivian has stipulated for normality and Delphi will do her best.

In a sudden impetuous rush she says, 'Mama, I know you don't want to talk much, but I need to say one thing?' Delphi is already wondering if this is a mistake to bring up.

Vivian looks detached, her gaze far away, out across the river, already merging with the horizon.

'Mama, I want to tell you… I want to ask for your forgiveness?'

Vivian is drawn back. 'For what, my flower?'

'For baby Arthur.' A tectonic rift rips through Delphi. She refuses to allow tears to flood her and forces them back with the same power one would wield a sword.

'My girl, that wasn't your fault, it was an accident. If anyone is to blame it is your wretched father not you, my love.' Vivian rubs her daughter's cheek. 'What kind of parent asks a six-year-old to babysit a toddler, particularly in a house with a pool and a pond.'

Delphi paces. 'I think about Arthur all the time. I still dream of him. I'm so sorry.' Delphi is unable to support the weight of her skull and drops her head to rest in her mother's lap.

'Darling,' Vivian sounds exhausted, 'I never blamed you…' she says, her gaze again drifting out to the river.

'But you sent me away to boarding school right after and we never spoke of it, none of us. And then the family blew apart.'

'Delphi, Delphi, stop. This is ancient history. The family was already disintegrating. Your father with all his affairs… You are not accountable; you were so little. There is nothing more to say. The death of a child is an atomic desecration. In a way we all died that day.'

Vivian pushes Delphi's head from her lap and calls for Pilot to jump up, closing the conversation. Delphi is reminded of her mother saying *it's easier to love a dog than a child* and she makes room for the tubby dachshund.

Delphi rolls back onto her heels and stands, her legs burning with pins and needles. 'I shall get us tea.' She staggers a little as she walks into the kitchen. She continues out into the back garden, up the stairs and along the overgrown path until she is high above the house. She looks out over the rooftop at the river and covers her mouth to stifle a howl.

*

Delphi sits down gently on Vivian's empty bed. The death manual is back on the bedside table. The cover has a coffee cup stain and

Delphi runs her finger around the ring of it. She picks up the book and flicks through the pages looking at the diagrams and photos again. Delphi shuts the book and closes her eyes for a long time. Her mother is dozing in her armchair in the sitting room, the house is quiet. The whole wide world has stalled. The angels have hushed and are watching from above with sorrowful faces.

Vivian's wardrobe door is open and Delphi notices a package on a shelf just below eye level. She reaches for it and as soon as her fingers touch the plastic she recoils. It's the death hood. Delphi is atomised but commands herself to regroup. She reaches out and, suppressing her revulsion, unfolds the bag. She lifts the bag and puts it over her head. She tightens the cord at her throat, her fingers trace the Velcro, the plastic is pulled toward her mouth by her inhalation. Shockingly quickly she observes the air running out yet Delphi holds her course, she feels nothing, she is an empty echo chamber. Her chest begins to burn and with that sensation rational thought returns. Delphi yanks the bag off her head, scrunches it and puts it back where she found it.

Her spine melts and she liquifies down onto her mother's sheets. Delphi smells lavender and talcum powder and inhales deeply. She'd recognise this scent anywhere. It's the primary, the foundational smell of her life, it's part of her DNA, encoded through her umbilical cord. It's the smell of safety and peace.

'Soon,' Vivian has been saying for days. 'Soon, my darling girl, it will be my time called forward in the queue to the "Ultimate Reckoning".'

Now *soon* is today. The hourglass has nearly run through. The last grains of sand rapidly funnelling down.

Delphi is terrified of death. She has spent her life trying to outrun it. To get away from the image of her little brother's face, so still and white under the water.

This evening her mother will die and Delphi will help her. Vivian gave Delphi life and now Delphi will complete the circle. A witness for a witness. Spring and winter. Tide in and tide out. Delphi will walk into the Valley of Death and shout out into the blackness, 'I'm here again, I know you know me by my name!'

*

'Actually, darling, I won't eat this.' Vivian pushes her dinner away. 'You have it. I shan't need it where I'm going.' Is that the trace of a smile Delphi sees on her mother's face or is it the resignation of one already out the door?

Today has been the most peculiar of Delphi's life. After their conversation this morning they've not returned to the shadows, they've stayed in the light. They've spoken of books, of Pilot, they had a lengthy conversation about the wonders of David Attenborough. They circumnavigated innocuous memories. They avoided any topic that might excoriate, barricading themselves up against the foe that would demand more of them than is already being taken.

Vivian struggles to stand and Delphi swoops around to help her. 'It's nearly time for *The Bill*,' says Vivian and they both shuffle towards the sofa. Pilot jumps up on his mistress's lap. Delphi turns on the television.

'Are you sure you don't want some wine, Mama?' Delphi's own glass stands untouched on the dining table. She's not managed to swallow a single morsel of food. Her throat is fused shut.

'No thank you, my flower. Can you turn the telly up a little? I do so love the music at the beginning, it's exciting, don't you think?' Delphi sits down beside her mother. Pilot uses his nose to lift up Vivian's hand to demand more patting. Delphi finds this so poignant her breathing stops. What's that boy going to do when Vivian is dead?

Giant brutal waves of anxiety crash though Delphi. It's as if she's drowning in the surf, the power and turbulence of the ocean pinning her below the waves, and just as she's about to lose her mind, she breaks the surface and drags air into her desperate lungs.

Dusk is falling fast. Delphi asks if she should shut the curtains. 'No, no,' says Vivian, 'I want to see it… or maybe I don't…' and she trails off gobbled up by the flickering screen. The two women and the dog sit together quietly watching the program. The police on the screen are racing about the wet cobbled streets of London.

'Mama, I called Dr Edens this afternoon.'

Vivian isn't interested.

'She said she couldn't talk to me because her phones are bugged.' Vivian doesn't even nod, the light of the television casts strange distorting shadows on her face. Delphi wants to turn on the lamp, but she's not prepared to give up a single second sitting here with her mother.

*

The closing theme music has only just begun announcing the end of the program and Vivian is wrestling to get up. Pilot jumps out of the way and Delphi pulls her mother to standing. Vivian doesn't look at Delphi and sets off in the direction of her room. 'I'm going now.' Delphi is cleft in two like a tree struck by lightning. Her arms like charred branches outstretched, reaching for her mother.

'Mama, can I help you get into bed?' Vivian doesn't say no, so Delphi moves into the room too. Navigating around the bed Delphi shuts the curtains and turns back to help her mother remove her dressing-gown. Vivian fumbles with the sheets and Delphi helps to clear the way. Vivian slumps back against the pillows and Delphi lifts her mother's legs up and onto the bed. On the right calf a perfect round mole, the size of a five pence piece. Delphi recalls a photograph of her mother as a child; cascading curls, a smock dress, swinging her legs from a bench and that mole, as if God herself had touched Vivian, leaving a brown, round fingerprint.

Her mother is struggling to pin a *Do Not Resuscitate* sign to her nightgown. Delphi helps manoeuvre the safety pin and flattens out the piece of paper. Apparently medical teams ignore these signs but Vivian is adamant she wants to use it anyway.

'Water.' Vivian asks and Delphi runs to the kitchen, returning with two full glasses. She makes sure they're the crystal ones her mother loves. Vivian has a bottle of pills in her hand and everything is moving fast. 'The bag, Delphi.' Vivian points towards the cupboard. Delphi slides it open, retrieves the hood, unfolds it and places it beside her mother.

'Go now.' Vivian is a train moving at speed on solitary tracks. Delphi blinks, blinded by the brightness in the room. She turns to go but Pilot dashes under the bed. Delphi squats down and tries to call him out but he won't come. She decides to leave him, it's probably his proper place anyway, right here in the room with Vivian. Is this where she should be too? Delphi stalls, she can't find the will to leave. She returns to and kisses her mother again and says, 'I love you.' Vivian looks up from opening the bottles and her blue eyes look directly into Delphi. Their connection whole. Then Vivian retracts, making herself insular again. Her focus fortressed she starts to put the pills in her mouth, a small handful at a time.

'Mama, shall I stay?' Vivian shakes her head putting more pills into her mouth and swallowing them down with glugs of water. Delphi wants to scream out 'Don't go! Please don't leave. I'm begging you.' She has the sensation of being at a theme park, trapped on a ride that is cranking out of control. She is completely powerless. Her worst fear playing out before her. With the death of her mother the polestar of the family will be extinguished. Hysteria goes to work inside her. She can't stay here.

Delphi leaves the room, shuts the door and moves into the kitchen, stunned. A swarm of violent bees are marauding through her veins. Refocusing, Delphi starts cleaning up, gathering plates from the table, scooping dirty pots off the stove. Her hands plunge into the sink with the dishes covered in suds, so much detergent frothing. She pulls on the brakes and screeches to a stop. Delphi is lifting up and out of her shoulders. The out-of-body experience is so disorientating, so nauseating that she drops to her knees gasping and presses her head against the cabinet. The tiles beneath her are cracking, the panes in the windows are shivering in horror. She can hear someone mumbling. Talking. It's her own voice. She is praying. Begging. Beseeching for her mother to be released. For Vivian to take flight on broad wings. For this to all be over.

Delphi hears a heavy thump and she's back up on her feet, racing into her mother's room. Vivian has fallen from the bed and is on the floor. Pilot is jumping on her, barking, and Vivian is laughing, delirious with the drugs. Delphi is down on the ground with her mother. 'Mama, have you taken all the pills?' Vivian is too far gone to respond. Delphi shouts at Pilot to get out of the way and to stop barking.

'Mama, we have to get you back up on the bed.' And Delphi tries to direct her mother up, but she is so very heavy, a dead weight.

'You have to help me!' Delphi calls out, but Vivian's head is lolling back, her eyes are unfocused, and her laughter burbles on.

'Okay, Mama, I'm going to push you up and see if you can pull with your hands?' It is impossible, a thousand volts of panic course through Delphi. She holds her mother's face and yells at her. 'Mama, we are getting you up on to the bed and you have to help me!' Somehow Vivian turns over and Delphi manages to get her top half up on the mattress. Vivian is pulling with her arms, all the while Pilot is splitting the air with his barking.

Delphi is shoving her shoulder hard against her mother's thighs and using all her strength to push. An alarm begins to wail. Delphi realises that Vivian has forgotten to remove the panic button she wears around her neck in case of emergency. She had made such a fuss about not wanting it a year ago, but after she tumbled and broke her hip, she acquiesced and has worn it ever since. If it's pressed it triggers an alarm and then the company will ring to see if Vivian is in trouble and needs help. If she doesn't answer the phone the people will start calling assigned friends and send an ambulance.

'No… no… no…' Delphi stammers and she screams again at Pilot to shut up. The alarm shrieks on and on and Delphi's heart is beating so hard it's as if her ribs will shatter.

With a final desperate push, Vivian is back on the bed, and she slurs, 'The bag, Delphi, the bag.' Delphi grabs it and hands it to her. 'Put it on, Mama, put it on.' Her mother's hands stay limp at a weird angle by her sides. Delphi's mind is racing, she is cornered, trapped. Then the phone begins to ring. The sound explodes. Delphi grabs the bag and puts it over her mother's head. Once it's in place, she holds it closed at her mother's throat and struggles to fasten the Velcro. Vivian's face under the plastic distorts and Delphi starts to whimper. She pulls her mother towards her and holds on with all her might. They rock back and forth. The dog is barking madly, the phone rings on and on. Delphi explodes, she's sobbing, 'I can't do this! I can't! I can't! I can't!' She breaks and pulls the bag off her mother's head. Vivian is unconscious. Delphi is trembling, charged with terror and adrenaline.

She knows she has very little time before the ambulance arrives and she thinks back to Dr Edens' warnings about incriminating evidence, and now races around like a mad woman. She takes the glasses from the bedside table and throws them in the kitchen sink to wash off her prints. She grabs some Windex to spray the outside of the hood and stows it away in a drawer. She wipes down the empty pill bottles that she's touched, then she dashes frantically about but can think of nothing else to do. She grabs her keys and races barefoot out into the night.

*

It is a release to run. Night has fallen like black velvet cloth. The street is empty and it's raining. Even the skies are crying tonight. Lamp lights come into view and track over head as she races below them. Her breathing is ragged and loud, she consciously tries to slow it, to calm herself. Her left hand is aching, she loosens her fingers that are crushing her phone. Rigor mortis, I am the living dead she thinks. Why she brought her UK mobile on the run with her she has no idea. When she's charged with murder, maybe her location will be tracked by the telephone towers she moves between. Fleeing the scene of a crime. Delphi is winded as if punched in the stomach and she buckles over to be sick. The contents of her stomach splatter onto the pavement. Her mouth tastes acrid and toxic. Everything is spinning.

Panting, she regains her balance. Her feet are sore, running barefoot on the bitumen has chewed them up. She hears an ambulance siren in the distance. They're coming for Vivian. Terrified, she knows it will pass her as this is the direct way to her mother's house from the hospital. Delphi scans the driveways to see where she can hide. Up ahead is a bank of small trees and Delphi throws herself into it. The water from the ground soaks her jeans and she pulls her knees up to her chest. Her teeth are chattering and the ambulance is upon her now, blue and white lights violate the landscape as it thunders past.

Delphi hopes the time that has passed has been enough for the pills to work. Maybe if her mother hasn't vomited them up, perhaps if they don't resuscitate her, Vivian may get her wish and die tonight. Delphi says the word *please* repeatedly.

The siren retreats, dissipates, drawing her out of her hiding space. She must go back and she turns her bloodied feet towards her mother's home and forces herself to walk.

*

Approaching Vivian's driveway Delphi sees the house bathed in light. Lit up like a Christmas tree is how Vivian would have described it. There is the ambulance and two police cars. Delphi is confused, how did the police get past her on the road without her seeing them? They must have come from the other direction. Or maybe she's lost track of time and space? A black hole of horror having devoured her. All the flashing lights. Looking at her mother's cottage it's as if an alien invasion is taking place. Her mind isn't working properly.

She climbs the stairs and sees the front door has been bashed open, people in uniforms are milling about. Something has happened to Delphi's ears; her hearing has shut down. A policeman comes out of the kitchen, sees her and asks who she is. Delphi answers, 'I'm her daughter.' But she can't hear herself. She's stunned, trapped at the bottom of the ocean. More police step into Delphi's view; faces, chunky belts with batons and handcuffs, ironed blue shirts, black army boots. She pushes into her mother's room and it is crowded with ambulance workers. Different uniforms, less bulky, one attendant has three earrings in his earlobe, another has his hair tied up in a bun. They all look at her, faces neutral but purposeful.

Vivian lies on the bed, her mouth gaping, her nightie twisted as if she's been attacked. The crew are discussing what to do, Delphi can see their mouths moving.

'She's wearing a "Do Not Resuscitate" sign.' Delphi says to no one in particular and her hearing reboots with a jolt. A woman on her right says, 'We can't honour that I'm sorry, sweetie.' She touches Delphi on the arm and says, 'Maybe you want to wait in the lounge room?'

Delphi moves to get onto the bed with her mother, but she's held back and she asks, 'Is she dead?'

'No, sweetie, she's not dead. She's unconscious and we are going to take her to the hospital and look after her. We'll take good care of her. What's her name?'

'But she doesn't want that,' Delphi wails. 'Just leave her be, please, please!' She surges forward again, but an officer grabs her around the waist, lifts her off her feet, Delphi is screaming out, thrashing and kicking. 'Leave her alone, don't you touch her!' Spit and tears whip from her face as she's dragged back and out. Deposited in the sitting room and told to calm down, an unfamiliar blanket is pulled around Delphi's shoulders.

A female cop stands square in front of her and says firmly, 'Alright, we need a few facts, then we can help you and your mum.' A list of questions is peppered and Delphi answers them as truthfully as she can, until, 'Did you know your mother was going to try to kill herself?' Delphi lifts her eyes and looks the officer straight in the face and says, 'I knew this was what she wanted, everyone does, she has an incurable brain disease. It's not suicide, it's euthanasia.'

The officer repeats the question. 'Did you know your mother was going to do this tonight?' Delphi exhales and says evenly, 'No. I didn't.' Delphi can't tell if the officer believes her or not. Delphi hopes her own poker face is as good.

'Okay, we need your help. We can see what your mum has taken, the team in there are talking to her even though she's asleep, but we can't get to her because of the dog under the bed.' Good old Pilot. 'When we approach he attacks. Can you get the dog out of the room, Delphi? Is that what you said your name was?' Delphi nods to both questions.

She gingerly walks back to her mother's room. The ambulance team are pressed against the walls eager to get to their patient. Vivian looks waxy. Delphi sinks to the carpet and sees Pilot bunched into a ball under the bed. She calls to him, but he's not having a bar of it. She stands letting the blanket fall from her shoulders. She goes into the kitchen and finds some cheese in the fridge. She brings it back and throws a chunk to Pilot. He gobbles it up. She intones gently to him; 'It's you and me, bud, you're such a good boy protecting Mama, but now we need to get you out. Follow the lumps of cheese.' Delphi thinks of Hansel and Gretel and throws another chunk and another. Pilot follows the cheese trail right out of the room and into the bathroom across the hall. Delphi places the rest on the tiles, pulls down towels for him to nest in, kisses his head and says, 'I'll be back as soon as I can, buddy. What a good job you did. I'm proud of you, sausage.' Pilot lifts his furry face, his fear and confusion are as plain to see as Delphi's.

Vivian is on a stretcher being lifted out of her room. Delphi asks, 'Can I go with her?' The female cop from before steps into view and says, 'Yeah, you can, but we're going to need to speak to you tomorrow and I need your phone number.' Delphi nods without taking her eyes off her mother. They're careful of the paintwork as they inch around the corners. Vivian would be pleased. Delphi realises how insane that thought is, and she watches a medic pull down the hem of Vivian's nightie so her legs are no longer exposed even though dignity and privacy have been immolated.

She delivers a bowl of water to Pilot, grabs her bag, some shoes and goes out the front door. Her mother is put in the back of the ambulance and Delphi waits for instructions. She's told to get in the front beside the driver and two staff jump in to flank her mother. The rain is coming down hard. Everyone is glistening, they look celestial, hyper-real. Delphi lifts her face to watch the rain. Above the rain, there is space, there are planets, and multiple galaxies, she thinks. The back door of the ambulance clunks closed and Delphi climbs into the front cab. She looks at the house, the door still wide open like a puncture. All the lights on, people, strangers working in there. Delphi wonders if they will talk of her mother when their families' ask how their shift was in the morning. Just another grizzly suicide attempt.

'Belt please,' says the driver. Delphi blearily looks over, and he doesn't seem much more than a boy. He's wearing a black puffer done up to his throat and has an angry pimple on his cheek. 'Rough night?' he asks with a trace of misplaced excitement. Delphi can't think of how to respond so she stays silent. 'Let's get your poor old mum some help then, hey?' Delphi closes her eyes tightly. He throws the machine into gear, and they carefully descend the steep driveway.

CHAPTER 7

The Jurassic-sized wipers move across the windscreen of the ambulance. The hypnotic rhythm comforts Delphi a little, like a metronome tocking out structure. When Pilot was a puppy in the UK, Vivian put a clock under his bedding, the ticking intended to soothe by mirroring his mother's heartbeat. This memory rises in Delphi like flood waters and spills out her eyes and down her cheeks.

Delphi's arms are wrapped around her body, her hands balled into fists. The driver makes conversation incessantly, Delphi responds with wet crumbs yet he keeps persisting.

'Well, here we are,' he chirps as they take a final left into the accident and emergency forecourt. 'I hope everything goes well with your mum.' He pulls to a stop. Delphi opens the door and lets herself out.

'Hey,' calls the boy driver as he leans across to hand her a piece of paper. Delphi looks at him confused. 'That's my number. I'd get in trouble for that so don't tell anyone.' He smiles idiotically, 'If you want a drink or a chat, give me a call, pretty lady.'

Delphi blinks at him then shuts the door, letting the piece of paper flutter to the ground.

Vivian is being whisked away by the triage team. A short woman wearing green scrubs and an aggressive fringe approaches Delphi. 'Hiya,' she says in a broad Australian accent. 'Can you come with me and we'll get through the paperwork while they work on your mum?' Delphi can't tear her eyes from the swing door through which her mother has been swept. The Fringe says, 'This way, please,' as she ushers Delphi into a room illuminated space-station white. Plastic chairs in rows, a vending machine, people wilted about waiting.

They turn a corner. 'Let's go into the small room here,' says the Fringe. Her vocal inflection rising at the end of every sentence robs her of the power of a declarative statement, tossing her into the abyss of eternal questioning. Delphi lifts her eyes with a herculean effort and is startled to see a police officer standing in the middle of the corridor looking directly at her. She knows he's there because of Vivian. Delphi's face aches, and she drops her eyes to the ground.

'Here we are,' the Fringe says, and Delphi is relieved when she shuts the door with the policeman safely on the other side of it. After many boxes have been literally and figuratively checked, the Fringe says, 'So your mum is having gastric suction which is a fancy way of saying she's having her stomach emptied. You can sit outside in the waiting room, and someone will come and get you when she's stable.' Delphi is unsure if that's a question. 'There is a counsellor available to you if you need one.'

Delphi holds her head still in case that one truly is a question.

The Fringe, shuffles her papers and says, 'You look so upset.' She pulls a sad face. 'Any questions?'

'Might…' Delphi asks, 'Might she die? Do you think?'

The Fringe flickers with mangled understanding and says, 'Look, I've not seen her condition firsthand, but from what the response team said en route, she will be just fine. You don't need to worry.'

Delphi envisions her heart beginning to decompose in her chest cavity.

*

Delphi has been sitting beside her mother's ER bed for twenty monstrous minutes waiting for her to surface. A curtain has been pulled around them both and Delphi is shivering, dread coursing through her veins like poison.

Vivian's head starts to move slowly from side to side, she's trying to swallow, but her mouth is painfully dry. Delphi leans in and takes her mother's hand. Vivian's mouth is moving but no words are forming.

Then as if waking from a dark spell Vivian's eyes fight open and then close. Tears start to tumble down her face. Delphi is too distraught to speak.

'Why?' Vivian's voice rasps weakly. 'Why?'

Her mother's desperation overwhelms Delphi; she is smashed and grief-stricken. She whispers so they can't be overheard. 'Mummy, I'm so sorry.' A new form of grief develops like a viscous membrane over Delphi's eyelids, nostrils and mouth. 'You took so many pills so quickly, you fell, your clicker… I couldn't… Mama, I couldn't…' Amelioration is impossible.

Her failure is spectacular; she couldn't go all the way for love, she wasn't capable, wasn't strong enough. Delphi has proof now that she's not the person she needed herself to be. The reckoning arrived and Delphi was weak. She failed the test.

Vivian is weeping, her shoulders heaving. Delphi gently strokes her mother's hair and bites the insides of her own mouth until she can taste blood.

*

'This is dreadful,' spits Vivian.

They've just been informed that she is to be transferred to the psychiatric ward as anyone who attempts suicide is deemed mentally unwell.

'I absolutely refuse to go, Delphi. I will not! If they trap me, I won't be able to get out and I mean to die as soon as you can get me home.'

Delphi is perched on a leatherette armchair. The disgusting tea in the Styrofoam cup in her hand is tepid, like her insides. Someone has drawn a lopsided love heart in blue biro on the armrest. Hospitals, hotels, life… all of us just passing through… thinks Delphi.

Vivian carries on objecting and frothing.

'Okay, Mama, but they say the only other option is for you to go into palliative care.'

'I'm not doing that either! It's ridiculous. I don't want my pain managed. I want it to end. I choose as a sane adult that *now* is the time of my death and bureaucracy is shaking its moronic, domineering grey beard at me and shouting *No*. Well, I shan't be chained up in the system, Delphi. Like an appalling Kafka story. If they entrap me I shall stop eating and drinking. An awful, protracted way to die but it will still serve my ends.'

Vivian first asserted this contingency plan yesterday and Delphi had googled: *How long does it take to starve to death?* Thirty to forty days if one is hydrated. *How long does it take to die without water?* Three to four days.

'But the hospice representative said they would intubate you with a nasogastric tube, Mama. Whether you choose it or not they'll pump nutrients and fluid into you.'

'And I would just pull it out, Delphi!' Vivian looks wild and dishevelled, the fluoro tube light beating down harshly from above. The disease is making her eyes water and her words slur. Before she was diagnosed several people at the library where Vivian worked had thought she'd turned into a drunk.

'Look, Mama, let's just calm it all down and see what happens. I'll keep talking to the staff here; they're not all devoid of compassion.'

'Delphi, promise me you will get me out of here? If this goes on too long, I will lose the last of my strength and won't be able to kill myself. I can hardly brush my own teeth as it is. They will institutionalise me and then I will be imprisoned. I can't have that be my life, rotting away in a hospital bed year on end. You must promise me, my darling?'

Delphi rises, puts her cup down then sits on the side of the metal bed. The starched sheets and plastic mattress protector crunch as she holds her mother. 'Okay, Mama, I promise, but please relax and breathe.' The fight goes out of Vivian and the women soften in each other's arms. Delphi thinks about a study she read that explained how the vital signs of people who love each other sync up. Their heart rate and breathing patterns mimic each other. Women are much more apt to do this than men, underscoring an increased capacity for empathy. Delphi is sure she and her mother are tracking in perfect unison.

There is a knock at the door. Vivian calls 'Yes' and a small, hirsute man with thick glasses pops his head around the frame. Delphi warmly thinks of Mole from *The Wind in the Willows.*

'Hello there,' says the man. He's wearing a bow tie and has three coloured pens lined up in his shirt pocket. Delphi wants to draw whiskers beside his nose and be done with it.

'Hello,' the women answer.

'I've come from Christ,' says Mole, turning to address Vivian, 'He is so sad you've tried to take your life, the precious, sacred gift he gave you.'

Delphi feels as if a grenade blast has gone off in the room and all she can hear is a dreadful ringing as her eardrums reverberate.

Vivian's face crumples in distress. Delphi tunes back in as Mole mentions *eternal damnation* and then says, 'You must be so terribly lost, I've come to help you.' He's taken a step into the room and has a bible in his hands. He's quoting scripture or speaking in tongues, Delphi isn't entirely sure. Vivian is crying now and every tear makes Delphi wild with the necessity to protect her.

'No thank you,' she says to Mole but he ignores her, focusing on Vivian.

'For no one is cast off by the Lord forever. Though he brings grief, he will show compassion, so great is his unfailing love. For he does not willingly bring affliction or grief to anyone.'

'Seriously?' Delphi is on her feet and pulling up to her full height. Her mother has been through enough; this is all completely perverse. 'That seems a pretty bloody shaky argument to me.' Outrage is infectious in the room and now it's Delphi's turn to detonate. 'He doesn't bring *affliction or grief*? Shall we pop across to the paediatric oncology unit and see if your opinion holds there?'

Mole looks embarrassed. Delphi can't tell if it is for himself or for her. She gives absolutely zero fucks either way.

'You feel you have the right to come in here and pass judgement? You claim to be a representative of Jesus when His whole deal was forgiveness and love, yet in His mighty name you pedal fear and sin?'

Delphi's wings are stretched across the room; she has tripled in size. 'We don't want what you're selling. Take your brand of faith and get the hell away from my mother!'

Mole opens his mouth, closes it then dashes off the sign of the cross and backs out of the room.

'Well, darling,' sniffs Vivian, 'I think we both need a nice cup of tea.'

Delphi agrees but first trembles her way into the bathroom. She shuts the door and holds herself up against the wall. She swirls with a grief so extraterrestrial she thinks she's going to pass out. Delphi refuses to give in. She makes stern eye contact with herself in the mirror and demands fortitude. Hold it together, sister, hold it together. The two Delphis claw back to solidity, stare down at their purple Converse high-tops, take a few deep breaths, then return to make tea for their mother.

*

'Please follow me, Miss Hoffman. I'm Inspector Dutton.' They don't shake hands. He is about forty, blond, was once thin but has gone to fat. The inspector has a tanned face stencilled with much paler skin around his eyes from his sunglasses. Delphi wonders if he's a sailor because he obviously doesn't exercise. Maybe he plays old boys' cricket and doesn't wear a hat? Delphi's brain chatters and races from place to place. The fear coursing through her feels very much like speed. Manic and dirty. Delphi gathers her bag, book and jacket and follows him down the corridor and up a flight of stairs.

Inspector Dutton stops, reaches for a handle, opens the door wide and stands back to let Delphi through. 'Please take a seat at the table, and I will be back in a few ticks with Constable Carter.'

His casualness is like a strong aftershave. Cloying. Overstated. Worrying.

Delphi nods and does as she's told. She wonders if she looks as terrified as she feels. She's struggling to breathe and is screaming at herself to calm down, which is compacting her stress, making room for more rather than reducing it.

Eleven minutes pass. Delphi counts every one on the wall clock. She wonders if this is a technique, if they're letting her sweat it out. Is she being filmed? The blinds are hanging lopsided in the small window and Delphi resists the urge to straighten them. Someone has deposited a grind of pink chewing gum in the bin. Delphi shudders to think of being forced to chew it.

The door opens and in swaggers Inspector Dutton with a woman, presumably Constable Carter. She looks smart, direct, as if she won all the sports awards at school.

Introductions are made and the women shake hands then Delphi sits back down on her side of the table.

'Okay, Miss Hoffman,' he opens, 'You're aware you're here to give a statement about the attempted suicide of your mother, Vivian Heath, in her home yesterday evening, which was Thursday the fourth of March, today being Friday the fifth?'

Delphi swallows and nods. Inspector Dutton leans towards the recording device that's sitting in the middle of the table against the wall. 'Miss Hoffman has nodded in assent. From here out, please state your answers *aloud* so the recording can catch them.' His face isn't unkind, but Delphi can tell he doesn't like her. She wonders how he votes, not left that's for sure.

'Ah, sorry, yes,' says Delphi. She determines that the smartest way to play this is from underneath. Her strength will irritate this man, he likes his women submissive. Delphi lets her spine collapse a little, drops her chin and tilts her head, so she's looking up and out from under her eyebrows. An anatomical play immortalised by Princess Diana.

'In your own words can you please tell us what happened yesterday during the day and into the evening?'

Delphi is sitting on one of her hands and it's starting to go numb. She shifts her weight further on to it hoping the pain will crystalise her focus.

'Um, well… I arrived in Hobart last week. I live in London.'

Constable Carter is taking notes in a jarringly red pen.

'My mother Vivian has a terminal degenerative disease and ever since she was diagnosed has been determined to euthanise herself when things got too bad. And, well… that's what happened yesterday.'

The couple in uniform sit in silence waiting for Delphi to continue.

'Um, we spent the day together. We talked, we hung out with her dog, we watched some telly. In the evening she went to bed and I tidied up then I went out for a walk.'

Delphi has absolutely no idea if they're buying it. It's coming out of her mouth just as she rehearsed it but she's so tired with her adrenals jammed on that she can't properly distinguish which way is up and which way is jail.

Inspector Dutton leans back in his chair, 'So you went for a walk without the dog?'

Delphi hadn't thought that bit through. She's been talking for only two minutes and is already making a mess.

'Yes, that's right, the dog is obsessed with my mother and he won't walk with anyone else. That's why I left him at home with her.'

'And you didn't feel the need to take your shoes either?'

Delphi leg starts to shake at the knee and she forces her foot into the ground to stop it.

'Ah, um… I often do that, I like to feel the ground, re-wilding, you know?

'Nope, I can't say I *actually* do, Miss Hoffman.' His deliberate leaning on the word 'actually' freaks Delphi out.

From there the three of them spend some time unpacking the day in more detail and Delphi by-and-large tells the truth. Dutton leans forward with renewed interest and asks, 'Miss Hoffman, did your mother tell you she was going to try to take her life last night?' Delphi answers him with a straightforward 'No.'

Dutton circles around pressing harder.

'Did you help your mother try to end her life, Miss Hoffman?'

Delphi holds his gaze with her deferential chin still tucked in and repeats, 'No.'

'Will your mother try again do you think?'

'Yes, yes, I do… it's what she wants, her quality of life is terr–' He cuts her off, his energy is barrelling into Delphi.

'Do you intend to help her?'

Delphi takes her time and answers. 'She has never asked me to help her. She wouldn't want me to get into any trouble.'

And with that Inspector Dutton shakes his head quickly, as if flicking water from his hair and sits back in his chair. He swings a look to Constable Carter and something passes between them. The three sit awkwardly for a few moments and Carter asks, 'When your mother had gone into her room and you hadn't quite finished tidying up, where did you walk to, Miss Hoffman?'

Delphi furrows her brow and answers, 'Down to the reserve below my mother's house. I sat by the river for a while and when I came back to go to bed, all hell had broken loose. The house was full of people and my mother was unconscious. I think she waited for me to go out, to protect me, to keep me out of it.' Carter takes copious notes.

How can she possibly be writing so much after those few sentences? 'And did anyone see you? When you went walking?'

Delphi shakes her head and then remembering the recorder says, 'No, it was late, and that area is very quiet. I don't even really know anyone here, in Tasmania. I've only visited a few times since my mother moved here.'

The police look at each other again, and Dutton formally closes the interview for the recording.

'Thank you for your time, Miss Hoffman.' And as an afterthought, 'We hope you understand how serious this is.'

The uniforms are both standing and Delphi feels very small and frail on her chair. She nods and says, 'Of course.' She raises herself up hoping her legs will solidify and support her.

Dutton says a dry goodbye and leaves Constable Carter to show Delphi out. They make their way silently down and when they reach the front door Carter looks at Delphi, and gently asks, 'Are you doing alright?' Delphi's sore eyes brim again but she holds herself rigid, frightened that the dam will break and she will become hysterical. Carter places her hand on Delphi's forearm momentarily and says, 'Please be careful, okay?'

Delphi looks at the woman's face, and recognises a well-loved human. Constable Carter's parents have always been proud of their girl, and they've told her so. Delphi struggles to pull on her jacket and says, 'Yes, I will, thank you.'

Delphi stumbles a little down the front stairs. She doesn't look back because she's sure Constable Carter is watching her.

*

'Pilot, my furry friend, would you like a scotch, too?' Delphi scratches him under his chin and swallows the dregs in her glass. She has been procrastinating calling her brother in Paris.

He's a sculptor but she's only seen his recent work online and it's good, classical. He has a baby daughter called Zenia and Delphi has heard virtually nothing about the mother. So many locked rooms. Delphi is confounded by how relationships can just drift into oblivion, particularly those forged in blood. The estrangement is as bewildering as it is sad. The riddle to solve seems to be *how does one repair a damage one doesn't even understand?*

Delphi refills her glass, grabs the phone and sits herself down on the hallway floor. She's left the front door open so she can look out into the blackness of the river. There are no lights on the grazing land on the far side so her imagination fills in the blank. She lifts the old school receiver to her ear and twists the numbers into the rotary dial. The international ring tone buzzes and Delphi senses an adrenaline drop hit her bloodstream. Pilot waddles over and puts his head with his fairy-dust eyebrows on her thigh. *Animals know.*

After five or six rings the call is answered by an answering service. A French humanoid requests that she leave a message. Delphi inhales, winding her finger into the coiled cord of the phone and says, 'Jack… It's me, Delphi. I'm sorry to call you like this but Mama is in the hospital. She tried to kill herself a few days ago. It didn't go well. I… well, I wanted to call you earlier, but Mama forbid it… I think she actually used that word, forbid… forbade… it's lovely in the past tense too, isn't it?' She can't believe she's talking vocabulary now.

'Anyway… it's all a bit of a mess. The palliative care administrator told Mama today that she was selfish and destructive… That suicide detonates a guilt bomb that destroys families. And what else… oh yeah, a nurse wearing a gay pride badge asked me how I was coping with the stigma of suicide. Stigma. He used that word.' Back to more language analysis? Delphi pinches herself hard on the cheek.

'I'm sorry, I'm prattling.' Delphi gropes around in her brain for other topics. 'I heard from Mama and Hugh that you have a baby girl. I'm happy for you, Jack. I hope you got the present I sent. You'll be an amazing daddy, I'm sure.'

The pause swells as Delphi canters back over all the inanity she's just recorded.

'Okay, well, it's very late here. Pilot and I are going to go to sleep now. Do call if you want to.'

'And Jack… Jack, I really want to say that–' Delphi knocks her scotch over and the liquid spills across her mother's carpet. 'Shit! Oh sorry, I spilt my drink. You know if Vivian were here she'd be going off her dial.' Delphi releases her grip on the fraying rope of this message. 'Bye Jack. Bye…' she says hoping he can't hear the defeat in her voice.

She replaces the receiver and stares at the phone sitting moss green and squat. She pulls off her t-shirt and drapes it over the booze on the floor to sop it up. Delphi exhales hard. 'Oh bloody hell, Pilot, that was not what I hoped.' The dog yawns then hops up on his little stubby legs and trots off around the house. He does this every half hour or so, checking the perimeter for Vivian, wanting her home. Delphi sprawls out and watches him from a weird angle on the floor. Her eyelashes blinking against the carpet. 'I miss her too, bud, yes I do.' He comes back and snuggles into her side and she curves to make a more compatible space for him. 'Mammal Tetris,' whispers Delphi and shuts her eyes.

'Stuff it!' she says with sudden conviction and Pilot starts with a jump. Delphi finds the number she wrote on an old bill earlier and dials her mother at the hospital. It takes forever for Vivian to answer.

'Sorry, Mama, were you sleeping?'

'Delphi darling? Yes, sort of sleeping, not dead I'm sad to say.' Her words slosh together.

'Mama, let's bust you out. I'm going to come to get you right now. Pilot and I want you home. It's called a "discharge against medical advice" an officious doctor tried to warn me off it. The hospital won't like it, legally they're in the wind if you die, but I don't think that's ours to worry about. It will be a skeleton staff now so let's just make like bandits.'

'Make like bandits? Darling, that means to profit greatly not to dash over a prison wall.'

'Oh really? That's a bit disappointing, Mama, I was happy with that phrase.'

'Yes, I understand, my flower, but if it's inaccurate it's not right, is it? Now come and save me. And bring my dog, Delphi, bring that soft boy.'

'You've got it. We'll be there in fifteen minutes.' Delphi smiles and hangs up to find the car keys. Action is much kinder on the nerves than suspension. She is grateful to be able to finally help. Her sense of uselessness recedes. She knows what she can do for her mother and it's edifying. She couldn't kill her, but she can bring her home. It's not enough but it is practical and achievable, and Delphi will wholeheartedly take that. Her grandpa used to say *a single twig is weak but a bundle of them are strong*. Maybe actions for good are like that too. Maybe it's an equation that can be true of people also. Alone weak, together strong. She calls for Pilot and they run outside and into the car. Once the dog is settled on the passenger seat, she plunges the key into the ignition and turns the stereo on. Metallica's 'Nothing Else Matters' is playing. Delphi whoops with the serendipity and Pilot wags his tail madly. She lowers the windows so he can stick his head out as they drive. 'Consider my lap your seat too little guy.' Delphi gives him a pat and turns the stereo up to full volume.

*

Delphi and Vivian are sitting on the back deck of the house drinking tea in the flaxen sunshine. A butterfly is circling close by. Delphi hopes that it's loving it's horrifyingly fleeting twenty-four hours on earth. Vivian has watched Delphi paint her toenails Smurf blue and Delphi is reading out loud to her mother. The two have settled into a domesticity that belies what has gone before. Delphi thinks about the stillness in the eye of the storm. She sees herself and Vivian sanguine inside the central calm of a tornado. Delphi reaches out to touch her mother's hand. She's aware it's the first time since her arrival that is peaceful, and the dreadful tension in her shoulders has eased. Vivian closes her eyes dreamily against the sun and Delphi smiles, imprinting the moment of her mother's beauty. Vivian is expanded with restfulness, her white skin luminous. Delphi takes the photo with her mind and thinks of Sally Mann and of Orlo. Delphi notices the butterfly approaching Vivian. With all her heart she wills it to land on her mother. The butterfly dances about for some time, Delphi is aware she's holding her breath, and then it touches down on Vivian's thigh. It carries on moving its delicate wings and Delphi is filled with joy. A sacred omen of hope. Or maybe a benediction from the gods. Delphi can't explain it but she accepts it as precious and wonderful.

The doorbell rings and Pilot cranks up his barking.

'Are you expecting anyone, Mama?'

'No, I am not.' Vivian shakes her head clumsily, bovinely, struggling to open her eyes against the sun. The disease is bleaching her neurons.

Delphi skips to the front door telling Pilot to knock it off which is pointless as he furiously carries on yapping. She throws open the door and standing there with a large soft bag by his feet is her big brother, Jack. Delphi is delighted and wants to launch her arms around him but is warned off by his energy. He looks older now, thinner in the face. His hair is dark, long and unruly, Byronesque. He's wearing jeans with a rip in one knee and dilapidated boots. Jack is wiry and lean, and yet he's always moved slowly as if carrying a great weight. His eyes are tired and sad, but he smiles. Delphi is struck by how wonderful he is, how fiercely she adores him, and how hurt she is that he doesn't stay in touch.

'Hello Del.' He leans forward and gives her a stubbly kiss on the cheek.

'Wow, you're here from Paris?' Delphi is stunned.

'I am. Thank you for your message. Where is the Queen Bee?'

Delphi steps back and gestures for him to come indoors. 'She's here, out the back.'

Jack pats the now twirling dog, drops his bag in the kitchen and walks out to find Vivian. Delphi follows to see her mother catching sight of her prodigal son and Vivian's face exploding in adoration and disbelief. The two cuddle each other and press their heads close like primates. Delphi's torso heaves with contained emotion and she retreats to settle herself and get drinks from the kitchen.

Delphi puts the kettle on, finds and opens two Cascade lagers, searches out a suitable teacup for her brother, he used to be picky, and another one for her mother. Delphi listens as they reconnect. There's laughter. Gathering her hostess offerings on a tray, she re-joins them and hands a green bottle to her brother and a fresh cup of tea to her mother. Delphi raises her bottle in a toast.

'We three reunited. It's good to see you, Jack.'

'And you too, Del, and you, Mother.'

Vivian is holding on to Jack's hand and patting it, her eyes thirsty for her son, tracking every contour of him and sporadically pulling him back into a clumsy embrace.

'So, Delphi, this stunning arrival makes everything a good deal simpler.'

'How's that, Mama?'

'You need to go, flower. You can't be here when I die or the police will hound you. They came to interview me in hospital.'

'You didn't tell me that.'

'I didn't want to worry you, my love, but they know you tried to help me.'

'But how? Was it the dog thing or my shoes? I don't think I handled that interrogation well.'

'No, love, it was my bruising. The nurses reported the marks on my arms and legs, all fingertip-sized and apparently I have one on my back that looks almost like a complete handprint. A Rorschach test of blood rather than ink that incriminates you, my darling.'

Delphi is appalled.

'So, my girl, I want you to leave, to be safe.'

Delphi puts her head down on her knees and tries to sift through an exploding big bang of thoughts. Is she being released or cast out? Where will she go? In which direction does a child face when they're leaving a parent for the final time?

Failure and shame make a crown on Delphi's head. She hasn't managed to help her mother. Once again she's the little girl who needs to be managed. Shunted off to boarding school. Secrets withheld from. Moved out of the picture. Told the way to help is to keep out of the way, to be at a distance. She is being passed over and Jack will step in to do, and be, what she is incapable of. She remembers being very young and Vivian in a drunken rage about her father. She was smashing crockery. Delphi had tried to calm her, begging Vivian to stop. Jack had come in and Vivian had screamed, 'Get her out! Take her away!' He'd picked Delphi up and she had resisted, reaching out desperately for her mother. Jack had put Delphi in her room and told her to wait, that he would come back, but it had taken hours to talk Vivian down. He'd still only been a boy himself, he was exhausted, he'd forgotten his promise, and Delphi sat all night alone in the dark, waiting.

She looks up and the eyes of her sibling and mother are resting on her. She inhales sharply and says, 'Let me get you another beer, Jack.' She stands and as she walks inside lifts a hand to her throat unsure if it's failure or exclusion that is blocking it.

*

Delphi's bag is packed. She has absolutely no idea how she is going to survive what is being asked of her.

'Mama, do you know Leonard Cohen had a love affair with a woman named Marianne Ihlen? She was a documentary maker and his muse. She inspired his "So Long, Marianne" and "Bird on the Wire".'

'No, my flower, of course I know him, a great man, a poet but I've not heard of her.'

'They were together in the late sixties and maybe early seventies. Before Cohen died, he was told that Marianne was dying of leukaemia.'

Maybe this is a dreadful idea.

'He wrote to her just before her death and I wanted to read you his letter… only if you're interested of course… but I found it moving.'

Delphi can't bring herself to be more explicit, that this letter is about saying the ultimate goodbye in the face of a great love. Just as she and her mother will be doing within the hour.

'Yes, read it to me, my darling.' Vivian resettles in her chair.

Delphi sits on the floor and pulls out the transcribed letter she's been keeping in her pocket.

'Well Marianne, it's come to this time when we are really so old, and our bodies are falling apart, and I think I will follow you very soon. Know that I am so close behind you that if you stretch out your hand, I think you can reach mine.'

Delphi struggles to stay the course, but she wills her voice to steady and ploughs her eyes along the trembling page.

'And you know that I've always loved you for your beauty and for your wisdom, but I don't need to say anything more about that because

you know all about that. But now, I just want to wish you a very good journey. Goodbye old friend. Endless love, see you down the road.'

The women sit in wretched silence. Delphi refolds the paper and tucks it away. She is unable to lift her eyes to her mother as tears are freely flowing down her chafed checks. She leans forward and with both hands encircles her mother's bare ankle.

'Mama, you are just going first. You'll take a part of my heart, and in some years, I will follow you back through the stargates. There on the other side, reunited with you, and with baby Arthur.'

Jack has already said his goodbyes to his sister, and thanked her for returning his hire car to the airport. He calls from the kitchen. 'Del, you need to go now or you will miss your flight.'

'I know. Thank you,' she answers wiping her face.

She sees Jack scoop up her bag and take it outside to put it in the hire car.

The mother and daughter help each other up and move to the front door. They stand holding each other for the last time. Delphi breathes in every particle she can. She is incapable of speech. Delphi looks into her mother's blue eyes and Vivian caresses her child's cheek. She proffers an immutable truth. 'I love you.' Delphi cannot answer, the internal pressure generating an earthquake of unbearable emotions. Delphi kisses her mother on both hands, then on her cheeks. She backs down the stairs crushing the railing in her grip. All she can do is to move and to stay connected with her eyes.

Jack is waiting by the car; he kisses her and shuts the door as Delphi mechanically sits behind the steering wheel. Key somehow finds ignition. She starts to reverse and part way down the drive she looks back. Her mother is standing with one hand on her heart and she raises the other high in a salute. Delphi presses her hand to the glass. Vivian offers a final sad smile of farewell.

Once Delphi has the car at the bottom of the driveway she drives for a minute or so before pulling over to the side of the road. Out of Vivian's sight Delphi is engulfed by fire. Her emotional pain and psychic pain register as physical pain. The three cannot be separated.

CHAPTER 8

It's cold, even for the tail end of a British winter. The trees are still naked, the colour palette greys and blues. She knows this neck of the woods, the streets of her childhood. Delphi pulls her scarf up to cover her chin.

She caught an early train from London and the morning fog is still sitting low. Delphi stops on the stone bridge and looks at the freezing Thames gushing underneath her. Surreal to think that just three days before she was standing on a concreate seventies bridge, on the other side of the planet, scrutinising the Derwent River. Looking at her reflection now she wonders if she's rippling with courage or if it's the quivering of a fool.

Delphi presses on towards her childhood home. She's not seen her father for several years. The last time was when her best friend from school told her that Edward had seduced her when she was sixteen. Delphi had been furious and when confronted her father had denied it resolutely, rendering Delphi swirling with revulsion and a keen sense of betrayal. She had sworn to herself that she would stay away from him but her conviction has dissipated, Delphi yearns for him now. To be reunited, amalgamated, held. To be parented. Delphi doesn't want to be an orphan and spending time with Vivian these weeks has further impressed on her how precious time is and that it's truly a commodity that runs out. She remembers when she was little, Edward used to read to her. She would climb onto his big lap, and they'd sit together as he expertly did all the voices from the

Roald Dahl books. He taught her how to ride a bike when she was four. She'd fallen several times. One of her knees was quite badly grazed but she'd kept getting back on. And when she managed to make the bike balance and circled her feet with determination and speed, Edward had danced in the street, bellowing with delight.

*

The house looks the same. Victorian era, the symmetrical frontage, triangular roof lines, the gabled entrance, ivy triumphantly covering the stone. Delphi doesn't pause to look too carefully as she walks up the path to the front door. She bangs the lion head knocker. 'Hello lion,' she whispers and traces his nose with her forefinger.

Delphi tries to stop herself dancing from foot to foot with nerves. No response from inside. After a few moments, she gives the lion another rap. It clonks out peculiarly loud to her alert ears.

Delphi pivots around slowly on the stoop. Nothing. The place is shrouded in stillness. She jumps down and wades through the flowers to check in the front window. The roses claw and ladder her stockings. Excellent, she thinks looking at her snagged left leg. She presses her face to the old, warped glass; inside looks tomblike. Juliet could be slumbering on the coffee table in there waiting for Romeo.

The place has been redecorated. The walls are apricot, the colour of suburban death. Edward got the family home in the divorce and Vivian got crumbs. Beyond the sitting room Delphi can see into the dining room. One night, in her teens during the school holidays, her father was having a dinner party. Delphi was taking off her shoes in the boot room. She could hear the crowd guffawing with laughter, they were drunk and boisterous. In her socks, Delphi went into the kitchen to make herself some toast and heard her father's voice speaking in an exaggerated and mocking tone. Another round of laughter erupted and someone hooted. Delphi drifted towards the dining room, a slice of bread in one hand. From the doorway she saw her father reading to the group, reading from her diary.

With this, Edward had delivered the purest experience of humiliation she'd ever known. He'd later defended his actions by calling her overly sensitive and saying she must have wanted him to read it because she left her diary on her desk, inviting it to be read.

Delphi frees herself from the bushes and sets off around the front lawn. She's leaving tracks in the dew, feeling like a burglar. Scanning all the windows looking for signs of life Delphi makes her way around the side of the house. There, under the huge oak tree, are the little submerged headstones of their dogs past. She sends them all her fondest love. Delphi's hamster Poseidon is also buried there. She'd thought that name was hilarious.

She circumnavigates the conservatory. Vaguely she remembers her parents putting that addition on; it must be one of her first memories. The excitement, yes, but the real magic came in the discovery of how the glass magnified the sun's rays. Delphi would stretch out on the tiles and study the red membrane of her closed eyelids, being warmed and baked to her core. Vivian used to sail past, clopping on high heels, bracelets clinking and say, 'You always turn towards to the sun like a flower, Delphi.'

Edward had called her a lizard, which Delphi can see is ironic as it's his blood that runs cold.

The garden looks just the same, the wonderful, majestic tangle of trees ringing the expanse. The long-abandoned swing waiting to be re-animated. The birdbath green with moss. The many-windowed house looks on with empty eyes. Before Delphi focuses on the swimming pool, a wave of nausea rises in her. After Arthur's death, her parents had the pool fence fixed, too late, but it stands here still, rebuking, rudely defiant.

The water is hidden beneath a grey pool cover. A single leaf blows about, but many others are clumped by the ladder. Delphi presses her lips with her fingers as she's slashed by the image of Arthur's face suspended below the surface. His blue eyes staring calmly up at her. His blond curls drifting as if in a celestial breeze.

*

Delphi hears the crunch of tyres on the driveway and is electrocuted back to the present. She runs around to the front of the house to see a Mercedes pull in beside the garage. Instinct makes her stay hidden. The passenger doors open and out tumble people unfamiliar to her. Soon they are all in view, laughing, joyful, pastel, radiating health. They look as new and fresh as a soap commercial. The children, a boy and a girl, talk animatedly. The mother, her soft blonde bob refusing to stay tucked behind her ear, laughs. The father goes to the boot to remove some breakfast supplies in brown paper bags and the four make their way into the house, into their home. Delphi recognises the familiar sound of the knocker giving a little clunk with the energy transfer from the door closing.

This is not her home anymore. It's not her father's home either. She has no idea when he sold it, something desolate and miserable presses into her. Nostalgia, sentimentality, the past dissolving. This honeyed quartet of functional familial happiness, of impertinent unbrokenness, have claimed this house and they've made it their home. Apricot walls and too many scatter cushions. Delphi is confused by how she feels; she's unfamiliar with jealousy.

Those lucky chosen four have something she covets. Envy tries to work its sickness and she retreats into the thicker grove of trees. She turns, moving diagonally through the foliage until she hits the perimeter's wooden fence. She jumps it, her breath billowing out like a dragon's.

A story she once heard comes to mind, it was about a snail looking for its home. It tried everywhere; a house, a tin can, a bucket, all are no good. In the end the snail realises that its home has been right there all along, on its back.

She walks onwards, but without direction.

*

'I think I know you,' says the publican. Delphi smiles weakly and sips her pint.

'Probably, I've been coming here all my life, not for a while, but mostly with my mother. We came here a lot when I was younger.'

'Who's that then?' He has the lilting accent of a Yorkshireman.

'Vivian Heath.' Delphi takes another deep sip.

'Oh, aye, I remember her. Very glamorous your mother, moved to South Africa or was it Australia? Loved a Bloody Mary.'

Delphi laughs. 'Yes, that's pretty much right.' And the publican nudges away her attempt to pay. 'Nope this one is for your ma. I liked her.'

Delphi opens a discarded newspaper but is interrupted by a man perched on the stool to her right.

'I'm sorry to disturb you, Miss, but I think I know you and your family too.'

Delphi looks up to see a man with a boozer's nose and a tweed flat-cap on his head.

'I'm Angus McCawley. I used to be with the police force before I retired.'

Delphi shakes his hand and wonders how quickly she can escape him.

'Tell me if I'm mistaken…' He leans in conspiratorially and Delphi becomes drunk from the whisky on his breath.

'Tell me, lass, did a great sadness befall your family? I can't remember the details exactly, but…' Delphi hopes he will stop, but he presses on.

'Is your father Edward Hoffman the psychiatrist?'

'Yes,' Delphi says, shielding her face behind her glass.

'Aye, then it is your family. Your old man is a great doctor, a great man. He helped my wife when she was very low.'

This happens to Delphi fairly often and every time she's intrigued by the irony that her father is celebrated as great. A healer, a person of emotional and intellectual intelligence, and yet with all those skills offered to the outside world, few were reserved for his kin. Jack had fallen in love with his English teacher in senior school. Delphi never knew if they became lovers but in retrospect, she assumed they had. Edward had had an affair with the same woman. There was a cruel timing overlap and the fight between son and father had shaken the house so hard it cracked the foundations. It was before the divorce between Vivian and Edward was finalised, which took them years to sort out as periodically they would make a stab at reuniting. This time the eruption blew when the family were all together for Christmas. Delphi was ten and Jack sixteen. A table was upended. Jack had frothed and sworn. Edward had denied and minimised. Finally, Jack hit his father in the face, stood over Edward's fallen form and shouted, 'I will never forgive you.'

The whisky soused man has a golden retriever slumbering at his feet, and Delphi intends, as soon as manners permit, to redirect this conversation to that safe furry terrain.

'And your mam, always so put together.'

Delphi looks about to see if she can move elsewhere.

'Your mam had a breakdown and tried to kill herself. The reason I knows is I was on duty that night and I always felt good that your da saved my Cathleen and I, and in my own small way, I saved your mam.'

He rubs his stomach with both hands like a jovial Humpty Dumpty.

Delphi had no idea her mother had ever tried to commit suicide before. No idea she'd had a breakdown.

The man's nicotine-stained fingers tap the wooden bar. 'That's right and you were there, a little girl, maybe six or seven, in your nightie. You'd found your mam and called us. I remember your face clear as day, you were crying like a leaking pipe. You looked like a doll, 'cos you weren't making any noise, but dem tears flowed out of you so. I was worried you'd clean dry out.'

Delphi has absolutely no memory of any of this. The revelation makes her feel like she's peaking.

'Geoffrey!' He booms as someone he recognises comes into the pub. He offers a hasty, rambunctious farewell to Delphi and then crashes off to play darts. Delphi is left stunned, as if her ears have been cloched. She grips onto the stool tightly to stop herself slithering to the floor.

*

'Grandpa, it's me, Del.' She speaks loudly over the noise of the pub and pops another coin into the payphone as her mobile is out of credit.

'Dear, how lovely to hear from you. Just wait a second while I turn off the television.'

Delphi hears his receiver clatter down and she is filled with soft undulating love for him. She thinks of his cobalt blue eyes, the same shade as Vivian's. There's a sweetness about him that makes Delphi always want to hold his hand.

'Right, I'm back. How are you, dear? When are you coming to visit me? I hear from Mummy that you're back in London.'

'I'm okay, thank you. And I promise I will come soon. I miss you.' She avoids telling him she's not very far from his house.

'And I miss you too,' he says in his gravelly voice.

'Grandpa, how did Mama sound when you spoke to her?' She knows Vivian has told her father of her plans, but so far, he has never wanted to discuss it.

'She sounded pretty well. Loving having Jack with her.'

'Yes, it's good they're together.' She leaves a space for him which he doesn't use. 'Grandpa, I was calling to tell you I love you, but also to see if you have Edward's new address. He's moved from Twiborn Lane.'

'Oh yes, quite a while ago now, maybe a year. You know I don't see your father, but I do have his address. I'm sorry I didn't mention that to you, my brain is mostly porridge these days. Shall I find it for you?'

She smiles and scratches her eyebrow. 'Yes please.'

A woman in a knitted beanie squeezes past Delphi to get to the bathroom.

'Righty-o. Got it. Do you have a pen?'

*

Delphi is sitting on a freezing park bench watching two hot air balloons prepare for take-off in the field. The orbs inflate, the silk technicolour swelling and listing, nodding back and forth like creatures coming to life. People looking competent with a dash of urgency fire up the burners and then call out for the passengers to clamour aboard. The ropes are released and Delphi watches the baskets rise into the thick dawning heavens. She blows on her numb fingers and is awed as these whimsical vehicles ascend into the 'Great Above'.

A single snowflake floats down and rests on Delphi's check. Very strange at this time of year. This forerunner opens the gates and its ice-friends chase it down. Delphi sits in wonderment as over the space of an hour the field is enveloped white. A new dimension is added to the quality of the silence. An early spring miracle.

She observes the visible in-and-out of her breath. Delphi is calm and capacious. She wonders how her mother is, she misses her and thinks of Vivian, Jack and Pilot sitting together.

Delphi inspects her thighs, her feet, her hands, all snow-covered. She's sentient, she's completely present and wide awake. She draws resolve up through the ground and she calls it down from the skies. She imagines her entire bloodline, all her ancestors standing, flanking her, their faces all turned to her with curiosity. This makes her stronger. She is not alone. There are all those that have come before and those that will come after. Delphi is just one of the whole. Vivian read her a story years before about a little wave bobbing about in the ocean. He's enjoying the wind and the fresh air until he notices the waves in front of him crashing onto the shore. 'Oh, this is dreadful!' the wave says. 'Look what is going to happen to me!' Then along comes another wave and she sees the first wave looking grim and she says to him, 'Why do you look so sad?' The first wave says, 'You don't understand! We are all going to be crushed! Us waves will be nothing! Isn't it terrible?' The second wave says, 'No, little one, you don't understand, you're part of the ocean. You are part of the ocean.'

CHAPTER 9

HE LOOKS OLDER, STIFFER, more creased. His grey hair is thick and unruly. Even depleted by age, he still emanates power. He is at his front door, bending down as he tries to attach two bounding Tibetan Spaniels to their leashes. He's wearing khaki-coloured Hunter boots and the trout fishing jacket he's always worn when he goes out walking. Delphi's heart expands, despite everything. Love has such valour in its stride. Her mind is telling her to protect herself, that he will hurt her again. And yet her heart wants to love him, to be loved by him, to be family. To love without limits, to blissfully surrender to the unconditional. To vanquish judgement and accept it all. Fear and hope surge forward, racing for dominance.

Eventually he gets the dogs hooked up and cool as ever, as if he's been expecting her on this exact day, he stands and looks at Delphi.

She's confronted by the genetic link, her own eyes looking back at her but detached like a reptile. He was always better at battle. He runs cold and she runs hot – opposites in all things. Delphi pushes against her desire to flee but is also held by the gravitational pull of the parent.

They stand like this for a vibrating moment. He waits for her to speak as he's generally not one to make the first move. His strategies are calculated with binary clicks. Her voice has abandoned her but she stands straight-backed, aiming for open.

'Hello Delphi,' he says. His capacity to indicate disinterest towards her is always unnerving. A father carved from stone.

'Hello Edward,' she says evenly.

'I was just off for a walk with Tobias and Guinevere.'

She looks at the puppet dogs with their wet, loose eyelids. She can't see their souls; they're fuzzy, like battery operated toys.

'I presume by that bag you intend to stay?' he says.

'Um, well yes, if I may? If it isn't an imposition to you or Clara?'

Edward had married Clara just before Vivian had hightailed it to Tasmania. Even though Vivian claimed these events weren't connected, Delphi knew they were. Just because someone breaks your heart doesn't mean you can stop loving them. Just because someone doesn't deserve your love doesn't mean you won't love them.

'Go inside. The dogs and I will be back in an hour.'

'May I come with you?' Delphi asks.

'No, thank you.'

She is winded but employs her manners to stabilise. 'Enjoy your walk.'

'Thank you,' he says. He doesn't look back as he sets off chatting to the dogs with a tenderness Delphi can't recall him offering her since she was a child. She has distant memories of playing childhood games with him. Hide and seek in the garden. If she'd been hiding too long she'd become afraid and would make a noise leading him to her. He would grab her, delighted, lifting her high, smiling, and then hold her to his chest as he'd run about. She remembers the happiness, the playfulness. She remembers the feeling of their delight but as she grew it disintegrated. For him relating to a small child was different to dealing with a young woman. When his eyes looked down it worked, but when they were level with hers it didn't.

The deficiency in their relationship jabs her in the ribs. She shoulders her bag and walks into her father's house.

*

They've eaten roast chicken with all the trimmings and Delphi resolves once again that eating meat is a crime. Tasty but wrong.

She downs the rest of her red wine and Clara is quick to refill it. It's essential to celebrate everything one is grateful for Delphi thinks. Her stepmother cooks well and sloshes booze about with a heavy pouring arm.

'Thank you, Clara. And thank you again for letting me stay.'

Over the last few hours, Clara has hardly drawn breath with her incessant talking. Neither of them has asked about Vivian. Delphi stands to clear the dishes. Clara catches her arm to study the long rope of pearls that Delphi has twisted around her wrist.

'Your father gave you these pearls, didn't he, Delphi?' Clara's eyes glint.

Delphi gently takes her wrist back and rolls the palm of her other hand over the luminescent beads.

'Ah... no. My mother gave them to me.' Danger! Danger, Will Robinson! Vivian has finally been mentioned and her spirit has entered stage left carrying a Molotov cocktail.

Clara doesn't accept this. 'No. That is not right. I remember your father giving those to you. They must be worth a fortune.' Her botoxed brow would lift if it weren't immobilised.

'My mother bought a rope of pearls for her mother with her first pay packet, and when she could afford to, she bought a matching set for herself. After my grandmother's death Mama had them combined into one long rope. That's the story,' Delphi says neutrally lifting the pearls to feel their warmth against her lips.

Clara looks irritated. 'Does that sound right to you, Eddie?'

Something about infantilising her father's name makes Delphi want to throw the plate she's holding against the far wall.

'Let me see?' he asks and puts his glasses on.

'Oh, yes, I recognise these. Your mother wore them all the time.'

'But Eddie,' Clara says, 'you gave *me* those pearls and you *took* them back to give *to her*.' Clara points at Delphi.

Edward looks shifty and diverts the conversation, but Delphi knows precisely what's occurred. She scoops up another plate and seeks asylum in the kitchen.

After the separation but before the divorce there was a dreadful row and her father had taken Vivian's jewellery box and had, over time, given the contents to various women. Vivian had risen with biblical fury. She demanded the return of the pearls, lest her anger engulfed the whole of England in vitriolic flames.

It took Edward years but ultimately, he relented and presented Delphi with them on her twenty-first birthday. She recognised them as her mother's and had returned them to her. Last week Vivian had taken the pearls from her neck and placed them into Delphi's hands. No words had been needed, they were passed to the third link of the generational chain. Three women connected. Just as each of them had been created. One inside the other, like genetic Russian dolls.

Delphi scrapes the remains of the dinner into the bin as both spaniels jump up on her legs scratching for attention. They're actually pretty sweet, she thinks, and finds some tasty leftovers for each. Dogs make everything better.

*

'Do you come to watch the rowing, Edward? When it's regatta season?' He'd been a keen oarsman at Cambridge University. The best years of his life he is wont to share. He nods in answer.

Edward and Delphi are sitting on a bench. They're drinking takeaway Pimm's by the river in the weak mid-morning sunlight. The crotchety ducks honk and quack for bread and the village of Henley-on-Thames bustles around them.

Delphi steadies herself as if preparing to climb a cliff face.

'Edward, I wanted to tell you about Mama. I came, in part, to tell you she will die soon. In case you wanted to write to her… or, well, I don't know… I just felt you should know.'

Edward doesn't move and after a minute without taking his eyes from the passing boat he says, 'I will fly to Tasmania for the funeral.'

Internally Delphi slams a door so hard it splinters off its hinges. She finds her composure.

'You know Mama doesn't want you there which must be painful for you, but you two–'

'The funeral is not for her, Delphi, it's for all of us.'

Delphi looks at his profile, his face collapsing with age yet the scaffolding of his sculptural nose is still striking. Vivian used to say he exuded unparalleled charm and was devilishly handsome. 'His face, like Caesar's, was made for gold coins,' and 'You should have seen the way he danced, my flower!' Sitting with him Delphi can still see the truth of that resplendent history but also he looks like a man who has not lived a kind life. We get the faces we earn.

'I don't understand why you want to go. You don't like Mama. I can't remember you ever saying anything kind or loving about her.'

Edward doesn't react. Delphi wonders if he wants to come to support her and Jack, and her heart opens like an aperture.

'I was her husband for many years. I'm the father of her children. It's the right thing that I should be there.'

There it is, the moral imperative. When it suits him, Edward has an inflexible and robust sense of what is correct. Delphi's chest fills with stones but she decides not to go to battle over this now. She wonders if she's a masochist, drawn back time and again to get her teeth kicked in. She knows this pattern needs to be broken and recast if she's to get free of this emotional straitjacket.

In for a penny, in for a pound, Delphi thinks, and she again reaches up the cliff face.

'Edward, will you tell me about Arthur?'

Nothing.

'I think about him. All the time. And I think being with Mama, being in a death space with her, it's opened all those old wounds. I don't think they ever actually close. Maybe I hoped for too much. Has your hurt from his death eased?'

Edward gives no indication he's listening and takes a sip of his drink, his eyes moving with a boat.

'I said this to Mama and I want to say it to you. I am intensely sorry that I let him drown.'

Edward snaps.

'Why do you want to rake up the past all the time? All of your life you've whipped up frenzies.'

Delphi has heard all of this before. She used to believe it, every toxic word, but not so much anymore. Be like a duck she says to herself, shake it off.

'That's not true. I don't.' She thinks again how strange it is that he has so little interest in people and yet became a shrink. Jack's theory is it was because it was prestigious and that Edward wanted to mend himself after his own painful childhood.

'Did Mama have her breakdown before or after Arthur?'

Edward wipes his mouth and takes a moment to choose his course. Delphi wills him to tell her the truth. It's impossible to put together a puzzle with pieces missing.

'After. It was after his death, but she was always mad.'

And there it is. A piece that has been withheld from Delphi joining the messy pile.

'And what happened then? Was she put into a clinic?'

'Yes, she went to Northampton because she couldn't cope and she'd tried to kill herself. She made me promise never to discuss it with you. She was ashamed and paranoid.'

He is looking at his daughter now, trying to read her. 'You don't remember, Delphi? Truly?'

She shakes her head.

He says, 'It was you that found her. Near dead, up to her eyeballs in pills. She was in the clinic for months. I don't know how long, six maybe, and you whimpered around the house pining for her, you hardly spoke. I couldn't comfort you. God knows I tried.' He looks as if he is going to weep. ' You refused to go to school, refused to eat or get dressed.'

Delphi swallows to clear her mouth. 'I'm sorry.' She can feel her return to the default position with her father but his evident pain is excruciating for her.

'And Arthur's death was your mother's fault. If she hadn't been drunk... well, it's all water under the bridge...'

The metaphor strikes Delphi as grotesque.

'I don't want to talk about it, Delphi.' He stands, waits for his spine and hip to settle and declares he's off to stretch his legs.

Delphi offers to hold his drink, but it drops to the grass, his hands shaking. She watches the ice, strawberry and cucumber tumble out. All of it makes her want to cry.

*

The central heating system is clicking and the thick wool carpet is soft underfoot. Delphi is alone in her father's home and she's moving from room to room. The coffee table is covered with aesthetically stacked hard-backed books, bought as decoration rather than to read. Clustered on side tables and shelves are trinket boxes, coloured glass vases, candles and small statues. The mahogany sideboard groans beneath two large candelabras and a mass of silver frames. Photographs of Clara and Edward on their wedding day, their dogs, of Kate and Josh, Clara's children from her first marriage, who live with her ex-husband. Delphi picks up a photo of her step-siblings and studies it. Matching sailor outfits. Pudgy faces. She wonders how Clara had mustered the justification to run off and leave them when they were so little. There are no photos of Delphi, Jack or baby Arthur. A previous life wiped clean.

Delphi opens a cabinet drawer and runs her fingers over a silver cutlery set, a wedding gift to her parents that Edward took it in the divorce, along with almost everything else. Just as history is written by the victors, in divorce the spoils go to the one who can afford the most savage lawyer.

She pads up the stairs and passes the guest room she's staying in. Her bag is open on the floor as there's no room in the cupboards because they're crammed with the overspill of Clara's clothes.

She walks past a bathroom and into her father's study. His grandfather's desk stands proud in the middle of the room. Reportedly it has secret compartments, Delphi made several committed but fruitless endeavours to find them when she was a child. She sits down in his leather chair and swivels around looking at his blotting-pad, his fountain pen, the paperweight with his and Clara's initials intertwined. It all reads as expensive but self-consciously staged. Delphi resists the urge to look in the drawers but picks up a discarded t-shirt and brings it to her face. It smells like Edward, of oak trees in the rain. Love rushes up in her dancing all over rationality. She folds the shirt, replaces it and pauses before she gathers it up to breathe it in again.

Further down the corridor she comes to the master bedroom. The door is slightly ajar and she pushes it open with her big toe. It's pastel on pastel and there are cushions with the embroidered faces of the dogs on the bed. Books on his bedside table, magazines on hers, half-drunk glasses of water, reading glasses and more framed photographs. Delphi stands in the doorway and lets her eyes touch the details. Looking up, she is nearly knocked off her feet. Above the king-sized bed is a painting of her mother. Done in the nineties, not commissioned but a gift from the artist whom Vivian had befriended. Delphi didn't know where the painting had gone but to find it here, hanging above Edward and Clara's marital bed is a perversion she can't process. Vivian abstracted but identifiable looks out of the canvas, replete and knowing, her hair dissolving into the frame, a pre-Raphaelite goddess. 'Hello, Mama,' Delphi whispers. She leans in, takes hold of the handle and pulls the door closed. Delphi is tired of all her feelings; she wants to be absolved of them. A tall order, so distractions of the body it will have to be. She sets off to the pub to find trouble.

*

'Where are you going to, Delphi?' Clara's in her teeny white tennis dress. She puts down her racquet and bags on the entrance-way parquetry. She's in full make-up with an energetic ponytail caught up in a ribbon.

'I'm just ducking out to the pub, I'll see you later,' Delphi answers.

Clara greets her dogs and stumbles a little. As she regains her balance she says, 'Whoops, I'm a little bit tipsy, we didn't play much tennis today, it was too cold, but we did have a few bubbles. Come on, Delphi, put your handbag down, come and have a glass of chablis with me.'

Delphi doesn't know how to extricate herself without being rude so she follows Clara's spray-tanned legs into the kitchen. The dogs settle into their baskets and Delphi props herself against the counter as Clara clatters about retrieving the wine and glasses. She uncorks, pours and hands one across.

'So, Delphi, you wanna know something?'

'Okay,' Delphi says amenably, taking a sip of the wine.

'Your father is having an affair.' Clara totters sideways, yanks out a chair and falls into it where she starts to cry. Tears gush from her face and mascara runs black rivulets down her Restylane plumped cheeks.

They don't have a history of physical intimacy, but Delphi places down her shock and her drink, goes over and tries to put her arms around Clara. To comfort her, to ease her distress. 'I'm so sorry, Clara.'

'Don't do that,' slurs Clara, pushing herself clear. Delphi resumes her position by the counter and Clara collapses with the energy of someone who needs the release, and is committed to having a good cry. Delphi's mirror neurons make her step-mother's pain her own, igniting her capacity for deep empathy.

'Oh Clara, it's terrible to see you so upset. Have you spoken to him about it?'

'Talked to him? Screamed at him, you mean? I can't think of anything else. Your father says it's over with her,' Clara's face distorts and twists, 'but I don't know… He doesn't want to have sex with me and when a man doesn't want that, then he's either dead or playing away.'

Delphi curls her toes up inside her boots.

'And you'll like this, Delphi, she's only twenty-two. A bloody baby! And guess who she looks like?'

Oh no, thinks Delphi, that's not rhetorical.

'Um, I don't know, Clara… Does she look like you?'

'Me… no, not me! The last one looked like your mother and I thought that was bad enough, but this one looks like *you*.'

The edge of Delphi's vision blurs. Something rank is gyrating its way up through the floorboards.

Clara seems to have forgotten Delphi is in the room and addresses the dogs. 'What am I going to do? I love him so much. I can't live without him. I can't, I just can't.' Then, looking at Delphi, 'I will forgive him anything but I won't share him.'

'He loves you, Clara. He loves the life you've built for him. It will all be okay. I really think it will.'

'Why am I not enough for him?'

'You are, of course you are.' Delphi's heart tears, registering that yet another woman has been made to feel less-than by her father. 'Why don't you have a bath and get into bed, and I will make you some soup and toast.'

Clara processes this slowly then nods her sad head. Delphi helps her step-mother to her feet and guides her upstairs to the door of the master bedroom.

'Are you alright from here?' she asks. Clara waves her away.

'Yes, I'm okay.' Her voice is thick with booze and emotion. She turns away and with a wave of her hand announces, 'I always hated you, Delphi.'

Clara closes the door without looking back.

'I know,' Delphi says quietly. She lets the side of her head rest on the doorframe and stares out through the window at the end of the corridor. It's getting dark and maybe the rain will come. The light looks improbably orange as if there's been a disturbance in the Force.

Delphi walks gingerly down the stairs, scoops up her handbag and closes the front door behind her.

*

They lie in the wet grass breathing hard. It's not been raining so it must be fog that has settled. It is freezing and Delphi lifts her naked pelvis to pull her coat back underneath her.

'Can you see where my shoe is? One came off,' she says. The man gropes around until he finds it and hands it across to her. He does up his trousers and flops down again on his back. It's so dark that she can't see his face and she's too drunk to remember what he looks like.

'Is your hair dark or light?' she asks.

He laughs. 'Jeez, did I make that much of an impression?'

She pushes into her boot and is grateful she kept her sock on. Her back is starting to ache, her jumper must have ridden up, she hopes she's not too grazed.

'I look like Brad Pitt,' he chuckles. 'Okay, it's bloody cold, let's get out of here.' He stands and offers her a hand up. She sways to her feet and tries to assess just how smashed she is. The intel comes back immediately and she sits back down.

He laughs and picks his coat up from beside her.

'Oh shite, my wallet.'

'What?' she asks.

'Oh nothing, just all me stuff's fallen out and I can't see a feckin' thing.' He's crawling about blindly.

Delphi finds her phone and fumbles on the torch function. It wobbles around like a crazy beam but she steadies it, and there is his wallet, his phone, some keys, a pack of chewing gum and something glinting. Delphi reaches out and picks it up. She holds it beneath the pool of light between her knees. A simple gold band.

'What's this?' She looks at his crouching form and he tries to take the ring from her. She closes her fingers around it and holds it away.

He stands, stuffing his possessions into his pockets.

'Will you give it to me, please?' A crack of desperation runs a seam in him. Delphi opens her fist and holds the ring under the light again. Her skirt has ridden up and she notices bruising blossoming on her inner thighs. She's disgusted by the colours and what they represent. Her throat constricts making her voice distort as she speaks.

'This is your wedding ring.' Delphi's revulsion swells.

He groans and vigorously rubs his hands together. 'Yeah, yeah okay, but what's that to you?'

'What's that to me?' Delphi has an acute desire to have a bath and scrub herself.

'Oh, come on, you knew I was hitched.'

She lifts the light to see his face.

'You wanted to get off from the get-go. Don't come over all high and mighty now.' He snorts and stands over her, his features distorting in the shadows.

'No, I didn't know.'

'Well, no harm done.'

Delphi spumes with self-loathing.

'Relax, no one need to know.' He extends his hand out for the ring.

'But I will know,' she says, her stomach clenching.

Delphi struggles to her feet and lobs the ring as hard as she can into the blackness.

'Work hard trying to find that, you disloyal shit. And then work hard at your marriage. Loyalty matters. Love is the point of all of this fucking madness!'

He is scrabbling in circles as he peppers the air with obscenities.

Delphi grabs her bag and stumbles herself back to the solid earth beneath the streetlights. She resists an urge to drop to her knees.

'I want to do better.' She passes under the light of another lamp and her breath curls around her.

A keening sound escapes her as anxiety and dread go to work with their unstitching. Delphi pinches the skin on her cheeks to release some of the pressure and she breaks into a run.

*

'God, you look a fright, Delphi. Why don't you put some make-up on?' Edward says as he crunches the end of his toast at the kitchen table.

Delphi is too hungover to rouse any response and shuffles about making herself a coffee.

Edward has chosen his moment. His voice has the quality of someone making a declaration in a town hall.

'You need to leave. Today.'

Delphi lowers her cup and turns to face her father.

'You're upsetting Clara, and the dogs.'

Delphi coughs to clear her throat and clarifies. 'I'm upsetting Clara. And the dogs?'

'Yes. And I won't have all the upset. You need to go.'

'Where to?' It tumbles out before she can stopper it.

'You're an adult, Delphi. You decide where you want to go. Have some grit, choose a path, don't you want to make something of yourself? Carve your initials into the Tree of Life?'

Delphi is close to puking over the kitchen floor.

He continues, 'Clara told me how rude you were to her yesterday. She had to stay in bed all evening to recover.'

Delphi is about to defend herself but knows nothing productive will come of it. She's seriously lightheaded. Maybe when she's sick it will relieve the intolerable pressure that's building up inside her.

'You and Jack are wastrels.' Edward is warming to an old theme. 'And your mother, what a disgrace. Euthanasia. It's suicide! A coward's way out.'

Delphi's head is pounding and her mouth feels stuffed with metallic cotton balls. Rage starts to erupt within her so she puts down the cup to prevent smashing it through the closed window.

The kitchen is spinning and Delphi is smacked by the fact that her father is a different species. His coldness is a tragedy to her. She would never let herself move through the world like that. She wants the opposite in all her relationships, the connections to be strongly held by deep caring and empathy. She will not build a citadel around her heart like he has. She wonders again at the lived traumas that inform that choice for him. She wonders if his own parents had loved him more generously, if he'd be more whole now. Surely so. All his behaviours of control and destruction stream from feeling worthless, she is convinced. And she wishes she could lay her hands on his cold armour and remove it, to let him feel the lightness and joy of being unburdened by it. She wishes she could hold him in her arms and whisper that the armour doesn't keep him safe at all. It just keeps him hidden, and what is shielded from the sun ultimately rots and dies.

He stands, his breakfast things discarded on the table. 'And another thing. You're out of my will, Delphi. I intend to spend every pound and every penny I have before my death, but if anything is left over, it will all go to Clara. And she's quite sure you only returned to grease your way into an inheritance.'

Delphi observes this injustice from a dispassionate distance.

'Clara's the one who looks after me. There will also be a small provision for Jack's daughter and some money for Cambridge.' Edward is going out of his way to clarify his position. She doesn't give a damn about the money but what its removal represents, that makes her bleed.

His face settles into a mask. His eyes are like stones.

'You are one of the greatest disappointments of my life, Delphi.'

Realisation knocks. Something extra and starved of oxygen is fuelling his need to crush her today. Clara has worked behind the scenes to have Delphi removed. Any person taking his attention, even Edward's child, is a threat and she's operating from a place of searing jealousy. She must feel exposed having told Delphi about the affair, and the sober discomfort of that has twisted her into malevolent action. Delphi isn't angry; she is sorry for her step-mother. She is sad for all of them. It's not evil that makes Clara behave like this, it's fear.

'I'm heading out and I expect you'll be gone by the time I get home this afternoon.' He re-tucks his shirt into his salmon-coloured trousers and leaves the room. Delphi hears him gather his keys from the hall table and go out the back door. She drifts to a chair and sits down. Was it William Faulkner who said if offered the choice between grief and nothing he would choose grief? Delphi doesn't know where to find the salve for this much grief. Through the window she watches a robin alight on a tree.

CHAPTER 10

DELPHI IS ROCKED BY the rumble of the train as it tracks south to Brighton. She rests her head on the window and looks from the flat countryside to her reflection. She's a stranger to herself, appearing translucent and ghostlike. Delphi wraps a scarf around her head and bunches further into herself, curling in like an animal into a shell.

She's on her way to her friend and the seaside. Looking out over large bodies of water has always offered her a broader perspective. Her fingers are covered in coloured ink and she rotates the drawing in front of her. It's of interlaced hands. She turns it over and writes a note to Hugh:

Godfather o'mine,
I loved seeing you. I always do.
I hope all is well with you.
All the love, D

She folds it up and will post it when she gets to Brighton along with the drawings she's done for Vivian. Her mother will be doing her rounds of doctors again, gathering up a fatal number of pills. Delphi doesn't know how long that will take but she will send love through the post until the end. She violently wants a cup of tea but can't lift herself to bump along to the dining cart. She modulates her breathing, and envisages air moving in and out of her like a prayer.

The train lurches and an elderly woman walking down the aisle falls. Delphi jumps up to help her. The woman is on the floor, jammed between the seats. A few other passengers look up but no one moves to help other than Delphi, who is out of her seat immediately.

'Are you alright?'

'Yes, yes, I think so…' says the woman, looking herself over. Her face is flushed red.

Delphi squats down and says kindly, 'Stay where you are for a moment to catch your breath.'

The woman wilts a little more towards the floor.

'I'm always falling,' Delphi tells her reassuringly. She hopes if she chats it will expunge some of the woman's fright and embarrassment. 'It's shocking, isn't it? Falling is a primal fear. I read once that after abandonment and hunger it's the next fear we experience as babies. Making it an elemental fear. None of us ever wants to fall.'

'Yes, yes that seems true. I most certainly don't,' the old woman answers as she awkwardly twists to sit up. Delphi rearranges herself to be level and they hold forearms. The woman has pale peach nail polish. She's applied it herself and it's wonky. She's still auditing her akimbo limbs.

'Do you think you're ready to stand yet?'

The woman nods. Together they rise off the floor and Delphi asks again, 'Do you feel alright now you're upright? May I help you back to your seat?'

'No thank you, pet. I am quite alright; I'm just getting old. Thank you for helping me.' She reaches out and rubs Delphi's cheek. 'You're a kind, dear girl. Your parents must be very proud of you. Thank you for looking after me.'

Delphi wobbles against a seat. Her mother is proud of her. One out of two.

The unsteady woman with her peach nails shuffles away and when she reaches the door between carriages, she turns back to Delphi and gives a little queen-like wave. Delphi returns to her seat to study the precious gift the woman has given her. Kindness.

The horizon rips past and Delphi wonders if her saviour is alive out there, busy doing other things.

*

Adarsha has an unusual beauty. A sensuality underscored by a palpable strength. She's as direct as an arrow. Delphi spots her moving up the platform and crackles with happiness. A mermaid's tumble of dark hair to her waist. A long black skirt with a belly dancer's belt, twinkling and chiming on her hips. As she throws her arms around Delphi she smells like orange oil and cloves.

'My love! So good, so good to see you. Now, I'm parked illegally so let's go.' Excitement mixed with a potential parking ticket fuel Adarsha's usually languid pace.

They have known each other forever as Adarsha's father delivered both Delphi and Jack. And even though Adarsha was a few years above, Delphi had begged to transfer from her conservative school to Adarsha's much more progressive one – Bedales. But Edward was resolutely against boys and girls being educated together. An insight into his belief that the sexes are fundamentally different and that boys need insulating from their unruly desires and girls need protecting from teen pregnancy. Delphi had put her case forward over and again, that the sexes learning together was surely a shot at better balanced adults and that she wanted male friends too. Edward, immovable, banned her from bringing it up and Delphi had been unhappy at her school from the first day to the last.

The dilapidated Volkswagen is parked, un-booked beside the station. They cheer, pile in and accelerate off, the car coughing with age. Below Delphi's feet is a mess of detritus. Adarsha is driving while removing her bag from across her body and then scrabbling on the back seat hunting for something but she soon abandons her search. 'Ach, never mind.' Now she is fixing on Delphi. 'My love! It is good to see you!' Adarsha is so alive and vibrant that Delphi is nourished just sitting beside her.

'Thank you for collecting me and thank you, thank you for having me to stay at such short notice.'

'But of course. My home is your home. I even had time to buy the Israeli dates you love. So what's going on?'

'Ah too much. I'm bored with myself. Tell me your news?' Delphi delights looking at her friend's profile, her hands covered in silver rings clutching the thin steering wheel.

'I am well. I'm poor because I just got back from Burma. Three months of silent mediation. I can't wait to tell you about it. It was so extreme but amazing. I will save that for when we can properly talk, but I think one day I will give myself over entirely, shave my head and take the vows, but I'm not ready, I love my life too much. I'm shameful,' she laughs.

'That's not true, Ada. You're totally wonderful. And are you back working yet?'

'Yes, of course. I am massaging my usual clients and a few extras. I've been running some women's groups, which you would love, and still doing the full moon gatherings. But I need to focus on abundance; it's hard living hand to mouth. And I'm trying to get back to India as soon as I can.'

They make their way slowly through the congested city. It's raining non-committedly, and the VW's windscreen wipers are broken so stay unresponsive.

'Okay, Delphi, your turn, tell me everything? I've not seen you in too long. I do love your emails. I keep them in a special folder on my computer.'

'I do that with yours too. I seriously don't know where to start.'

'Your work? Your mother? Have you heard from that brother? Love?' With this, Adarsha takes her eyes off the road to look at her friend.

'Eyes forward, you'll kill us both.' She does as she's told and Delphi chooses where to start. 'I will give you the headlines. Are you in the brace position?'

'Consider me braced.'

'Mama, she's not at all well. I want to talk to you about that, but not straight out of the gate and not in the car. It's too much. She sends you her love, and to your parents. She's always loved you.'

Adarsha takes a deep breath in. 'And I her. Go on.'

'As I mentioned in my message, the visit with Edward was a disaster. Same old but still awful. I saw Jack in Hobart… it was complicated but good too. And love? There was someone but I've only got a broken heart for my troubles.'

'Boy or girl?'

'A man, Ada… it was brief, devastatingly brief.'

'Why?'

'He had another woman.'

'A liar?'

'He didn't lie. I hadn't asked.'

'And now?'

'I'm trying to get him out of my system. Withdrawal hell. And it fucking hurts.'

'Oh babe…'

'You know when I looked at him for the first time, when his eyes met mine I felt it in my body. Right through me. Like an electrical charge. Which I know is such a cliché, but I didn't know that's because it happens. Have you ever felt that?'

'I need to see a photo.'

Delphi takes Ada's mobile from the pocket by the gear stick. 'Can I use your phone? I can google one.'

'Do it.'

Delphi puts his name into the search bar and presses the images button. In no time at all photographs of Orlo from interviews and gallery openings square across the feed. Looking at him she wants to push herself into any one of those frames, pull him into her arms and remind him that he belongs with her.

'Show me?' Adarsha asks, grabbing at the phone.

Delphi leans across and puts her hands on the steering wheel as Adarsha all but abandons responsibility for driving and lifts her sunglasses to get a better look.

'Jesus, Delphi! He is a beauty. And an artist. Of course he is. Has he seen your work?'

'Nope, we didn't have enough time for that, but I saw his and it was incredible. I think that's maybe why I've fallen so hard.'

'Darling, that face alone is explanation enough. Makes me rethink my vow of celibacy.'

'When did you make that?'

'Thirteen days ago and counting.' Delphi laughs hard and then so does Adarsha. They take a right at the light.

'I'm sorry it didn't work out with the artist, Del. Maybe it just wasn't your time?' Delphi looks out of her window and lets her eyes bump over all the people out there. Not a single one of them is Orlo. She looks for him in every crowd. She did it even when she was on the other side of the planet. Adarsha reaches out and they hold hands until the gears need changing.

'Can I do it?' Delphi asks remembering when she was small and played this game with her father. Sometimes he would let her sit on his lap when he was driving. Her feet couldn't reach the pedals so she must have been young, before Arthur died. These are happy memories. She bookmarks them for herself.

'Okay. Clutch now,' says Delphi and puts the bug into third.

'Clutch again.' And they move into fourth and increase speed as they hit the more open road of West Hove.

'There are lots of people at my place. If you were after quiet I'm sorry I can't offer you that this time. There are nine of us because tomorrow we are coming together for an ayahuasca ceremony.'

'Ada, being around people is probably exactly what I need. I'm not the best company, but I will pull it together for your friends.'

'Why don't you join us for the ceremony? It's such a great group and Shaman Puma is incredible, his intuition, his knowledge is next level. He's visiting the UK from Peru. He's a fifth generation Shaman. We've been together for six days, meditating, eating well, abstaining.'

'We'll see, Ada. I'm a bit smashed at the moment. I think if I took part I might go somewhere bad. Maybe I can help out, support you all. Although with all that purging… you know how much I hate vomiting.' Delphi shudders.

'I do know this about you, my love, so squeamish with the contents of tummies.' Adarsha is so articulate that the occasional idiosyncratic jumble is disarmingly charming.

'I have no quarrel with the contents when they stay put. It's when they come out that I get upset.'

'Okay, no need to decide now. I'm not sure if Puma would allow it anyway, without the preparation. We're nearly home. Do you recognise where we are? You'll be in sleeping with me. Be warned there are mattresses everywhere. I'm so happy you're here.' Her sweet monologue bubbles on. 'And Del, I won't press it now, but I can see you need to talk…' She slows the car down as they reach the top of the hill and makes a turn. 'We will find the time, I promise.'

'Thank you, my sister. It's good to be here, to be near you. I'm a bit of a hot mess, but just being with you makes me feel better.'

'I get it, my sweet, I get it.'

They take a right and trundle down a smaller road. The trees on either side fatten up and the potholes widen. They turn into Adarsha's dirt driveway and pull up in front of a blue cottage. A few people are scattered about on the front verandah. A bearded man in a woollen hat is playing the guitar and they all lift their faces warmly as Delphi gets out of the car.

Adarsha puts an arm around her waist. 'Come, let me introduce you. You've really come at the most perfect time.'

Delphi observes Adarsha's strength transmitting into her body and a Walt Whitman quote comes to mind. *Keep your face always toward the sunshine, and shadows will fall behind you.* Family aren't just the people you're related to by blood, and the sun isn't just up in the sky.

*

The heat from the bonfire is roasting Delphi's face so she leans back a little, sensing her eyebrows are about to singe. Everyone is sitting on the ground facing the flames and talking. A woman with a liquid voice is singing and playing the banjo. As the light changes angles across her face, she's momentarily amorphous and then becomes recognisable again. No one is smoking or drinking alcohol. Adarsha explained the group have also cut out sex, meat, gluten and sugar. A spiritual detox, a purification before they drink the wisdom plant.

'So, you're Delphi?' a jovial Scottish man with a subtle overbite says.

'Yes, hello.' They shake hands.

'I'm Billy. You obviously mean a lot to Ada. She was so happy to have you arrive today.'

Delphi smiles and shreds a leaf between her fingers. 'And I'm happy to be here. Thanks for letting me intrude.'

'No intrusion at all. The more the merrier. Are you joining the ceremony tomorrow?' His soft dialect burrs all the edges off his vowels.

Delphi looks up into the blackness. 'I'm not sure.'

'Have you drunk ayahuasca before?'

'No, I haven't. I'm interested, but I'm not sure on the timing.'

Billy grins. 'When's the timing ever perfect?'

'I don't know,' Delphi concedes.

The light flickers on the trees making them gambol.

'So what's stopping you?' he asks.

'Well, I have a rule that I never take drugs when I'm unhappy.'

He looks into the flames. 'That's a good rule. I like it, but ayahuasca isn't a drug, it's medicine, it's the teacher plant.' He scratches at his chin and Delphi notices that near the wrist of his jumper he's worked a hole, and his thumb is poking through like a child's. It's endearing.

'You see Sue, over there.' He points to a woman with a Modigliani face on the other side of the circle, 'She's my partner. She's a therapist and has done a dozen ceremonies.'

'Sue?' Billy is calling out to her. 'Sue?' She lifts her eyes towards her man. She extracts herself from her conversation and walks around the circle to bob down beside Billy. She slings an arm around his shoulders and his energy dilates.

'Sue darlin', have you met Delphi?'

'No, not yet, hello.' The women smile warmly at each other.

'She isn't sure if she wants to join us for the ceremony.'

Delphi likes this couple and their decent, open faces. 'Billy was saying you've done it a lot?'

'Yep, it's fascinating. And I'm not trying to pressure you, but for me, the psychological and spiritual insights have been amazing.'

'Life-changing is what she usually says,' Billy adds.

'Wow, really? In what way?' Delphi asks looking back towards Sue.

'Ah… I used to be a hard-core atheist, but I'm not anymore. And I struggled with depression on and off since I was a teenager, and that's gone. I was also really anxious, but I'm much more calm. Would you say that's true, Billy?'

'Oh for sure. Sue gave me this great book and the quote I keep thinking about is how ayahuasca delivers ancient wisdom for our modern problems.'

'Which book is that in?' Sue asks.

'The one with the blue cover and all the light pouring out of the top of that person's head.'

Sue nods emphatically and says, 'Oh yeah, and why that quote specifically?' Delphi likes how curious and delighted they are in each other.

'It's that whole section, looking at the madness we all accept; poverty, environmental destruction, war, inequality… that we have habituated to a psychotic *normality*, this idea that we're separate, individual, whereas the truth is that we're all connected, everything is connected and infinite. And there are a million practical examples like God Particles in quantum physics. Or that the neurons in my brain allowing thought fire in the same way as lightning in a storm. Or that we're all made of stardust!'

Adarsha arrives and all three look up. 'You've turned up just in time, Ada, as I'm nerding out about connectivity all over your friend.' Billy laughs.

'No, I'm loving it,' assures Delphi.

'Ah well, I'm sorry/not-sorry to interrupt that then. I need to feed and hydrate this one.' Adarsha extends her hand to Delphi, 'Come, my travelling psychonaut.'

Delphi lets herself be pulled up. 'Psychonaut?'

'It means sailor of the mind.'

'Sailor of the mind. I want to be that.' And turning back to the couple, 'It was good to meet you both.'

'You too.' Billy stretches up to offer his hand for Delphi to high-five, which she does. And Sue blows her a kiss which Delphi returns in kind as Adarsha pulls her away.

*

Adarsha passes Delphi a glass of water in the kitchen. 'So I asked him and Puma was pretty reluctant for you to join the ceremony without the proper preparation, but I talked him around. He said the decision is ultimately yours, but to remember the plant will give you what you need, not what you want. And you'll have to fast from now. So it's just water for you. You in?'

Delphi is excited. 'Nothing ventured, nothing gained, right? I'm in.' She takes a big sip. 'Hey Ada, do you still have bicycles? Want to go for a night ride for old time's sake?'

'Delphi Hoffman, I thought you'd never ask.'

And they run out to the shed to find the bikes.

*

It is midnight the following night, and they've gathered in a field. The night is clear, stars are sprinkled about above them, the majestic firmament.

Everyone is reverential as Shaman Puma welcomes them to the ceremony. Delphi tries to listen to every word but she's anxious. Each participant sits in the semi-circle, a bucket behind them and a candle burning before, Puma cross-legged in the middle.

In his rolling South American accent he says, 'The plant will do fifty per cent of the work; healing, cleansing, awakening and harmonising, but you must set your intention and do the rest. As your consciousness separates from your body, all your understandings, the paradigm you've always accepted will be changed.'

Delphi makes eye contact with Adarsha. Billy and Sue are side by side listening intently. There's an intensity and wakefulness on everyone's faces.

'This is experiential spirituality. Open yourselves to the plant's teachings. Give yourself permission to go through the barrier and into other dimensions. Beyond waking, sleeping and dreaming there is another state of restful alertness. Find that place tonight and be in conversation with universal consciousness. Be at one.'

He lifts his arms above his head, his robe falling in soft waves around him.

'Why suffer when you can liberate yourself and be available for higher service?'

Somehow Puma looks more substantial than he did when Delphi saw him earlier in the day. Now he seems ageless, genderless and of an unknown ethnicity.

'Ayahuasca is a very powerful transformational tool. It must be respected. My ancestors have used it for religious divination for over 5000 years, and with an open heart I share it with you.' He bows low, his forehead touches the ground.

'Let the plant be the mighty hand of grace that lifts you to reveal the top of the mountain.'

A breeze blows Delphi's hair across her face and she strokes it away.

'This gift, this sacred plant will take you up to God. The songs I will chant are traditional and called Ikaros. They help grow feelings of courage and peacefulness.'

As he starts to sing Delphi shuts her eyes, listening. Her heart is beating hard.

Puma's helper moves gently into her space by touching Delphi's hand. 'I will be here to help Shaman guide you. Please if you need help just ask. In a moment you drink, then you turn to truth.'

Delphi nods gratefully and senses the focus of the helper shift to the man to her left.

When Puma stops chanting, Delphi opens her eyes. It is time to drink the tea. One by one they enter the circle, kneel before their Shaman, accept the cup and drink the bitter, dark liquid. When all nine have drunk and are returned to their places, Puma sings again. Delphi lies down, giving herself over to what has been irrevocably set in motion.

*

Sometime after drinking the first cup Delphi accepts a second. Clutching a bucket between her knees she loses track of how long she has been vomiting. Delphi wipes her mouth on the back of her hand and lies down. Her vison is altered, the outline of objects and people blur and throb but she's not hallucinating wildly. Puma is singing and the sound is bewitching. Delphi closes her eyes and the auditory becomes visual. She can see the form of the sounds in her mind's eye. Colours and shapes kaleidoscope and a sense of wellbeing thrums through her. She becomes aware that her hands and arms have sunk into the earth on either side of her. She doesn't need to look to know that the molecular structure of what was her flesh has dissolved. If she were to lift her hands in front of her face she would see nothing of herself at all. This idea forms as a peculiarity to be inspected, yet Delphi intuitively understands she must stop assessing what is happening through her brain. To stay tethered to what is rational is an attempt at control. She must not fight the plant. She lets go and clocks herself internally changing direction. As if standing in a hallway of mirrors, infinite Delphis turn.

She hears whisperings. A little boy's voice. She knows that voice. Her hands are being held. She knows this touch. Her eyelids separate even though they are already open. A second, then a third set of lids get out of the way of her vision, and her brother Arthur is before her. He is smiling broadly. His baby teeth so white and defined. He ushers her up. They're travelling at enormous speed and yet the hair on their heads moves in slow motion, licking and twirling.

Delphi is laughing. She, them, everything, is entirely whole. She knows beauty as if for the first time but also simultaneously as if perfectly remembered. Opposites touch each other to forge a circle. A double helix twirls. Something is submerged into a river. Then reefed out reconfigured. A porcelain doll hits a wall and shatters into pieces. An altar bursts with light. There is rushing and noise so loud she covers her ears only to find she has no head. The channel is switched and the silence is miraculous. Delphi witnesses the earth suspended in black, eternal space. She recognises the infinite with unbridled awe.

Arthur is the age he was when he drowned, in his striped t-shirt and corduroy pants, his cheek curved with toddlerhood and health, but his eyes are as knowing and wise as a monk's. He points out the moon to Delphi. It is massive and seems close enough to touch. Arthur introduces Delphi to the moon and the moon to Delphi. The moon glows its celestial light and her soul responds in kind.

Delphi is back in time as Arthur dies. She is bending over from the waist repeatedly, a glitch, ever recurrent. Cracks appear all over her and she can see through the parts of her broken self to the empty void beyond, but the moon comforts her, soothes her, telling her to relinquish her tears. Telling her that the tears don't belong to her. That she is confused. That she doesn't understand.

Instantaneously the weeping vanishes and Delphi is kneeling before Arthur. A wound opens in her chest and she looks down into the cavity to see her heart, motionless and black inside her. Horrified, Delphi looks up but the moon and Arthur both smile and observe her putrid heart without attachment. Delphi is terrified. The black fear moves through her like a hurricane. Arthur steps forward, she notices the buckles on his navy-blue sandals. He puts his small hands into Delphi's chest and holds her heart. As soon as he does her heart begins to grow. It becomes red, flushed with life-giving blood. It bursts with vitality and her heart jumps; it begins to beat. The tidal wave of fear starts to move in reverse, rewound out of existence. Arthur removes his hands and the siblings embrace. The clean oaty smell of him infuses Delphi with peacefulness. The moon shines on so brightly with unadulterated joy.

Arthur tells Delphi that she is doing well. To not lose faith. To keep seeking growth. That he is proud of her. That there is nothing to forgive, and now it is time for him to go, but he will leave her with God. He vanishes and the gash in Delphi's chest is closed. She inspects it and as she does, she notices that her belly is beginning to swell. In time-lapse speed, she is nine months pregnant. A searing pain explodes from her back and cramping beyond any physical agony she has ever known buckles her. She falls to the ground writhing and God says to her, 'You are birthing. You can't resist it. You must take part.'

Delphi can't open her eyes due to the pain but she desperately wants to see the face of God. She is alternating between screaming and panting. She is slick with sweat. She begins to bellow and bear down with all her might.

Then it stops.

There is silence.

Delphi is floating serenely in her mother's womb. She senses Vivian's whole life. All her pain and ebullience and their unequivocal, unbreakable connection. Delphi sees their umbilical cord float up by her face and she feels pure wonderment.

The experience collapses and is deposited into Delphi's belly and she is in a new space. A different world where everything is made from books. Delphi's fingernails are covered in a tiny alphabet. Her clothes are made of paper covered in writing. She is euphoric, and she starts to run. She runs as fast as the speed of light. As she races, all the lies and mistruths blaze past her, and understanding replaces them. The Buddha and Ganesha wave to her as she runs through history and space. She is made of pure light. Then a door slams shut in her face. There is a blinding flash. Everything goes white and she can hear Arthur's voice. She spins around looking for him, but he is nowhere yet everywhere. He tells her it is time to go home. She is moving backwards, her feet and hands floating, weightless. She drifts down to a set of Roman gates. Vivian walks inside the gates and holds the suspended Delphi in her arms. She kisses her and then Delphi floats through. She carries on descending, still backwards, watching her mother until she fades out of view.

*

It is daylight when Delphi wakes. She is in bed beside Adarsha who is still sleeping. Delphi watches her with a clarity and love that evokes an extraordinary sensation of peacefulness. Delphi reaches out her fingers and touches Adarsha's hair. The texture is wildly vivid, all of Delphi's receptors exquisitely sensitive.

She needs to find paper and pencil so she can write everything down. Quietly she gets out of bed and goes to her bag on the chair in the corner. She digs into it and retrieves her pencils and notebook. She sits down, her back against the wall, facing the window. It is open and the cold breeze is gently filling the curtains and making them billow. The whole world is breathing. Delphi spends a long time watching the beauty of this movement. She's never felt more awake. As if a hood has been removed from her head. Living in darkness, now the lights are on. She opens her book and begins to draw.

*

Adarsha picks up her plate, recrosses her legs and spoons food into her mouth. They are alone in the back garden. 'Okay, Delphi, I've talked enough, now you tell me about your ceremony.'

Delphi is conscious of a pervasive sense of wellbeing, of robust health and she stretches out her limbs across the earth and looks at the clouds drifting above.

'It was incredible, Ada. I'm grateful to you for giving me this opportunity. Is that the right word? Maybe experience is better? Or rite of passage?' She is like a failing plant uprooted from the shadows that has been replanted in the sun.

Adarsha is listening and eating her meal.

'I'm obviously still processing it all, this rebirth, and several times today I've thought about *The Matrix*, you know the red pill and the blue pill?'

'Oh, I hate that film, Delphi, glamorising violence. Although Carrie-Anne Moss is a goddess boss. Whatever happened to her? Go on, but we must talk about Trinity later.'

Delphi laughs. 'Okay we will, but do you know what I'm trying to get at, regarding the choice to stay sedated or to wake up?'

'Yes, my love, of course!' Ada is wonderfully emphatic about pretty much everything. 'It's not romantic, but I've been thinking of myself like a computer having been refreshed, or rebooted.' Adarsha picks an olive off her plate and tosses it away.

'You remember in *Brave New World* when the government issues Soma?'

Adarsha shakes her head.

'It's a kind of opiate that diminishes negative feelings and enhances the good ones.'

'Like MDMA?'

'Sort of, yes, except Soma's sinister because it keeps the people distracted so they don't realise they're living in a dictatorship. They can't face life without it. Maybe how we are with mobile phones now. But what I'm getting at is that ayahuasca is the counterpoint to Soma. It doesn't put you to sleep, it wakes you up. I found it seriously confronting, and painful, and, oh God, the vomiting was disgusting.'

'I have little burst capillaries around my eyes. But it's purging, yes? Getting out the negativity, clearing the way. Don't forget to really brush your teeth well, Delphi, to protect the enamel.'

The women simultaneously run their tongues over their top teeth. Noticing their synced up action makes them laugh. 'So what was your intention?' Adarsha asks.

'I asked to be shown who I've become, which felt terrifying.'

'Ah good one! Ayahuasca is the best at exposing the gap between who we think we are, and who we actually are. It's the most powerful ego dissolving medicine on the planet. *Fact.* Tell me some of your visions?'

Delphi rolls over onto her stomach.

'Well, it was all so vivid, like a waking dream.'

'What was the most extreme moment?'

'Ada, Arthur was there.'

Adarsha stops chewing.

'And I died.'

Adarsha swallows and puts her plate down. 'You died?'

'Yes, or I was dead. My heart wasn't beating. I was also back in my mother's womb. There was a lot of emotion but there was also acceptance. I've read a bit about what the Buddhists, conative scientists and philosophers have said about the "fixed self", no thinker behind our thoughts, no doer behind our actions. That there's only consciousness and immediate experience, everything else is the result of the mind projecting into the past or the future. I had glimpses of the absolute truth of that.'

'Wow.' Adarsha exhales and lies down beside her friend. 'Now your job is to integrate all of that. Don't let it flow through your fingers. Use what this has shown you to come to a new understanding.' She strokes Delphi's hair. 'Hey, when we were riding the bikes and we talked about what happened with your mum in Hobart, all the shame you feel. Can you now see it was an impossible thing she asked of you, that you asked of yourself? I'm so sorry you've had such a brutal time.'

'Thank you, sweet Ada. When I arrived yesterday I felt dreadful. And shame is the right word but it was coursing through me like unadulterated fear. It's still impossible right now to reconcile that I couldn't help Mama die. I can't express how much I wanted to be able to do that for her. On the night, I was like an animal. My rational mind had to be overridden, my emotions disavowed, I was pure instinct and terror. The only other time I've experienced anything like that is when Arthur drowned.' Adarsha carries on playing with Delphi's hair. 'And when Mama woke up in the hospital I felt so useless. And worthless. And of course that was all compounded by Edward. Yesterday on the train I was back in that old loop, of what on earth is wrong with me that my own father hates me.'

'He doesn't hate you, darling.'

'I know... he just doesn't know how to love and I'm frightened I've inherited that, but I know that's not true and last night was such a gift. Today is the first day I've not felt saturated in fear. I need to quieten down, make friends with myself a little, and what's meaningful to me, what'll give my life purpose, I'm sure now, is love and belonging.' She looks at Adarsha, 'I feel that with you, with my mama, with Romy and Hugh. I believe deep down it will come back with Jack. And I felt it with that artist, Orlo. Maybe it's okay if it doesn't always last a lifetime? Maybe a brief glimpse of it is also sustaining? I wouldn't take back meeting Orlo, the pain is worth the gift.'

'Delphi, you're brave. And so tough on yourself. I think you are Christmases.'

'Christmases? Plural?'

'Whoops. Actually, yes, lots of Christmases, all the Christmases!'

'I like it.'

'Now can we watch some crap TV?'

'I thought you got rid of your telly as it was *impeding your spiritual growth*?'

'Yeah, well, turns out I missed it. All meditation and no Netflix makes Ada a dull girl. I have lots of crystals in the sitting room to balance it out.'

Delphi rolls onto her side laughing. 'Excellent logic. I'm sure that holds water. Which season of *Drag Race* do you want to re-watch? Nothing with everyone being nasty to each other. Or *Glow Up* is a new show on BBC3? Or what about the *Great British Bake Off*?

'No, that's boring and it always makes me hungry.'

'I'd like to eat Noel Fielding.'

'Babes, we all would. Although, do you know, fun fact, gay men don't love Noel the way we do?'

'What madness are you talking?'

'Well not all gay men, I've not polled them all, but some that I respect and have discussed this with in depth, they say no to the Noel.'

'Interesting. What do they think of Paul Hollywood?'

'They all want a piece of that.'

'Quite right. I want him to shake my hand and burn all my defenses to the ground with his blue-blue eyes.'

'Okay, let's start with *The Bachelor* and then *Bake Off*.'

'Done. I'll draw while we watch. I wish I had some paints.'

'What do you want to paint?'

'You. The Noel. Everything.'

They stay lying together, side-by-side, chatting until darkness arrives and reminds them it's time to go inside to watch TV.

CHAPTER 11

It's getting dark on the pier as Delphi presses her mother's number into her mobile again. The first time around it hadn't connected but now it's ringing. Delphi's anxious about calling Vivian so early in the morning in Australia, but the time difference keeps thwarting contact.

The seagulls are flapping about gobbling up discarded chips and sticky children are being ushered home for bed by their parents. As the ringing continues, Delphi looks down over the balustrade into the dark grey water. The recording clicks in and her mother's voice invites her to leave a message. It is astounding the power of hearing the voice of someone you love. Someone you're worried about, someone who is dying. The longing in Delphi is making her giddy so she steps back from the railing.

'Hiya, Mama, it's me again. I hope you're okay. Sorry, that's a stupid thing to say. I'm standing on Brighton Pier. The spiritual home of fish and chips, do you remember calling it that? Please call when you can? Or ask Jack too. Um... okay, well, I've posted lots of things to you, I hope they don't take too long to arrive. I love you very much.' She decides not to say goodbye, worried that it might be the last one. Delphi kills the call and looks at the inert phone in her hands.

'Delphi?'

She looks up to see who's addressing her.

He clocks her freefall. 'Peter Channing. Your art teacher from school.'

She bursts with recognition. 'Ah, Mr Channing! Yes, of course, I remember you. I'm sorry, I was a million miles away.'

They shuffle through greeting options then awkwardly choose a hug. They mismatch the timing of the cheek kisses and very briefly touch lips – both flare with embarrassment and jostle about like foals.

'Peter, call me Peter or Pete, please? Bloody hell, I'm only thirty-eight.'

Delphi nods and slips her phone into her pocket and readjusts her beanie.

He has a London haircut, short on the sides and long on the top. Elvis meets hipster, Delphi thinks. She would put money on the fact that he's obsessed with coffee. She notices his jeans rolled up at the ankle and he's wearing hot pink socks with black and white chequered kicks.

'How have you been? I was so happy to hear you'd gone on to art school.'

'Ahh…' Delphi pulls at a button of her coat. 'Yes, I did, and it was as incredible as you said it would be. And you? Are you still teaching? Are you on holiday here?'

He's shifting his weight from one foot to the other. 'Yes, I still teach, but here now. I moved down, ah, let me see, nearly two years ago, and it's good, I like it here.'

Delphi's attention is drawn to a portly set of twins in their sixties attempting to struggle out of their deck chairs. Their tummies are big and their limbs stiff with the cruel atrophy of age. They can't get their legs underneath themselves to stand up.

'Do you want a hand?' Delphi calls but is waved away as the sisters, wracked with giggles, wriggle about but fail to extricate themselves. They're dressed in identical outfits and have the same dyed red hair.

'Like upturned turtles,' Delphi says. 'So Lynchian.'

'Kind of, yeah,' Peter nods. One twin liberates herself and joyfully fist pumps the air. Then turns to tug and heave her sister up.

'Tell me about your painting, Delphi? You really were so talented.'

She grimaces at his use of the past tense and at having to confess to her impoverished career. 'Sadly, not much to tell there, I was sort of taking an unintentional break but I plan to get back into it, Mr Channing.'

He pulls a face and she rebukes herself, 'Sorry, Peter. And what about you?'

He studies his shoes earnestly. 'I guess I'm sort of having a break too. Until recently I painted most days but having those unsold, un-exhibited canvases stacking up in my flat was doing my head in. I'm sad to hear you stopped though, Delphi. Don't let that drag on too long. You know it's a sin not to use your gifts?'

'A sin? That's a big word, I mean technically it's little, only three letters, but big. Are you religious?'

'No, but I was raised a Catholic so I have a PhD in guilt.' The joke doesn't land as he hoped so he attempts to overlay it. 'I parted ways with God when I was about ten. I wasn't convinced he had my best interests at heart.'

Delphi watches the freshly liberated twins potter away. They're holding their matching handbags on the outside of their bodies, their arms are intertwined. There is something crazy and magical about their duplication. She wonders if they inoculate each other from loneliness.

Peter asks, 'Do you have time to walk for a bit? Maybe to the end of the pier? I could buy you a doughnut.'

The invitation catches her around the waist and she answers, 'Yes, I do have time and I do love doughnuts.' He beams and slowly, side by side but with a clear space between them, they walk over the old planks.

'I just read on that plaque before I spotted you that this pier was built in 1823 and is 1870 feet long,' he says.

Delphi knows it's 1722 feet, but it would be churlish to correct him.

'It was entirely rebuilt around 1890 because it was destroyed in a storm.' He adds.

'Wouldn't that be useful,' Delphi muses.

'What?'

'To be able to be entirely rebuilt after a storm. I'd be on rebuild number three.'

She catches a look on Peter's face so she energetically collapses the moment and replaces it with a smile. They walk on towards the belly of the English Channel.

*

'Come in, come in, put your coat down and I will get cracking on dinner. Would you like a beer or glass of wine?' He's taken off his coat and thrown it over the back of the sofa.

'A beer, thank you,' Delphi replies, as she looks about his flat as he beetles into the kitchen. Shades of brown mostly, the furniture, the carpet, the curtains are beige. Bleak comes to mind but there are books scattered about, which is a good sign. She picks one up off the floor and flicks it open. It's second hand, the original owner's name has been crossed out and replaced with Peter Channing. She wanders over to the bookshelf and places it into the jangled stack where she notices a book of Orlo's work. She touches the battered spine, and her body teems with the silver fish of yearning. She turns away and holds her own hands, comforting herself.

The blistered wallpaper is covered with posters. Many of them are of planets or the solar system. The largest, which has been torn and stuck back together is of the earth. Someone has scrawled HOME in black marker across the bottom.

Peter comes back in, managing to look lost in his own apartment. He has two beers and hands one to Delphi.

'It really is so good to see you after all these years. And all grown up. I mean you were always very mature. Bloody hell, that sounds even worse. Now I'm Hubert Humbert.' His mouth twists. 'I'm going to stop talking.'

Delphi takes a sip of her beer and shakes her head. 'No, it's okay. Oh, I'm not meant to be drinking.'

'Are you on antibiotics? he asks.

'No,' she answers. 'I did this ceremony...' She is protective of her experience so diverts the conversation, spotting his guitar. 'Do you play?'

'I do. Not terribly well.'

'Do you write your own songs?'

'Um, yes I do. It's really poetry with a few strummed along chords.'

'Cohen-esque? Will you play something?'

'I certainly wouldn't compare myself to Leonard Cohen.' He looks sweetly terrified and she backs off.

'You don't have to.'

'No, sure, sure I will play for you.' He picks up the guitar and settles himself on the sofa to tune it. Delphi sits down on the leather chair adjacent. The stuffing bulges from a deep laceration in the seat cushion.

'I wrote this after the break-up with my ex.'

His face is gravely serious, and Delphi wishes she hadn't put this train in motion.

He starts to sing and she is willing it to be better than it is. After a few lines, he abruptly places his hand flat across the strings and says, 'You know what, I'm not nearly drunk enough to perform for you. And I think rolling out my heartbreak isn't going to work for either of us.'

Delphi is relieved he's pulled the pin and she assures him it's completely fine.

'More beer?' he asks and he jumps off the sofa and retreats into the kitchen. Delphi wonders if she should get into the car and drive back to the cottage now but that would be rude and he's sweet and a bit damaged which evokes compassion in her.

*

Delphi is drunk and has Peter's sketchbook open before her, some of the work is really strong. An erotic through-line runs like lightning from this moment to Orlo's studio. She's aware she finds Peter more interesting having looked at his work and it opens up small wounds in her; that she's been wasting time – Orlo kissing the sole of her foot – that she has to create – Orlo's hands encircling her waist, anchoring her to the earth – Vivian bolting down fistfuls of pills – paint, she must paint – she misses her big brother – why the hell has she been spinning her wheels – her father telling her to leave – she wants little Arthur to hold her heart again.

The acidic churn of all that makes her reach for an old salve. She leans forward and puts both her hands on Peter's knees. Reaching for sex is probably not the solution she tells herself, and yet; 'I'm not sure what your story is Mr Channing, but I'd like to invite you to take me to bed.' Even as the invitation is coming out of her mouth it saddens her a little. Delphi has not consciously recognised this in herself before, that she sometimes internally separates and observes herself as if a passenger. Fledgling learnings shelter as old survival patterns take the controls. Through sex she has reached for many things; for fun, distraction, to give pleasure, to be chosen, to see the view from the cliff's edge. To have hands on her body kneading out her humanity, to expand her identity, to frolic in her femaleness, to crush boundaries between her thighs. To dissolve into the starburst of sexuality, to tap the carnal creative wellspring, to bathe in the sensuous, to see herself in the relief of the other. To quell oblivion and her deep burning hunger, to stave off death, fear and loneliness, but the core, it's always the same, the attempt to be in connection. To feel wildly alive; seen, met and heard. Good sex is like art, it says yes to life and makes the collective constellation glow, rendering us whole, but bad sex leaves grime and replaces soft parts of us with brittle, parched ones.

Peter sifts about inside the pause assessing if she's joking, then reaches his hands behind her head and kisses her with a ferocity that hurts her mouth. His energy cranks up further. His breathing becomes ragged, and he's pulling at her hair. She leans away and places her forearm across his chest, 'Slow down, slow down.' He nods and responds by kissing her more gently. 'It's just...' more kissing, 'that I...' he's biting her lip, 'want to...'

'Let's just take our time.' She stands up and pulls off her t-shirt and bra, dropping them to the ground. She folds her arms around him, and he attempts to devour her with an untrammelled energy that makes her clench.

'Peter,' she says trying to control the pace. A shot of regret races through her, robbing the heat. She tilts him back in his chair then unbuttons his shirt. He looks more like a boy. A collapsed chest but Delphi refuses to turn back, she's gone too far to extricate herself. She unbuckles his trousers and her hands look like they belong to someone else. Someone sure.

'God, I love you,' he whispers.

She ignores this, tossing it into the barrel of alcohol that's sloshing in her brain.

He's moving her back and supporting her awkwardly onto the floor. Together they tear away her skirt and knickers, arranging their limbs between the table legs. He pushes himself into her, she grits her teeth, and he is watching her, greedily pulling in the imagery. He watches a lot of porn, she thinks. He tucks his head beside her shoulder and whispers, 'Will you hurt me?'

'What was that?'

'I'd like you to hurt me.'

She hears him this time and her heart constricts.

He lifts up so they're looking at each other. He's apologetic but also hopeful.

'What do you mean?' Delphi asks. 'In what way?' Christ, she's even trying to be a helpful girl when she's getting clumsily nailed on a kitchen floor.

'You could hit me. Or choke me a little.'

'Hit you? Peter… I can't do that.'

She's pinned under him and he tries to pack his request up by saying, 'Okay, that's fine, let's just carry on like this.'

But for Delphi what was only partially alive is now completely dead and she wants to get away.

'No, Peter, we should stop.' She lies rigid under him as he takes long moments to make his decision.

He groans defeat and rolls off. 'Shit,' he says. 'I'm sorry I mucked that up, Delphi. Are you okay? I didn't mean to freak you out.'

'It's okay,' Delphi says as she finds her t-shirt and wraps it across herself. 'I'm just not into that. I don't want to hurt anyone.'

'Yeah, sure, sure, no, of course.'

He's lying on his back rubbing at his face. Delphi's pierced through with the acute need to get out. She sits up, finds her underwear and starts to stand.

Peter springs onto his knees and says, 'Don't go. I know I've made things weird but let's have a drink, and I will make it better. I've had a rough time, Delphi. That ex, it was a terrible break-up. That's why I moved to Brighton.' He simpers with dejection and desperation.

It's smothering Delphi, making her claustrophobic.

'This was a bad idea,' she tries to appease him. 'You're hurting, too raw to do this. I am too. I'm sorry, I really am. We miscalculated. I have to go.' She leans down to pick up her skirt and his hand slaps her hard across the upper arm. The thwack reverberates around the tiny kitchen. Delphi reels back. He's over her, words pouring out of him.

'Oh my, Delphi, I'm so sorry. I have no idea where that came from, I can't believe I…' He's recoiling, his wretched face is pressed to the tiles.

Delphi is appalled, by both of them. She has stepped into the internal warzone of another human being. How did she misjudge this so supremely? She felt so connected and love-filled after the ceremony, a whole new lens on life, and yet she's chosen this?

'I'm so lonely,' he keens.

'Peter, listen to me. I am going to get dressed in the bathroom. You should get dressed too. And then I'm going to come back in here and we can decide what we are going to do.'

She doesn't want to touch him, but she leans closer. 'Peter, does that sound like a plan?'

He's crying. 'I'm so sorry, how can I even look at you?'

She reaches out and strokes his protruding spine. 'Let's get dressed. I will make us a cup of tea. Good people do bad things all the time. Get dressed, Peter. Please, just get dressed.'

*

Delphi rushes to get her clothes on and washes her face in the grubby bathroom sink which has his toothpaste spittle caked in sad lumps. She smarts where Peter slapped her and in other places where he didn't. She looks down to inspect the welt. It's not bad but Delphi is polluted by the knowledge she's squandered something. Looking up into the mirror she sees the potential of victimhood and squints her eyes closed tightly against it. Blame is less destructive internalised. No, she won't do that either. Vivian wouldn't abide this. Delphi straightens her back. What she accepts is what she thinks she's worth. And she doesn't want this.

*

Peter and Delphi sit at the tiny kitchen table and pass the last cigarette between them in silence. The tea stands untouched, getting cold.

'I am so ashamed,' Peter says. He looks at Delphi's red arm and quails. 'Does it hurt very much?'

'Not physically,' Delphi answers.

'Look, this is an insane proposition, but I'd love you to stay tonight. It's a huge ask I know, but what I most want is to sleep with you in my arms.'

Delphi looks at his pleading face. 'Peter, that's not going to solve anything. And I don't know if I bring out the best in you.' The line between tending to the aggressor and standing up for herself is undeniably blurry. The story is frighteningly malleable.

'What happened wasn't your fault, Delphi. Something in me snapped. I think it was terror at you going, at being left. Which I know makes me needy and weak as shit. I guess I am those things, but I'm also a whole lot of other things. If you give me a shot, I'm sure I could be good for you. I would give the best of me to you. You could live here, not as my lover if you didn't want, but…' He leans forward, his face a childish composition of sincerity. 'I would love you to live here with me. I have enough money for us both and you can paint here. I have so much love to give. I'm tired of being on my own. Humans aren't designed to travel solo. Creatives, artists like us, we could be an amazing team.'

She inhales the cigarette smoke down into her toes and releases it with a measured slowness. She looks at the ember at its end and stubs it out.

'Peter, I'm not trying to be cruel, but you don't even know me. And what happened here tonight was a disaster.' He shakes his head.

'Please don't cry any more, Peter. We're both lonely and I think what we need in our lives is calmness and clarity. God, I know I do. It seems that neither of us is capable of making that sort of healthy decision right now.' She notices a postcard tacked to the wall. It's a painting by Winslow Homer of a fisherman in a dismasted, rudderless boat struggling against the ocean. 'Who was it that wrote about being in a sea of troubles?'

Peter's voice is raspy with emotion, 'Oh… um, Shakespeare, I think.'

'Probably,' she answers, 'such an awful image.'

Peter drops his head into his hand.

'I'm going to go,' Delphi says. They sit for a moment in their separate reveries.

Delphi stands, and Peter gets up as if his body is filled with shards of glass. She steps forward and leans in and kisses him on the cheek.

'I do wish you well, Peter. Don't go hitting any more women, okay?'

'Delphi,' he says as she moves towards the doorway of the kitchen, 'I think you're amazing. I always thought so and I hope you find what you're looking for.'

'You too, Peter.'

'Can I walk you to your car?'

'No, thank you. I can manage by myself.'

She turns and leaves the flat. Once out of his door she checks her phone to see if her mother has called – nothing. The threadbare hall runner leads her down the building stairs, out into the ink of night.

*

The VW is very noisy, resentfully trucking up the hill. Delphi lowers it into second gear and eases off on the accelerator. The night is pitch dark. Delphi feels like she has journeyed through a sandstorm. Her skin is lashed and raw. Soul dermabrasion.

Puttering over the crest, Delphi and the bug are relieved to be on flat road. Their speed quickens, the headlights paving a narrow path. Into fourth and cranking now, Delphi thinks about a hot shower and curling up in bed in the cottage.

Her vision picks up the smallest static flash, but there is nothing obscure about the reality of the crunch.

'Holy shit!' Delphi breaks violently. She sits panting, clutching the steering wheel. Insects dart about in the light beams. Ominous silence. Delphi releases the seatbelt and gets out of the car. She moves to the front and on the road is an animal. 'A wolf,' she says disbelievingly, the world tumbling in an avalanche.

'Oh God no!' she pleads out to the night as she kneels beside the animal. In the spill of the headlights she can make out the huge prostrate form. She is ashamed of how terrified she is. It looks like a monster. You're the monster, Delphi, she cuts at herself.

She hears her phone ringing from the passenger seat. Stumbling, she retrieves it. Her mother's name is lit up. She diverts it to message bank. Her hands are shaking violently as she turns on the torch function and returns to the animal. She shines the light and the dog lurches and Delphi screams. It howls, its teeth white, gnashing at the air.

'Oh, dog, calm, calm. I'm so sorry. I am going to save you. Just hold on and I will find a vet to come.'

The dog flails, trying to get to its feet.

'Oh God,' Delphi beseeches. 'Please lie still, boy.' She moves closer and the dog lunges at her, snarling. The fear radiating from it infects Delphi. They're in a terror feedback loop and she falls backwards. The sounds the animal is making burns Delphi's insides. She starts humming discordantly to block it out so she can function. It's macabre, the dog howling and Delphi humming. She checks her phone but can't find any reception – not a single bar of helpfulness.

'Are you kidding me?' She squeezes the phone in jagged rage. Frustration is bursting blood vessels in her temples. She turns the mobile off and on again. All the while the animal is keening. Delphi has a visual flash of Pilot the night she tried to kill her mother and she doubles over, winded.

'Okay doggie. Okay my friend, lie down. I'm doing all I can.'

What directory can she call? Her mind is splintering. The police? The fire brigade? Adrenaline has her on the move and she's pacing. Delphi straightens up and walks around trying to find reception. Stretching her mobile towards the sky a bar appears.

Delphi decides on the police, calls and after six rings, which she counts, it cuts out, the reception disappearing again.

'No!' she screams into the blackness. Swooping down to the dog she says, 'Not you, sweetheart, not you. Please hold on. Please, buddy. We are going to make this.'

The dog stops howling and settles into an intermittent whimpering. Delphi shines her torch near his face. His fur is matted with blood.

Delphi slumps to the ground and scrabbles about looking for a course of action to cling to. The dog whimpers again, a different tone and Delphi recognises that he's fading. She brings her voice way down and whispers to him. 'Oh darling, my poor, poor darling, you're going, aren't you?' Her voice breaks as her grief smothers her vocal cords.

She reaches out her hand, the dog watching her and this time he doesn't try to bite her. She places her palm on his soft coat and tracks his struggling breath. She refuses to let herself cry.

'You know, doggie, I'm going to stay here with you. I'm going to stay right here. You take all the time you need to find the doorway.' Her throat is on fire.

The dog's eyes close and Delphi carries on stroking him gently. His whimpering is very quiet now. Her voice seems to be comforting him.

'It's okay. It's okay.' The car engine is tinkling as it cools down. The driver side door is wide open like a mouth in a perpetual scream.

Delphi lowers her face to the asphalt and looks into this animal's face. A calmness has melted over everything. Visually, the world now looks like it did on the ayahuasca journey, colours gently kaleidoscope and throb.

The dog is silent, his ribcage continues rising and falling. 'Don't be afraid. You can let go.'

Under her fingers the movement stops. Delphi shuts her eyes.

Shock steeps through her until every part touched is discoloured.

*

The sun is beginning to rise and Delphi looks at the dog's blood on her hands. He had been so heavy to drag to the side of the road. She will come back with Adarsha to bury him. He wasn't wearing a collar so she will have to find his owners some other way. She'll make signs, knock on doors.

Delphi gets into the car but can't quite bring herself to turn on the ignition.

She finds her phone in the passenger footwell. She stays twisted over low down not wanting to lift the mobile out of the small zone of effectiveness and presses her mother's number. It rings and it rings until the recorded mother voice activates. Delphi finds she doesn't have any words. She sighs and presses 'end'. She rests her head on the steering wheel and listens, attuning her ear to her surroundings. And as she becomes attuned she's aware a state of grace has arrived. And with it she's reminded that life is the most magnificent gift. It's painful and complex to be sure, but its majesty is in part due to the mystery. Delphi lifts her eyes to the dawn light again. Her whole being is vibrating.

She turns the key and the VW grumbles awake. The dog is safely hidden under a tree, shrouded in her favourite skirt. Delphi's takes a tiny crumb of pleasure in this. She checks the rear-view mirror; she's alone so she pulls out and drives.

CHAPTER 12

'DELPHI, CAN YOU HEAR me?' Jack's voice is perfectly clear even though he's on the other side of the planet.

'Yes, I can, I've been trying to get a hold of you and Mama. Is everything okay?' She places the book she's reading on the arm of the sofa and stands up.

'Where are you? Are you with anyone?'

'I'm at Ada's, in Brighton. She's sleeping. What's the time there?'

'It's early. Listen… Del, Mama is dead.'

A nuclear bomb detonates.

Delphi's heart beats.

An inhalation of breath.

Disorientation.

Then post-explosive ringing ruptures Delphi's skull.

What was she doing when her mother was dying? Images from this afternoon flash. The burial of the broken wolf-dog. Billy digging a hole. Adarsha singing. Delphi cradling the dog's head in her lap. The others picking flowers.

'Del, are you still there?' Her brother's voice sounds exhausted.

Pushing thick clods of soil over the dog's fur. Adarsha's friends in a circle kneeling around his grave.

The phone is so heavy in her hand. The air has become viscous. Her limbs are alien.

The dog fully covered. They set down flowers and assemble rocks as a gravestone. It is reverential. Loving.

Delphi places a hand on the back of the sofa as her bones melt. 'Oh… Jack…' Gravity has changed its force, and she's free floating. It's all peculiar and disarming. Then she's plummeting. Submerged.

The dog is alive again. He and Delphi are playing in fallen leaves. She throws them up in the air and the dog pounces and barks, his tail wagging.

'Delphi, it's going to be okay.'

The dog is moving backwards, as if reversed, and goes back into his grave and Delphi is covering him again. She can smell the earth. Her hands are covered in dirt.

'Del?'

'Jack, where is she now?'

'She's here, at home, in her bed. She looks very peaceful.'

Delphi gasps for breath. 'When? When exactly did she die? How?'

'Let's talk when we are together,' Jack answers.

'Don't let them take her, Jack. Don't let them take her away. I'm coming. I'm going to come as soon as I can get a flight. Please, Jack, don't let strangers take her and put her in a fridge. Oh God, will they do an autopsy, will they cut her apart?'

She's racing blind down tunnels, smashing, deskinning herself on the walls.

'Delph, go and wake up Ada. It's good you're with her. Get a flight. I will come to the airport to collect you.'

'But will they take her? I don't want them to take her.'

'Yes, Del, they will have to take her.'

'But I need to see her, Jack. Can I see her?'

'Yes, yeah, you can, just breathe.'

The siblings hold on to each other across the world's oceans.

She takes a breath. And another. 'Are you safe, Jack?'

'I'm fine. Just come, Delphi. Don't be alone tonight, okay? Let me know your landing time.'

The kaleidoscope turns again as numbness starts to set in.

'Del, I have to go now. I need to call the police.'

'Okay, Jack. I will come as soon as I can. I love you.'

It's been years since she's said those words to him. Longer still since he's given them to her. She holds them out with an open heart.

'Yes, I know. I love you too. See you soon,' he answers softly and hangs up.

Delphi presses her phone to her chest. The numbness is greedy and she stands suspended as it claims her, then beneath her a trapdoor opens and below it is another and another and another. Delphi falls through each and every one of them.

*

'Thank you for driving me all this way, Ada, you are such a good friend.'

'Are you sure you don't want me to park up and wait with you until you have to board?'

'No, this has eaten up enough of your time.'

Early morning Heathrow is grey and the skin below Delphi's nose is chafed red. The women embrace for a long time.

'You will survive this, Delphi. I truly believe this will make you stronger in ways neither of us can fathom. If that's possible, my love. In my experience devastation can be a seedbed for renewal, for new life.'

Delphi shoulders her bag, 'Thank you, Ada.' Delphi feels infinitesimally small. They hug each other again. Delphi holds on to her friend. Reluctantly she drops her arms and kisses Adarsha goodbye. Picking up her bag, Delphi turns towards the airport to swim the next stretch of desolation alone.

*

The plane cabin is dark. Black ocean below, indifferent infinity above. Delphi has her legs and arms tucked up, the origami folding in of grief. The airline blanket smells weird and her face is pressed to the window frame. An emotional roulette is playing out. She lunges from sadness so acute that she struggles to breathe, then swings to a fear so all-pervasive she can barely contain the need to scream. Delphi craves oblivion, sleep, to feel anything else, but she is trapped. A moth pinned to a board desperately trying to flap its pinioned wings. Her mother is dead. Vivian is gone. Delphi is in freefall.

She tries not to make eye contact with anyone. She refuses food and drink. The poor man beside her leans away as if her brand of madness might be contagious.

Tears plummet down her face. They're made of acid and burn. How will she carry on? How will she stay upright? Why does everyone else seem so normal? Don't they know everything is changed, that the whole world is now spinning on a new axis. Vivian has left our shores for eternity. A majestic library has been burnt to the ground. Its ashen contents disseminated into the ether.

Delphi wants to pull the sword from her heart but she doesn't know how, so she sobs the particular tears of the child who has lost her mother. She knows this place. She came before to trudge the waist-deep mud when Arthur died.

Delphi tries to meditate. To simplify it all down to her breath. She lists all the things she's grateful for: painting, art, cups of tea, books, sunlight, the smell of pencil shavings, love, sex, her friends, her Converse high-tops. And somewhere deep into her list, the angel of sleep arrives and flies her away to a safe dreamless space, holding her in its arms. Its feathered wings outstretched and kissing her gently on the forehead.

*

She reclaims her bag from the conveyor belt and walks stiffly out of the small terminal to find her brother. There he is, ambling heavily towards her. They find each other's eyes and speed up into each other's arms. She buries herself in his chest and cries. He smells like wool and scotch.

When she can finally speak, she asks, 'Did she have a good death?'

'Yes,' he answers, gravel texturing his vocal cords.

'Did you help her, Jack?'

He is ruddy with grief. He shakes his head. 'No.' Fresh tears tumble, her voice breaks and she quietens back into his arms.

He holds her tightly and drops his lips to the top of her head. Delphi and Jack, two of three people who were brought into being from Vivian's womb.

'Where is Pilot?' Delphi looks around their feet.

'Oh, he's not doing so well, poor little guy. He's under Mama's bed. He won't come out.'

'Bloody hell.'

The colours are reconfiguring. So many tears and so many emotions have bled out of her. Delphi has arrived at her destination and everything is slowing down. It gives her body a weight she's never previously known. She observes the sound of her throat swallowing and it's strange.

Jack takes her bag and leads the way to their mother's car. Delphi looks up at the clear sky. So unpolluted here at the bottom of the planet. Such fresh, clean air. The sun is shining, which seems a dislocation, the frolicking birds are also discordant. On the wheels turn, how can it be? Hobart, Tasmania, the location of her mother's death.

*

Jack unlocks the front door and steps back to let Delphi in. She stands at the threshold and looks inside. Vivian has not come to welcome her. Pilot is not yapping his intruder alert. Delphi feels like she's peering into a counterfeit version, an alternate reality devoid of a heart.

'Go on, Delphi, in you go,' encourages her brother.

She steps inside and looks around. It's all the same. She's not sure why this surprises her. How can it all be the same when it's so irrevocably altered? A paradox. A sleight of hand. A death theft. Delphi looks at the squat phone on the glass hall table. The matching coat stand shaped like a tree. Pilot's lead, her mother's cardigan, several of her hats, all hang there. Placed there by Vivian. Last touched by Vivian.

Delphi drifts into the sitting room. Vivian's chair dented with her not-forgotten weight. Outside the large square window, the river carries on. A huge tanker is gliding down into port. Delphi presses her hand to the glass and watches it for a long time. No one on board knows Vivian is dead.

'Do you want a cup of tea?' Jack calls from the kitchen.

'No, thank you,' she replies and turns to look at the bookcase, the inactive screen of the television, the striped pattern of the open curtains. Vivian loved that fabric. Delphi moves into the dining room. Her mother's upright piano on the left, sheet music open on the stand. The table covered in rows of paper, bills, letters, lists. That will be Jack's work.

Her brother is moving leadenly in the kitchen. Delphi passes him to go through the back door. The maroon painted boards underfoot, nails working free, she looks up at the wild garden. To her left, the brick steps where her mother broke her ankle four years ago. To the right, the laundry with its smell of cleaning products and weatherboards long baked by the sun.

'Here you are.' Jack hands her the cup of tea she didn't want.

'Thank you.' She takes a sip, barely able to swallow. They stand looking at the trees whispering to each other.

'I want to see Pilot.' Delphi puts her cup down on the counter as she moves through the kitchen, through the hall and into her mother's room. The bed is made, it's completely tidy, no proof of what has passed here in Vivian's blue cube. Delphi kneels and rests her face to the carpet. She looks under the bed and there he is. Pilot the furry womble is tucked against the wall.

'Hey boy,' she coos. 'Hey buddy, it's me, your friend.' She reaches out her hands hoping he will come towards her. His eyes move about in recognition, his tail gives two half-hearted slaps and then he is still again.

'Pilot, she's gone, buddy. You need to come out and have something to eat. A little drink maybe?' He is unresponsive. Delphi pats at the carpet, hoping the drumming might draw him out. 'Okay, dear boy, you rest up and I will come and see you soon. The door is open so when you want to come out, do that.'

She stays slumped there for some time in yoga child's pose. A child kneeling beside her mother's forever more empty bed.

Delphi has a brutal headache; she needs Panadol. She heaves herself up and holds on to the bed-end as her blood settles. Vivian's half-read book on her bedside table, her reading glasses beside it. Her clothes abandoned in the wardrobe. Her cherished special box crammed with letters, baby teeth and first curl hair clippings. Delphi moves as if she's sustained a blow to the head.

She crosses the hall into the bathroom and towards the cabinet under the sink to rummage for pills. Around the basin are talcum-powder fingerprints. Her mother's. Delphi leans in to study them. Those fingers are gone, she thinks, never again to leave their mark on any surface. My mother's hands, the ones that held me to her breast as a baby and nurtured me, are gone.

Careful to keep her sore head upright she opens the cabinet, finds the pills, frees them from their packaging and takes four. They stick in her throat so she gulps water from the tap. Delphi releases herself to the tiles and rolls onto her side.

This is the recovery position, she thinks. Foetal, maybe I should spend the rest of the time like this. *S*he shuts her eyes and pulses with the awful throb of her head.

*

'I wish Pilot would come out from under there,' Delphi says and sips the spicy Bloody Mary Jack has made her. It's the middle of the night and they're both lying on their mother's bed. Jetlag and grief have scrambled their circadian rhythms.

'When you were taking your nap on the bathroom floor earlier, he did go out for a bit, but then he darted straight back to his vigil. Didn't even pause at his water bowl.'

'How long can he carry on without drinking anything?'

'He'll be okay, he's pining I guess, but I'm sure he'll come out soon. When he's ready. Grief has its own clock.'

'It reminds me of those stories you hear about dogs sitting on the graves of their masters for years.'

Jack makes small circles with his glass so the ice clinks. A Bloody Mary was one of Vivian's favourite drinks. *Lots of vitamins whilst it takes the edges off, what a friendly drink!* She used to say that, past tense. Almost everything regarding Vivian will be in the past tense.

'What time did you say we are due at the funeral place to see Mama tomorrow?'

'Midday. Are you sure you want to do it, Delph? I don't think it's a good idea.'

'I'm sure. I don't really believe she's dead. I mean, I know it intellectually, but in my heart, in my body, I can't accept it. I need to see her. The idea of never seeing her again is intolerable. I can't…' she trails off and looks at her feet. They seem so far away.

A dog from next door barks out into the night and Delphi wonders if it will stir Pilot into action.

Nothing.

She turns her worry towards her brother.

'Jack, are you alright?'

'Yes,' he moves a slice of lemon aside so he can drink unimpeded. 'I'm okay.'

They make eye contact briefly. His eyes are darker than Delphi's but the same almond shape. Heavy lids. *Romantic, intelligent eyes,* their mother would say.

'You called the police; they came with an ambulance and took her away?'

He nods.

'Two mornings ago? At what time?'

'Around 9 am. I called them right after I called you.'

'Did the police interview you?'

'Sort of, they took fingerprints, photos, the bag. I may have to go in and give a statement.'

Delphi treads carefully.

'What time did she die?'

'Around midnight I guess. We had dinner together. She went to bed early. I had cabin fever so went to the pub. When I came home I watched some TV, then went in to check on her before I went to bed.' An insect is darting back and forth demented by the light of the pendant. 'I'm so sad she died on her own but I'm also really proud that she managed it.'

'Me too. And what happened then?'

'I sat with her holding her hand. I sang to her for a bit. Then I tidied the kitchen, just pottered about.'

'What, all night?'

'No, I came back in here and I combed her hair. Then I lay down with her.'

With this image Delphi is introduced to a sadness so all-encompassing she is cut adrift.

'You are a good man, Jack. And such a good son.'

'I don't think I'm a good person, Delphi.'

'Well, you are. I know you are.'

Silence returns to recoat all the surfaces.

Delphi forges a crack in the imperviousness of it. 'I miss you, Jack.'

Nothing from him.

She circles back. 'What happened to us?'

She holds her breath and watches the side of his face carefully. He exhales exhausted and swings his legs off the bed.

'Delph…' As he gestures his glass tumbles and the dregs of the tomato juice splatter across the carpet.

They jump to their feet. 'Oh no! Mama's carpet!' Vivian had always been obsessed with her carpet and the fear of staining it is ingrained in them. The antiquated irrelevance of this strikes them and they start to laugh. The energy and release fuel them and soon they are both laughing hard.

'Ah, she would hate that. We've got to clean it up.'

'Yeah, I know. I will get a cloth.' Her brother leaves the room.

'You still breathing under there, Pilot?' The dog doesn't respond. 'Okay buddy, as you were.' She resettles on the bed and pulls the blanket over herself. She wonders if she's getting the flu. Nausea is painting the room yellow. A jaundiced world. Delphi breathes deeply until the swell passes.

*

'Do you remember that old telly series *Six Feet Under*?' Delphi asks Jack.

'I didn't watch it.'

'It was amazing. I loved it. It's about a family who run a funeral home. I think in the States it's called a parlour. What a gross word. Parlour. Parlour.' She stretches out the sounds. 'This place reminds me of it. It's all so heavy, so woody, so much furniture polish… and that guy who let us in, a twenty-five-year-old in a grey suit? Grey loafers? He moves like a sixty-five-year-old. He had pens lined up in his pocket.' Delphi wonders if he smells like embalming fluid when he's naked.

'Delphi, can you stop talking so much?'

'Sorry. I'm nervous. I feel like I'm going to be sick.'

Delphi stands still hoping the lifting sensation will subside.

'I'm not in control of my body,' she says.

'We're not in control of anything at all,' Jack answers.

The sombre grey funeral attendant returns holding his hands clasped in front of his groin like a fleshy fig leaf. He has a signet ring on his little finger that has swivelled around. It's too big for him. Someone has died in your family too, Delphi thinks. Clark and Sons' Funerals the sign had read. Maybe his father, Clark senior is the original owner of that ring. A bigger man, maybe he owned more pens.

'Jack and Delphi, when you are ready your mother is right through that door. Visit with her as long as you would like and I will be out here if you need anything or have any questions.'

He shakes both their hands which seems peculiar timing to Delphi but she's grateful for his sincerity. What a job, taking care of people at their lowest ebb.

'Thank you,' Delphi says, hoping he understands she means for everything.

'Are you ready, Delph?' Jack asks, his hands anchored deep inside his pockets.

'I am.' Reading his body, 'You're not coming, Jack?'

'No, you go. I'll wait here.' His face has the quality of a crumbling mountain. Grief eroding his thirty-two-year-old youth.

Delphi slides open the pine door and steps into the room. To her left is a bank of floor-to-ceiling windows. Yellow sunlight is spilling across the floor. She wonders if the glass is tinted. To her right, at the far end of the room, is a coffin. Seeing it Delphi reels with a horse-kick of shock. Reality is sometimes so extreme it can only be felt in jolting increments.

She steps into the room, a stop-gap animation of the macabre. She's careful to keep her footsteps as quiet as possible. She doesn't know why. Don't wake the dead. She moves towards the coffin. It is a pale wood, silver handles, sitting on a metal trolley.

Closer and she sees there is no lid, then discerns the shape of a body.

Delphi steps closer and looks at her mother's face. Vivian is deformed and in that instant flashes ghoulish and unrecognisable, like something zombified from a horror film. Delphi gasps and steps backwards. She can't do this. She runs back down the room to the door. Sliding it open, Jack is where she left him. He looks at her and doesn't need an explanation. Trembling, she reaches for him and he takes her hand.

'Will you come with me, Jack?'

He squeezes her fingers. He is steady, earthed, strong, such a contrast to her shivering translucency. Delphi feels like a coward.

'Of course.'

Together they enter the room and walk to their mother.

Snatching a look at Vivian, Delphi ventures, 'Her lipstick is the wrong colour.' It's peach, Vivian would hate that.

'We can ask them to change it,' Jack says quietly.

'That lace is tacky. Can we take it away?'

Jack carefully removes the fabric from around their mother's head. Vivian's face is collapsed, it's settled into a death mask and the fear this unleashes in Delphi is riding roughshod.

'If you squat down a bit, Delphi, if you look at her from this angle, her profile, it's her.'

Delphi does as he suggests and there is her mother. This liberated updraft of recognition is complicated. It's a swirling mess of love, anguish and loss. This pushes Delphi over another edge and she is wracked with sobs. Jack places a hand on her spine and stands present until the storm has passed.

Delphi wipes the tears away on the backs of her hands. She studies her mother again. Vivian's wearing her pink dressing-gown.

'I like that you chose that Jack. Is she wearing slippers too?'

'Of course.'

Vivian's chest looks inflated and boxy. Delphi thrusts away the thought of the autopsy. She'd read that they take out the organs and once examined, slop them back into the body any-which-way. Who knows, Vivian's heart could be down in her pelvis now. They will have taken her brain out too. What horrors the back of her head must now conceal.

Delphi reaches out and touches her mother's hands which are resting on her stomach. The flesh is frozen solid; the texture and temperature make Delphi invert. Her brain hadn't expected this. The warmest flesh of all, the mother skin, ice cold now. She's been slumbering in an industrial fridge. Delphi recoils. Her anger at not being able to keep Vivian at home until the funeral doubles down.

But Vivian's hands, they still look like her mother's. Imprint she commands herself, imprint that. Those hands that helped you learn to walk. Those hands which also struck you across the face. Those hands that put the first paintbrush between your fingers.

Delphi recalls a photograph of herself with Vivian when she must have been three. They're at a party, Vivian glamorous in a soft blue corduroy suit, pearls and a thick gold chain around her neck. Delphi is crying for some reason, and Vivian is looking at her with tender empathy as she strokes away a tear. Mother-love is ferocious in its power.

'Mama. You're free now.'

Jack takes his hand away and the two stand looking at the starkly vacated body of their mother. Vivian has gone. Left. Vanished.

Delphi takes a letter, some drawings and photographs from her pocket. She wants to tuck them into position under Vivian's hands but realises the sinister mortuary freeze means the only option is to place them on her chest. A photo of the three siblings when they were little all smiling and shiny in their pyjamas. Another of Pilot. A third of a man named Oliver whom Vivian had long said was the love of her life. A romance truncated by his early death. When Vivian and Edward had divorced her mother framed this photo of her dead lover and placed it on her bedside table.

Vivian wore a locket around her neck. A small flat one of creamy gold. Inside it, a photo of Oliver, smiling, wholesome looking in front of a green hedge. He'd been twenty-seven when it was taken and he'd been killed four months later in a car crash. Edward, their father, had screamed in some horrendous argument, 'Who can compete with a dead saint, Vivian?' and had lobbed a vase across the room, hoping to smash his then wife to pieces. Poor Edward, doomed to never be loved enough to stop his own pain.

'Do you think Mama really loved Oliver more than Edward?' she asks.

'No, I don't think so. She just said that because loving Dad was so painful for her.'

'Hey, where's her locket?'

Jack pulls his shirt open at the throat and Delphi sees it. 'Oh, it looks good on you. Is Oliver still inside it?'

'For now. Which is a bit weird, I guess. I will put a photo of Mama in.'

Jack is distracted, taking something from his wallet. He leans forward and places it into the coffin.

'What's that?' Delphi asks.

'Her frequent flyer card. I thought she might need it.'

The siblings smile.

'You remember, Jack, how she dreaded the idea of standing over either of our coffins. At least this is the natural order of things. She had to do that with Arthur…' Delphi doesn't finish her thought out loud.

'Come on, Del. Let's go.' Jack tugs gently on her.

'Okay,' she replies. 'I just don't know how to take my eyes away from her.' This final time looking at her mother. It's a Sisyphean task.

'Del, come on now,' Jack calls again gently.

Her vision is blurred with tears as she leans forward, kisses her mother's frozen and distorted cheek. 'I'm so sorry I let you down, Mama.'

She walks towards her brother with her head hanging low. He takes her in his arms and then ushers her from the room.

'Let's go and stand in the sunshine,' he says. And that is what they do.

CHAPTER 13

THE PHONE IS RINGING. Delphi calls out to her brother, wherever he is, 'I'll get it.' She jogs along the corridor from her room.

'Hello, Delphi speaking.'

'Hello. This is your father.'

Delphi had wondered when he would call. She knew Jack had told him of Vivian's death days ago. She takes off her mother's ugg boots as her feet suddenly feel hot.

'So, your mother is dead.'

The saddest statement ever to be said. She stretches the phone cord so she can open the front door to look out at the river.

'When's the funeral?'

'It's in three days.'

'Good. That's enough time. I'll be coming.'

Delphi reels.

'Mama doesn't want you there. I know that's painful for you. But she made it clear.' Delphi braces for the backlash.

'I don't care what your mother wanted. As I've already told you, funerals are not for the dead, they're for the bereaved.'

'Are you bereaved?' It sounds churlish but Delphi is interested.

'Of course I bloody am. I was married to her for years. A disaster, but still a marriage.'

Delphi shrinks like Alice in Wonderland. Down, down, down she reduces. Now a tiny little version of herself. Edward is speaking on but she can't listen, as she's busy galvanising her strength.

'You can't come, Edward. Please, I don't want to fight. Let's have a memorial with Jack and your friends, if you'd like, back in England.'

He falters. 'It's not your decision.'

'You're right, it's Mama's. You can't bulldoze this one. You've not been a part of her life for years so you don't get to be a part of her death.'

He's quiet. Delphi holds on tightly to her resolve and asks, 'I don't get it. Why do you want to celebrate her life when you can only speak of her with contempt?'

Once in therapy in senior school, her counsellor had told her that when one parent hates the other and expresses that to their progeny, the child learns to hate themselves – the half that they associate with the vilified parent. Delphi hadn't liked that thinking because both her parents savaged each other violently. It followed that her entire being was swimming in transferred hate.

Edward is still silent. She imagines him in his sitting room, steam jetting from his ears, his eyes pitch black. Clara sitting attentively at his feet making sure no threatening paternal intimacy can blossom.

'When you and Jack divide up her things, some of them need to be returned to me.'

Delphi shuts her eyes tightly. He hasn't rung to commiserate, to comfort, nor offer any familial kindness. He has rung to bully, transgress and demand. She's such a dolt, always hoping he will step up, just a little, and be a father.

'Are you serious, Edward?' Delphi explodes. 'You call me, right after my mother's death to stake your imaginary claim on her tiny estate? You have no capacity for empathy. You're a sociopath! Don't you dare turn up at her funeral. Do you hear me?'

She swings around. Jack is standing a few feet away from her.

'Del?' He has the body language of someone approaching a lion mid-kill. His hands are held up in a placating gesture. And just like that, the revving engine falls out of Delphi. Her weapons tumble from her.

She realises that the phone line is dead. Her father has hung up. Of course, he has. Never would he willingly enable her to take the power, to speak her truth. A woman's rage revolting to his misogynistic sensibilities. The other truth is his own mother screamed at him enough to break him to pieces before he'd even had a chance to choose what kind of man he'd like to be.

Delphi slumps to the floor. The fuel of rage violently spent.

'Jack, I want our mum. I miss her so much and she's only just left.' Her tears drop. 'Where is she now? This is insane. It's cruel.' Her words slur and Jack bends down and puts his arms around her. Delphi sobs for her mother, for herself, for her father, for all the sadness that's ever befallen anyone. She's swept into the collective highway of trauma and Jack holds her tightly.

*

Delphi drains the last sip of whisky from the tumbler and stands unsteadily to pour herself some more.

'I feel terrible.' She slurs using all her concentration to get the liquid into the glass.

'I do too. It's been a dreadful few days,' Jack says.

'A dreadful few years.'

'Really, Delphi? Has it?'

She moves the burning liquid around in her mouth. Her throat is telling her she's had enough but she forces it down.

'Well, you wouldn't know, Jack, as you've chosen to bow out of my life.'

He looks back at her, inscrutable.

'Why is that, Jack? You have a baby I haven't even met. Does that make me an aunt or just some sort of discarded option?'

'Del, you're her aunt. And you will meet her.'

'What the hell happened to us? You were there and then you just vanished.'

'I don't have an answer. It's not about you, believe it or not.'

'Not that again, Jack, *Delphi the self-obsessed dramatist*. You get that language from Edward.'

'Don't compare me to him.'

Delphi goes back to the dining table and sits opposite her brother. She stares at him; her vision is out of focus.

Jack speaks slowly. 'I didn't make a single decision. I guess I drifted. Mama and Edward were such nightmares and after finishing school I got as far away as I could and never really went home again. Not in any meaningful way. It was always so painful and ugly and I made my own life. It's a clean world I've carved out for myself with Marie and Zenia. We are good. The baby is miraculous.' A smile spreads across his face. 'We live quietly. We love Paris. Marie's family are really supportive and involved.'

This pierces Delphi through the heart. She would give anything to be allowed to be involved.

'You, Del, you're so wild and full of passion. You remember when we were kids, I called you Passion Fruit?'

She loved it when he did that.

'I'm not like you. I was ground down, defeated by them. I tried but I ran out of steam. All the lies.'

'You left to save yourself?'

'I wouldn't say it like that... but I couldn't be there anymore. Particularly not near Dad.'

'Do you love him?'

'In a way, but I don't respect him.'

'Will you grieve when he dies?'

'I'm not sure. I don't think so. What would I be grieving?'

Delphi pulls her shoulders down.

'You never answered my emails or calls, Jack.'

'Yeah, I know, I read them. The painting you made for Zenia's birth is above her crib, but I just couldn't reach back. With all the mess... in a way you were collateral damage.'

'Collateral damage?' Delphi winces as the knife pushes in deeper.

Jack is watching her tenderly and he offers her a small inadequate smile.

'Then I was away so long it was impossible to find my way back, even if I'd wanted to.'

'Did you want to?'

'Not really.'

The knife twists.

'Jack, do you promise me you'll help with this Edward mess? The funeral and things of Mama's he says he wants?'

Jack leans back and rubs his face.

'Look, that old man isn't getting any of Mama's stuff, but in relation to the funeral does it really matter?'

'Yes, of course it does. It was Mama's wish. Surely honouring her is all about making sure that's respected.'

'Okay but I don't know how much fight I have in me, Delphi. Maybe some compromise could be good. I sure as hell know we never learnt that skill from our parents.'

'No way,' Delphi digs her heels in. 'He can't come, he's just cashing in on the drama of it all. There is nothing loving in his motivation.'

'No, but he's weirdly sentimental. It will mean something to him, Del.'

'He doesn't deserve that. Not when it rides over Mama.'

'She's dead. She's gone. What are you fighting for?'

'For love. For respect. For the bloody truth.'

'Okay, okay.' He shuts his eyes and exhales all the air from his lungs. At that moment Delphi can see Edward in him and it's confusing her.

'Jack, please tell me about Arthur?' She's probably too drunk to push down this road.

Jack's face changes. It calcifies.

'What about him?'

'Well, anything. I can't remember. I guess because of the shock. I have massive gaps. He was happy that afternoon. I was playing with him. It was windy, and then he was under the water. I tried to get him out, but he was so heavy and thrashing, and I wasn't strong enough. I wasn't a good enough swimmer. My feet, they didn't touch the bottom.'

Jack looks down at the carpet and lines his shoes up so they're perfectly side by side.

'It's such a long time ago, Del. Arthur drowned. Dad wasn't home. Mum was drunk. Afterwards, she had a breakdown and you kinda went off the rails too. That's why they sent you away to boarding school. That's it.'

'And that's it?' How can you sum it up like that? Arthur is our brother. Were you home? Did you see anything?'

Jack wavers so Delphi presses on.

'Jack?'

'Yes, I was home. I was inside. You were screaming. It's all over now though. What good does this do?'

'What good does it do? I have never moved on, Jack. I'm still that girl, that girl who let her brother drown. And we as a family have been so screwed up about it. So English, never any talking. It became like Arthur never existed. Don't mention him or Mama will break down and Edward will become furious. I turn it over and over and I can't make sense of it. Like a page of writing where all the letters are jumbled up.'

'Del, it's time for bed. You're wasted. We are both smashed. Let me help you up. I'll get you a glass of water and let's get some sleep.'

'Jack, what's happening here? You're shutting me down just like Edward does.'

'Oh, for Christ's sake, I've had enough. You're not the only person suffering.'

Delphi struggles to her feet and is swaying in the middle of the dining room. She moves towards the kitchen counter so she can hold on to something.

'Jack, one last question and then I will stop, I promise.'

He's rinsing his plate and glass in the sink.

'Did you really not help Mama?'

Jack finishes and turns off the taps. He looks at his sister and says, 'I've told you, Delphi. I was at the pub. I know you hate the idea and so do I but she was alone, and as tragic as that is I'm also proud of her.' He runs his hands through his hair. I'm going to check on Pilot, see if he's touched that food.' He turns and leaves the room.

Delphi focuses on a scratch on the counter. It looks like a great big letter Y.

*

Delphi spends hours examining her mother's books. The occasional relevant paper clipping tucked inside a cover, but not a single section underlined, nor a corner turned down. Her mother was fanatical about respecting books but Delphi would give anything to have a trace of her mother in those pages now. Several times she presses her lips to her mother's signature, always fountain pen, and feels the groundswell of loss.

The depth of her wallowing crystallises into something akin to panic. She envisages herself as an astronaut, air cord severed, floating away from the mothership into a black abyss for all eternity.

Unable to find the strength to stand, Delphi crawls along the corridor. Nudging her mother's bedroom door open with her head, she sprawls out on the carpet. Pilot is still holed up under the bed. He's not eaten nor drunk anything for days and his suffering is terrible. Delphi stretches her arm under the bed towards him.

'Buddy, please come out. Come here and let me cuddle you, dear, true boy.'

She drums her finger to make a luring sound. He looks dreadful.

'Pilot, sweetheart, our plane is crashing. Protocol and my heart require me to fit your air mask first. Please, I'm begging you, come out, come to me.'

The dog lifts an eyebrow and after a moment he shuffles forward a little so Delphi can reach his head. 'Thank you,' she whispers. 'You're so lovely, Pilot.' The dog closes his eyes and Delphi does too, letting herself float beyond consciousness.

*

The siblings are in the police station waiting to be interviewed. Jack sits reading *The Great Gatsby* on the other side of the room from his sister.

Delphi is unwell. She wonders if she has a fever and quietly touches her forehead and then the back of her neck. She's sweating but chalks it up to nerves. Spotting the water cooler, she debates getting herself a cup but gives up, deeming it too hard.

Jack is deep inside his book. His legs crossed, his face is sad and closed. His skin replete with hedgehog quills.

The policewoman behind the counter is listening patiently as a man, who's obviously eaten all the drugs, is blathering about a payphone stealing his money. As she answers him she uses the word *mate* as firm punctuation to the end of every sentence.

Eventually, a great relief to Delphi, the stoner breaks off mid-sentence, stumbles his way through the glass doors, down the stairs, and resumes fuming once he hits the pavement.

Delphi watches the policewoman for any sign of relief, but there's none. She's a professional and Delphi guesses she has skin as thick as a rhinoceros. Delphi is full of admiration.

The surge of seasickness pushes up in Delphi and she races to the bathroom. She only just makes it in time. She carefully cleans up then washes her hands and holds her wet hands to her face. Coming out, Jack is waiting for her in the corridor.

'You okay? You look white as a sheet.'

'I'm sorry, Jack.' She makes a circular gesture with her arms, trying to indicate she means for everything.

'It's okay, Passion Fruit. I'm sorry too.' The siblings take each other's hands and walk back to the waiting room.

*

Inspector Dutton hasn't become any more charming since the last time she was sitting in this chair opposite him. Delphi wonders if the air-conditioning has been deliberately turned off or if she's just a paranoid mess. Constable Carter is riffling through papers. She looks at Delphi and smiles.

'We have one final question for you, Delphi. Thank you again for being so helpful and understanding why we needed to interview you separately to your brother.'

Delphi holds the woman's gaze and tries to set her face into a non-combative mask. In reality she wants to stand up and throw the table across the room. She wants to tear at her flesh and scream out for her mother to come and take her away.

'It's fine, Constable.' Delphi wonders if she's said that too many times during the interview and resolves not to repeat it. Overly accommodating may be incriminating.

'It's imperative you answer this honestly, Delphi.' Both detectives watch her intently.

'Do you know and or believe that your brother Jack Hoffman aided your mother in her death in any way, shape or form?'

Delphi observes the air enter her nostrils and she traces it as it passes the back of her throat. She listens to the clock ticking, tick tick tick, and feels the smoothness of her skin as she holds her hands in her lap. With her chin at 90 degrees and her voice as steady as an ocean liner in calm waters Delphi answers, 'Jack had nothing to do with it. As you know, Mama tried once before and this time she was successful. She achieved what she wanted to achieve. She set herself free.' Delphi's inner voice warns her to say no more so she shuts her mouth and aims to emanate serene conviction.

Constable Carter writes something down then turns to look at the inspector. He holds his eyes on Delphi for several beats then abruptly and formally terminates the interview. He stands, shakes Delphi's hand and as they all prepare to leave, he says, 'I am very sorry for your loss.' Delphi is startled. It's such a weird expression, but she searches his face and he means it.

'Thank you,' Delphi swallows.

'My mother died last year,' he adds.

Delphi, with her head cocked to the side, waits to see if he has anything else to share. He adjusts his heavy-duty belt and she understands the exchange is over.

*

Jack goes home to sleep so Delphi walks into the first bar she comes to. It's an ugly seventies besser-block situation. She orders a bottle of wine and the first of many whiskys. She sets herself up in a sticky corner table, sitting with her back to the room and takes out her drawing things. She stays there until closing, drinking hard and endlessly drawing pictures of her mother. The barman approaches, lifting stools and inverting them onto tables saying, 'That's it darlin'. The good times are over.'

'Do you think so?' she asks. He looks perplexed and she brushes away what she said by packing up her things. She stumbles needing to steady herself against the brick wall, which scratches the skin off the top of her hand. She tries not to stagger as she clears the door. The street outside is empty. Delphi wants to see the water so she heads for the docks. It doesn't take her long to get there, and she finds a spot where she kneels and supports her torso over the wooden barrier and looks down into the black water. She envisages Virginia Woolf filling her pockets with stones and walking herself into the River Ouse.

If Delphi were to dive in, Virginia might swim up to meet her. Embracing, cheek to cheek, their hair moving back and forth, in the slow currents of the river. And Virginia might swim them into the abyss or maybe Delphi could pull them both to the surface. She rests her head down on the barrier. She has to get away from the river and she heaves herself onto her feet and leadenly walks into Parliament House Gardens. She lies down and waits for the tears to drain out so she can see the stars.

*

She wakes pulverised. Confused, she shields her face from the invasive fingers of sunlight prising into her eyeballs. Discerning the grass beneath her, Delphi slowly sits up. People are milling about, off to work. They all look so clean. So unburdened. She waits for her head to stop spinning. She needs to get home. Jack will check in her room at some point and she doesn't want to add to his worries. She gets to her feet like a newly born giraffe and sets her course to the bus stop.

*

Delphi hauls herself up the steep driveway. Godfather Hugh is sitting drinking tea on the front verandah of Vivian's cottage. His white linen suit and Panama hat are gleaming in the morning light. He looks at Delphi as she hobbles towards him.

'Look at what the proverbial dragged in.'

'Hugh. You're a sight for sore eyes.'

'Did Jack tell you to expect me today?'

'No, he didn't.' She rubs at the dirt on her hands.

'Fem, come here.' He opens himself towards her.

Delphi takes the stairs gingerly and gratefully tucks into his embrace, careful to keep her grimy face away from his suit.

'Sit down a moment. God knows you look like you need to.' He plucks a stray leaf from her shoulder.

Delphi does as she's told. He takes the cane chair beside her and holds on to her hand. His brown flesh and clean nails contrast Delphi's chipped black nail polish. She takes a skull ring from her middle finger and studies it. She wonders why she ever chose it and lobs it from the balcony.

'Fem, I don't want to harangue you, but Jack has updated me and, looking at you, it seems you are in a bit of a mess.' Delphi squints out across the river and wishes she hadn't lost her sunglasses.

'Delphi, may I speak to you?' She likes his gentle manners and arcane politeness. He hands her his cup of tea and she sips at the remaining lukewarm fluid. Delphi nods in assent.

'My girl, your mother has died. And in terrible circumstances. You are in agony. Grief is like swimming solo across an inclement ocean at night. I wish I could protect you from all of this, but sadly I can't, this is your path. Delphi, listen to this old man, you must travel it and you can choose to rally grace or you can collapse and wallow in the chaos.'

Delphi is listening.

'Fem, you are old enough and God knows smart enough to be making better choices.' He gently disentangles a twig from her hair. 'I don't say this with judgement but with love. Delphi, less drinking, stop the raging and take more sleep and food. You are too thin. Even Audrey Hepburn would agree with me. If you *feel* your vulnerability, you won't die, there will be relief. When my June died I thought I would never recover. She was the greatest boon of my life. Without her, meaning and purpose were elusive, but I rallied, as you must, as life is the most precious gift.'

Tears slip down Delphi's face and pool on her chest making her t-shirt wet.

'You are mistaken if you think you can force your way through these black days. Stop thrashing. Soften. Surrender. And I promise the desperation inside you will slowly alleviate. If you can't love yourself enough to do this, then do it for your mother and let's bury her tomorrow with open hearts. Rage will burn you to a crisp, and it will repel all wonder and grace from your path.'

He sits quietly letting Delphi do as what she wants with his words.

She tries to speak, but emotion is clogging her throat. He puts a paternal hand on her leg. She calms enough to stammer, 'I feel like my life has been cut to ribbons… a world without her… I can't make sense of it…'

His kind face furrows with understanding.

'There is no making sense of death. It is the ultimate mystery.'

'Everything is a mess, Hugh. This overwhelming sadness, Jack, Edward, the police. Pilot is not doing well. And our baby Arthur, his death… It's as if the grief of Mama has brought up that ancient grief. It's all alive again. I'm nearly through my savings. No proper job. I don't even have a home. And that's just my tiny sphere, what of the refugee crisis, gender inequality, global warming and–'

'Delphi, Delphi,' he interrupts. 'You are flooding. Slow down. Let's talk about you now, and we'll tackle the rest of the world another day. I don't remember which wise soul said it, but you can't go back and make the details pretty, but you can move forward and make the whole beautiful. I believe that. You have been dealt quite the hand, but you have also been given many gifts. I'm not telling you not to feel your pain, quite the opposite. I hope in some small way my arrival will help you feel supported. Collapse here with me, you are safe right here, but stop railing out as you're hurting yourself even more.' He lifts his eyes to the river.

'As usual I have used too many words, Delphi. The distillation is this: to take stock one must stop running. Does that make sense to you, darling Fem?'

He hands her a handkerchief, and as she unfolds it, notices his embroidered initials. June loved to sew. 'This is too good for me to use,' she says trying to return it.

'Oh, nonsense.'

'Thank you, Hugh,' she says, blowing her nose.

'That's quite alright, darling girl. Quite alright.' He leans back, the cane of the chair creaks and they look out at the water together. 'And don't worry about your coffers being impoverished. I will write you a cheque to tide you over. All you ever need do is to ask. And I spoke to your father. He won't be coming to the funeral, so that's another worry off your list.'

The river is so beautiful it hurts.

'Hugh?'

'Yes, Fem.'

'I love you.'

'Excellent, because I love you too.'

CHAPTER 14

DELPHI BLINKS UNDER THE halogen lights at the differing brands of pregnancy tests. She picks up a box and looks at it hard. *Clear Blue* with its massive plus and minus signs. Maths to make you cry, thinks Delphi. Then another brand, *First Response* – pink, yellow, white. Comforting playful colours, she notes while swallowing down her hysteria.

Delphi has never kept track of her cycle, but an hour ago it occurred to her that she's late. She'd stepped out of the shower and thrown a towel around herself. Still dripping, she'd dug out her diary and leafed through it in an attempt to track a timeline. Her fingers making the paper wet, a corner of her handwriting forming ink tears and dribbling down the page. Delphi's face had become very, very hot.

She was probably due to bleed a week ago, maybe only five days, but then she's not always regular, and she's been on international flights which can scramble things. But what of the vomiting at the station? The low-grade nausea? Was she just unwell or is this another aspect of grief? Maybe a freak out about nothing.

Delphi replaces the box and lifts the one next to it. This has two tests and says it is 99 per cent accurate from the day your period was due. The cellophane is perfectly wrapped around the rectangular box making it shine like giant confectionery. She's holding it with both hands in case it tries to run away.

Unable to sit in the discomfort of indecision for a second longer, Delphi makes her choice and takes the test to the cash register. A boy of about seventeen is vacant and powered down behind the counter. He has a weak chin and is wearing glasses chosen by someone unkind. His striped tie must only be an inch across, an ungenerous amount of fabric and his name tag reads 'Brenton'. What parent would call their child *'Brenton',* Delphi wonders. 'Brenton' will never be prime minister. 'Brenton' will never be written within the script of an ardent poem. No sane person will ever scream that name in the throes of ecstasy.

Brenton takes the box from Delphi. Scans it. Offers the machine to process her credit card, puts the test into a paper bag and then looks at her and says, 'Good luck.'

Delphi is caught by his choice of words. It's so clever. She blushes as she tucks the test and her purse away. Delphi says, 'Thank you' and he smiles with wide-open warmth. He is radiant in his well-meaning simplicity. Delphi thinks Brenton might just be the loveliest name that ever was.

*

'How do you want to do this, Delphi?' Jack drains the last of his beer.

'I don't know. You can have it all. I don't want it and anyway, I've nowhere to put any of it.'

Delphi and Jack look around the sitting room as if seeing it for the first time.

'No, Del, Mama wanted us both to have half. She told us that often enough. We can arrange for it to go into storage until you have a home of your own.'

Delphi rubs at her red eyes. Jack is sitting on the floor too, one of Vivian's wigs on his head. The thick red curls make him look fabulous. Years before, their mother had had breast cancer. When the chemo took her hair she bought wigs, and Jack had found a box of them. Delphi is wearing a blonde one that is cut into a shiny bob.

'I will get a marker pen, and we can put a J or a D on things. I know it seems vulturous, but it has to be done. The timing is shitty but when is this sort of thing ever–'

'Can't we wait until after the funeral?'

'We can if you want but we've still got so much to do: get to her bank, the lawyers for probate, find a home for Pilot.'

Delphi groans and falls backwards so she's lying on the ground.

'Excused me, be-wigged siblings.' Hugh walks into the room with Pilot in his arms. 'I'm going to try to get this hound to drink and have a little roam in the garden. I may even bath him as he smells decidedly zoological.' Poor Pilot looks like an unpotted plant.

'Thank you, Hugh,' the siblings say in unison.

Delphi sits up. When she's vertical her blood pressure plummets. To prevent passing out she bends at the waist and takes a few breaths.

'You okay, Del?'

'Yep, I'm fine. A bit lightheaded.' And probably pregnant, she thinks. Oh God, I hope I'm not. I hope I'm not. Please don't let that be happening.

'Del?'

'Okay, let's do this. You pick first, Jack.'

'Alright.' He walks to the nearest painting of a crush of figures at rush hour on a train. 'Do you particularly love this?'

'No.' Delphi lies.

'Then I will take it.' He writes a small black J in the bottom corner with a marker.

'Your turn.'

'This breaks my heart, Jack.'

He turns to her and rubs her cheek. 'I know. It's awful.' She has a preternatural flash of the scene from a distance. An uncanny Haruki Murakami moment. As if viewing herself and her brother from outside the big square window. Jack in his red wig and she in her blonde one, tethered by his arm. Something about the tableau gives her strength. She covers his hand with her own and is revived by the warmth of his palm.

'Onward, brother, onward.'

*

It's a perfect day. Bluebird sky, fleecy clouds. It's been art directed for absurdism. Sitting in the back seat of her mother's car, her brother and Hugh are up front, Delphi observes her hands resting in her lap. Surely, they belong to someone else? Foreign fingers. Plastic-y flesh. Distance distorted. Vivian's pearls hang heavy around her neck. She concentrates on their micro movements as they roll on her skin. The three passengers are all dressed in funereal black. Delphi wonders when and where that colour tradition began. The men travel in silence. Delphi studies the backs of their heads the same way one would peer through a telescope – with one eye closed. When her working eye tires she swaps over to the other eye.

Today is the day they are to bury Vivian.

She didn't take the pregnancy test this morning. She's not entirely sure why. There wasn't time or maybe she wasn't brave enough. She hasn't felt at all nauseous, so it's probable she's drummed up the whole thing. It's logical that with the shock of Vivian's death, Delphi's rhythms are a mess. She prods her flat belly. Impossible to believe a human is growing in there.

Looking out the window, it's as if perspective has been tampered with. Everything is different but she can't put her finger on how. A small child on a tricycle is furiously pedalling along the footpath. His carefree father following behind is chatting on a mobile. One day they'll both be dead too, she says in her head and waits to see if it makes her feel anything. No, nothing. It's as if she's hollowed out, just an outline.

'We are here,' Jack says. Delphi swivels and recognises the funeral home. *Home,* she thinks, that's weird and sort of wonderful. We all go home in the end.

They pull into the carpark. A few people Delphi doesn't think she knows are milling about by the front doors. Her brother chooses a car space, drives in, turns off the ignition and pulls on the handbrake. The three of them stay still and silent as if the journey were continuing.

Jack inhales so sharply, it sounds like a stick being cracked in two. He cranes around to look at his sister. 'Are you ready?'

'No, brother. I will never be ready.' Her voice is thick as if she has not spoken at all today.

Hugh turns to look at her and says, 'Fem, make your mother proud.'

Delphi nods.

The men get out of the car and their movement creates a tsunami of noise. Delphi opens her door and heaves herself to her feet. She's tall in her mother's heels. The ground is bizarrely far away. She is an alien newly arrived to earth. She wonders if she will pass as human.

Jack takes her hand and squeezes her fingers. Together they head towards the cream building. Hugh, arm in arm with his own grief, following behind.

*

The attendant Delphi met before spots the siblings and walks towards them. With a Tom Cruise intensity, he shakes their hands. Delphi's fingers are crushed. That must be how he handles the insensitive dead. He reassures Jack that the funeral is all set to start in ten minutes and asks if they have any questions.

A ceiling fan rotates slowly overhead. Watching it Delphi quivers.

More people are arriving now. Delphi doesn't recognise many of them. They seem to recognise her and Jack though. Their faces emanate solidarity and something else that Delphi can't yet decode. Is it embarrassment? Or maybe fear? Delphi is dazed and lets her thoughts slip away. It's less awful to drift than to think.

Jack turns to her and whispers, 'Do you want to stay here for a bit or go in and find a seat, Del?'

'Let's go in.'

They move through and as it did last time the sunlight pours in from the left. People are finding seats in the pale wooden pews, talking quietly. This place is non-denominational but it has the feel of a modern church. A strong Ikea influence in the décor, crucifixes not included in the flat pack.

Vivian's coffin is at the end of the central aisle. A large bouquet of white flowers rests on the closed lid. Delphi wants to scream and scream.

Jack is shaking hands with people and simultaneously leading her towards the front. He gets stymied by a woman with a little beard. Profuse whiskers spike at crazed angles from her chinny chin chin. She looks to be wearing a harlequin costume. Vivian always loved the eccentrics. Hugh assumes the mantle and steers Delphi onward. He intuits that anchoring her to a chair as soon as possible is the preferred course of action.

Close to the coffin, Delphi can't take her eyes from it. My mother is lying in there, in the same position as if she were sleeping. And soon we will put her in an oven, Delphi thinks. Her dressing-gown, with the flammable warning on the tag, will ignite in an instant. Her flesh and fat will bubble and burst. Her eyeballs will liquefy. Those astonishing bluebell irises will blister. Her skeleton will reanimate and clatter against the box. Her teeth will sear loose from her skull. She will be desiccated, turn black and convert to smoke and coal. The cycle complete. Ashes to ashes. Dust to dust. Are we really all made from the same stuff as the stars? Delphi drops her head and a tear falls in a direct line from her eye to the floor where she observes it settling into a round tiny pond by her foot.

A man with the posture of an ex-soldier introduces himself.

'Hello there, I'm Ian Tanker. I'm sorry for your loss. I will be conducting the celebration for your mother today.'

Delphi thanks him and wonders about that bizarre expression. Why sorry? He's not culpable. And what loss? Vivian hasn't been misplaced. And celebration? That is perverse. The intention is obviously kind, but the words are euphemistically mangled. The other phrase that gets stuck in Delphi's throat is 'passed away'. And she thinks, Are we really so terrified, so estranged from the ultimate destination, that we can't plainly state the words died, die and death? We have bleached the words from our language but that doesn't keep us safe. The grim reaper finds us wherever we are. He's still going to separate you from your heartbeat and all you hold dear.

Delphi notices a pin on the celebrant's tie. A swallow soaring in flight. 'I like that,' she says pointing at it.

He is pleased. 'Oh, yes, a gift from my daughter,' he stammers as he calculates if that was insensitive to say to a girl who's burying her mother.

Delphi smiles gently at him to relieve him of his concern and looks to her seat. Before sitting, she lifts the order of service and studies it. A wildly glorious photograph of Vivian on the front. She's twenty-eight, not much older than Delphi, on a beach in Spain. Wearing a tiny yellow-striped bikini, a man's straw hat perched at an angle on her head. Her earrings are bunches of glass grapes. She is bursting with life and beauty. How can she be gone? Delphi thinks. How can one make sense of so much wondrousness now vanished, dematerialised, evaporated… almost as if she never were here at all? I know her smell. My children will know her stories. My grandchildren will know her name and the next generation will probably know nothing of her at all. Delphi clenches her teeth together as hard as she can.

*

Jack's eulogy is succinct, loving and composed. He plays a Debussy piece on the piano that undoes every stitch that is holding Delphi together. Hugh reads out a poem about trees. He and Vivian had a shared obsession with maples.

It's Delphi's turn to speak. She steps up to the podium and looks at the group. Their expectant faces upturned, smoothed out with deference, masking the cowering horror of all our impending deaths. Her voice sounds peculiar as she starts to speak, reading from the pages she wrote the night before:

> I love my mother. She defined for me what it is to be a woman. What it is to be a thinker, an artist, a contributor. She was complicated, passionate, sometimes irrational, but she blazed bright with curiosity and love. To be in her company was to know what it is to be chosen, what it is to be beloved.

She drank wine from cut-crystal water glasses. She smoked Peter Stuyvesant reds down to her toes. She loved that people throughout her life told her that her nose was just like Meryl Streep's. She was a wild mother to the three of us. And, for a time, she adored our father with her whole being.

Our mother was a force. She loved her dog, Pilot, her job at the library, England, and her life here.

She elevated me with a pride I'm yet to deserve.

When I was lonely at school, she'd brush my hair and say, 'Who cares, who wants to be chosen by everyone. Just find the precious few.'

She gave me her watch before she died. I'm wearing it now and it reminds me of when I was a child lying in her arms, and I'd listen to it ticking – the metronome of security.

She was so very nearly destroyed by Arthur's death, yet she managed to crawl forward. I wish I were a person of religious faith. I wish I knew for sure that Mama and Arthur were reunited. I don't and can't know that with my mind but I feel in my heart.

Tears try to break the dam, but Delphi does not release her grip. Carrying on in measured dignity she says, 'I want to finish by quoting a poem of WS Merwin's. He's dead too.'

This erupted correlation burns Delphi's lips, she presses them together and stutters out a small 'Sorry.' She looks at the audience and from memory incants.

Your absence has gone through me
Like thread through needle.
Everything I do is stitched with its colour.

*

Vivian's wake is in full swing. Her home is filled with people. Delphi looks out at the garden from the deck. It's packed with guests smoking, drinking, talking animatedly into the still night. It looks just like a regular party. Vivian would approve. Nina Simone's voice rumbles and soothes. Delphi spots Jack smoking a joint.

She makes her way to her brother and whispers that maybe smoking pot now isn't wise. He nods and crushes it under foot into the grass.

Delphi is exhausted. What she desires is to collapse into bed and stay there for a year. She wonders when it will be appropriate for her to dissolve away.

She moves between elbows, avoiding eyes, back up to the verandah, through the packed kitchen, into the front hall and impulsively turns into the vacant bathroom. She locks the door and stands alone in the darkness for a few moments. Through the frosted windows she can see people outside. Their silhouettes in a dance of sorts. Shadow puppets. The bereaved. The left behind.

Delphi turns on the light. She double checks the door is locked and goes to the cabinet to retrieve the package she'd stuffed at the back.

She removes the brown paper bag, then the cellophane, opens the box and takes out one of the packets. She uses her teeth to tear off the end and looks at the white plastic stick.

Lifting her skirt and pulling down her knickers, she takes the cap from the test and urinates onto the exposed strip. She returns the cap and sets the test down flat to wait for the results.

Delphi takes out her phone to look at the time. Eight-seventeen pm. This must be the longest day in history. She thinks to look at Instagram but can't face that. She flips to her message bank and sees a long list of missed calls. The one that collars her is the one bearing her mother's name. She looks at the date and time it was logged. It is the call she missed on the road in Brighton with the dying dog. Her mother never left voice messages but this one indicates nineteen seconds of recording. How had Delphi not spotted that? Delphi has the sensation of falling off a cliff in slow motion. She presses play and holds the phone to her ear to listen.

'Delphi, flower. This is Mummy. My love, I am calling to say I love you. You're an incredible woman. So vibrant and creative. So very beautiful. I know how cross you get when I tell you that but it's true. Delphi, I wish we had more time, but it's all run out now. Goodbye, my daughter. Always remember to be brave and kind.'

And the phone is hung up.

Delphi sits in a trance. She presses replay to hear the words again. She sits still, narcotised. The yearning in her chest changes shape; with each iteration, Delphi feels it anew.

Her hands shaking, she puts the phone down beside the test and takes some paper to blow her nose. She straightens her back. Picking up the test she holds it up and there is a clear blue cross. Pregnant. Delphi shuts her eyes and counts to three. She opens her eyes to see if there is some mistake, but the cross adamantly remains.

Someone knocks on the door and Delphi jumps.

'Hey, you going to be long in there?'

'No. Sorry.' She stands wondering what to do with the test. She stuffs it into her jacket pocket, then checks that the wrapping is hidden deep within the bin. She changes her mind and yanks the test from her pocket and stuffs it into the bin too. She washes her hands and moves to unlock the door as another knock cracks into the room. Her legs are trembling like a colt.

*

Delphi had intended to seek shelter in her bedroom, but she's swept back into the party by friends of her mother's wanting to say goodbye. She musters her remaining strength to listen, give thanks and farewell. Words of consolation are offered. She is kissed and patted. She's told stories, some she knows already, but many she doesn't. The well-meaning folk collect their belongings and wave sad, serious goodbyes as they're released.

Delphi turns to make her way to solitude when Cathy approaches. She used to work with Vivian. Her make-up-free face is blotched with emotion. In her arms she is carrying a sleeping baby. Delphi can't hear very well over the rush of blood through her ears. Cathy is talking and Delphi is watching her mouth, unable to decipher a coherent meaning. She nods, hoping this situation will magically retract but it only escalates. The baby is passed into her arms as the mother goes off to find her partner. Delphi looks down at the infant, at its tiny hand over the yellow blanket. At the plump curve of its cheek, the lift of its nose, the delicacy of its eyelashes resting closed. Delphi is transfixed. She is in awe with the perfection, the clean, fresh being of this baby. She has one of these inside her now. It's growing, cells dividing and divining. Maybe Delphi's baby dashed through the star gates when they were opened for Vivian? What crazy magical thinking. That timing doesn't lend itself to sense. But Delphi is convinced that truth isn't always logical.

Cathy returns to scoop the baby out of Delphi's arms. Delphi is weightless. As if the babe were keeping her tethered to the earth. She accepts more words of commiseration and Cathy says, 'I'm sorry we can't take Pilot. I've asked around. No luck but I'll keep looking for you, I promise.' Delphi hugs the couple goodbye, thanking them and congratulating them on their child. She moves to the front door to wave them off and as she does, she places a hand on her belly. Then she goes off to see if Pilot is alright.

CHAPTER 15

THE SUNLIGHT IS BRIGHT white making Delphi squint, an action which lends itself to nostalgia. Delphi thinks about *The Virgin Suicides* and *Picnic at Hanging Rock*. Both books had bewitched her with girls in white dresses, sun-bleached worlds, ghastly, deathly endings.

The funeral yesterday was Everest. Gratefully she slept, thanks to Valium, and now she's lying in the front garden watching clouds reshape and move gently above. The *Star Wars* theme music plays in Delphi's head as she watches their undulating forms.

Vivian loathed kitsch but when she bought this cottage, she inherited an ancient garden gnome. Idiosyncratically she was fiercely loyal to it, referring to him as My Dear Friend. Delphi tilts her head back to look at the battered smurf. He's very battered with his hat chipped off at the top, his colours faded, his once rosy cheeks still apple-round with laughter. Frozen mid-chuckle waiting for Snow White to return.

'You've got quite some wait ahead of you, buddy.' Delphi reaches out and dislodges a flake of paint from his waistcoat with her nail. She traces a circle on his portly belly. 'You're made of cement and I'm made of cells.' New DNA is spiralling inside her womb. A big bang of celestial majesty in minuscule proportions. Delphi wonders if what's within her is still called an embryo or if it is now a foetus? Is its heart beating? Does it have fingers, fingernails? 'Oh God,' she says aloud.

Delphi can't be a mother but the alternative is terrible and she shoves the word *termination* away. Up rises *abortion* then *killer.* Delphi covers her eyes with her hands, rolls onto her side and pulls her legs up. She is lying as if she were a baby and a wave of nausea slops within her.

Delphi is pro-choice but she's blindsided by how conflicted and frightened she is, and how alone. How did she let this happen? This fledgling human will pay the price for her stupidity and rashness.

And the father? She's counted and recounted the days in her diary; sex, ovulation, missed period, and it must be Orlo. She obviously miscalculated her fertility cycle when she'd clasped her legs around his waist and whispered, 'Don't worry it's safe.'

When does the soul enter an embryo? When does that divine alchemy occur? The transition from meat to life. Delphi wonders if she will go to hell. She doesn't even believe in hell and she isn't convinced about souls either. She muses torpidly about reincarnation. Where is Vivian's soul now? Her mother would be appalled by this pregnancy development. Delphi's skin swarms with mortification. Once a killer, always a killer. She says the word 'infanticide' out loud several times.

A choice must be made as soon as possible. A referral to a clinic from a GP. Is termination even possible in Tasmania? And then a black secret. More loss burnt into her. A shucked out, hollowed-out cave of regret. A womb of grief. Will she ever deserve to be a mother if she chooses this path? Is it morally okay to use the money Hugh gave her to do it? Will the Devil chase her for his due? Awful thoughts pool in her and she sits up in an attempt to drain them.

Delphi stumbles to her feet, collects her discarded sunglasses, an old pair of Vivian's, and pushes them onto her face. The gnome is still transfixed in raptures of laughter. Delphi stabilises and chooses strength if not a solution. She channels Hugh; forward reckless girl, forward into the fire.

*

Jack is smoking one of Vivian's cigarettes at the kitchen bench as Delphi makes tea.

'Jack, what are we going to do about Pilot? I've called all of Mama's friends but no one can take him and no one has answered our advert.'

Her brother inhales the last drag of the cigarette and stubs it out in a large silver ashtray.

'I called Michael Cooper.'

'Who's that?' Delphi takes a cigarette from the packet and puts it between her lips. She lifts the lighter but is unable to hurdle the implications of smoking.

'Pilot's vet. Mum liked him. He's a sort of Peter Pan man.'

Delphi puts the cigarette back in the packet and shakes her head. She envisions a man-child dressed in green tights swinging a stethoscope about like a lasso.

'No, I don't know him. What did you say to him?'

'I told him about the Queen Bee dying and how Pilot won't come out from under her bed. That he won't eat or drink and, well, Cooper said he's seen this before. Pilot is pining. No surprises there.'

'What can we do? Can he prescribe antidepressants? Did you tell him when we've got Pilot and shut him out of the room how he howls?'

'Del, try to keep your cool, but I think we need to put Pilot down. It's the kindest, most humane thing we can do. He's beyond miserable.'

Delphi can see how dire the situation is with Pilot but to kill him, to not be able to save him feels like a travesty. A faithless torching of duty of care.

'Del, he can't live with me in our tiny apartment in Paris. And you don't know where you're going to live and wouldn't be able to keep a plant alive, let alone a dog.'

His words lacerate. Death is hounding them. Vivian used to say tragedy comes in threes. Delphi had concluded the dark trilogy to be Arthur, the divorce and Vivian. Maybe, horrifyingly, it's actually Vivian, Pilot and Delphi's undeclared baby.

Jack comes around the counter to his sister. He stoops to look closely at her crumpled face.

'Sorry, Passion Fruit, I didn't mean to make you cry.'

Internally, Delphi is racing away from herself, feet slipping out from under her as she hurtles around floodlit corners.

'Can't we try harder to find him a new home, Jack?'

'Cooper doesn't think rehoming Pilot is an option.'

Jack worries at a pimple on his cheek.

'Del, he's not a young dog. He's a very old boy whose had a great life with Mama. It's pretty clear he wants to follow her out. It would be a kind act. Putting him out of his misery.'

Delphi attempts to marshal thought out of the turbulence. Pilot is deteriorating fast and she can't save him. She reaches up around her brother's neck, the only life buoy available to her, and clings to him.

'Jack, this is vile.'

'I know, Del.' He kisses the top of her head.

*

It's close to midnight and both siblings have been drinking hard but feel anomalously sober. Vivian's entrance light is on and Jack has opened the garage door so the light from inside spills out. The siblings are piling up the most intimate possessions of their mother's beside an old surfboard. The ones that are too personal to throw out or can't be given away but make no sense to keep. Vivian's knickers, her stockings, her comb, some lipsticks, perfume bottles she's half used, which neither sibling associates with her true smell, and a few of her favourite books.

'Is that sacrilegious?' Delphi asks. 'To burn books?'

'Not in this case, Del.' Jack takes a deep breath looking up into the black expanse above. His warm breath rolls like smoke. Delphi can't see any stars.

'What else?' Jack whispers. They're keeping their voices down so as not to wake Hugh. He's flying back to Melbourne early in the morning, and they don't want to disturb him. Their farewells earlier were painful for Delphi. She wanted to clamber into his shirt pocket and stowaway to dry land.

'I can't think of anything. But shall we write a note?' Delphi retrieves a lipstick from the pile and bends down to write her mother's full name, birth date and death date across the surfboard. Jack gets another lipstick and they add their names, Arthur and Pilot's names along with love hearts.

'Oh wait, I nearly forgot.' Jack runs back up to the house and Delphi starts stacking the objects onto the surfboard.

He returns with Vivian's handbag and fishes out her purse. He takes out her credit cards, her library card, a dilapidated packet of mints and puts them all on the pile.

'Nice work, Del, good stacking. I think that's it. Let's do this.'

'What about lighter fuel?' Delphi asks, rubbing her cold hands on her thighs.

'I have that and some matches,' he answers shaking the Redheads box.

'We're set then. Jack, do you want to take the front, that might make it easier going down the driveway.'

They move into position at either end and lift the board, carefully balancing Vivian's intimate things. The physical surge trumpets a change in Delphi and hysteria is dancing through her like a whirling dervish again and she has to repress the need to burst out laughing. She fears for the hundredth time that she's going mad.

They slowly walk down the steep drive concentrating on the angle of the board. It's heavy but Delphi has no intention of complaining. Unsurprisingly there's no traffic on the road. The streetlights struggle to fend off the gloom. They cross and take the pebble-strewn dirt path down to the river.

'We should have brought a torch,' Jack says and they slow down on the uneven terrain.

'I wish this was a proper Viking funeral, Jack. With eight black horses, black swans weeping diamonds and a barge waiting to be incinerated.' Delphi's arms are aching.

'I don't think the Vikings had swans, Del.'

The waterfront house to their left is in darkness. Its occupants long since tucked up in bed. As they reach the bottom of the path, the trees and shrubs clear. Their breathing and the lapping noise of the water is all that can be heard. Just as Delphi curses the darkness, the clouds shift and moonlight erupts. The river is exposed in its liquefied stateliness. It could be pure mercury, the runway of unicorns, but it smells earthy and dank.

They hobble across the riverbank's stones and place the board down. Jack is taking off his shoes. Delphi does the same. The ground is bracingly cold and slimy underfoot. The siblings pull off their jeans awkwardly, trying not to tumble.

'Make sure you put all your clothes together, Jack, so you can find them when we get out.' Delphi releases her t-shirt directly over her already vanished jeans. She tries to take a mental picture of their location. Futile in the indistinguishable blackness but it seems sensible to try.

Jack clamps the matches between his teeth. They pick up the board and make their way into the river. The water is freezing against their ankles and Delphi inhales sharply. Rudely sober now, they press on and the water rises above their stinging carves.

'The fin will be clear of the bottom so let's put it down, Del.' With the board bobbing in the water, they reassemble behind it and start pushing it out toward the deep. The water rises to claim Delphi's waist and then the tender flesh of her breasts and armpits. Her skin is shrieking in outrage. She doesn't fight the cold, instead she welcomes it in.

'Jack, this is as far as I can go without swimming.'

'Okay. It's far enough I think.'

He gropes for the lighter fluid from the stack and squirts it over the board. Dunking his hands clear of accelerant, he turns to his sister but he can hardly see her as the moon is back in hiding.

'Are you ready to let go, Del? When I say, give it a big push out. We don't want you going up too.'

'Okay,' she says through chattering teeth.

Jack strikes a match, but it fizzles out. The second time it snaps in two.

'Ah, my hands are too wet.' He waves them about trying to dry them.

'Here, use my hair.' Delphi tilts her head towards him and her brother wades closer to rummage a hand about in the long strands.

With the third attempt, the flame fights into life and burns true. Jack throws it onto the board and the pyre ignites with a whomp.

'Now!' he calls, and the two of them push the board out as hard as they can. The flames are taking hold and the current scoops the board onto its shoulders. The siblings break the quiet with their yells and wet clapping.

'Goodbye, Mama, we love you!'

'Travel safely!'

The flames lick the sky. The blazing love riot defying the abyss.

Jack wades back towards his sister.

'Give me your hand, Passion Fruit.'

Hand in hand, their arms above the frigid water, they watch the flaming board sail further and further out until it is a far-off thing.

'I hope it goes out to sea, out to the wilds of the ocean.' Delphi starts to hum to dissipate the uncomfortable clattering of her jaw. 'I'm reminded of a quote I read somewhere, by Brené Brown, I think. I will probably make a mess of it, but it goes something like *The dark does not destroy the light; it defines it. It's our fear of the dark that casts our joy into the shadows.*'

Jack squeezes her fingers.

'Let's go in,' he suggests and they begin to wade back.

'I think Mama would have liked that.'

'Yes, she would,' he agrees.

'I like how the Greeks do it. All those black veils. Everyone weeping for days around the body. And the Maoris, such dignity with those hakas. I want singing over my corpse, Jack. I want to have loved ones sing and sing and sing. I think that's the atheist replacement for prayer.'

'Are you an atheist, Del?'

She stumbles on the underwater rocks.

'No. I guess I'm agnostic. Or maybe I'm spiritual. Mama hated that term but it's probably the one that best suits me. Now she's dead I should just claim it. Sometimes it seems so blatantly obvious to me that we're all connected, like when I meditate or when I burst with empathy to see people reunited at the airport. I can't always hold on to that grace, that knowledge, because fear destroys it.'

'Ah, Passion Fruit.'

They support each other back to the shoreline. Their outraged flesh is smarting. The siblings find their clothes and dress stretching the fabric with their wet limbs. After a comedic struggle, Delphi abandons her jeans. She bunches them into a ball and holds them against her belly.

Jack is watching the blaze recede and Delphi joins him, close enough so that her shoulder touches his. She wonders what he's thinking but doesn't want to intrude. She waits for him to turn to her and then she takes the leap. 'Brother, I'm pregnant.'

There is no response from him and Delphi gropes in the darkness of his silence.

'Shit,' he eventually says. 'Are you intending to keep it?'

'I don't know. I'm thinking… maybe. So, much has been taken away…'

She sees him rub at his face. 'Having a kid isn't like getting a toy, Delphi. And it's sure as shit not a replacement for Mama.'

'Of course not.' She feels belittled.

'Or Arthur.' And this one really winds her.

'I know that Jack.' She realises she wanted him to be happy. To reassure her, but she refuses to take a step away, to put herself beyond striking distance, because out there you can't be held either.

Jack bends down, finds a stone and throws it hard into the water. They're standing only shoulder distance apart but for Delphi he's once again unreachable.

*

It takes ages to coax Pilot out from his hiding space and when he finally emerges Jack scoops him up and whisks him straight into the car and onto Delphi's lap. The journey is without words. The three sit in suspended silence. In the carpark Jack opens the car door for Delphi and she carries the dog into the building past a mural of animals smiling with human teeth. Pilot is trembling. Delphi sees the waiting area is empty and claims an orange plastic seat. Jack taps the bell on the counter. The siblings still can't bring themselves to talk but Delphi rains kisses down onto Pilot's head. He's now agitated by the intensity of animal smells.

The vet bounds into the waiting room and waves heartily. 'Hello there, I'm Michael.' He has the energy of a Labrador puppy or a children's performer. Delphi and Jack are the polar opposite with their black clothes and condemned demeanours.

The vet's wearing what appears to be a boy scout uniform. Noticing Delphi's interest, he takes hold of the scarf tied around his neck and gives it a yank. 'Yes, I'm a scout leader, or a Scouter.' He gives a thumbs up and smiles a guileless smile. 'I am all gussied up like this because I have a troop meeting later.' Delphi wonders when she last saw a grown man wearing knee socks like a schoolboy.

'A woggle,' Delphi says into space.

The vet looks delighted. 'Yes, that's right.' He takes a look at the fastening device on his scarf with pride. 'Were you a girl guide?' He is on alert, his openness and excitement bouncing. She wishes she could say she had been to make him happy.

She shakes her head and he looks momentarily crestfallen.

'What can I do for you today?' he almost sings.

Delphi and Jack look at each other.

Jack gathers himself. 'We're Vivian's children and this is Pilot. I spoke to you on the phone. We're here to have Pilot put down.'

The vet's smile turns upside down into a pantomime of a frown, but then he rallies.

'Oh, of course. Poor old Pilot.' The vet bobs down and starts patting the dog's head warmly. 'What a loyal boy you are.'

He stands up and directs them into the room behind. Delphi guesses he's going to be the type that won't mention the death of their mother at all. She thinks it's generally embarrassment rather than disregard. Either way it's inexcusable.

'Pop him up on the table,' he says pulling on a white coat. 'You both know this won't hurt him? I'll give him an injection then he will go to sleep and his heart will stop beating. No pain at all.'

It doesn't feel right to put Pilot down on the table so Delphi asks if she can stay holding him.

'Oh, of course. Good choice,' says the vet, and he gets a chair for her to sit in. He then busies himself listening to Pilot's heartbeat, looking at the file for his weight and finally preparing the injection. A vial of eternal sleep. The liquid is bright green.

'It's so vivid,' Delphi says.

'That's why it's called the green dream,' Jack answers.

'Oh God,' she responds.

The walls are covered in posters. Different breeds of cats and dogs, sketches of skeletons, animal drawings done by children or the demented.

'Pining is such a sad business,' the vet chats on. 'If only more humans knew loyalty like this, hey?' The radiant innocence of the man is disarming and Delphi is grateful this court jester is leading them through the ghastly woods.

'Are we all ready?'

Jack gets down on the floor and kisses Pilot's face and scratches behind his ears. Delphi holds him close and lowers her face and starts to sing. After a few words, Jack joins in.

Frère Jacques, Frère Jacques,
Dormez-vous? Dormez-vous?
Sonnez les matines. Sonnez les matines.
Ding, dang, dong. Ding, dang, dong.

Vivian used to sing this to them when they were little. It's the most comforting song Delphi can think of.

The vet expertly presses the hypodermic needle into Pilot. The dog squirms but doesn't yelp. The siblings keep singing as the syringe plunger is compressed into the barrel. The green poison surges into Pilot's little body.

He wags his tail a few times and isn't afraid. His brindle eyebrows move as his eyes travel between Delphi and Jack. The siblings sing on. Astoundingly quickly Pilot closes his eyes. He loosens in Delphi's arms and he dies. There is no mistaking the transition. It is like a candle being snuffed out.

Michael listens to Pilot's heart again with the stethoscope. The vet tells Jack and Delphi he will step out of the room to fill in the paperwork and give the three of them some time. As the door closes, the tears race from Delphi's eyes, along her nose and onto Pilot's head. The siblings hold the dog and each other – a huddle of grief.

It was peaceful, dignified and loving.

'It should have been like this for Mama, Jack.'

'I know, Passion Fruit, it should have been.'

The circle of three stays together and Delphi is struck dumb by the realisation that on the outside of her belly is fresh death and on the inside is fresh life.

*

Jack drives to town to speak to the lawyers. Delphi can't face it after the vet and sets off to walk home but her feet are failing her. She drops her bag on the kerb and lets her knees buckle. She slumps down towards the pavement. To take stock is terrifying. Her mother is gone, Pilot is dead and an unplanned, monstrously timed baby is forming within her. She has no home, no job, no lover and a cloak of grief so heavy around her shoulders she can stand up no longer. She can't have this child. She's not ready, not able, and not willing.

Delphi holds her head with both hands and rocks back and forth.

'Are you okay?' It's a blossom-textured voice from above. It belongs to a lady with silver hair braided around her head like a crown. Even full with troubles, Delphi recognises how much she likes the woman's hair. It's romantic and eccentric. The lady is wearing a blouse with small turtles printed on it, a royal purple corduroy skirt, and on her feet, slippers. That reminds Delphi of her mother and a surge of love takes flight inside her. She blinks, looking into the woman's unclouded face. For a moment they are quiet together, connected by the silver thread of a shared gaze.

'Oh dear, you look sad,' says the woman.

She mustn't be much over five foot. Delphi would tower over her if she were to stand.

'I know it's none of my business, but I saw you from my window and I wanted to bring you a cup of tea.'

The old lady moves forward and the comforting scent of talcum powder wafts like a spell. In her extended hands is a delicate china teacup that is the softest blue, the saucer rimmed in rubbed-away gold.

Delphi is moved by this sweet act of kindness. It transfigures all that is darkness within her into mellower hues. She takes the cup and she does something ancient and unplanned, she dips her head. And the little old lady smiles and curtsies in return.

'I live in there.' She points a crooked finger at the house across the street. 'If you want to come in you are most welcome.'

Delphi uses the sleeve of her jumper to dry her face, careful not to disrupt the teacup in her other hand.

'God bless,' says the lady and Delphi dives into unchartered waters by echoing the declaration.

'Yes, God bless.'

As the lady turns away Delphi calls after her. 'May I ask you something?'

'Yes, dear.' The lady's eyelashes are pure white and catch the light.

'Do you have children?'

Her sparse eyebrows raise in surprise.

'No, I'm sad to say. I was never blessed with any. We did try, oh how we tried, but no, dear, no. Everyone has their cross to bear and that was mine.'

She waits to see if Delphi has any further questions. But Delphi is running equations on crosses carried and babies denied. Sensing the conversation is over and the tea has been received as she intended, the old lady totters little steps back towards her house. Her glorious sparkling wings flap out wide before folding back down against her blouse.

*

The police are on the phone to Jack, and Delphi is hovering close by trying to pick up on what's being said. She's wearing an old flannel nightie of her mother's and still has Vivian's long ropes of pearls wrapped around her neck. Her fingers are curled around them. They're warm from sharing the heat of her body.

'Okay, okay, no problem, I'm happy it found a home. Thank you, Detective,' Jack says and then he returns the receiver to its cradle.

Delphi stares at her brother, waiting for him to speak.

'They're not pressing charges.'

Relief feels like levity.

'The detective said so many people knew of her intention to commit suicide. That their investigation also confirmed she shut down her bank accounts herself. That she got her affairs in order, her will, her superannuation, everything, and–'

'And what?'

'And that she left you and me those envelopes of cash. The ones on her bedside table.' The police had taken them away as evidence.

'The detective mentioned those envelopes twice. It was clear Mama had an evident intention.' Jack sweeps his long hair out of his eyes. His irises are normally hazel but are very green today – the same as Delphi's.

'The detective says we can collect the money and her other belongings whenever we want. Probate can conclude, we can sell the house and are free to leave the country.'

For the first time in Delphi's life she reconciles that liberty is as light as sunshine.

'Jack, what was the bit at the end of the conversation when you were saying you're glad something found a home?'

'Oh, I gave Constable Carter the Queen Bee's washing machine.'

'What? When?'

'At the wake. She was saying hers had broken so I offered Mama's. A couple of us disconnected it and put it in her truck before she left.'

'Couldn't that be perceived as bribery?'

'Del, that's a bit paranoid.' It's so typical of Jack, always offering to help.

'That was sweet of you.' Delphi loves him. 'Anything else?'

'Not really. Well, they determined her time of death incorrectly. They thought it was between 4 am and 8 am.'

'But you said it was close to midnight, right? How do you account for that?'

'I guess because I was cuddling her after I found her. My body kept her warm.'

Delphi reels as the exquisite tenderness of this image forms for her. A son spooning his dead mother through the darkest of nights.

'Your body and your love, Jack. That's what kept her warm.'

*

Delphi lies in the bath making soap bubbles between her hands. The overhead light is off but the rays of the sun at day's end are colouring the room buttery gold. The steam is thick, and the condensation glistens on the tiles.

Delphi looks at her naked body in the water.

She's done nothing about securing the termination. After all that's happened Delphi finds it impossible to see how she will. This isn't what she would have chosen, but it is what she has been given. Delphi places both her hands over her stomach and says, 'Let's do this.'

She will make it work. She will come up with a plan. Plenty of women have children on their own. Edward will be livid. Hopefully Jack will want to be involved when he gets used to the idea. Orlo will need to be told. Imagine if the baby looks like Vivian? Delphi smiles. This is wild, it's completely full-on but it feels right to say yes.

CHAPTER 16

Vivian's house is empty and spotlessly clean. Delphi has been directing removalists and cleaning like a demon for days. This morning, Jack cuddled her goodbye and flew back to his life in Paris. He promised to stay in touch, to lock in plans for Delphi to visit, but something in his eyes told Delphi she shouldn't hold her breath. He'd asked her again if she was keeping the baby and when she told him she was he looked oddly blank.

'Be happy for me?' she'd asked him.

'For sure.' He'd answered looking down at the ground.

Delphi now lies alone on the floor of Vivian's empty bedroom. She lifts her arms and draws circles in the air. As a small child she remembers lying in bed and playing an invisible piano just like this. She assumed she'd learnt the skill and the next morning when she'd sat at the family piano and discovered she had been unable to play she'd been disappointed. That was the day she asked for lessons and had diligently practised for years. It had been different with art. She had no memory of a first time, of not being able to do it, as if she was born with it already formed inside her. Of course her skill evolved but she'd never felt constrained or the need to effort. Passion carried her onwards and upwards. Perhaps talent comes with its own fuel.

The neighbour's dog is barking excitedly. A car whooshes around the bend in the road at the bottom of the drive, but quiet soon reclaims its throne. Pilot gone. Vivian gone. Jack gone. A lifetime of possessions sold, given and thrown away. Reassigned. Disbanded. Erased.

Delphi needs a home. For herself and her baby. The bottom tier of Maslow's hierarchy demands her serious attention. Fleetingly, she'd thought she should stay in Tasmania, in Vivian's house. But Delphi knows she doesn't belong here. This is not her corner of the world. She wishes she knew where that was, but her intuition is telling her to return to England. On the London streets she often thrums with the knowing that she's on the right road. Once she extricates herself from the emotional quicksand and the ground solidifies under her feet she can make plans for the future. It's all overwhelming but Delphi figures she will start by getting her waitressing job back. It's as if she's staggering forward in the dark with a tiny torch. She can only see the area directly in front of her.

Delphi mustn't miss her flight. Her credit card is maxed, and she used the envelope of cash her mother left her to pay for the removalists. She does have what remains of the money from Hugh. It's already been whittled down substantially due to her share of Vivian's funeral costs and her second round of flights. What's left she's committed to rationing out with maniacal frugalness, and repaying it to Hugh as soon as she can. She stands up and her head spins. She braces until the room re-finds its level. She moves to the window to drink in the view for the last time. The river is prepossessing, swollen with splendour.

'Goodbye river,' Delphi says aloud. Moving out towards the hall she calls out, 'Goodbye blue cube, goodbye corridor.' She makes a pilgrimage to each space: the kitchen, the back deck, the laundry, the dining and sitting rooms. All so sterile in their shucked-out state. Drained of proof, bleached of history. It honestly looks like Vivian was never here at all.

Delphi's interrupted by the toot of a taxi's horn. She steps out and waves at the driver to let him know she's coming. She retrieves her suitcase, bag and coat and closes the front door. She studies it for the final time. There is a small diamond shaped window in the middle of the door. A boat at full sail is carved into the glass. Vivian loved it. 'I hope those warm winds have found you Mama,' Delphi whispers.

She puts the keys under the doormat for the real-estate agent and clatters down the stairs. Before she gets to the taxi, she steps into the garden to grab the gnome. She's taking him with her. She wraps him in her jumper and stashes him in her handbag. He's heavy, but Delphi doesn't care. She doesn't look back. The driver is obviously not going to help her with her load, but she isn't resentful. Delphi is anticipating struggle. She is resolved to what lies ahead. She can and will do this. All by herself. With a belly full of baby and a bag full of gnome.

*

The taxi driver grumbles when Delphi explains she needs to make a quick stop on their way to the airport. She ignores him and watches the sedate city slip past her window as they drive. Arriving at the crematorium she says, 'I will be as fast as I can.' The driver is bristling with irritation.

Delphi races inside and the desk attendant smiles and stands to greet her.

'I'm Delphi Hoffman. I rang earlier. I'm here to collect my mother.'

'Oh yes, of course,' the woman says, moving out to a back room. How peculiar that this is part of the woman's everyday life. Yet for Delphi this is as untravelled as if she were walking on the moon.

Delphi spends the moments alone listening to her heart pounding in her ears.

'Here she is, Miss Hoffman, I will just need some ID please and your autograph here.'

Delphi ignores the rectangular box that is placed on the counter and fishes out her passport and signs where instructed. The woman checks everything is in order then she comes around the counter to where Delphi stands. The woman lifts the box and hands it across. 'Good luck, Miss Hoffman, and our deepest condolences for your loss.' Delphi feels the weight of the box, then she rallies and lifts her face to this benevolent stranger and nods. Delphi turns and pushes out through the glass door to the waiting taxi.

*

'Thank you,' Delphi says. 'Now I've collected my mama let's get to the airport as fast as you can.' His brow furrows low like monobrowed Sam the Eagle from Sesame Street.

Delphi is learning people don't like death. It makes them uncomfortable. She smiles and shakes her head. Her mama can shock even when she's ashes. The driver cranks the volume on his radio coverage of the cricket. Delphi suspects he's attempting to drown out his discomfort or build an auditory barrier between himself and his death-tainted passenger.

Delphi studies the box on her lap. It is smaller than she expected, decorated in a mauve paisley pattern. Vivian would hate it. Delphi was given some paperwork to ensure safe transit to the UK. Apparently, customs sometimes gets tense about dead loved ones being trafficked in boxes. In case they explode or double up as heroin. Delphi imagines herself being aggressively instructed to open the temporary urn, sneezing and her mother erupting in a cloud of ash. The official would then have to cough naughty Vivian out of his lungs.

Delphi unfolds the paper and sees it authenticates that her mother is indeed the contents of the box. Delphi looks out of the window as the taxi drives up and over the Tasman Bridge.

I don't know what lies ahead for me, she thinks. But I'm not trapped. I have options, I just need to find the best one. I don't have to be defined by the past. This baby represents all that is good in the future.

But her optimism quavers under the fear of the unknown, of the threat of poverty, isolation and solo parenting. She checks to see she's wearing the seatbelt and clamps her hand around the buckle until her knuckles turn white.

*

Delphi arrives at Heathrow Airport thirty-eight hours later. She is a husk. The queue at customs is brutally long and as she waits for her suitcase she is hypnotised by the rotating conveyor belt. Clammy, pallid passengers shift from foot to foot like zombies. A furious hot-cheeked toddler thrashes out. The smell of armpits and liberally applied cheap perfume mingle. Delphi becomes aware that she's staring into the middle distance blankly.

Finally clearing the cattle grid, she buys a coffee and finds a spot on the ground out of the thoroughfare to sit. She puts her suitcase close beside her and tries to work out what to do. Her eyes feel like someone has thrown sand in them and her mother's recently adjusted watch tells her it's 10.42 pm. Sleep deprivation is its own special brand of torture.

She left Hobart in such a rush that it wasn't until Singapore, during her second stopover, that she had texted her close friends asking for a place to crash when she landed in London. Reading through the responses her heart is taking a ride south. Adarsha is in India. Romy hasn't responded as she's probably lost her phone again. Other friends all have their valid but equally unhelpful reasons for being unable to save her.

Delphi bends her knees up and rests her head on them. She's not sure what to do and it's so late now that it would be rude for her to hassle anyone. Vivian taught her that 10 pm was the cut off for calls unless someone had died. Delphi thinks about the box of her mother's ashes and can hear her mother saying, 'No, that's cheating.' Delphi turns her head to the side and sees the shape of the gnome in her handbag. She stretches out and pulls the protective jumper away and frees the gnome's head. 'So, you can breathe, My Dear Friend,' she says to him. She tries to ignore the chronic inflammation of feeling that's progressing to an all-out haemorrhaging of emotion.

As a backup, she'd thought that she could get a train to Berkshire to her grandfather. Walk to his house and sleep on his stoop until morning when he'd shuffle out to retrieve his newspaper and delivered bottle of milk, but she hadn't factored in that the country link trains have already well and truly stopped by this time of night.

Delphi lets out a sigh. A woman in a Primark dress with sunflowers all over it bends into view and drops some coins into the dregs of Delphi's coffee. She marches away as Delphi's exhausted brain crunches the information and realises that the woman thought her homeless.

'Bloody hell,' she says to the gnome. He laughs as usual.

Delphi realises she mustn't atrophy with indecision. She stands up, wobbles, shoulders her bag and grabs her suitcase which has apparently been filled with lead. She looks for the signs to the tube station and follows the bleary red arrow to her left. She will get on the Piccadilly Line, and in an hour she will be in the Circus. From there she will find a hostel.

It's not much, but it's still a game plan. She adjusts My Dear Friend's head so he can see over the rim of her handbag and tells him they're going to be okay.

Delphi's worries her screws must indeed be loosening because she could swear she had heard the gnome giggle.

*

She'd chosen the Phoenix hostel for three reasons. Firstly, it was cheap. Secondly, it was stumbling distance from Piccadilly Station. And lastly its name represented what Delphi was hoping for herself. To rise from the ashes reconfigured. If she also scored a set of golden wings she'd be thrilled. Cyclical regeneration and metamorphosis sound like the business to Delphi.

The last fragile vestiges of her levity are exorcised as she stands, waiting to be checked in. The place is like something out of *Blade Runner*, a post-apocalyptic hovel. The broken tiles underfoot are sticky and streaked with mud. The neon lighting shouts on and off with every strobe. To her left, the wall is spattered with what looks to be chunks of tuberculosis-spackled sputum. A filthy mop is leaning further off against a wall. The bucket next to it is filled with stagnant, grey water, coagulated with unrecognisable gore.

The attendant is a mountain of a man with hair as rapacious as Rasputin's. Behind a Perspex security screen he photocopies Delphi's passport. When she handed it through the round hole, his nail-bitten fingers grappled her as he'd smiled lasciviously. She wondered if the clear plastic was to protect him or her.

A sound on the stairwell draws Delphi's attention up to the right and she sees a person of indecipherable gender. A hardcore punk or an emo well over 6 foot in platform black boots. The person's frame is skeleton-like, sheathed in multiple layers of black, dissected by clinking chains. Their face is painted as white as a geisha and the tiny eyes and mouth are lacquered black. Delphi is stuck by how much she wishes Romy were with her, her friend would think this person awesome. Romy had her own six months deep in the world of emocore before she found punk. The emo doesn't acknowledge Delphi and continues their glide outside and are absorbed into their natural habitat of the night.

'Vat's twelve quid, fanks darl,' Hostel Rasputin's voice is muffled through the Perspex. She counts out her pound coins, placing them on the rotating metal tray.

'Dorm vat way, all the way to the top.' He points an index finger towards the stairs, leaving a smudge where it contacts the plastic.

'Pick an empty bunk. Or an occupied one for all I care,' he laughs with a smoker's wet lungs at his own joke. 'You need to be gone by 10 am, or you pay anover day.'

A fly lands on his shoulder and clambers about in the forest of hair.

Wife beater. That's the term Delphi has been searching for as she clocks his grubby white singlet.

Hostel Rasputin doesn't like being studied by this girl whom he assumes is off her chops. He hoists his thick-as-a-tree arm and pulls down the blind between them. He has vanished, and Delphi moves to make her way up the stairs to her purchased place in hell.

*

Groping in the darkness of the dormitory she chooses the first vacant bed she can find. Delphi only just manages not to cry out and wake the whole room when she discovers that her chosen bunk is actually already claimed. She notices a padlock gleaming in a shaft of streetlight, from it a chain connects a woman's leg to her backpack and the bed frame.

She finds another bed, removes her boots and lies down. The single mattress is thin and smells dank. She is forced to cover her mouth with her sleeve and take shallow breaths. Delphi spoons her suitcase and keeps her clothes on. She grabs fitfully at sleep with one eye open and sleeps as badly as the Princess and the Pea but with cause.

Less than five hours later Delphi needs more sleep but has given up the fight. She lies glassy-eyed, staring into the dark above her, listening attentively. She guesses between five and ten women are in the room with her and some bastard is snoring hard. The ragged jackhammer of an alcoholic, she thinks. Delphi has been counting each arpeggio of snorts and tries to talk herself over tidal waves of resentment.

She runs through her limited options and decides to get going. She will find breakfast and then look for work. She wishes she could go home to her apartment and thinks of the lucky occupant sleeping safely there. Delphi peels the sheets back and they feel weird as if woven from pulverised moths. Sitting on the bedside, she shoves her socked feet into her boots and doubles over to lace them up. With her eyes adapted to the dark and the scratchings of streetlight, Delphi can see the grim landscape beneath the bed, a cityscape of human detritus: lint, hair, skin and unrecognisable matter clumped together. Delphi is mesmerised until the build-up of blood in her head forces her to stand up.

She pulls on her jacket and, as quietly as she can, takes herself and her stuff out of the room, closing the door behind her. She gingerly tracks her way down the first few stairs and pauses, waiting for the light sensor to pick her presence and turn on. It doesn't. She waves her free arm around. She gives up on the light and accepts it will be a descent by brail.

As she reaches the next landing impoverished dawn light creeps its way in through a small, barred window. Delphi swaps her suitcase to her other hand and shuffles on to take the next flight of stairs. Grasping the handrail, she continues on her way down, comforted that she is nearly out of this place.

A serpent strikes and grabs her from behind. A large hand is pressed across her mouth, another is pinning her arms. Usually when Delphi's amygdala fires up she invariably chooses the fight option but, thinking of her baby, her body goes still.

A heavily accented voice hisses into her ear. 'Don't you scream or I will smash you. Give me your handbag and you can go.'

Delphi is trapped in the disgusting embrace unable to answer with his hand clamped across her mouth. Disturbingly, he sounds more frightened than she feels.

'Do you hear me?' He swings her hard into the wall and her suitcase falls.

The air is forced out of Delphi in a rush.

'Yes,' she says with a calmness that sounds bizarre to her.

'Move very slowly. And no sound!' Delphi can feel the man vibrating with mental illness, drugs or desperation. She hopes it's not all three.

'Don't you look back at me or you're dead.' He smells like urine and petrol.

'I won't look at you,' she reassures him. 'But you can't have my suitcase. My mother's ashes are in there and nothing of value to you, just old books and old clothes.' Delphi has a clear snapshot of a frozen lake, with an anchor suspended in the ice below.

The mugger, still holding her from behind, is breathing jaggedly in her ear. Delphi is the supernaturally calm. It doesn't even occur to her to scream for help.

'I need you to let go of my arms so I can give you my money.'

He releases his grip long enough for her to open her handbag. Moving aside the gnome she takes out her wallet.

'Can I just give you the cash and my credit card?' she says. 'My license and the photos won't be any use to you and my mother bought me the purse. It means a lot to me.'

'Give me the whole purse!' He grabs it from her. 'And where's your phone?' His voice slashes at her in a hot whisper.

As she digs around in her handbag, her hands are shaking. She retrieves the shitty old iPhone with its long-ago shattered screen. She doesn't want to give it to him, she abhors bullies, but she counsels herself for sense over principles and heroics. Her choices affect her passenger. She hands the phone over her shoulder. He grabs it and bolts, nearly knocking her down the stairs in his furious wake. A moment later the front door slams behind him.

*

Delphi places one hand on the wall and the other on the balustrade. She sits down waiting for rational thought to return. The first one that crops up is that she needs to move. The mugger may look at her near-empty wallet and come back even more enraged with the world. And she will fight him to the death for the ashes and the gnome.

Delphi pats at herself, assessing and self-soothing. Nurse and comforter. Grateful to be in one piece. She gathers her suitcase and tentatively carries on down to the entrance foyer. The Perspex above the counter is still blanked out by the drawn blind, like a giant's closed eyelid. Delphi wonders if she should wake Hostel Rasputin and get him to call the police. She's alive, that bastard didn't kick her belly, rape her or take her mother or gnome so she decides against it. She has her passport, the credit card is maxed out and her travel card is safe in her jeans pocket. Dear Hugh's money is in her account. She'll need to get that debit card cancelled and reissued too. Delphi chooses to stay her course. She needs a home. If she goes to the police, they will waste her time and that's a precious commodity when one is holding the deck Delphi has been dealt.

She knows she must carry on moving forward or risk drowning in the undertow.

Delphi elbows the door open, takes a tremulous breath and exhales slowly to calm herself. A sign reads 'Please stay again, at the Phoenix!'

'No, I don't believe I will,' Delphi says out loud. 'And your punctuation is shitty.'

A headache is pressing in like a severe weather front, and dawn has painted London similar turbulent greys. Delphi walks down the road towards Piccadilly and finds herself standing at the base of one of her all-time favourite fountains, 'The Horses of Helios'. The four bronze beasts rear up and burst out of the water. Their mouths gape, their eyes are wild, their spines are arched, their hoofs raised, veins ridged on their bellies. This equine quartet of strength and power is breathtakingly beautiful.

Delphi puts her suitcase down and stands before the horses. Aethon, Eous, Phlegon and Pyrois. These spectacular bad boys belong to Helios, the Greek God of the Sun.

In comparison to the beasts, Delphi feels incredibly small and weak. Her adrenaline has been spent and her strength has bled out. She looks for it to see if it is a puddle under her feet. She turns towards the horses. She wishes she could drape herself across their backs, but she sits down on the pavement as close to them as she can. She pulls her suitcase alongside her and shrinks down. Self-preservation issues orders for Delphi to sleep. Early morning Londoners don't even notice the homeless woman unconscious under the awesome drove of protectors, the four horses, riding out of hell, just as Delphi is intent on doing.

*

Delphi's mother's watch-face is smashed. It must have happened when she was slammed into the wall. She looks at the maze of fractures and notes her irrational thinking, that it's a sign of some kind, a sinister declaration from the gods. She only looks for patterns and symbols when she's careening out of control. Delphi doesn't need a watch to know that she's spent hours and hours revisiting her old places of work and each time they've told her there are no shifts available, but they'll call her if and when there are.

She was embarrassed having to explain that her phone had been stolen. Maybe they assumed she was lying, that she'd just been hopeless and lost it. Her pride prevented her from falling to her knees to beg for work. The collective noun for a pack of lions is pride and Delphi feels it stalking back and forth within her.

She is hungry and still has no idea where she will sleep this evening. All her contacts disappeared with her phone too. Is there something wrong with her brain that the only telephone number she has memorised other than her own is that of her childhood home?

Maybe she should seek out Orlo and tell him she's carrying his child and that she needs a place to sleep? She pictures herself anchored inside his arms. Envisages raising this child with him, a whole family. Her fantasy twists and distorts with her recognition of its delusion. She will not live her mother's life, smelling her lover's clothes for the scent of deceit. And Edward, he has never had any faith that Delphi can fend for herself. She is defiant that she will never go to any man to fix or save her. Delphi refuses to collude with either bleak narrative. She will write her own story. She will be the hero of her own journey.

Delphi decides to leave her suitcase in the station locker for another day. She will get on the tube and head up to Belsize Park to knock on Romy's door. It was too early to disturb her and her parents this morning but now will be okay. Delphi's feet ache and she's longing for a shower. She touches her near-empty Oyster card to the panel of the stile and nudges through. The crowd is thick as it is rush hour. Delphi waits in the crush to catch the elevator below ground. She reasons that if she makes it into this next batch of commuters everything will be alright, and if she doesn't, disaster will reign. Delphi recognises that this is another form of thinking that comes into play when she's anxious. As is counting, silently chanting from one to ten over and over or allocating the initials of loved ones from the letters of number plates. When she was little, all the negotiations were for the safety of her family rather than herself. She would make deals with herself – if I can get through that door in time or catch that falling leaf before it hits the ground, so-and-so will be safe.

The elevator door opens and the crowd seethes forward. Delphi is interested to learn her fate. Just as she is about to make it and step across the threshold she becomes aware of a young mother carrying a baby in a papoose. Delphi is momentarily conflicted, then shifts her body and indicates to the woman that she should step past her to take the lift. The mother looks at Delphi and smiles.

'Thank you, you're very kind.'

Delphi smiles back, 'My pleasure.' And wonders if she's doomed.

*

Neither Romy nor her parents are home when Delphi knocks so she loiters on the stoop until darkness arrives. As they moved flats last year the family now live on the 5th floor. Delphi knows she could scale it, but a concerned and intuitive Romy made her swear that she would never try. And to Delphi a promise is a promise. She jogs on the spot as her bones are freezing and her nose is streaming. She has to get moving as she has no idea how long it will be before they come home. Delphi figures she will come back in a few hours so sets a course to the verdant lushness of Hampstead towards Keats' home. According to legend, he wrote 'Ode to a Nightingale' beneath the plum tree in the garden there. He died of tuberculosis at the age of twenty-five, younger than Delphi is. She loves the Romantics and between blowing on her frozen fingers, recites snatches of his poems to herself, and makes her way towards his house.

She passes a sitting room window that is wide open, which is unusual in this cold. The light from inside the house spills out with warm radiance. Music is playing loudly. Delphi doesn't recognise it but it sounds to be Latin American; it is jubilant and irreverent. The notes are packed full of vibrancy and elation. Delphi stops to listen and peers through the window. An old man is sitting blowing the smoke from a cigar out into the night. He and Delphi regard each other and his face transforms as he recognises her.

'Well, well, it's you. The Oliver Sacks reader. With the dying mother.'

The link is forged, the control panel lights up and Delphi places the kind, gentle man she'd had a drink with at the Holly Bush.

He's smiling at her mischievously.

'Hello,' she says. 'I'm sorry, I've forgotten your name.'

'No, I don't believe we actually exchanged monikers. How do you do, angelic nightwalker? I'm Arthur. Call me Art.'

Delphi hears a Tibetan bowl chime just below her thoughts. 'I like your name. How do you do? I'm Delphi.'

'Delphi? The shrine where the oracular god is consulted? How absolutely marvellous.'

'Yes, that's the one.' Plumes of visible breath escape Delphi as Art releases another dragon puff of cigar smoke.

Her hands are stuffed deep into her pockets and the couple assess each other.

'Are you coming in, Delphi?'

And it's as natural and straightforward as that.

'Yes please,' she answers. She moves towards the railing and lifts her foot to get purchase, careful to avoid the spikes.

'Are you choosing to come through the window rather than taking the door, child?

'Yes, if I may?'

'Indeed. How delightful.'

Delphi grabs the black railings, stabilises her foot on the narrow crossbar and pulls herself up. She stretches herself wide to transfer across to the large stone windowsill. Art offers his hand, but she worries she might pull him through; he's as delicate as a bird.

'No thank you, I'm alright but do stand back so I don't bash you on my way in.'

She launches and sails through the massive sash window and finds herself standing inside Art's oh-so-lovely home.

CHAPTER 17

'SHALL WE DO IT formally this time around?' Art stubs out his cigar, briefly touching the scarf knotted at his throat. Beaming and regal, he offers Delphi his crinkled hand. The music is so loud they need to shout to hear each other.

'Art Horowitz.'

Delphi places her hand in his. 'Delphi Hoffman. Delightful to re-meet you.'

'And you and your frigid hand. Child, would you like a cup of tea, something stronger or a hot-water bottle?'

'Tea please. That would be perfect.'

The old man is barefoot, his trousers rolled up at the ankle, a loose linen shirt draped around this tiny frame. The scarf is covered in words. When they'd been touching, Delphi had noticed a Star of David tattooed onto the web of flesh between his thumb and forefinger.

She is wide-eyed in this wonderful room. The overhead lights are off, but it's warmly lit by lamps. The walls are crammed with art. The sofas stacked with cushions. The floorboards are covered with Persian rugs, and thick velvet curtains are sashed back at the window, giving the whole room the feel of a luxurious Bedouin tent.

Art has spirited himself to the open plan kitchen in the far corner and is busying himself making tea. Delphi can feel the music throbbing inside her chest, twinning with her heartbeat and her baby's. The thought makes her feel peculiar.

Delphi turns slowly, taking everything in. Books, vases, trinket boxes and talismans are scattered and assembled into curated arrangements. A taxidermied owl peers down from the top of a bookcase. His snow-white face still wise in death. Art's aesthetics have thrown their arms wide to beauty and waltzed it in. A gorgeous crush of a life lived large and exultantly.

She sits down and takes off her boots, feeling unusually self-conscious of their utilitarian heaviness, and tucks them discreetly beside the sofa as she watches Art sing along to the music in Spanish. She notices that all the art is of men, mostly oils from the golden age of European painting. The men are being gored by bulls, are supine in forests, drinking from streams or taking part in philosophical circles and all of them have somehow lost their clothing. The walls are a celebration of the male form.

Art turns down the music and invites Delphi to the dining table. He pushes a space clear for her and indicates where she should sit. He has laid out cheese, bread, salami and olives. He pours a tiny portion of red wine into delicate glasses. Delphi can't find the words for her gratitude and she looks at this sweet man, desperately hunting for them. He graciously swats away her efforts.

'Eat, drink, revive.'

She sits and runs her fingers over the table's carvings.

'Ah, yes, my Good Guest List,' Art explains. 'If I love the company of people who eat here I ask them to sign their name. Then every few months I carve the signatures to make them permanent. We shall see if you receive the honour, child.' Art sips his tea and claims the seat opposite Delphi. This, for some reason, doesn't feel right to him so he Goldilockses to another chair and the way he settles indicates it's just right. His interior life is evidently as vivid as his external one.

'May I ask how your mother is?' He is looking at her with his chin tucked in and his cup held high in the air.

The bit of bread that Delphi is chewing lodges in her throat. Struggling to breathe incites primal panic and Delphi's eyes stretch wide. Art quickly gets up and returns with two glasses and a Frida Kahlo jug filled with water.

Delphi drinks the water and when she can she says, 'Thank you for the water, and the food. This is all enchanting.' She knots her hands in her lap and Art is waiting at attention.

'My mother is dead.'

Delphi hates herself as tears rise and fall down her face, her lips tremble as she weeps. Internally, she shouts at herself to stop.

Art makes soft comforting noises similar to those one would use to reassure a baby animal.

Delphi swabs at her face and apologises. 'It still feels raw. I'm very tightly in the grip of... Maybe I'll never outrun it.' She gulps for air. 'Sometimes I can't...'

Art nods compassionately.

'Ride the wave, sweet child.' He pushes some Turkish delight towards her.

She places a piece in her mouth then brushes the icing sugar off her fingers with a napkin embroidered with two tiny ships. He's pleased and jostles the dish towards her again. Delphi notices a piano groaning beneath manuscripts, the white keys discoloured with age.

'Horowitz? Are you related to the pianist?'

Art's face is fantastically mobile, rearranging as the conversation changes tack.

'Yes, actually, we are related, although tragically I am no musician – a true dilettante in that regard. Acting is, or rather I should say, has been my art, but I would have loved to play an instrument properly. To be a musical conduit.' He looks theatrically towards the heavens, opening his chest and dropping his head back as if waiting for divine instruction. When it doesn't arrive, he pops an olive in his mouth instead and asks with keen interest, 'Do you play?'

'Yes, but not very well. I play from my brain, like a competent robot, which is odd because my heart rules me to a fault, apparently. My brother Jack is good. My mother played too. She wept through it. She never played for joy.' She looks at the walls. 'But painting is my thing.'

'I saw you appreciating my collection.' He makes a sweeping gesture. 'What do you make of it?'

She considers his question.

'I think they're wonderful. And they tell me we have a third thing in common.'

'Indeed, what are the three?'

'Our love of Oliver Sacks, Turkish delight and men.'

Art is entranced and he raises his teacup. 'Let's drink to that. To our love of men. You at the beginning, and I, the old sop that I am, at the end.'

They touch their teacups together and drink.

'Do you still act, Art?'

'Not for some years now. My eyesight is poor and my balance is abandoning me but I had a good run.'

Delphi wants him to talk on and on. Happily this man needs no encouragement. Storytelling is in his veins.

'I joined the Royal Shakespeare Company in my late teens. I worked with them all: Olivier, Jacobi, Dench, the delicious Ian McKellen, whom I was profoundly in love with. I probably still am. God, how ghastly.'

'What were your favourite roles?'

'Oh, the mad and the bad boys – Hamlet, Macbeth, I'd have adored to play Othello, but he never came my way.' He taps his white forearm. 'I was, however, Desdemona once or twice in my off-stage life.' He flutters his eyelashes and feminises his body.

Art talks on about London in the seventies, about theatre versus screen acting, about a book he bought on dwarfs at a flea market and his deep enmity towards coriander. Delphi is heavy with exhaustion and is holding herself tightly to stop evaporating, but the reality of her accommodation woes pinches her awake. She initiates her leave-taking by standing. Jetlag has mashed her. She fears she may have overstayed her welcome. Art stands too and asks her where she's off to. A pause opens up and Delphi can't find a place within it to jump. She chooses not to lie, that option seems repugnant after being offered such civility and kindness.

'I don't exactly know, Art. I was thinking to go to my friend Romy's house, she lives with her parents down in Belsize Park Gardens.'

Art looks aghast. As if Belsize in this cold were the same as declaring an intention to dash barefoot to Siberia.

'Well, you are very welcome to stay here for the night. You've gone quite pale. I have a spare room, I have terrific towels and a claw-foot bathtub from Greece, but you really must promise,' and he takes a perfectly timed pause, 'you must swear not to rob or murder me during the night.'

It is Delphi's turn to look aghast, and Art realises she is too tired and battle-worn to saddle up to the joke.

'Come along, child, it is far too late and frigid to be setting out. To be frank, you don't look well enough, but if you insist, you may borrow my bicycle and maybe that's a negligent offer on my part, but I don't have a motor or I should drive you like the gentleman I am.'

Delphi wraps her arms around herself and when she's sure she has control of her voice she thanks Art. 'I would love to stay, I'm so grateful, I don't want to impose on Romy's parents and I don't even know if she's home. And I promise not to steal from you or kill you while I am under your gracious roof.'

'Well, how marvellous, a chance encounter, twice over, and now we've evolved into a slumber party. Here let me show you the way to your room, dear child, you look utterly wan.' He offers her his arm as if he were about to usher her into a banquet at Versailles with the Sun King himself.

*

'Most excellent to see you on this splendid fog-heavy morning.' Art is standing by the sash window, inspecting the low-lying clouds. He's wearing a royal blue floor-length gown with a stenciled dragon poised furiously along the length of his spine.

'Isn't the mist mysterious?' He grins like a little boy. 'I'm waiting for Her Majesty's horses.'

Delphi walks over to join him and they wait together.

'I took the liberty of setting out breakfast for you. Please eat whatever you'd like, although I don't have coffee in the house, being a firm tea man myself. Nor juice, it is quite evil to pulverise fruit into liquefaction. I cannot abide it.'

Delphi smiles at him and he catches her warmth.

'What are your plans today, dear girl?'

She picks at a hangnail. 'I need to do a few chores, bank, phone shop and I will try knocking on Romy's door again.'

'Goodness, that's a packed diary. How sweetly old fashioned of you, though, with your friend. I thought you young people texted each other rather than turned up in person.'

Delphi turns back to look out of the window. Condensation trickles. Vivian would have called this fog *as thick as pea soup*.

'I'm sorry, Delphi, I didn't mean to be condescending.'

'No, not at all. You're right in a way. I would text her if I could, but my phone was stolen. So, you see last night you actually saved me from something pretty awful.'

Art melts into deeper concern. 'Oh, dear girl, were you mugged on the street? In Hampstead?'

'No, in the hostel I stayed in, but please don't worry. The man didn't hurt me, he just made off with my mobile and my wallet.'

'Good lord, your wallet too. Did you contact the police?'

She shakes her head and explains she couldn't see the point.

'I certainly don't mean to overstep, but if Romy isn't home, you are welcome to stay tonight. I do so love the company. Unfortunately, tomorrow I must turf you out back into the arms of your loving family as I am off to France. But please do tell me if there is any way that I can be of service.'

Delphi touches the soft red velvet of the curtains and wonders what familial loving arms would feel like now. 'Thank you, Art.'

They hear the clip-clopping of horses' hooves and Art presses excitedly to the window.

'Every third week they come down this road and every single time I feel like a great celebration, a private pageant is occurring.

Something completely resplendent about so many horses moving through the London streets together.'

Art is right. The Queen's Guard comes into view. They've walked up from their stables in Regent's Park. The riders are not in uniform as they're exercising the beasts, but there is a stately dignity all the same. The animals are huge and flanked two by two. As they pass the house, Art lifts the sash window open and calls out, 'Good morning horses, how noble you are!' Some of the riders smile, one discreetly calls back, 'Morning Mr Horowitz,' and touches the brim of his hat. Delphi feels herself transported back to when she was a little girl, bursting with wonder. Another rider with high cheekbones is looking at her and she meets his gaze. After several seconds the rider winks at her. Delphi takes the tiny gift and stashes it away as she moves from the window towards the teapot.

*

Delphi gets in and out of Barclays Bank as quickly as she can. She cancels her old cards and is enormously relieved that what's left of Hugh's money is still safely nestled inside her account. She makes a withdrawal and then does battle at the Carphone Warehouse leaving interminably later, her hair greying around her temples, with a new phone. She walks down the hill and presses Romy's buzzer. The inactivity within is deafening. Delphi sighs audibly. It feels good so she does it again and then feels idiotic. Casting herself as a Russian longing for Moscow over the snowfields isn't going to cut it. She does miss her friend, though, and thinks about other people she could contact, but it's Romy she wants. Delphi takes out her new mobile and tries to guess Romy's number but she just can't retrieve it from her brain. She makes a note to memorise it so this doesn't ever happen again. She logs into iCloud, retrieves Romy's email and fires off a message giving her new number and asking her friend to call back ASAP.

Delphi sets off walking and it takes her half an hour to reach Fitzrovia where the Women's Health London clinic is. A radiant young man checks her in and she settles down in the plastic chair to wait.

The room is full of women. Some with children, all look harried or bored. A television bracketed in the corner plays a soap with the sound turned down. The pastel palette and subtitles mesmerise Delphi. Pamphlets are stacked on the table beside her. Everything one could want to know about sexual health.

Delphi looks down at the cover of a particular pamphlet. There is a picture of a grinning couple holding a baby with 'Adoption?' written on an umbrella that is held over the baby. Delphi reaches out to pick it up but pauses, her fingers hovering as if the paper may scorch her. She clambers over her resistance, opens it and reads about the ins and outs of giving up a baby. There is lots of supportive language directing the reader towards a website where 'one can learn more and book an appointment!' Why the exclamation mark? It seems pushy and inappropriate. Delphi wonders if this is an option for her baby. Static begins to crackle and erupts in Delphi's brain. An internal power surge crashes through her. Delphi shoves the brochure into her bag and she zips it up quickly. She can't conceive of a life where she would be alive on this planet knowing she had a child walking the very same earth, and yet being raised by someone else. Delphi thinks of toddler Arthur's death. Would her baby be another lost child in her life? She stands up suddenly to halt the downward spiral and a teenager chewing gum looks at her to see what's happening. Delphi offers a smile, but the girl stares on, chewing open-mouthed, unimpressed, as if Delphi were just another lame adult. Delphi wonders what happened to the girl to have removed all trace of softness from her. Delphi sits back down and bites at her lip. She makes a resolution to not to become battle-hardened.

Delphi's eyes return to the boy doing the checking in. He is stunning. Like a young Idris Elba. She wonders if he's a model. Surely he is. He has the self-consciousness of someone who knows they're always watched, a feigned casualness. She studies him as he goes about his work. He wears a badge that states: *I'm here to help,* with a big yellow smiley face. Delphi would bet that his family adore him. That man-child knows what it is to be beloved. He is so undamaged.

*

'Thanks again for letting the students be in the room with us, Delta. Such an important part of their training.'

Delphi nods and decides not to correct the name slip. She is sitting knee to knee with Dr Smithsen in the cramped room. The doctor has an Irish accent and her thick hair is cut into a sensible bob.

Nine gormless students stand pressed to the walls giving the impression that the tiny room is shrinking further. They all wear white coats and are holding clipboards which makes them look even more awkward than Delphi feels.

'Delta, that's an unusual name,' Dr Smithsen says reassuringly.

Delphi agrees.

'What can we do for you today?'

Delphi swaps the way her legs are crossed and accidentally kicks the doctor on the shin with her boots.

'Oh, sorry.'

Dr Smithsen makes a gesture for Delphi not to worry.

'I think I'm pregnant. Um… well, I am pretty sure I'm pregnant.'

Dr Smithsen swivels to face her computer. She asks questions and touch-types in the answers, moving her head from Delphi to the screen like a sideshow clown. Delphi finds it eerie.

'Have you taken a test?'

'Yes. Three.'

'When was your last menses?'

'Um, I'm not entirely sure, but I think about five weeks ago.'

'Any live pregnancies before?'

'No.'

'Any stillbirths?'

'No.'

'Any terminations?'

'Um, surprisingly no.'

'Do you have a partner?'

Delphi observes the drip of intergenerational ignominy but refuses to cower.

'Uh, no. I mean I did, he helped me to get pregnant, but he's not… um… no,' she stammers.

'I am going to arrange for you to get some blood work done.' The doctor taps into the computer. 'And we'll need a urine sample.'

Delphi lifts the brown paper bag she's been awkwardly cradling in her lap. 'Ah, the nurse asked me to do that already. It's here.'

The doctor smiles 'Oh that's fantastic. I love efficiency. Did she test it?'

'No, not yet.' The doctor pulls on some rubber gloves, takes the bag and places the specimen jar on her desk. She unscrews the lid, opens a strip test and dunks it in. The doctor explains this process to the baby doctors and Delphi feels exposed. That private fluid of hers that's sitting on the desk renders her shockingly exposed. She avoids looking at anyone and just fastens her eyes on the test.

Dr Smithsen lifts it up and says 'Well, you're right. You are pregnant.' This is the first time Delphi has heard anyone say these words aloud and she draws them into herself in awe.

'Right, so what would you like to do today, Delta? Are congratulations in order?'

'I beg your pardon?' Delphi doesn't understand the question.

Dr Smithsen softens. 'Do you want to keep it?'

'Oh, yes. I want to keep it,' Delphi answers slowly and the doctor smiles warmly.

'Okay. Let's get you up on the table and I will do a sonograph and we can see what's what.'

Delphi nods and presses her nails into the palms of her hands.

'As you are so early along the scan will need to be internal. I will insert a probe into your vagina. Don't worry it's no bigger than an average-sized penis.'

Christ.

'If you would like to go ahead with that, slip off your clothes from the waist down, including your underwear, hop up on the bed, put your legs in the supports and pop the blanket across your stomach and thighs.'

The doctor is so efficient that Delphi struggles to keep up. Will the students all watch her undress? Dr Smithsen is on her feet, navigating the furniture, ushering the students out quickly, saying, 'Just call out when you are all set.'

Delphi keeps her eyes averted as the room empties. She undresses, disentangling herself twice from the chair arm, then climbs up onto the table. A paper mat is under her bottom, and she places her legs in the stirrups. She hurriedly unfolds the blanket and covers as much of herself as possible. She is not yet done when a rap on the door makes her jump.

'Are you ready for us, Delta?'

Delphi answers, 'Yes,' when everything inside her is saying, *No.*

The students file in. Delphi wishes she hadn't consented to the audience. Why in sod's name does she always try to be so bloody helpful? She suspects it's because she wants to be loved or maybe it's just the awful conditioning of being female.

The androids flank the walls again, Dr Smithsen turns on the monitor and prepares the probe with a condom and lubricant. If only Delphi had been similarly prepared the night she'd spent with Orlo.

'Are we ready? Just breathe and relax.' This seems improbable as a woman wielding a phallus heads towards Delphi accompanied by a pack of acne-ridden virgins looking on taking notes. She hasn't even been bought a drink.

The probe is cold and despite herself, Delphi gasps as it's pushed inside her. She shuts her eyes tightly and counts to three, repeatedly.

'I'm just inspecting your ovaries first. Very nice. All healthy. Looks like you ovulated from the right side. That's a fun fact. And… there it is, Delta, your baby, you can take a look on the monitor.'

Delphi opens her eyes, turns her head and shadows fill the screen. She can't make anything out. It's a snowstorm of static. The doctor points out what looks to be a prawn from outer space.

'Here is the head,' she says circling a blob on the screen, 'and here are the tiny legs. That fluttering is your baby's heart beating.'

Delphi looks at the image as if she has just been bestowed with the miracle of sight. She is awash with feelings of joy and awe.

'Shall we see if we can have a listen?'

Delphi is entranced.

A sound is emitted in the room, like the feet of stampeding mice.

'And that is the sound of your baby's heart. It's completely normal to be that fast. The range at this gestation is around 110 beats per minute so that looks very healthy too.'

Delphi is free-floating. The cornerstone of her identity is reconfiguring. The molecular structure of her heart is undergoing a transformation.

The doctor is taking measurements of the foetus and explaining various things to the students. Delphi becomes aware that her ankle is being tapped.

'Can you hear me, Delta? Good girl. Pop your clothes back on and then let's have a chat, but the measurements tell us your baby is very new, not yet quite six weeks, and as we calculate gestation from the first day of your missed period, rather than conception which happens in the middle of your cycle, your baby was conceived three to four weeks ago.'

Delphi struggles with the calculations, but this revised plotting means there's ambiguity about paternity. It could be still Orlo, but it could also possibly be the art teacher's. Delphi shudders. It's impossible to say for sure as her cycle was messed up.

'Okay everyone, let's leave the room for the mummy to get dressed.' Dr Smithsen presses Delphi's shoulder cheerfully.

'I have two little girls. You are going to love being a mother. It's the hardest job on earth but, oh golly, it's the most rewarding.'

*

Sitting back at Art's table that afternoon looking at the old man and Romy laughing together makes Delphi happy, but she's also numb, as if she is outside, looking in on real life.

Tea has been made and her new friend and her old one are riffing together like jazz players. Delphi wants to offer them something but she's incapable. Occasionally they look at her sympathetically and their pity serves to cast her further out to sea. Romy's been trying to convince Art about the power of punk and he sets off to change the music. Once he's moved away, Romy leans over and squeezes Delphi's knee and asks, 'Del, hey Minx, earth to Delphi? Do you have any painkillers in your bag? My head is on fire.'

'Um, yes, if I do, it's in the inside pocket, help yourself.'

Romy gets up, lifts the handbag and rummages for the pills. Before finding them, she removes the gnome, studies it and looks at Delphi. Delphi doesn't notice as she's re-sunk inside her glass of water, trying to recall a Sylvia Plath poem. Romy puts the gnome aside intending to circle back to him once she has drugs in her system and Delphi is less maudlin. She carries on digging when she notices a white folded card branded with the Women's Health London logo.

'Yikes, Minx, what's this?'

Delphi turns and Romy is holding the baby scans.

Art has returned, the sounds of Chopin are filtering through and, sensing the air has changed quality, he hovers unobtrusively on the far side of the table.

Romy looks down at the images again and then back to her friend.

'Are you pregnant?'

Delphi tries to say *yes* but no volume accompanies her intention. It's akin to looking into the blazing sun to finally tell Romy, brilliant but frightening.

Romy moves over and puts her arms around Delphi. The women hold each other in silence and Delphi sees Art withdrawing from the space.

'Oh, please don't go, Art. I don't want you pushed out of your own sitting room. Please stay.'

He returns and scoops up a glass of wine before taking a seat in an armchair. He looks rattled. Delphi regrets bringing this into his cocoon. 'I'm sorry, Art.'

'Sorry? What on earth for, child?'

Delphi doesn't quite know.

'Who's the father? What are you going to do?' Romy is riding a pendulum swing between shock and consternation.

Delphi tucks her hair behind her ears and exhales. 'I'm not entirely sure who the father is. Do you find that dreadfully unseemly, Art?'

'Not at all, child, it's actually rather decadent of you.' He sips at his wine conspiratorially.

Romy isn't taking the news as gracefully.

'What the hell, Del? Well, who *might* it be?'

'I think it's probably that artist Orlo, the one I told you about, but there's an outside chance it's this other guy I hooked up with in Brighton.' Delphi decides to hold off telling her in front of Art that it was her old teacher. 'It's probably not him as we only had sex for about three seconds but according to this dating scan today and the doctor's timeline it could be either.'

'Right, anyone else?' Romy's mouth is pulled down on one side.

'Well, there was a man in Berkshire but we used protection and I've excluded a woman in Hobart for obvious reasons.'

Romy refolds the images, places them down on the table and claims a chair.

'And?' she asks pointedly.

'And what?'

'What do you intend to do about it?'

'Obviously the timing is not good, in the beginning I assumed I'd get a termination, I mean look at my life, but now, after Mama… I just don't think I can.'

'Christ, you're kidding me, right? Tell me you're joking?'

'I know I stuffed up. I know I'm not fit to be a mother, but I can't kill it, there has been enough death already.' Delphi is white-hot. 'And where is your Buddhism now by the way?'

'If you abort then that's the baby's karmic lot.'

'I can't listen to that bullshit.'

Romy looks wounded and Delphi grabs her hand and gives it a firm kiss. 'Don't be upset, I love you, just tread carefully with me because I'm just holding on. I'm doing the best I can. I'm sure from where you're sitting it doesn't look like I am, but let me reassure you. I'll come up with a plan.'

The three of them sit silently, all bubbling until Art speaks.

'I'd have cherished parenthood. My family were mostly wiped out in the Holocaust.'

Delphi's mouth drops open.

'Truly, as I approach my death, I think I'm seventy-three but I may be a year or two older, I've lied about it so much I've actually lost track. I don't so much lament not having a life partner as I've known love and spells of great if dysfunctional companionship. What makes me sad, makes me certain I've missed out, is that I never had a family of my own. I have never held my child in my arms. I've mourned that lack almost every day of my adult life.'

Delphi identifies a large piece of the Art puzzle slot into place. 'Art,' she tells him, 'You would have made a wonderful father. I wish…' she wonders if she should say it, but stuff it, truth and vulnerability are superpowers, 'I wish I were your daughter.'

His breathing alters and a tear chases down his wrinkles. 'I was reading Kübler-Ross today, prompted to do so by your grief and I read something there that struck me as a perfect description of you. I actually wrote it down.' He pulls out a slip of paper and he reads it. 'People are like stained-glass windows. They sparkle and shine when the sun is out, but when darkness sets in their beauty is revealed only if there is light from within.'

He hands her the piece of paper. 'I can see you miss your mother most desperately. But, Delphi, your light still burns brightly.'

Delphi reads the quote again and Art declares the music no longer suits his mood and must be changed again. 'Time for the big guns, *Adagio for Strings,* I think. Samuel Barber, make our souls swell!' The violin trembles and the lower strings join in. The melody suspends and then lifts as if climbing up a staircase towards God herself.

Romy runs her hands through her peroxided hair, listening, and eventually says, 'Tell me about that gnome then?'

Delphi takes a small sip of water. 'His name is My Dear Friend. A poor and stiff substitute for you, sister.' Romy dips her head to the side and smiles.

'He's been guarding Mama's house for years but now he's hopefully going to guard me. And stuffed into his cavity are my mother's dog's ashes.'

'Seriously?' Romy turns the gnome upside down, inspecting it. 'Very bloody heavy to be lugging around in your handbag, sweets.'

'Yes, he is. But I'm lugging around much heavier shit than him at the moment.' Romy sets the gnome down on the table then punctures the packet of pills and swallows several of them, drinking from Delphi's glass. Delphi studies the laughing face of the gnome and reaches out to give him a pat.

'I'm sorry I didn't tell you, Rom. I was planning to later tonight. I've only told Jack and that didn't go well. I'm sorry.'

She reaches out and takes her friend's hand.

'It's cool, Minx.' She leans in and they hug.

'Art!' Romy yells over the music. 'Do you know DJ Tiësto?' She pulls her phone from her jeans pocket and opens Spotify. 'Let me crank this baby, let's power mix this shiz and you can hear your *Adagio for Strings* ramped up and rather than us all sitting here sobbing our guts out we can bounce!' She plugs her phone into Art's stereo and the techno interpretation of the classical music thunders through the house. The floors and walls throb. Art rapidly dials up from curiosity to ecstasy. He turns the volume up full and stretches his arms above his head and begins to move. The bass kicks in and Romy starts to jump and romp about. The panes of old glass come alive in their frames. Delphi gets to her feet and joins them and the three pounce and cavort and twirl. They lift off, their bodies warm, and they laugh, twisting hands, pulsing their limbs and Art clicks off the lights and they dance around the candlelight ecstatic, elevated, transcendent.

*

Delphi is leaving the bathroom with a towel wrapped around her body and another around her wet hair. It's not that late, but she's well and truly ready for bed. Romy had offered to have Delphi stay with her, but as much as Delphi loves Romy's parents she just couldn't face the questions they would have about Vivian. Art calls to her and she turns in the hallway to see him walking towards her.

'A blanket in case you get cold tonight. The BBC just told me the temperature is due to plummet.'

'Thank you.'

'And, I also wanted to give you this.' He's holding out an envelope. 'Inside is a little money.' Delphi begins to protest, but he talks over her. 'No, please, it's not much, I wish it were more, but hopefully it will alleviate your immediate pressure.'

'I can't take money from you and I'm not strapped, my godfather has lent me some.'

'If you won't take it as a gift, think of it as payment for one of your paintings. There is also an address in there. It's for a commune that I know of. I've not been there myself, but I have actor friends who've spoken highly of it. It was originally founded by a great man, whom I knew, sadly not in the biblical sense, named Lorenzo. So handsome it would make you weep. Now his son Christoph, I think he's called, whom by all accounts is also an exceptional human; a meditator, environmentalist and pacifist, runs the place. They don't condone alcohol so obviously that's desperately odd, but the community have built a life, an aspirational nirvana and I think you and your baby could possibly find a home there. I may be entirely wrong, but the idea struck me, and now I can't shake it.'

He offers her the envelope. Delphi stares at it with a furrowed brow.

'Why don't you google Lorenzo. I've watched some of his talks online and his son's, and there's something special there. Have a look and see if it resonates with you.'

'Thank you, that's very thoughtful.'

'Child, do your research and if you're interested I could write a letter of introduction for you to take along as the community is not on email.'

'You're not sending me off to a cult are you?'

He chortles. 'Oh goodness no. I'd not send you off to something like that. An old chum of mine, Jane, was in distress a decade ago and she went there. I've not spoken to her extensively about it, but I do know for her it was a safe harbour. She got her life together and has gone from strength to strength. I know you meditate and I saw you doing those yoga stretches in the sitting room this morning. They're very big on all of that. Downward dog. Appallingly hard. I've read that's meant to be a rest position. What madness. Salute to the sun! Now that I approve of. Très pagan.' He raises his hands above his head.

Delphi smiles. Art is so charming and he looks almost elfin with gentle overhead lighting distorting his features.

'Okay, I will have a look. Where is it?'

'It's in Tuscany or maybe it's Chianti. So, you either fly into Roma, Firenze or Pisa.'

'Italy? Seriously? I was assuming rural England. Wow. Okay. You sure think outside the box.'

'And that, as they say, makes all the difference.'

'Who said that? Originally?'

'Oh, I have absolutely no idea. Some pioneer.' He taps the envelope. 'Just sleep on it. You can always take Romy up on the offer of her sofa in her parent's sitting room. And find yourself a menial job to work yourself to the bone. How that will pan out without maternity benefits in seven and a half months, I shudder to think.'

She laughs. 'Tell it to me straight why don't you?'

'Italy! What a country. The men are fantastic there! And all that delicious pasta. You need some fattening up.' He brings his fingers to his mouth and kisses them, tossing his kiss to the sky. 'I feel badly you can't stay on in the flat tomorrow. I leave for the Eurostar at 4 pm and I've lent this place to a prickly character who wouldn't tolerate a flatmate one little bit. Even one as lovely as you, Delphi.'

'Art, you're not responsible for me, but thank you for being so thoughtful and generous. You've already gone above and beyond. I would love to paint you something, that would be an honour. I will give you the cash back anyway, as soon as I can, I promise.'

She reaches out and cuddles him. It's the first time they've embraced. He feels minuscule and bony in her arms. She says a silent prayer of thanks for having been put on his singular path.

'You're a wonderful man.'

'Well, I do so like to be helpful. And I'm a nurturer from way back. You should have seen me with my dolls when I was little! My father was appalled. And you're a wounded jaguar.' He pats her hand. 'I know it's very difficult for you to trust as you're in the blackest part of the night, but sunlight will return to your world. And do you know what I think is the absolutely bravest thing any of us can do?'

She shakes her head carefully so as not to dislodge the towel.

'It's to own our stories and to love ourselves through that process. Please don't forget to be on your own team, child.'

He gives her hand another pat. 'Now off to bed with you and make sure you dry your hair so you don't get a chill.'

He smiles and turns back towards the sitting room. 'I hope I don't bother you if I turn the music up. I feel something wonderful brewing!'

He is well out of earshot but she sends her love down the corridor after him.

*

Delphi slips into bed wearing her mother's flannel nightie. The sheets are soft linen. The counterpane is from India and Delphi watches the tiny mirrors sewn on it flash as she settles. Vivian's ashes are in her arms, pressed to her chest.

Alone, she is able to feel her grief full force. She has no one to protect. No one to behave for. Grief stalks in through the doorway, shimmies down the drainpipe, swells up the central heating ducts, floods in through the window and pulses out from the light bulb. Assembled, it pauses for a moment to celebrate its awesome power before it falls on Delphi and devours her.

*

Delphi shifts in Art's office chair, stiff from sitting in it for the last few hours. Dawn is arriving and the light is shifting in this little room crammed with books. Art had offered the use of his computer and wrote down his password for her – 'Open sesame' – and he'd done a line drawing of Delphi beside it, which had the feel of Quentin Blake. Unable to sleep she'd come in and fired up the computer.

Images of Christoph, Lorenzo and members of The Bodhi Famiglia fill the screen. Delphi is surprised by how impressed she's been by the information she has managed to find. It's a private organisation, and Lorenzo was the original founder. There is footage of him holding meetings and giving speeches from as far back as the seventies. It appears Christoph took over the figurehead role in the last decade after the death of his father. Both men speak eloquently and with a marked equanimity. They speak out against war, calling for nuclear disarmament. They ask for racial equality and, more recently, for inclusivity for the LGBTIQA+ community and express the moral imperative to act in the face of climate disaster. Lorenzo in his prime was a powerhouse of conviction, intensity and idealism. Delphi is drawn to him as he's evidently a revolutionary for peace.

There is less to be found on his son, Christoph. In photos he radiates serenity and love for his father. Delphi leans closer to the screen to look at a grainy photograph of him meditating with a large group.

There are several articles on the community but little substance is offered. Words like pacifists, vegetarianism, hippies and commune are tossed about and Lorenzo is always mentioned with respect. He had intended to join the seminary as a boy but moved into politics as a young man. According to him, the municipal corruption and ineffectually of what he found there resulted in him establishing The Bodhi Famiglia in the sixties and the community has existed in Italy where they were gifted land ever since.

Delphi clicks on a tab she's already looked at several times and rough footage of Christoph speaking fills the screen. He is in some kind of hall. It's difficult to tell from the angle how many people are listening to him but it looks like a lot. He is dressed in white and sits cross-legged on a raised stage. He has begun his talk earlier as the energy of the crowd indicates they're well down the path together.

The richness of his voice softens Delphi and she takes her head off her hand to give him her full attention.

'All people are equal,' he says. 'But some are seekers.' There is no sound from his audience. 'Everyone suffers. But some don't want to live like that. They refuse to be passive. A victim of their lives, pushed along by the current, without true autonomy or self-determinism. They don't want to turn the wheel for distraction, isolation, corruption, and capitalism. We've been sold a lie. But, and this is important, some people know that the true point of our existence is to be in connection and in service. Not to skim along the surface, but to go deep. That was my father's life work, which I, with humility, will carry forward. To live a life of wakefulness, of love, of activism and thoughtfulness. To quieten down the noise that's in our society, all the distractions. To live mindfully and peacefully with my brothers and sisters. To do good in this world. It's as simple as that.' Delphi's heart beats erratically in her chest and she presses her fingers to the pulse in her wrist to track its irregularity. 'There's another way to live.' Christoph's charisma is palpable. 'It's being brave and being ready to choose it.'

He thanks everyone and asks for questions. Delphi scrolls through the first few but stops on the one that moved her so much earlier. A young man in the crowd has had a death in his family. He doesn't get his question out because he is overwhelmed with emotion. The camera swings back to Christoph, who has stepped down from the stage and is moving through the crowd with a look of compassion on his face. The people move out of the way to let him through and when he reaches the young man Christoph wraps his arms around him. The young man relaxes into the encircling arms and weeps. They stand there together and tears flow down Delphi's face as she watches. She looks at the clock on Art's desk, it's too early but she doesn't want to lose the impetus. She unlocks her mobile and presses in the freshly googled number for Horizon Art. She lost Orlo's direct number along with all the others on her stolen phone. The message bank kicks in and she leaves her name and number asking Emma Moorfield to have Orlo call her back. Then she stretches back in the chair and puts one hand on her heart and the other low on her belly.

CHAPTER 18

THE EASYJET FLIGHT IS nearly two hours late arriving at Ciampino Airport. Delphi collects her suitcase and walks outside to find the bus to the centre of Rome. It's the same season, but the light is entirely different from London. She left grey and has landed in yellow. She hopes it is a metaphor.

Taxi drivers spruik noisily for business, their cigarette smoke obnoxious. They see she is disinterested and quickly move their hustle to the tourists in Delphi's wake. One driver kisses his fingers and flings them at Delphi: '*Ciao bella, ciao!*' She'd forgotten how intense the men are here. A bubbling pot of Christianity, sexual frustration, vanity, misogyny, and mother dominance – it's a fertile brew producing some of the world's worst hecklers.

She presses on past one bus company and then another, looking for Flixbus. They're the cheapest at six euro and she's pre-bought her fare. Even though the airport isn't big, she's reluctant to keep lugging her suitcase in the wrong direction. Vivian's ashes and the gnome's combined weight in her handbag are carving a welt in the soft flesh of her shoulder.

She asks a sun-toasted man with thick black hair for help. The buttons of his cream shirt are straining and the fabric is puckering over his big stomach. Delphi tells him the bus company name several times. Finally, the penny drops and he points in the direction she was heading. She hopes this is another good omen. Maybe she's aligned with the great compass.

'*Grazie,*' she says, forcing a smile. She's so anxious her jaw is aching.

'*Arrivederci, bella donna,*' he responds, stepping back so he can ogle her as she walks past him.

A green coach with the branding she's been hunting for comes into view. The female driver is loitering at the front of it, committedly chewing gum. Delphi identifies herself as a passenger in rusty Italian and the driver smiles sunnily, revealing tiny white teeth like an infant's and helps Delphi with her suitcase. It goes in the back door and Delphi goes in the side and claims herself a seat.

She has about thirty minutes before she will be dropped at the railway station. She'd intended to catch a train north today but with the flight delay it's too late. The upside is she adores Rome. She has enough money for a hostel, but she's gun-shy and decides to spend that money on visiting the Keats-Shelley House instead. She wants to see where her beloved poet died. Maybe she should lie down on his single bed, beneath the roof of carved roses and see if she can follow suit?

The driver gets into her seat and swivels back to do a final headcount before strapping on her belt and cranking up the soft rock. She turns the ignition and the bus rumbles into life. The vibration is strong beneath Delphi's legs and the window rattles within its frame. Hello Kitty is hanging from the rear-view mirror, jiggling maniacally. Just like me, Delphi thinks. She takes out her mobile to check again if Orlo has called. Still nothing. His silence, his absence feels solid. The driver throws the bus into gear and sets off to Rome.

*

Delphi locks up her suitcase at the station and finds the most direct route to the Spanish Steps, which are heaving with tourists, selfie sticks and tour groups jockeying. Lovers canoodle, limbs intertwined, and locals walk at speed looking impossibly stylish. Delphi doesn't have the time to linger, but she intends to spend the night walking so she will have plenty soon.

To the right is the Keats-Shelley House. She unbuttons her coat and goes in through the enormous doors. The inclemency of the years has petrified the wooden shutters; they look like stone. It makes Delphi worry protectively for her heart. The tiling underfoot is coloured hexagons, and high above the dark-beamed ceiling is an elaborate crystal chandelier twinkling with opulence. She pays the entrance fee. The cashier explains it's less than fifteen minutes before closing. Delphi thanks her, picks up a leaflet and walks to the parlour. In Keats' time it was divided into two and he shared it with his landlady, but now it's been returned to its original form of one long thin room. Wooden cabinets filled with leatherbound books line the walls, and more cabinets run along the centre displaying open manuscripts and letters. Delphi thinks there is something so moving about the handwriting of the dead. They were here, their scrawl a vapour trail, and now they've vanished. As if erased by an irreversible magic trick. Difficult and painful to reconcile. Above the bookshelves the plaster is painted burnt apricot and the ceiling is intricately carved with flowers set in grids.

Delphi is elated to be here. Keats stood here, and now, for the blink of an eye, so does she. Between the large windows at the end of the room is a marble bust of Percy Bysshe Shelley. Delphi walks towards it and looks into the carved eyes. He is fine-featured, windswept, an intelligence and radiance about him transmitted despite the inanimate stone. Delphi leans forward and kisses him on the mouth. Her lips of flesh and his lips of marble. Another great person cut down in their prime. He drowned; his heart plucked from his funeral pyre by a bereft friend. In the short twenty-nine years he was alive, Shelley created poetry and essays of expansive romantic and moral wonder. Delphi is suddenly struck by the thought that she will never contribute anything of merit. If she is unable to create, does that mean she will lead a life without wonder, denuded of meaning, bereft of any real contribution? Her fingers trace Shelley's cheek.

She walks on towards Keats' bedroom. It looks just as it did in the postcard she had pinned above her desk throughout her teenage years. Along the bottom of the card was written his gravestone quote: 'Here lies one whose name was writ in water.' Delphi stands motionless by the window absorbing the view. She always does this, wants to see what is without before looking within. It reminds her of Art's parting words to her as he waved her goodbye from his front window, that in life, *the only way out, is in.*

Aware she's pressed for time she turns back and walks the few steps to the sleigh bed where Keats breathed his last. She disobeys the sign, kneels on the floor, leans over and rests her head on the mattress. 'Thank you,' she whispers. 'Look out for my mama. I think you'll like each other.' She shuts her eyes and intuits the baby in her belly understanding all of this better than she does.

A tannoy crackles in Italian, then in English, and she is told the house will be closing.

She crawls over to Keats' death mask displayed to her right but regrets looking at it. It makes her impossibly sorrowful. It's shocking after seeing her own mother's face similarly pulled flat.

The cashier sticks her head through the doorway and sees the young woman on her knees praying. She thinks to leave her for a moment but then remembers that she's hungry and wants to get home to her cats.

'English lady, it is closed now. Please up and out.'

Delphi stands and does as she's told but she looks back. Savoring. Wishing there was more time.

*

Delphi's feet ache from all the walking and the night is colder than she expected. For the last hour she's been sitting in a pew in Santi Vincenzo e Anastasio. She's trying to decide if she should risk it and find a place to lie on the floor to sleep but the idea of being so vulnerable keeps her sitting. Also, the marble is freezing and only the aisle is carpeted. Poor long-suffering Jesus is strung bleeding from his cross. Delphi looks at his ribs, the wounds in his hands, his resigned tragic expression and she thinks how distressed his mother must have been.

Delphi hears the clock tower outside start to chime midnight. She smarts with tiredness. A priest in brown robes walks out from a cloister, moves to the central altar, performs the sign of the cross, turns and arches an eyebrow to see Delphi sitting huddled up at the back. He approaches her speaking Italian and when she answers, *'Buona serata, Reverend,'* her voice breaks as if she's not spoken for days. Frightening how quickly one can drift out of orbit. He is about fifty and his flesh has the pink quality of one bathed and scrubbed with vigilance. A belt of beads like an oversized rosary is lashed around his ample waist, falling to the ground.

His swaps to English; it was the British pronunciation of reverendo that gave her away. 'Thank you for you visit. Is close now. Time to go.'

Delphi had hoped the church, with is frescoed domes and impressive altar, would stay open all night. She reluctantly shuts the book she was not managing to read and collects up her drawings. Not Orlo this time. All Mary. She wonders if she should beseech the priest for sanctuary? Isn't it an ancient juridical concept, the right of asylum? The priest stands observing her from a measured distance. Something ophidian in his eye. She keeps her head down, stands and turns towards the main doors when he asks, 'You tourist ere?'

'Si.' She clears her throat. 'I arrived today but I'm heading north to live.' She adds the last two words to give legitimacy and credence to herself. Silly, she thinks, what am I playing at? Trying to justify myself to a man I don't even know, attempting to stake a claim of belonging in his country?

He receives this information and rolls it over, his soft jaw moving left then right.

'Where you live up Nord?'

Delphi rubs her eyes and wonders if she shouldn't share, but then decides too much secrecy is another way of staying separated.

In Italian she answers, 'I'm going to Chianti in the morning to join a community called The Bodhi Famiglia.'

'The Bodhi Famiglia?' he asks, the sharpness of his voice pursing his lips. His watery gaze gives her the creeps.

Delphi turns to leave.

'Beez careful,' he calls after her. 'You will not find God there wid them. It…' He's hunting for a word in English and looks flushed with satisfaction when he finds it. 'Cult. It eez a cult. *Si.*'

The priest wants her out so he can lock up and go back to his crumpets, slippers and scriptures. He makes a shooing motion with his hand as if she were a stray dog. Deflated, Delphi steps out into the bitterly cold night.

*

It's a tonic catching the early morning train from Rome to Florence. Delphi tries to stay awake to drink in the flat countryside but exhaustion claims her and she wakes as the train screeches into the end of the line. Delphi wants to take a walk around, specifically to see the Duomo and kneel before Michelangelo's David, but after all the walking from the night before her body is sore and she decides to press on to her destination.

Delphi chooses a place to stand on the shoulder of the highway looking as conspicuous and pick-up-able as possible. She pulls out the sign she made on the train and hopes the black eyeliner on the flimsy cardboard is legible to the passing cars. Now she realises it would have been worth the hassle of opening her suitcase to find a pen.

It only takes a few minutes for a large pig truck to stop. Delphi's melancholy bubbles up like yeast as she sees the condemned pigs' snouts pressed out between the bars, snuffling in their last free air. She pats a snout and wishes the animal luck then wipes the gunk off her hand onto her trousers.

She reaches up and opens the passenger door. The pig farmer is wearing a sweaty hat and a necklace with a gleaming cross around his woody neck. He starts talking Italian fast. Her ear is still attuning but she doesn't try too hard to decipher the words as she's looking for instinctual clues regarding his sanity. She thinks he's okay so she shoves her case in and climbs up after it. The windows are open which doesn't help much with the stench, but that gets better as they pick up speed.

On his dashboard, looking out at the road, is a small garden gnome. Like a figurehead on the prow of a ship but less queenly. It's fixed in place by a large wodge of BluTac. Delphi points at it and smiles. The farmer looks at her confused, unable to understand her meaning. *'Lascia che ti mostri,'* she says digging around in her handbag, and brings out Vivian's gnome. She holds him up and the pig farmer hoots, slapping his knee. Delphi sees that joy sits close to the surface in him and it warms her.

'Umberto!' the driver explains the name of his gnome. And Delphi introduces My Dear Friend, having him bow to both driver and statue.

'Mio caro amico?' the farmer asks, as if this is the most hilarious name he's ever heard. Delphi confirms it and he slaps his knee with unabashed merriment.

Delphi props her own gnome on her knees so he can see where they're going, heading away from Florence and into the hills beyond.

*

It takes three separate rides to be delivered to the base of the driveway, up which Delphi lugs herself. For ten minutes she follows the dirt road, wending her way higher into the mellow hills. Poplars and olive trees flank her pilgrimage, dust is clinging to her boots. She's not seen any dwelling other than long abandoned stone ruins. This is Da Vinci country.

Large steel gates loom before her path. Delphi checks the rusty chain which is fastened with a padlock. She puts down her suitcase and stretches her back. What now? The gate is out of the question as impalement would be the most probable outcome. Also a break-in seems a bad choice, so Delphi settles down to wait for someone to come by. She will practice patience, not a skill she's ever worked on, but it's early afternoon, the temperature is pleasant, she has water. She hopes she is in the right place and lies down with her bag beneath her head. The blue sky is decorated with fluffy clouds and a small hawk glides by, hunting for prey in the long grass.

*

It takes her brain a few moments to get her bearings and recognise that someone is blocking out the sun.

'Ciao sorella. Parlare Italiano?'

Squinting and bringing her hand up to shield her eyes, Delphi answers, '*Si* or *Inglese*.' Her mouth is dry.

The women regard each other. One with open curiosity and the other with a rough attempt at composure.

The woman has flowers braided into her hair. With the light behind her it looks like she has a halo. Delphi rises onto her elbow.

'You were sleeping.' The woman's American accent is foreign in this landscape and goes against Delphi's expectations. 'I didn't want to wake you. You looked peaceful and seriously tired. Like you'd never slept before.'

It's disquieting to think this stranger has been observing her sleeping. That defenselessness and unfurled softness usually the privilege of kin and lovers.

'Is anyone expecting you?' the American asks.

Delphi sits up fully and shakes her head. She suspects her defensiveness is making her appear hostile. Strategically that would be stupid, as this American seems to be the gatekeeper.

Delphi can't find it inside herself to smile, to open, to radiate any warmth. All she can locate is her own desperation.

'Are you comin'?' the American asks, pushing the gate open.

Delphi jumps to her feet, panicking that the offer might be retracted if she delays.

'Can I take your bag for you, Sister?'

Delphi shakes her head even though her shoulder muscles protest. She takes her first step onto the land of hope and restitution.

'Thank you,' she says to the American and notices the woman can't be much more than nineteen. She has a smattering of freckles across her apple cheeks and a wholesome appearance. Delphi tugs at her AC/DC t-shirt and looks down at her leather pants and biker boots. She craves to swim in a waterfall. To scrub her face clean of the black eyeliner and heavy mascara. To acetone away the black nail polish. To wear a long dress like her companion, to feminise, to be in gentleness and in flow.

*

The American ushers Delphi into a large stone building. The cobbles are shiny underfoot as they walk into a quadrangle. Inside a man is sitting, chatting while shucking peas. Others are listening as they fold clean sheets. They look at Delphi and their smiles are welcoming. They address the American as sister and Delphi notices a room to the side which has a colossal loom in it.

'This used to be a nunnery,' the American explains. 'For eight hundred years or something. But it's been ours for the last thirty-five, and we feel lucky to be here, like the custodians of a powerful building and its lands. There are 106 people here who are part of the family. I came from the States eight years ago with my parents and two older sisters. We love it.'

The American directs Delphi up a flight of stairs. Each one is worn low from a million footfalls. Delphi looks at them and wonders who has walked here before her as she follows the American up to the top, where she knocks on a wooden door before turning the heavy metal latch. They step over the partitioning into a slightly musty room.

'Hello, Gita, I'm happy we located you so easily. I found this pretty lady sleeping at our gates.' Delphi is presented and observed. She puts down her suitcase and offers her hand to the erect woman in front of her.

Gita rises from her desk, ignores the hand and wraps her arms around Delphi. The physical intimacy takes Delphi off guard and she flushes. Don't let me go, Delphi thinks. Gita walks back to sit at her desk. A large painting of Ganesha is on one wall, on another is Buddha and beside him is a photo of Martin Luther King, Jr.

'Please take a seat,' Gita gestures to Delphi, and the American takes her leave saying playfully, 'Goodbye Sleeping Beauty. I hope I see you later.'

Gita's white hair is pinned back neatly from her square face. Her eyes are almost the same shade of grey as her simple dress.

'What is your name, young lady?' she asks. Her accent is too complicated to decode. Maybe she's Hungarian? Or from one of the Slavic countries?

'My name is Delphi Hoffman. I'm from England and my friend Art Horowitz knew Lorenzo. He suggested I come here.'

Gita is nodding, processing the information with focus.

'And why did Mr Horowitz send you to us?'

It's such a simple question yet Delphi struggles to answer. Gita waits, unflappable.

'I have come to a crossroads, I guess. I was hoping I might find a home here. With the community. Your ideology inspires me. I want to learn. I want to find my place in the world. Which sounds really pretentious, I know.' Delphi feels exposed and isn't happy with how she answered the question.

Gita's face doesn't change, but her demeanour indicates to Delphi that this was not an unexpected answer. Delphi wonders how many other lost souls have washed up here to be screened and processed. Stamped with a big red *Reject* or a heartwarming blue *Belong!*

'That won't be up to me,' Gita says neutrally. 'Christoph and our family, every member makes a vote, but let's not jump ahead. What I can offer you is a place to stay tonight and you can learn a little about us and we about you. You can meet Christoph, join us for our evening meal and in the next few days we can decide what is meant to be.'

Delphi has been drenched in apprehension for so many weeks that the upside is she'd be hard pressed to feel any more tense. She decides that she will let herself drift with the current. She hasn't the energy to dissemble and it is some relief to acknowledge she has no option but to let go and trust the outcome.

'A few ideologies and directives, for want of a better word, to make you aware of first, Delphi. Here we have no phones, no computers, no drugs, no malice, no meat, no jealousy, no lies. Everyone must work and put the Famiglia first. We believe the rise of individuality has a great deal to answer for, such as terrorism, environmental disaster, political corruption, isolation, greed and intolerance are all right up there on the very long list.'

'Over our time together we will unpack the philosophy of The Bodhi Famiglia but I must ask you while you stay with us to leave your phone and any iPad or computer if you have them, here in the office with me. I assure you they'll be quite safe.'

'Sure, fine,' Delphi agrees, wondering if she'll have time to email her brother and Romy to let them know she's arrived safely. She will post a letter to Art when she can but he won't be home from France for weeks anyway.

'And forgive the invasiveness of this question but are you addicted to any drugs? The reason I ask and I want to make abundantly clear, is that this is not a rehabilitation facility.'

'No,' Delphi reassures her. 'I'm not an addict, for love maybe, but not substances.' She hoped her statement would sound more playful and less true.

Gita tilts her head and asks, 'And are you a reporter? We have nothing to hide but we must protect ourselves from the aggressions and distortions of the outside world.'

'No,' Delphi says, and checks herself to see if this should raise a warning for her. It seems a little off but not unreasonable, at the same time, the hint of a red flag is raised within.

'Superb. Put your electronics in my cupboard, then I will give you a quick tour and find you a bed for tonight. You are encouraged to join us for our mediation which starts in the Buddha Heart soon and dinner is served afterwards. We are very proud that most of our produce is grown by us on our farm. In the early morning there is tai chi and yoga for those who are not milking the cows, feeding the animals or on breakfast duty.'

'Thank you, that all sounds wonderful,' Delphi says.

'I get a warm feeling about you, Delphi. I'm excited to introduce you to Christoph who is an astonishing man, a prophet and our figurehead. We think of him as our father and guide.'

They make their way out of the door and look down on the courtyard. 'You'll find us a very loving and warm community. We respect the planet and each other. It's as simple as that.' A trio below are laughing and Delphi is drawn to their levity. Her concerns about this choice ebb away. As long as she's not forced to wear tie-dye and listen to brainwashing claptrap, this might turn out beautifully.

'Welcome again. Oh, I forgot to ask,' Gita turns back to Delphi. 'You're not pregnant, are you?'

Confused and affronted Delphi stammers, 'What?'

Gita mishears her, 'You're not? Excellent. I'm thinking the blue cottage would be the place for you to rest.'

Delphi presses her hand to the cool sandstone wall, swallowing the impulse to be ill. Maybe this is actually a terrible mistake.

CHAPTER 19

GITA SHOWS DELPHI AROUND and everything springs with life and warmth. The vegetable gardens are lovingly organised. The chickens and cows, protected for their eggs and milk, are never to be slaughtered. Light-footed silky-coated dogs rumble and play in the long grass. Women in sundresses, some with scarves wrapped around their heads, pick flowers or tend to fruit trees. Two men stripped to their waists, and a woman with her skirt tucked up are mending a fence. Everything is suffused in flaxen light that would make Vermeer swoon.

Delphi is awestruck by the gentleness that she can see around her. She can almost feel the tranquility press soft against her.

The cottage she is to stay in this evening is lifted straight from a fairytale. Symmetrical, tiny, ivy grows thickly over it. Inside is warm, insulated by the foot-wide, white-washed stone walls: a small immaculately clean kitchen, spartan furniture, lace curtains filtering the light. Her share room has two single beds pressed to either wall and a wooden chest of drawers supporting an enamel jug of water beside two clean stacked glasses. Wildflowers are on the bedside table in an earthenware vase. It is monastic in its simplicity. Delphi loves it and she adds her own prayer of gratitude. The word 'salvation' echoes with the beat of her hopeful heart. She so wants this to work.

Gita introduces her to Sylvia, with whom she will be sharing the cottage and then takes her exit. Sylvia smiles uninhibitedly at Delphi. She's in her late forties and has silver bangles on both wrists. Her body is solid, yet she moves her head like a bird full of alert curiousity, radiating robust good health.

'Welcome.' Sylvia has a German accent. She takes Delphi's hands, shakes them and gives them a warm pat too.

'Are you going to come along to join us for meditation? It's about to start.' Sylvia's eyes twinkle, and Delphi notices the clear whites around her irises. This woman lives well, she seems to know how to be in the world. Delphi rubs at her own smarting eyes and feels squalid with travel and loss. Exhaustion yanks and tugs.

'I would like to come, thank you. May I wash my hands first?'

'Oh yes, the bathroom is behind you. We need to leave in two minutes as we cannot be late.' Sylvia smiles again. Delphi wonders where she's from in Germany and imagines she looks absolutely fantastic in lederhosen.

'Have you lived here long, Sylvia?'

'Oh yes, many years now. Back when Lorenzo was our guide. As Gita will have explained we have lots of people wanting to join as a kind of gap year or with unfocused or incompatible intentions. At the moment we are at maximum capacity and I don't mean to sound unwelcoming but I doubt you'll be granted permission to stay. We've not had a new member for well over a year now.'

Sylvia's well-meaning directness takes the wind out of Delphi's sails. She goes to the bathroom and busies herself. The soap smells like lavender, and Delphi steadies herself against the basin.

*

Sylvia takes off her shoes and holds Delphi's hand as they walk into the Buddha Heart. This is the only new building Delphi has seen on the property. It is filled with people sitting cross-legged on the ground, chatting. Delphi notices a group of children on the far side of the hexagonal space. Their ages range from ten down to tiny babes in arms. Delphi stops herself from instinctively touching her belly.

She follows Sylvia into the sea of people where she is handed a red cushion and sits, drawing her legs up so as to not take up too much space. The bald man beside her nods acknowledgement and the woman in front of Delphi is wearing a headdress of feathers. Diagonally across is a person wearing an Egyptian scarab t-shirt who is fiddling with his multiple beaded bracelets. Sylvia emanates inclusivity and excitement. A hush falls over the group as Gita stands in the centre of the round. She brings her hands to prayer position.

'Namaste Bodhis.'

The entire congregation answers her by gathering their hands into the same position over their hearts. 'Namaste, Sister Gita.'

Delphi notices how radiant everyone looks, their faces shining with happiness and presence. She studies them, hunting for anyone that looks evangelical or flat-out nuts, but what she sees is wonderful. It's multicultural, many aged, alert and manifest.

Gita gestures for the lights to be lowered and takes her seat within the throng. No one speaks. They sit in expectant silence. Delphi wonders what they're waiting for, but it doesn't take long for it to become abundantly clear. A man dressed in white has appeared. He is very tall and stretches his arms wide to embrace the room. He looks as expansive and solid as Apollo himself. He closes his eyes; the planes and contours of his face are extreme, black triangular hollows sculpt the space below his wide cheekbones. He breathes in and everyone takes his cue and does the same. He draws his palms together, opens his eyes, looks around warmly and says, 'Namaste family.' His voice is orotund, like a harnessed sonic boom.

Delphi is fascinated. So this is Christoph. His charisma is as powerful as anything Delphi has ever witnessed. Cynicism and suspicion prick her thoughts. She wonders if he has the substance to back up his genetic win. Just because you look born to godliness doesn't mean you are a power for good. Also, Christoph inherited this position as figurehead from his father. Nepotism is perennially undermining in Delphi's opinion. Privilege skews any playing field, entitlement renders everyone else handicapped. Delphi refuses to be hoodwinked by theatrics nor by hands that look like they could raise the dead.

Christoph sits down, arranges his long legs, his back perfectly straight, and invites the room to begin.

A fluttering of settling ripples around the room and when there is stillness Christoph speaks, 'Please set your intention for your mediation this evening.'

Delphi finds it impossible to shut her eyes as everyone around her is doing. She tries, but her desire to study this man sitting in the light is too strong. Delphi fears that she might have become a moth.

'Let us begin with three oms.'

She forces herself to shut her eyes and joins the gentle chant. The vibration of her voice buzzes comfortingly in her chest. On the third om she is more anchored. She opens her eyes and Christoph is looking at her. It is invasive yet altogether astonishing. She wants to look away, to protect herself, but she holds his gaze. A single beat and then he shuts his eyes, cutting her off, plummeting her into darkness.

*

After the meditation the group relocates to a hall to eat. Trestle tables run the length of the room, candles and jam jars full of flowers are placed along them.

Delphi is ravenous. She restrains herself at the buffet. Turning back to find a seat she looks at the community and is again struck by how lovely it all is. People laughing, pouring water, passing the breadbasket, talking animatedly. The energy is swirling with colour and enthusiasm. It is in her nature to safeguard against disappointment by holding herself apart. But at this moment she feels no cynicism. If religion is indeed the opiate of the masses, whatever is happening here is the reverse. Delphi is self-conscious in comparison to these activated souls. She feels so battered by life, to be accepted as part of this group seems like radical hope. These people are integrated, comfortable with themselves and sure of where they are.

'Excuse me, Sister?' Delphi turns to look at the young man who is addressing her. He has close-cropped blond hair and a well-mended harelip. The fine scaring across the tender flesh of his lip, running up and into his nostril, is both a tragedy and the making of him.

'I am Gabriel and Christoph was hoping you would sit with him.'

'Okay, thank you,' she responds. She is aware that a slight flickering has been set off in her eye, an unwelcome nervous tic.

Gabriel shows her to a seat, takes her plate and puts it down between a knife and fork. Delphi slips onto the bench and Christoph is talking to the person on his other side. He becomes aware of her arrival and turns to face her. Delphi's breath freezes. Without offering her his hand he introduces himself: 'So you are, Delphi? I am Christoph. Gita has told me you come to us via a friend of my father's?'

'Yes, Art Horowitz. He met your father briefly in London years and years ago and had a friend who came here for a time. I have a letter from him for you. From Art, that is. Not the friend. I don't know her. Her name was Alice, I think, but I can't remember.'

Christoph's wrists are roped with wooden prayer beads. Studying his face Delphi can't determine whether Art's name means anything. It certainly doesn't herald the opening of the drawbridge as she hoped. Delphi coaches her breathing back to some kind of regularity. Her natural impulse is to ask questions but he has her silenced. She twists a napkin in her hands beneath the table. His eyes are nearly gold, more amber, like a wolf's.

She wants to talk about their colour but fears it will be read as flirtation. She thinks about the dog she hit in Adarsha's VW. Him closing his saffron eyes for the final time. Her burying him as her mother lay dead on the opposite side of the planet. Delphi shudders.

'And what are you looking for here with us?' Christoph asks.

She stalls by taking a sip of water and a sprig of rosemary gets stuck against her lip. Delphi wipes it away, and he moves as if to help her but drops his hand instead. She forces herself to look at him.

'I want…' In for a penny in for a pound, she tells herself. 'I want a good life. And I don't… well, I don't think I, I want somewhere where I fit.'

He nods. 'Are you religious?'

She takes her time. 'I'm an agnostic, who… misses God. I want to be part of something, not have my life fade out wasted.'

'Wasted on what?'

'Um, on inconsequentialities.'

He nods. 'What else?'

'Illusions. Dead ends. Malformed love.'

She's not at all sure giving him this much truth is sensible. She doesn't want to sound like a fool and these are her most private thoughts and fears.

A pause sits between them, undulating. Then he asks, 'And what are you running from?' Delphi vaguely registers this as a question designed to reveal more of her than she'd like to give and his intentions, she instinctively registers, are not entirely good.

Delphi bristles with distrust. The focus and directness of him are derailing. She presses her lips together, relaxes them, scratches her cheek and answers, 'Death and loneliness.'

He leans toward her and she feels dizzy.

'And what would you contribute here? What is it that Delphi offers?' Is his tone playful or mocking? And why did he refer to her in the third person?

'I…' She falters, considering. 'I don't know, to be honest. I'm not afraid of hard work.'

'No,' he states and she's stumbled at the hurdle. He waits for her to get up and do better. He is deft at using silence to extract information from her.

'I can paint…' She hates that the words that escape from her sound like a question rather than a declaration. Her insecurity has betrayed her. Christoph doesn't miss a beat. Tilting his head, he gives her another chance.

Delphi shakes off incredulity. 'I'm in pain right now, but I've faith that I can heal and when I'm whole again I want to create, I want to contribute, and I want to love and be loved.'

He is so close she can smell his skin. He is looking at her as if he sees right through her, right into the darkest parts that she keeps hidden. She is frightened of him yet she aches to turn her face into the crook of his neck and dissolve into him. She imagines herself kneeling at his feet and is shocked at her subjugation and surrender.

Gabriel leans over and touches Christoph on the shoulder reverentially. The men's heads dip together intimately. Delphi thinks for a frightful moment that she has cut herself open, and Christoph is leaving her truth discarded on the floor. Christoph turns back to her and says, 'I'm not convinced we are a fit for you, Delphi from England. This is not a health retreat. People come here for life, not for a reset.' She is plunged into an ice bath. Christoph offers her his upturned hand. She slips hers into it and he turns it over to inspect her palm, drawing a circle on it with his finger. Then folds her fingers up, returns her hand and sets off in the direction he's been called.

*

Delphi guesses it's after 10 pm. She and Sylvia lie in their matching single beds talking and looking at the ceiling.

'Isn't he incredible?' the older woman asks, referring to Christoph. 'He is very different from his father, but such a gift. Truly the single most evolved human being I've ever met.' Delphi doesn't want to talk about Christoph anymore. She finds her thoughts circling back to him repeatedly and she refuses to foster a fixation on him. What a cliché for her to arrive at a commune, outrunning personal devastation only to throw herself at the guru who beguiles with his steady gaze and prayer beads.

'Sylvia, in the Buddha Heart I saw a group of children, but they weren't at dinner?'

'Ah, our children. They all live together in Cub House. You would have seen it up on the hill behind the kitchens. The house with the big verandahs? Such a view up there, right down over the valley. The adults are on rotation to supervise their care in the crèche, and for those ones old enough, their classes. They're having the most astonishing childhoods, surrounded by nature, and their learnings are underpinned by the best of Steiner and Montessori. They tend vegetables, interact with the farm animals, go on daily nature walks. They practice yoga and meditation. It's highly progressive and very loving.'

Delphi watches the shadows move and they look tidal, rippling across the ceiling. She thinks of her baby floating within the amniotic fluid inside her.

'That sounds so much better than my school experience,' Delphi offers. 'I was shunted off to a super strict boarding school. I don't think I learnt a thing, other than to rote learn and regurgitate.' She doesn't add that it was a prolonged study in loneliness. 'So, the children are up there during the day and then they go home to their parents?' She closes her eyes, the bed is so comfortable.

'Oh no, they live in Cub House all the time. In The Bodhi Famiglia we believe and put into practice the saying that "it takes a village to raise a child". Here we don't believe in ownership or the genetic link with the children. We are all mothers and fathers. Each and every child is our responsibility.'

Delphi's eyes flick open, she turns towards Sylvia in the darkness. 'You mean you take the children away from their mothers? At what age?'

'Take them away?' Sylvia sounds comically appalled. 'It's not like that, Delphi. This isn't *A Handmaid's Tale*. Biological parents don't expect to live with their child here. When a baby is born it has six weeks to breastfeed and then they are moved to the Cub House. I can take you up there if you're interested and you can see how wonderful it is and how well-adjusted, empathetic and thriving those small humans are.'

Delphi swallows.

'Gita asked me if I was pregnant before she let me stay. What was that about?'

Sylvia readjusts her sheets as she rolls over onto her side. 'Oh, that's because we don't accept unconscious conceptions anymore.'

Delphi doesn't understand what that means. She wants to ask but Sylvia is tired, and Delphi decides it best to tread carefully. Whatever the explanation, there's no way she'd give up her child to be raised on that hill.

Sylvia's voice is softer and her Germanic accent more apparent as she slips towards sleep. 'I heard you met Christoph at dinner. Did he mention your test?'

'My test?' Delphi asks. 'No, what test, what is it?'

'Oh, nothing to worry about. It probably won't even happen. I shouldn't have said anything. Gossiping is a pattern I'm working on. I'm such a blabbermouth. It was just that Gabriel said he thought you might have made an impression.'

Delphi is jolted awake by the possibility she's rippled the ocean that is Christoph. A test? She hates tests. She won't be part of any sacrificial ritual bullshit. She's read far too many books on the occult, but nothing that's happened here has given her pause, other than the Cub House separation business. This place is nirvana. It's a haven. Delphi suspects it's the conservatism and fear baked into her English bones keeping her shackled within traditional modes of living and freaked out by an idea like raising children away from their biological parents. Here they're doing something different, refusing a model of childrearing that doesn't work. Delphi thinks of her family and how things worked out there. Here the people are setting out to create something better. It's heroic, maybe even revolutionary. Delphi's feelings and responses are mixed. She observes herself justifying the information she has heard while being here. She also registers herself dampening down her instincts but the thought of being able to live striving towards goodness, and living in attunment with the planet and other people, it inspires her.

*

Everyone sits in the Buddha Heart in wrapped silence as Christoph concludes his sermon. He has been talking, teaching, musing, sharing for several hours and Delphi is blown wide open by his brilliance. Everything he's said has landed within her as a personal reckoning.

'Thank you all for being here. Thank you for turning up, truly choosing to be present today.'

He sits down cross-legged and drops his head in respect to his crowd.

'We are a flock, a group in flight together. Here…' he opens his arms wide, 'you have created something powerful. A culture based on kindness, inquiry and love. And just this morning together we have explored some immense ideas. What have we mined?' He holds a hand out to the audience indicating the question isn't rhetorical.

The group calls out the topics that interested them and Delphi trawls through her thoughts. It struck her when Christoph was unpacking the concept of wholeheartedness, that it's not about striving for perfection but embracing our brokenness as an inevitable and integral part of being human. And when he stipulated the difference between fitting in and belonging, Delphi had felt in that moment that she was having her deepest longing, her most elemental desire explained to her.

Christoph had invited the group to be vigilant about fostering self-compassion and put forward his fundamental belief that everyone is doing the best they can. Delphi had never thought that true before, but now she can see how it may be so. It redefines her father for her and she observes her love for him stir. As Christoph said, it can't be proven either way, but choosing to believe it will make life better, to move through the world in a spirit of generosity and non-judgement. Even exploring the surface of that idea had reduced the pressure in Delphi's head.

She makes eye contact with Sylvia and they smile warmly at each other.

'We can't know what we don't know,' Christoph says, and Delphi lifts her face to listen again. 'Our blind spots are un-seeable until we choose to actively seek them out and turn the light of awareness onto them, by employing rigorous self-enquiry. Do you want to live in the shadows or in the truth of the light?' He looks at her and Delphi only just catches the burning impulse to speak her affirmative answer aloud to him. His eyes move on.

'Last night I reread that terrific quote by Aristotle, that *real knowledge is finding the depth of our own ignorance*.' Delphi processes this and nods. The woman beside her reaches over and rubs Delphi's back and the unsolicited contact makes her uncomfortable. Delphi smiles awkwardly and returns her eyes to Christoph.

'So, you must all be hungry and forgive me talking too much but the last thing I want to say today before we all have lunch is the following. Every human being on earth just wants to be met.' This he feels is important enough to say twice.

'Please think about what that means to you. How do you like to be listened to? What does it mean to be actively engaged with? What is the difference between sympathy and empathy and how do you live more in the latter? Help each other, soothe each other, meet each other. You don't need to be alone here; you don't need to be afraid. Who was it that said, happiness is so amazing it doesn't even matter if it's yours? Do not combust with rage directed at shortsighted politicians. Live courageously. Be daring. One precious life. Well, until the next one.' People like his joke and they laugh warmly. Delphi tries to work out if he sincerely believes in reincarnation.

He smiles, presses his hands together into prayer position and releases the gathering with: 'Namaste Bodhis.'

The reply comes with sincerity: 'Namaste Brother Christoph.' People turn to each other and hug or help each other up. Some beeline for the dining hall, others loiter to talk further, sharing, questioning. Delphi is dazed. Dropping into the white space within her she retrieves a single thought. She is seduced. On an epic scale. Mentally and emotionally seduced and just to look at Christoph is to taste physical longing. She's vanquished by his energy alone. But Delphi doesn't want those feelings. It's all so touchy feely here.

Skepticism reclaims her and Delphi stabilises more sober and like herself.

*

During lunch, she's conscious of Christoph's eyes on her several times and finds her toes curling in her boots as she shields her face from him. Afterwards, she is assigned chores which she does committedly. She misses her mother as keenly as a trapped bird would the open sky, and being busy helps.

In the afternoon she rejoins the group outside the Buddha Heart for a meditation. Delphi has not done a formal walking meditation before. She falls into line and a woman she's not met before, Spanish, explains to her that all she needs to do is stay as present as possible. In her curling accent, she instructs: 'There's no getting it right or wrong. Just stay in observation. When distraction arises return to the breath.' She gives Delphi's forearm a convivial squeeze.

As they are about to set off Christoph appears and slips into the line directly behind Delphi. When she was a little girl, and Vivian was making the beds, her mother would raise the top sheet high into the air, and as it was aloft, Delphi would dive in under it to have it flutter down on her face. It was unadulterated joy. Delphi feels like that now.

She is flush with the effect of him, and when she finally marshals the courage to look, he is waiting for her. His face open, his soul lit, his attention placed on her like a garland of flowers.

The crocodile line begins to walk in slow motion. They are silent, eyes lowered, merely following the person in front of them. Delphi regulates her breathing and observes her mind thrashing against what is being asked of it. She focuses on the legs of the woman before her and inches forward. Considered, mindful. And yet every few minutes she's hijacked by his presence behind her. Christoph's proximity is as penetrating as the heat thrown from a colossal fire.

*

The last of the sunlight is blazing shafts between the clouds. Delphi is sitting alone in a field digging her fingers into the soil. She is exultant, a similar wakefulness to post ayahuasca. Her life force is palpable to her. During the ayahuasca ceremony Delphi had seen the trees breathing, and now each and every one pulses and respirates before her. What a place this is, what a community, and Christoph... with every interaction, she finds him more mesmerising. Yet she has enough self-awareness to know a woman in freefall doesn't have the wherewithal to understand true north. When it comes to love, Delphi's compass is scrambled at the best of times, and now is the worst of times. To fall for him would be insanity, and yet her crush is so visceral she's tempted to call it divine providence.

'I have been looking for you, Delphi.' She looks up, and it's him. She feels caught out and turns away.

'May I join you?'

Without looking at him, she says, 'Of course, sit, the sun is just about to go, your timing is perfect.' She lifts her face to the horizon and yet is attuned only to him as he claims the space beside her.

'Beautiful,' he says.

'It is,' she answers.

They sit quietly together. And yet Delphi is filled with him, permeated, inebriated, high. She wrangles the twirling girl within her out of sight. Falling for someone is a deranged business.

'Delphi, I have been thinking about you, and I have a problem.'

Oh God, this is when he asks me to leave, Delphi thinks.

He carries on.

'You and I don't know each other, not in the way it's usually spoken of, but I feel that I do know you. You are familiar to me. Recognisable. It's uncanny.'

Delphi is holding her breath.

'I can see you're in pain, in trauma. I want to be respectful of that, and in all honesty, I'm wary of it too. And yet I find myself sitting here with you and, quite simply, there's no place I'd rather be.'

Delphi turns to look at him. His face is directed down the valley. She is frozen like a deer listening for signs in the woods.

Christoph turns to Delphi and meets her head on. The curve of his eye, the broadness of his face; Delphi leans in to kiss him. Just as her lips touch his he recoils, tilting his forehead forward and she is left hanging. He closes his eyes and shakes his head, releasing a thousand insects to swarm across Delphi's pride.

'Incandescent, courageous Delphi.'

She tightens, trying to mask her distress.

He touches her hair. Then he presses the ends of it to his mouth and kisses it.

Nighttime has fallen now on both sides of her skin.

He stands: 'May I help you up?'

I hoped you could, Delphi says to herself, but to him, she offers a congenial: 'No thank you.' She stands and busies herself brushing her hands on her thighs. They cross the field and return to the path. A couple sees them and calls out. There is chatting about dinner, and the quartet moves towards it together – Delphi strategically using these bubbly carefree folk as a buffer between herself and the man she so desires. Nausea waves up. Is it morning sickness, lovesickness or both?

*

Delphi is woken very early the following morning.

'It's time to get up,' whispers Sylvia while shaking Delphi's shoulder.

'Am I being thrown out?' Delphi asks blearily, pushing her wild hair back from her face.

'No.' Delphi's brain is slowly coming online, and she allows herself to be led from the bed and out into the small sitting room. Two women are standing there waiting like handmaidens. There's a seriousness to them, but Delphi thinks she detects excitement too.

'Take off your night dress, Delphi,' and she does as she's told. Only when it's over her head does she think it's a little strange to be standing naked with three people, two of whom she couldn't name.

It's not the first time this has happened to her, but the last time she was high as a kite.

A white dress is dropped over her and falls long around her calves. Woman One takes a brush to Delphi's hair and twists it off her face, then Woman Two threads it with white flowers. Sylvia looks at her watch.

'My shoes?' Delphi asks as she's ushered towards the doorway.

'You won't need them,' says Woman One and they set off into the darkness following Sylvia's torch beam. Delphi can hear the animals beginning to wake and the rustle of wind in the big tree of indeterminate species that kisses against the cottage. In silence with her hand being held Delphi is walked past the vegetable gardens and along the stone wall. After a few minutes, they reach a gate and move through it into the orchard. The trees look spooky, illumined by the flash of the arm swung torch, but Delphi only shivers from the cold.

Getting to the far side of the trees, Delphi is now beyond where she's explored during her stay. She sees people, all women, up ahead. They are standing around waiting, flaming fire torches light them up. When they see Delphi they smile and each come to give her a hug. She recognises the bonnie American who rescued her from the front gate and is grateful for her extra warmth. Each woman takes a position, forming a circle. Delphi is mystified and yet stands un-cowered where she is placed in the centre of the ring. Sylvia switches off her touch and joins the circumference. Delphi looks at their faces, kind and reassuring. So, she's not to be sacrificed then? Which is a relief as this smacks of a coven – but in actuality, it scans as a ritualised expression of sisterhood. Delphi recognises that those two ideas are not necessarily mutually exclusive.

Dawn is beginning to break. Delphi tilts her face towards the heavens and the night sky is lifting toward purple. She sees the scene then as if from above – her standing dressed in white, surrounded by attentive women and dancing flames.

Christoph calls her name, and Delphi looks for him. He steps into the circle, and she instinctively wants to cross her arms over herself but she refuses to shrink.

He seems to be glowing in the shifting light. He speaks to the group, 'Dawn is such a powerful time, particularly for new beginnings.'

Delphi keeps her head level and watches him as he walks toward her. He stops two meters away and smiles.

'Delphi, we very much want you to come to live with us. To be a part of our family.' Delphi senses warmth spread through her body. So, this is her tribe after all, she's finally found them in her darkest hour. The women are all smiling, happy, eager.

Christoph moves a few steps closer. 'Delphi why are you in so much pain?'

She takes a breath and answers him. 'My mother died. Recently.'

'And?' he has an extraordinary ability to know when to keep tapping a vein.

'She asked me to help her… and I wanted to but I couldn't. And now I… don't…'

He looks suffused with compassion. 'You must learn to love your suffering. To sit with the pain. Don't silence it, fight it or run from it. Learn what it has to teach you. It is your antipathy to it that makes you suffer. As the Buddhists teach us through the notion of radical acceptance suffering is simply not accepting what is.'

Delphi thinks on this and says, 'That sounds clever… but it doesn't help me. I love her and now she's gone. Even if I give in entirely to that philosophy, the core truth remains the same. I'm without her.'

Christoph looks around at the women and they back at him. Delphi doesn't understand what has passed between them.

'What is your biggest secret?'

Delphi knows immediately that she won't tell them about her pregnancy, but she will give them a truth.

'My father doesn't love me.' She manages to get the words out dispassionately.

'And what is the worst thing you have ever done?' he asks.

'Why do you want to know that?'

'Because you have arrogance in you and strength in abundance. Put your greatest regret, your most appalling shame on the floor for us to see and let's become true family.'

Delphi, usually guarded, knows she has nothing left to lose and the answer doesn't require hunting for.

'I let my baby brother drown when I was meant to be looking after him.' She waits for a flicker of horror to race across Christoph's face. But he remains connected to her, with her. The longer she looks at him, the harder it gets for her to fight the tears, and they come, as there are just too many for her soul to hold, like a soaked sponge lifted from the ocean – an enormous outpouring of liquid grief.

Christoph walks towards her and leans so close she can feel his breath.

'Don't grow old together with what frightens you.' His arms encircle her waist, and then he kisses her. She reaches up around his neck and kisses him back. Her tears spill down her face. She can taste the salt of them along with him. Delphi senses the casing of her shell dissolve, and a softness revealed. She wants to stay within him. Consumed, enfolded, claimed, forgiven.

Christoph releases her and Delphi is acutely aware the women are watching them. She touches her lips with her fingers and looks down at her bare feet in the grass. There is more light now. Dawn has risen in celebration.

'So do you want to stay with us?' He asks.

'Of course,' she answers. And he picks her up and twirls her around. She hears the women clapping.

'Then it will be so, but two things. The first is you must commit fully to us. You must relinquish any family ties that you have out in the world.'

She thinks longingly only of her brother but cuts the cord on her pain. This man standing directly in front of her is more real and persuasive than an absent brother.

'Done,' she says. 'And what's the second?'

'That you receive a marking on your body.'

'I'm not sure. What's it of? What would it mean?'

Sylvia speaks up, 'It's a mark that we women all share. It means you are one of us.'

'Is it a tattoo?' Delphi asks.

'No, we use a firebrand. It's an ancient method.'

'Branding? Like on a cow?' Delphi suspects they are teasing.

Christoph smiles and shakes his head. He runs a finger along the exposed part of her collar bone.

'You are such a proud creature, Delphi. And you have a need to be perceived as special. To truly join us you must find a deep humility, and your reluctance is a good thing. Feel it. Study it. The discomfort you're experiencing is actually burning down the resistance to your own liberation.'

He leans in and kisses her. He cups the back of her neck in his hand and whispers, 'No rush. Think about it. But how wonderful that you've arrived.' He takes her hand and places it on his heart. 'I was waiting for you.'

CHAPTER 20

Waking up beside Christoph she can't remember the last time she felt so buoyant. The soft midday light looks to be sanctifying his sleeping form. She wants to reach out and run her fingers over his lips but is loath to wake him, to violate the divinity of the moment.

It is a pleasing room; his walls are wood panelled, his bed a four-poster, a few good pieces of art have been gathered up from his travels. Pens, leather-bound notebooks, jottings of quotes, are littered around. Vased flowers have dropped their petals onto his desk. A lone aubergine sits on an armchair, as sensual as any Renaissance painting. Candles stand along the windowsills. Their black wicks and uneven heights speak of nights past. Delphi wishes she'd been present for all of them. The only photograph in the room is of two women: one younger, the other older. Genetics alone could tell Delphi these are his mother and sister. They look out of the frame with the same fierce grace that Christoph has. It makes Delphi return to her wonderings about families that are unbroken.

She looks up and amber prayer beads hang from the light-fitting above. They glow golden like her joy. She gently presses her body down the length of his. She kisses his neck, holds her breath, kisses him again. He starts to wake, and she whispers into his ear; 'I'm falling in love with you.' She hadn't planned to say it, but the superb wonder of it billows inside her like silk caught in a breeze.

'What did you say?' he mumbles.

'I am falling in love with you.'

'Say it again.' He rolls on top of her and kisses her mouth, her neck, the line between her breasts and down over her belly.

'And right here is where my mark will be.' His lips warm the flesh of her hip.

'Your mark?' She shuts her eyes and tilts her head back.

'It's your mark too, but it's my initials.'

'Your initials? Seriously, you want to brand me with your initials?' She's laughing.

He moves further down her body and kisses the inside of her thigh. 'My darling, my love, it's a talisman, a symbol of belonging, not ownership. And it will also be my honour.' He carries on down her legs and when he reaches her feet he says, 'I am your servant.' He is looking up at Delphi traversing the curves of her naked body, and she is plummeting. Malleable. Dissolving. He tracks his way up the length of her, holding her gaze, and he lets his weight down and she feels the breath pushed from her lungs. The mass of him earths her.

Gesturing towards the photo of his family Delphi asks, 'Where are your mother and sister now?' He turns as if looking to be reminded who she means and then he places his head down on her breasts and answers, 'They're both dead too.' Delphi is paralysed by this and he says, 'Do you mind if we don't talk about that now? Ask me something else. Anything else?'

'Of course,' she answers and pulls the first thing she can think of from the sky.'

'Why didn't you let me kiss you in the field the other day?'

'Ah, I was still resisting. I don't want to be another person who hurts you.'

'I'm not a victim. I don't want you to infantilise me.' She is holding a second truth in her deck – that she also does long to be taken care of and protected – but the idea of transferring this to Christoph, of burdening him with the un-parented parts of herself is revolting to her.

As if reading her mind, he says, 'I'm not attempting to patronise you, I'm simply stating a fact that when there is a great love, there is extra responsibility. We are stronger together than apart. I will hold your hand, and you will hold mine. Me looking after you doesn't make you weak. With the roles reversed the truth is the same. I want to see how far we can go.'

'I think bravery is usually rewarded. And my tendency is to go all the way. I'm told this is another fault of mine, risk taking.' She runs her fingers through his hair.

Christoph kisses her and as he begins to make love to her he says, 'All the way?' Looking directly into her eyes. 'Let's see if I can match you. I want you to have my child.' The audacity of the statement is breathtaking. Delphi obscures her face from his gaze. The secret of her womb coils itself tightly like a snake.

She should tell Christoph now, but he is looking at her with adoration. The air is thick with desire and the necessary words don't leave her lips. She silences her fear and she gives herself over to this man as he pushes himself inside her.

*

It's bizarre to Delphi that she has been with The Bodhi Famiglia for more than six weeks now. Her days are taken up with meditations, sermons, yoga, chores and Christoph.

This morning she stood transfixed in a doorway watching a group singing. Their collective exuberance creating almost visible clouds of goodwill. The day before, she sat in on a lecture about the juncture between ancient wisdom and modern science where Christoph shone like the sun, all knowing and core warming. Afterwards, he caught her by the wrist and pulled her into a storage room off the Buddha Heart and fucked her. She thinks back to the intensity and wildness of him, of her legs wrapped around his waist, of the prayer mats that had fallen on them from the shelving. Of him covering her mouth to muffle her screams when she came. They had collapsed to the floor laughing, delirious, conspiratorial.

'What are you smiling about, Sister Delphi?' Her thoughts are interrupted by Layla, one of the people she regularly tends the vegetable gardens with.

'I think I'm just happy.'

'It suits you; you look radiant.'

Layla taps Delphi's shoulder and says, 'A few of us will come to collect you at 10 pm. This evening is your rite of passage. Should we get you from Sylvia's cottage or from Christoph's bed?' Layla's nostrils flair and Delphi tastes bile. This woman has been Christoph's lover too.

'Rite of passage?'

Layla's eyes are cold.

'Your branding.' She smiles and pulls Delphi into an embrace. Delphi's arms remain hanging by her sides.

*

'Christoph, I'm not doing it.' Delphi pushes his hands from her waist. This is something he does, always moves into her space, forever touching. She can't think straight when he's too near to her. Just the smell of him scuppers her.

The three people who were in the meeting with Christoph stand and leave the room discreetly.

'You're so angry, Delphi, so reactive. What would happen if you just let go? I can't set you free, and I know that's what you crave, you must do the work.' He tries to hold her again but she twists out of his grip.

'Delphi, I love you. The whole community loves you.'

'Christoph…' She so wants to believe he will take her by the hands and walk her into the light. It's all been so heady, so romantic, but this *ritual* she can't hurdle. Doubt, cynicism and suspicion canter into the centre of her vision.

'I won't have your initials burnt onto me. You want to brand me like an animal that belongs to you. It's obscene and makes me feel like chattel. Will you be getting my initials on your body too? Do all the women here have the same branding? Layla? Does she have one?' Rage is making Delphi rattle.

'Layla? Oh, Delphi.' Christoph takes a seat and Delphi notices his emotional withdrawal and it makes her feel like she's six years old again.

She's standing over him, her hands on her hips. 'How many of them have been your lover? How many of them still are?'

'You make me sad, darling Delphi. You're my lover. You. But let's not play at puritanism, I'm forty-one, I've slept with people before you which has equipped me with the skills to be ready for this love. For our love.'

His voice is emphatic. 'Don't get stuck on this one small thing or one day you will sincerely regret that you were unable to step up when your time came, that you were cowardly and small. That you turned your face from Truth. That you cursed yourself to live asleep, in darkness, absolutely and completely alone.' He stands and moves in close, his voice low. 'Do you trust me, Delphi? Because I trust you. I believe in you completely. We will have children together. I will marry you. Do this for me, but more importantly do this for yourself. This is the cave you fear to enter which holds the treasure you seek. Step over all your intellectualising. Let go and say yes. It will be such a sweet relief for you. Here is your blind spot my love. Choose to belong with us.'

And with this, he accesses the most hidden place inside her. Everything that has happened in the weeks, months and years preceding, swirl together and detonates. And when the energy is spent and her crying subsides, his arms are around her. He is kissing her face tenderly. Over and over, he consoles her and tells her of his love.

'You are infinitely powerful. That power is yours to harness. I see you, I see your true nature, Delphi. You are safe here with me.'

Delphi is out of fight and in love. She will do anything Christoph asks of her.

*

Delphi is tending to her chores, emptying the bins. She knocks on the cottage doors and if anyone is home she asks them for their rubbish and if they're not she has been told to go in anyway. The community prides itself on not creating much waste so it's not an arduous job, and Delphi likes talking to people as she does her rounds. Gita sees her through her office door but is on the phone. Delphi holds up her bag pantomiming why she's there. Gita beckons her in and Delphi moves inside as unobtrusively as possible. She fishes out the usual haul and transfers it to her canvas bag. She leaves with a smile and Gita gives her an affectionate okay sign, rounding her finger and thumb into a circle.

Delphi takes the stairs down and goes out the back door towards the storage room where she transfers any paper waste into a large bin where it's stored until it's either used for the fireplaces or it's incinerated in a bonfire, which Delphi looks forward to as the community makes it like a festival. She lifts the lid and turns her sack up and the contents fall out. Skittering across the top is a package and Delphi leans over, struck by the pink writing on its face. It's addressed to her and she recognises Romy's looping hand and her characteristic smattering of drawn stars. Delphi reaches in and lifts it out. Intuition makes her look over her shoulder to check that no one is coming and then she moves to the door, shutting herself in. She opens the parcel with her teeth and a letter, a small heart-shaped chocolate and a sticker fall out into her hand. Delphi opens the note:

Dearest De De Delphi!
Art (I completely dig him) reassured me that you haven't run off to join a cult. Have you left a breadcrumb trail so you can escape if you need too? You remember how intense we found the Landmark Forum? All that recruiting madness? You've seen the Book of Mormon *for f*&k's sake! Do the women there have long plaits and wear skirts with elasticated waistbands? If so, run!*

Dude, you've got to get in touch with me ASAP. I've been emailing but Art reckons you don't have your computer or phone, which is weird as f$k but explains why I've not heard from you. Jack called me which was lush after all these years. I still carry a little flame for him if I'm honest but I'm super happy he's settled. He's been trying to contact* *you too FYI. He told me some stuff about your dad. I don't know if you'll even want to hear it or if it's mine to tell but I wanted to raise a flag up the pole in case you do. Your dad is a bit of a specimen, isn't he? Reminds me of the Abraham Lincoln quote, 'I don't like that man. I must get to know him better.' That's awesome, isn't it? Not sure it would help with your father though. Sorry if that's super harsh.*

I hope you're getting stoned, sipping mineral water while patting a donkey. They're nice animals. I'm sure you've heard the theory that A. A. Milne created the animals in Winnie the Pooh *to represent different mental disorders?*

The letter restarts in a different coloured pen.

I've just googled it and here's the list:
Pooh is Impulsivity
Piglet is Anxiety
Roo is Autism
Tiger is ADHD
Eeyore is Depression
Rabbit is OCD
Kanga is Social Anxiety
Owl is Dyslexia
Let's go with that and you're Pooh (impulsive as all get out), and you're sitting (in an enclave with BO and patchouli-smelling recluses) patting Eeyore (depressed donkey). Well, I'm Piglet and I am anxious as hell about you my love, my turtle dove. I'm worrying about your aching heart. And pregnancy. How is that going? My mind is still blown. Call me as soon as you can, please???? I've strapped my mobile to my forehead with gaffer tape in anticipation. So, you have another visual, I'm wearing the most amazingly ace boilersuit I scored at Camden Market.
Lotza Love.
Sorry about the multiple question marks. I know you hate that shitz. Do you mind it as much as the !!!!! factor?
Ever, Rom xxx

Delphi is confused as to how her mail was thrown out. No one told her she couldn't have any contact with the outside world at all. She's not prepared for that, and to throw away her package and God knows what else, and from whom else, Delphi is affronted and sets off back to Gita's office to ask her about it.

*

The office is unattended and Delphi turns in a frustrated circle. She moves towards the cupboard where she placed her phone and computer and tries to open it but it's locked. She sees Gita's landline phone on the desk, as far as she knows it's the only one in the compound. She walks over, sits down in Gita's leather chair and when it squeaks she grimaces. She listens out but can't hear anyone. She scoops up the phone, and it takes her several tries to remember the number, but on the third go Romy picks up and Delphi punches the air in celebration. They both bubble with the happiness of hearing each other's voices. They cover ground quickly talking about Art's return to London, about Romy's band, Delphi's experiences getting to the community and her time here.

'But have you been abducted?' Romy asks with her usual intensity.

'No, of course not. What I'm trying to tell you is that it's a proper community. The foundation of it is about love and inclusivity. There's no goat riding, secret handshakes or bloodletting. Christoph's mind is like a diamond; brilliant at every single angle. He is so free and integrated. When I'm with him, Rom, I feel better.'

'Aye me, I'm not reassured. Christoph sounds like he could well be David Koresh's and Tony Robbins' baby.'

Delphi laughs. 'Now that's an image, but he's not. Christoph is… enlightened.'

'Okaayyy.' The women lapse into silence.

'Are you sleeping with him?'

Delphi doesn't want to answer. Which makes her uncomfortable. She usually tells Romy everything.

'Del, please tell me you're not sleeping with him.'

Delphi is vexed by her rising defensiveness, it nudges at something she's keeping hidden from herself.

Romy takes it further. 'Oh for God's sake, I bet he sleeps with everyone, with all the boys and all the girls. Why else be a cult leader?'

'All he's done is collapse the rules of convention. Here, tradition is thoroughly questioned and held up to the light. Sexuality isn't feared, it's expressed, it's a lens, Rom.'

'What do you mean a lens?'

'It tells powerful stories about who we are, how we see ourselves, about pleasure, our values, our hang ups, about power and connection.' She's quoting Christoph directly. 'Rom, I'm living from a place of love with people who are concerned about our planet, people who are pursuing lives of great meaning.'

'Great meaning? Holy shit, Del, you've drunk deep from the cauldron of Kool-Aid. You are so vulnerable at the moment and you're possibly ensnared by it all. That's the intention. You sound weird. Have you told him you're pregnant?'

Delphi freezes and Romy is strategically patient this time.

'No. Not yet.' It sounds feeble even to her ears.

'Riiiight…' her friend responds, her voice heavy with cynicism. 'Well, I guess if you don't tell him soon your belly will.'

Getting no response, Romy chooses a different tack. 'Minx, may I come to visit?'

'I'd love to see you, I miss you, but there's no rush, Rom. I'm just settling in here and I don't know what the deal is regarding visitors. I've not seen any. Christoph talks about protecting the energy at the property. That comings and goings dilute it. Christoph calls this "the great rewilding of our souls".' A stuttering release of anxiety flickers in Delphi's stomach.

'Christ, you, my dear friend, sound a bit nutso. What about you come to visit me?'

'There's nothing to worry about, Romy. I'm exactly where I need to be, where I choose to be. I'm rebirthing. Or shuffling out of the ashes. The paradigm is shifting. I promise to write to you lots when

I find some stamps. I can't email as you were right in your letter we don't have technology here.' Delphi wishes she could hug her friend, she suddenly feels very homesick for her.

'Rom, I can hear you pulling faces. I'm not explaining this well but it's as if a mosaic has been at my feet my whole life, confusing, disordered. I've moved the pieces around seeking their meaning and now they're aligning. I can see the picture, the narrative is becoming clear.'

Silence.

'Truly, Romy. Christoph is brilliant, what he's created here is inspiring.'

'It sounds like Jonestown. It sounds like you're stoned. It sounds like a cult. Are you sure you're awake and not just willfully lucid dreaming? Is it that you're so depressed that you want to be told how to live? You, a blazing feminist, you've found yourself a master? Is this father replacement bullshit? Have you thought about that? Because your dad has done a job on you. Does Christoph ask you to pull his ponytail and pledge your eternal love to him? Does he spit in your face while he pushes his fingers inside you?'

Delphi is winded, but she rallies. 'I know you love me. That you want to protect me, but you're dishing out advice which I've not asked you for. I truly believe that the more entrenched and reactive we are about an issue, the more we need to investigate it.'

'Minx that sounds like psychobabble.'

'Romy stop. It's not your job to fix me. That's my job okay?'

Again silence.

'Okay, Del. I am just afraid for you.'

'I get that but trust me, I'm good.' Delphi had intended to ask Romy what she thought about the branding, but can't bring herself to now. Delphi hears laughter rising up from the courtyard so she lowers her voice. 'You said in your letter Jack called you? What was that about? I didn't think you two were in contact after your hook-up?'

'That was 100 years ago, and no we haven't been in touch since, oh yikes I don't know when, before he moved to Paris, but I did email him after your mum died.'

'That was kind.'

'He responded and we back and forthed a bit. And then he called, primarily because he's worried about you and couldn't get hold of you.'

'Shit. What did he say? Is he okay?' Delphi is aware she's started whispering and tries to reclaim her normal voice.

'He's fine. He wanted to know if I knew about the pregnancy and what you're planning. If you're still in Italy. He got your email telling him you were going and um… he talked about your father…'

'What about him?'

Romy takes a big inhalation. 'Man, he's stewing in his juices, isn't he? None of what Jack said about him was very nice.'

'I'm not surprised.' Delphi looks out the window at the black night. 'Go on?'

'Your father for some bizarre reason and I feel awful repeating this…'

'That's okay, tell me…'

'He's decided he doesn't want you to go to his funeral. Whenever that will be.'

'That's suitably awful but it is a very Edward move.'

'Is he ill? Why would he want you to know that? It seems so mean. And the timing is all out vicious.'

'It's about power. I guess it's the last thing he can do to cause me pain.' Delphi tries to keep the agony out of her voice. His aim has always been straight, and his blade has run her through.

'Anything else?'

'Yep, Jack wants you to know that your grandfather has been ill.'

'Oh God, how ill?'

'I don't really know.'

'Oh no…'

'But Jack says he's better now so don't stress.'

Delphi chews at the inside of her cheek.

'Del?' Her friend sounds small. 'Are we okay?'

'Yes of course. Thank you for worrying about me. I'm sorry I've been so hard to get hold of. I will call Jack and my grandpa as soon as I can. Could you send Jack an email for me telling him that? And that I'm okay? And why I've not responded to his calls or emails. I hate the idea of him thinking I'm ignoring him.'

Delphi hears another noise in the courtyard below. People talking and it sends a thrill of urgency through her. 'I'm sorry, I have to go.'

'Okay, Minx. Promise to take care of yourself. I love you how squirrels love nuts.'

'And I you how salt loves eggs.'

Delphi hangs up the phone and the dim clock on the desk states it's nearly 10 pm. She feels a wave of yearning for her grandfather, and deep concern as to why and how Romy's package ended up in the rubbish. She will find out how that happened but now she's got to rush.

*

Layla is waiting outside as Delphi arrives. Delphi, panting, says hello and also acknowledges Layla's companion. A woman in her mid-thirties, short cropped blond hair, arm tattoos, wearing pink dungarees. She introduces herself as Astrid and gives Delphi a hug. Delphi has seen everyone in the family over her time there but there are still a few she's not properly spoken to.

'Ready to go?' Layla asks. All warmth this time around.

'Sure,' says Delphi and the women set off. The compound is generally quiet in the evenings. People go to bed early as they wake before the sun to meditate. Circadian rhythms are talked about and respected here. Delphi walks up the cobbled path following the women careful where she places her feet as it's not very well lit. Arriving at the courtyard, Astrid leads them down a corridor and at the end is a large door. She knocks, and another woman opens it from inside. Delphi steps in, and the room is covered with lit candles. Seven women, all of whom Delphi knows, are waiting for them. It smells like sage as Sylvia is smudging, lifting the lit herbs toward the corners and tracking it along the skirting boards. A large blanket is spread out in the centre of the room.

Delphi is gripped in the teeth of fear. She made her decision to do this for Christoph and for her own redemption, but now it's come to the crunch she's not so sure. Astrid takes Delphi by the hand and leads her behind a screen.

'Sister, don't be worried. It's all good. Everyone in this room has done this before you. We're so happy you're joining our family.' She smiles and gives Delphi another cuddle. 'Take off your clothes and wrap yourself in the sheet. Come out when you're ready and lie down on the blanket.' As Astrid turns to walk away, Delphi wants to hold her back but stops herself.

She takes off her clothes quickly and places them in a pile at her feet. She looks down at her swollen tummy. A small pot belly announcing to the observant that she has a secret. She pulls the sheet around herself, takes a breath, refuses to let her brain start a riot and steps back into the room. The women are sitting around the blanket, and there is an opening for her to walk into the centre. She sits down feeling self-conscious and readjusts the sheet to give herself something to do.

'Sister Sylvia, will Christoph be coming?' she asks, wishing her lover present to make more sense of what's happening.

Her roommate answers in a low voice, 'No, Sister, this is women's work.' Delphi mutes her disappointment. She looks around and recognises each of the women in turn and recalls moments of happiness and connection with all of them. They look back at her with love.

Sylvia explains, 'Each woman will wash your feet as a sign of our commitment to take care of you as one of our own. Then Sister Mata will lead a chanting meditation, and during that time Gita will join us. Delphi, it is painful but try to hold still. We will help by holding you.' She rubs Delphi's leg in what is intended as a reassuring gesture.

'Sisters, let us show our allegiance to Father Lorenzo.' The women swivel towards a painting on the wall. It's of Christoph's father in his prime, years before his death. The women raise their hands and clap. Delphi simmers with a peculiar embarrassment and thinks how deeply weird this all is.

'Alright Sister Delphi, please lie back. You'll find a pillow for your head, and sisters, let us begin.'

Delphi keeps her arms pinned against her body and tries to relax. Sister Mata starts the singing. The women chorus, incanting their mantra. Delphi doesn't recognise it, Indian probably, but it's soothing and rhythmic. Their voices surge forward and back like a tidal wash.

One sister and then the next wipe her feet with a wet towel. It is warm and comforting.

On the ceiling above is a vividly painted fresco. Delphi studies it carefully and recognises it to be a rendition of Dante's 'Inferno'. Dante is making his way through hell guided by the poet Virgil. The cloth of their luxurious blue robes billows out. Their muscular shoulders exposed. The nine concentric circles of torment are represented. A luminescent god is above it all. His arms outstretched, benignly waiting to be chosen by the recognition and rejection of sin. Beneath, seething depictions of purgatory: violence, licentiousness, horror, avarice, bestial appetites and perversion. Agents of Satan swirl with their black wings, horned heads and dripping mouths. Dante looks terrified. You and I both, thinks Delphi and abrades herself for being cowardly.

Delphi hadn't noticed the arrival of Gita, but she is now brushing the hair back from Delphi's face. It transports Delphi back to being a child unable to sleep and her mother stroking her, comforting her, loving her. Gita nods to the other women, who take Delphi's arms and legs and gently hold them out, pressing them into the ground. The sheet is unwound, exposing Delphi from the waist down. She shuts her eyes tightly and conjures Christoph's face but it's Orlo's which appears.

Gita strokes Delphi's forehead again and when she opens her eyes a small paddle is carefully pressed between her teeth. The women are chanting loudly now. Delphi's heart is pounding. She wants to tell them to stop, but it's gone so far. Delphi looks into Dante's anguished eyes above her.

The incandescent brand is brought down on the soft flesh of her pelvis. Delphi bites down with all her might. The pain is exquisite.

The women hold her firmly. Delphi smells her burnt flesh. She screws her eyes shut and hears Vivian's voice as clearly as if she were speaking directly inside Delphi's skull. 'Oh, my darling flower, what did you let them do?'

When Delphi returns to her body the room is quiet, and the last of the women are leaving. All but two candles have been extinguished. The only pool of light encircles her on the blanket. She is alone. When she has traversed the shock, she twists up to see what has happened and there on the inside of her hipbone are Christoph's interlocking initials. A furious burnt welt. A desecration. A blasphemy. Delphi covers herself with the sheet and rolls herself gingerly onto her side and draws the fabric up over her head.

*

She wakes to find Christoph lying beside her on the floor with his arms around her.

'Good morning, my love. I came to find you during the night. I put some burn cream on your mark. It was amazing you didn't wake. We've been together for a few hours. Even with you this close, I've been missing you.'

Delphi's mouth is dry. She has vague feverish memories of Christoph hovering above her.

'Was it so bad, my love?' He's nuzzling into her hair.

'It was terrible,' she says softly, licking her cracked lips.

He either doesn't hear or chooses not to and moves a hand to cup her breast.

'Christoph.' She must tell him before she has time to change her mind. 'I'm pregnant. I know I didn't tell the truth, but I was frightened. And I didn't expect to fall in love.'

Delphi feels his breath pause and his body stiffen.

'You're pregnant?' He lifts up onto his elbow. 'But that's wonderful.'

Delphi has an insane moment when she thinks about how easy it would be to lie but she knows if she does her soul will be lost. Her entire life polluted with unconscionable deceit.

'Christoph, it's not ours.'

He is watching her, expressionless. His voice neutral. 'I am confused. It's another man's child?'

'Yes,' she says, still not brave enough to turn her face towards him.

'Are you in a relationship with this man?'

'No. No, I'm not. I'm in a relationship with you.'

He unpeels himself from her and sits up. Delphi does the same, wincing. Christoph is sitting with his head in his hands. She reaches out and touches his back.

'I know this is a shock, but Christoph–'

He shrugs her off. Dawn is filtering through the curtains.

He stands up, adjusting the prayer beads on his wrist.

'If you want to stay here you will have to get rid of it.' His wolf eyes look down at her. His features have rearranged.

Pleading, she lifts her hand to him. The other is holding the sheet against her nakedness. 'Christoph, please? I can't do that. It's well past that. This is a fully formed baby inside me. I'm over twelve weeks.'

He steps away, looking at her in an entirely new way. He goes to speak but stops himself. He looks up at the mural on the ceiling and after a long, dreadful moment he covers his eyes and screams. Christoph then recovers, adjusts his spine and exits the room, leaving the door open in his wake.

CHAPTER 21

'Sister Delphi, are you okay? What on earth is wrong?' Astrid asks.

Delphi brushes the tears from her face and hides the knickers in her hand. The branding makes it too painful to wear them.

Lots of people are bustling about hungry for breakfast.

'I'm okay, Astrid.' The lie is so blatant that Astrid rolls her eyes.

'Come with me,' she says and takes Delphi's arm, guiding her across the hall into a little room that's filled with abandoned chairs, folded tables, drop-sheets and refuse.

'Sister, is it the ceremony that has brought on this sadness?' Delphi looks at Astrid's colourful tattoos which are as bold and graphic as a sailor's. On her upper arm is an old-school banner held aloft by two swallows and it reads *Mother.* This lances the last of Delphi's composure and she weeps openly. Every single tear holds the word, *longing.*

Astrid doesn't go in for emotional displays. She's not rude but she's impatient. 'What's going on, Delphi?'

'I'm in love with Christoph and I am pregnant, but it's not his. He says if I want to stay here, and I do, I have to terminate it. But I can't. And I won't. How can he love me and demand that? Do you ever think we're living some kind of perverse experiment here?'

Astrid's face is serious.

'I understand,' she says. Delphi waits for more, but that's it.

'Astrid, I am usually someone who can make decisions, not always great ones, but I generally know which way to swim, but right now I'm lost. What would you do?'

Astrid leans back and perches on the corner of a table.

'For me it'd be simple. I'd abort it, build a life here and try to reconnect with Christoph. You know everyone is in love with that man. Not all of us are lucky enough to be chosen by him.'

Delphi is shocked at how calculated Astrid is.

'He means it. He and Sister Gita won't let you stay here with a baby. But if it's a child you want it sounds like he will give you one. Or as many as you want. He has eight already. He's an amazing father.'

Delphi bends forward and takes some deep breaths. How has this happened? He has children already? Of course he does. Those children that look like him in the Buddha Heart. Delphi feels her extremities being crushed by a malevolent force. 'Was it real, Christoph's feelings for me, or was it all just a means to an end?'

'Sister Delphi, relax. You look like you're going to pass out. I've heard that Brother Christoph has been talking openly about you. That's a good thing. And, of course, it was real. You felt it, yes? Well, there you are. Life gives no more guarantee than that in my experience. It's actually an irrelevance what his reality has been. I envy that you can feel so intensely. I've felt half shut down all my life. Until I came here. And now I'm learning how to break the veneer. Don't walk away blithely from this community, Sister. It truly is a family. Ask Brother Christoph to explain his reasoning. He will have an explanation.'

Astrid looks at her Mickey Mouse wristwatch.

'In thirteen minutes, we have bashing in the Buddha Heart. You must come. It will do you good.'

Delphi blows her nose on her knickers and tries to pull her collapsed shoulders back into place.

'Bashing?'

Astrid pulls her out the door. 'Oh, you'll love it. A good old purging. You'll get to express all your rage. Put it all out so you can have some space in there.' She taps her fingers to Delphi's sternum. 'I will drop some antiseptic cream to your cottage. You'll need to be careful with your brand as they can get infected. We don't believe in antibiotics here so make sure you keep it clean and dry. We don't want you dying.'

Delphi shivers.

*

Marching down the hill, she tosses the chunk of bread Astrid gave her into the piglet pen as they pass. There's no way she could fathom eating. The pink, tubby little animals squeal with delight and rumpus about, their snouts and corkscrew tails such a crazy design. Their mother lies sprawled and exhausted, her swollen glistening udders exposed to the sun. Delphi wants to cover her with a blanket.

Astrid strides out ahead. She is the manifestation of strength and solidity. Delphi perceives herself to be a wisp of smoke trailing behind. A soul in limbo, trapped in the Bardo.

They round the bottom of the vegetable garden, and Delphi thinks to raise her arm to shield her eyes from the angle of the morning light, but she can't marshal the strength. It feels good in the darkened recesses of herself to have that sharp intrusion. Thinking about this, giving herself over to the discomfort she almost misses spotting Gabriel. He is standing in the field to their left. Completely stationary, watching her. She can't see his harelip from this distance, but his white-blond hair is easily identifiable. There is something decidedly odd about the way he's holding his body – the manner in which he's observing her. It is pointed and menacing.

Delphi decides to lift her hand across her face after all, as now she has a second and more pressing impetus.

*

In the hall she sees a circle of cushions on the ground and her friends standing around with bats, chatting and laughing. Music is playing loudly, something punchy and adrenaline inducing. Reticence tumbles out of Delphi and she tells Astrid. 'I don't want to do this.' Astrid hands her some gloves and a bat, 'Give it a go, Sister Delphi. You don't even know what this is yet.'

'Alright let's begin,' calls out Sister Mata, one of the three facilitators. The curtains are drawn. The lights dimmed. The doors shut and the music is turned up. Delphi watches as people start to bash their cushions. She reluctantly pulls her gloves on and brings her bat down a few times, feeling idiotic. Astrid looks at her and calls out over the music, 'Let go you control freak.' Someone from across the circle lets out a scream, Delphi looks up shocked, now the group are warming up it's as if a lid has been removed and they're starting to howl and shriek. Delphi is frozen and Sister Mata comes over to her and rubs her upper arms. Delphi has to tilt her ears toward Mata's mouth to be able to hear her. 'This is pretty full on the first time. The point is to unleash all the anger and hurt you've kept locked away inside you. Getting it out lets you get free of it. A sematic release. This is not performative or interactive. Keep your attention on yourself. Everyone else will do the same. You're safe, just give it a go.'

Sister Mata gives Delphi a hug, 'Sweetheart, if you don't like it you can leave.' Delphi takes in a big deep breath. She raises the bat and brings it down. She does it again and the action is foreign but curiously empowering. Sooner than she could have anticipated self-consciousness withers. She grits her teeth and brings the bat down over and over again. Around her, but beyond her field of focus is a scene of outpouring. Everyone is lost in their own world of expression. Bats are thwacking, smashing and in some cases splintering apart, to be quickly replaced by the facilitators.

After a lifetime of control, the invitation is to lose it entirely, to cross over an ever suppressed impulse. She coaxes her demons to the surface, and through her commitment and ferocity of action they begin bursting out and the catharsis is electrifying.

After the first hour, the anger begins to change its shape – to come in waves rather than as a wall of fury. Delphi sits on the ground, lampooning the cushion bayonet style. One of the facilitators rubs her back, 'Don't give up. Face it head-on Sister Delphi. Think about what causes you pain, imagine it on the cushion and then bash it! Bash it out of your life.'

The music changes, and the words of encouragement create a revitalised upswell. Delphi is back on her feet and raising the bat high above her head. With as much force as she can muster she arcs down, creating a sonic thud on the beleaguered fabric. Her inhibitions have been screamed from the building. Her thinking self-exorcised. She is all body. Entirely built of rage. A molten ball of spewing heat as she screams *No!* repeatedly; no to Arthur's drowning, no to her father's cruelty, no to her mother's death, no to the euthanasia laws, no to all the parts of herself that she despises. She bashes all that is bad, it is pouring out of her and she's euphoric.

An acute pain suddenly stabs her in the stomach. She bends double and sinks to one knee. Sweat splattering from her face. She presses on the point of pain low down on her tummy. In her mind's eye, Delphi vividly sees her baby. It is touching its face against hers, saying, *Enough now*. She sees herself holding the bag down hard over her mother's head. Vivian mouths through the plastic, *Stop this*, and grabs Delphi's wrists, digging her nails in until the blood runs in rivulets.

Delphi flattens and brings her hands over her ears to block out the surrounding cacophony. Vertigo. Fear. The cramping is a siren blaring.

An uncovered deep knowing is exposed to her – she is too broken ever to be fixed. She has snapped the last straw of self-deceit, and now she understands, and it's unbearable. She presses her face into the cushion. The revelation metastasises. She has always looked for others to fix her. To love her. To take the pain away. To lead her. If she were just good enough. Clever enough. Special enough. And they've never managed; her parents, her brothers, all the lovers she's invited into her body to fill the holes, to make her whole. Delphi collapses, decimated, into the river of selfhood. A lifetime of meticulously constructed bridges are yanked from their anchorage.

Debris churns in the broiling waters and all the rules Delphi has banked on are washed away. She gasps for oxygen as she is dragged down by the undertow.

She has to get out. She can't be in this room for a moment longer. Delphi stands unsteadily. Her bat rolls away. She weaves her way between flailing limbs to the wall and guides herself with her hands stretched out. She circumnavigates half the room and finds the door to the antechamber. Afraid she will be stopped she hurries through and is blinded by the light. With squinting eyes and pounding head she staggers out of the Buddha Heart.

*

Delphi shuts the door of the cottage and rests her head against it. She observes her pulse throbbing against the wood. Her ears are ringing. Delphi goes to the sink, draws a glass of water and sculls it.

She moves to the bathroom, rips off her clothes and drops them in a heap on the tiles. She struggles to remove her bra and pulling down her knickers she freezes. There in the gusset is a small puddle of blood. Delphi blinks. Her brain refuses to process the most logical explanation. She takes some paper and holds it between her legs. As she presses it there she calls in the Fates. Please, no.

Delphi grabs on to the basin and condemns herself. Was it the sex with Christoph? The travesty of the branding? Is it because she failed her mother? Or that her womb is doused in ingratitude? Because she wasn't sure about wanting her baby? Perhaps the gods heard her and have deemed her unworthy and are taking this child away? Everything precious gets ripped away in time. But please not this.

Delphi hears the front door close and her body jerks. She listens for activity but there's none. She grabs a towel from the railing, throws it around herself and steps out into the sitting room. It's empty. The door is closed. Delphi spins around to look into the bedroom she shares with Sylvia. On high alert she moves towards it, the hair on the back of her neck bristling. She inches the door wide with her foot. It glides all the way open, meeting the wall, and she accepts the relief by exhaling. It's empty. The beds are neatly made. Her book is on the bedside table. But the vase on the sideboard is recently toppled over. The flowers lie prostrate, the water is pooling and dripping to the floor. And her suitcase, just the corner of it is sticking out from under the bed. Not by much, but enough for her to know. Delphi reaches for the curtains and shuts them quickly, appalled by the idea that someone was just in here, and that someone might now be standing in the field outside watching. Delphi gets down onto the floor and drags out her bag, checking inside it. Everything seems to be there – her gnome, her books, her diary – but she can't shake the feeling of violation. Maybe she's mistaken? Perhaps she left the door ajar, and the wind blew it shut?

She sees the photograph of her mother. The one in a small silver frame which she's taken everywhere with her for years. It lies face down. She knows for certain that picture was upright when she was last here. Delphi reaches out and picks it up. A passport photo of Vivian. Magnificent at forty. Small gold earrings, a dark turtleneck sweater, long narrow nose, high cheekbones, hooded lids and an expression that reveals a woman of depth, of remarkable beauty and great disappointment.

Delphi encloses her fingers around the photo and draws it against herself. Is everything actually about returning to the womb? Finding safety and warmth? Pulling back the blankets Delphi climbs into her bed. The towel is bulky around her, she has to struggle to pull the bedding over herself, over her head. She curls herself tightly, to be as small as she can be. Her breath is warm against her thighs. She's running low on oxygen in her dark cubby but she has no intention of coming up for air.

*

Delphi hoped she might fall asleep even for a short time to give herself a break, but she's too wired, so pulls herself out of bed. She needs to speak to Christoph, to reason with him and argue her case.

To convince him that a compromise can be made but also to ask him about her post and Gabriel. She wants access to her computer, or any computer for half an hour. She needs answers.

There's no more blood when Delphi dresses, but anxiety about the baby shunts her organs up towards her throat and she struggles to breathe as she leaves the cottage. In her distress, time has distended. It must be the afternoon, but she can't seem to get her bearings.

She keeps walking. Her body is starting to stiffen from the exertion this morning. She feels like the Tin Man, atrophied and looking for her heart.

*

She is still searching for Christoph when Delphi spots Layla up near the dining hall.

'Layla, hello.' Delphi tries to smile. The other woman says hello and carries on walking in the opposite direction. Delphi switches direction and trots up alongside. 'Layla, I know we're not exactly friends but I need to ask you about Christoph. I want to know, if you'll tell me, what happened between you?' Layla comes to a stop and turns to face Delphi. Her face ripples with different expressions and settles on something close to compassion.

'Has he tired of you, Delphi?'

Delphi clenches her teeth to ward off sorrow.

'Well, we are teetering on the edge, that's for sure. I wonder, and I don't want to be intrusive, if he was ever violent with you?'

'Why do you ask?'

'I don't actually really know.'

'Do you mean emotionally or physically?' Layla asks without a shred of surprise.

'Either.'

Layla's mouth twists to the side. 'Listen, I could get into big trouble talking to you about this.' She pulls back when she hears footsteps.

Layla reaches for Delphi's hand and walks her around the side of the building.

'Sister Delphi, I was in love with Christoph, too. We all are, to differing degrees. This is what he does. Chooses you. Idolises you. Dismantles you so slowly and masterfully that you hardly know it's happening, until you feel you can't possibly live without him. Can't say no to any of his requests. Has he asked you to go to bed with another woman yet? That's what destroyed it for us. I didn't like it and when I jacked up, he sent Gabriel to ice me out. And that was it. It was over.'

'Oh my God, Layla, that's awful. Why don't you leave?'

She looks around checking to see they're still not being overheard. 'Because this is my home. These people are my family. I do love it here and where would I go? Because my child is in the Cub House and if I left, I would never see her again. And I will tolerate any indignity for her.'

Layla starts to walk away; 'I really can't talk about this anymore. Please don't ask me again.'

'Just one more question please. Are Christoph's mother and sister dead?'

Layla turns back and says, 'In a way, yes. They left the family a few years after Lorenzo died. And when you leave here, you're as good as dead. I have nothing else to say to you, Sister.' Delphi watches Layla's back recede until she turns the corner and is gone.

*

She takes a deep, centring breath and knocks on Christoph's door and after a minute he is standing before her. He is beautiful and wild-eyed. His arm is raised as he holds the door wide. Delphi wants to kneel at his feet and beg him to tell her that none of it is true, that everything will be alright. Her face collapses with misery, he catches her in his arms, and they are kissing. Christoph picks her up and carries her to his bed. So much of her is sore, her heart, her brain, her muscles, her bashing hands, her branded pelvis. And now pleasure is folded in amongst it.

He watches her face intently as he pushes up her dress and takes off her knickers. He whispers, 'Thank you, my love.' A high-pitched tone sounds in Delphi's middle ear. She coughs to dislodge the discomfort. He holds her jaw high, kisses her throat and inhaling her he repeats, 'Thank you.'

This time the sound claims its dominance and Delphi asks, 'For what?'

His hand is between her legs. She twists herself to the side immobilising his fingers. His brow furrows. 'I mean, Delphi, thank you for choosing me. For choosing us and The Bodhi Famiglia.'

Hopes falls like burning leaves.

'Christoph…' he is back tending to her body. 'Christoph?' She lifts his head. 'I'm not getting rid of the baby.'

They are frozen. In an instant their bodies make no sense pursuing unity when the opposite poles of the earth are calling them.

'Christoph, I do want you, and I want to stay, but surely my baby has a place here too?'

He removes his hand and Delphi wonders if it's printed in her blood. He drops his head to the sheets over her shoulder. She listens to his cogs cranking, and then he lets out an enormous roar. It is shockingly primal. Delphi unable to move as he's on top of her, turns her face away, shutting her eyes tightly.

Something exorcised in him, he rests his head on her chest.

'I am true to my world, Delphi. What I said before are the only two courses of action. You mustn't be greedy. You can't have it all. I won't raise your mistake – and nor should you.'

She uses her arms and twists her thigh, pushing him away. He smiles in such a peculiar way that Delphi momentarily fears he may strike her, but instead, he kisses her on the lips with a casualness that feels like distilled violence.

'You will be a bad mother.' His tone is flat. He is calm. 'Your own family rejected you. You couldn't keep your brother alive. You failed your mother. You have no idea who you are.' He wipes his mouth. 'I don't know who you are.'

Delphi scrambles backwards, pulling her dress down to cover her legs. A lock of air is travelling back and forward caught on her jagged breath.

'That's grotesque. To use things I've told you in trust and love. To weaponise… to manipulate my confidences to wound me.'

He looks benign.

'You know what Christoph? You've taught me so much. You've taught me about paradoxes. Right now, I'm learning about hatred. Say whatever you want, but don't you dare bring up Arthur. His death was the greatest tragedy, one I live and breathe every single day. And you don't get to wield that. You don't get a putrid version of your own because I own them all.' Delphi swings her legs off the bed and stands up, willing herself not to collapse.

'Christoph, I am leaving now.'

'Fine.'

She hesitates then says, 'You asked me the other day how I defined success and I said I didn't know but I've thought about it and my answer is this – it's to love. Do you know how to love?'

He pulls a shirt on over his head. 'You ask me that? Look at your life and look at mine.'

Delphi, outraged, bends down for her knickers and as she steps into them, a small trickle of blood travels down her inner thigh. She has set her course. She will choose this baby over this man, over this place, even if she is only given another 24 hours to be its mother.

*

Sylvia registers Delphi's packed suitcase. When Delphi offers no contrition, Sylvia takes herself into the bathroom and shuts the door.

So be it.

Delphi walks out of the cottage punch drunk and hurries up the path as discreetly as she can. The darkness of the night makes her less conspicuous and she hopes she will get to Gita's office unnoticed.

When she does, listening, she can't hear anyone within. She knocks and there's no answer. She waits, chewing the inside of her mouth, and knocks again. She tries the handle. It rotates but when she pushes her weight against the door, it doesn't budge. Locked. Delphi's mobile and computer are in there.

Delphi steps back and tries to think what to do. Her brain is addled. She attempts the handle again doubting herself but it's definitely locked. Delphi goes to the top of the stairs and leans out over the courtyard to see if the window to the office is open. It's not and even if it were stretching across to the tiny ledge would be extremely dangerous. Her desperation trumps the danger and she thinks she will give it a go.

Delphi hears her name called which blasts her with adrenaline. She leans further over the balcony to see who it is. Gabriel is standing in the far corner staring up at her, looking ghoulish under the stark courtyard lights. Very slowly, he shakes his head from side to side like a mechanical toy.

From behind her, along the black corridor, a woman starts laughing. Delphi grabs her suitcase and dashes down the dimly lit stairs three at a time. Turning the corner she nearly loses her balance and thumps hard into the wall. She pushes off and keeps descending. It's terrible to think that Gabriel will be waiting for her at the bottom but she intends to run right through him. She makes the ground floor and as she turns, he grabs her arm. Delphi swings her suitcase has hard as she can into him, twists her body and kicks out with her leg. He buckles, but as he goes down he grabs a fistful of her hair and she is pulled to the ground. She holds nothing back and punches him until he releases his grip. Back on her feet, scrambling to retrieve her suitcase, she's off, racing as fast as she can out of the building, taking the overgrown side path around to the front. Grasses and branches slash at her. She holds her suitcase in both arms as a shield and once she's clear and makes it to the driveway she races down it with the speed of someone whose life depends on it.

CHAPTER 22

THE MOON IS LIGHTING her way. She has been walking for hours to get as much distance between herself and the commune as possible. She scaled the fence without killing herself and is now aiming for the highway. From there Delphi will hitch a ride into Florence. She listens and can't hear a thing beyond her own breath drawing in and ebbing out. The few farmhouses she's passed are all shrouded in sleep. She could well be the only person on earth, except for the baby in her womb. Delphi thinks about the word miscarry and measures the terrible weight of it. She recalls when Adarsha had hers. The doctors could do nothing. The two of them were sent home from hospital and Delphi tended to Ada with hot water bottles and cups of tea. A week later they returned for another scan. Adarsha's womb was empty, no dilation and curettage needed. 'Nothing to be done,' the doctor said again and Delphi held her friend tightly as she wept.

Delphi turns to look back at where she's come from. Then turns to see where she's headed. The view in both directions is uncanny. Is it possible to have vertigo on flat ground? She must rest for a moment. Delphi sits and rolls onto her back. She allows herself to be held by the earth. The relief is radical. An otherworldly sensation begins to occur. A spell is taking effect. Delphi knows herself as a rock that has been on this land forever. She can clearly see the contours of her rock self. The weight, temperature, curvature. Lichen has grown over her like a shawl. She is at one. She is of the land. Human no more. The chaotic intensity of her-ness seeps away into the soil below. A peace is born. A tranquility only gifted by ancient wisdom. Delphi is reclaimed. Eternity embracing her with unassailable arms.

*

It's taken her all night walking and one hitched ride in the back of a truck but Delphi finally arrives into Florence mid-morning. A man tending his fruit stall hands her a peach as a gift and says, 'God bless you.' As she raises it to her mouth she whispers, 'God bless us all,' and she knows she must go into the Uffizi, her brand of church, it's calling her. She studies the long line of visitors and decides on a course of action.

A tour group trills and chirps in their matching fluoro caps. Delphi adeptly mixes herself into their throng. A roly-poly woman with two bright blue spots of eyeshadow sees what Delphi's doing and yelps in excitement. This is obviously a woman who broke all the rules in school and misses those heady days. She chomps at her gum double-time as she does a sweep of the ticketing staff. She takes the cap from her head and shoves it onto Delphi's. Then she raises both her hands five inches from Delphi's face and gives a zealous double thumbs-up. The gaggle bustle through the doors and camouflaged within their ranks Delphi skips the twelve Euro entrance fee as her wallet is empty of cash. For some reason the teller machine wouldn't acknowledge her card, denying her access to the remains of Hugh's money. She used Art's loan to pay for her flight to Italy so things are uncomfortably tight.

She returns the cap to the woman who hoots with laughter, slapping Delphi so hard on her shoulder she nearly crumbles.

With circumspection Delphi loiters for a bit, then checks in her suitcase and turns into the entrance hall to meet history.

*

For an hour she drifts through the halls, aimlessly floating down the galleria, her eyes gently touching the sculptures. She cranes her heavy head back and studies the painted ceilings and peers into framed works blinking.

Moving on she finds herself standing before Botticelli's *The Birth of Venus*. Delphi is jostled by selfie stick–wielding tourists and yet an aperture begins to open within her. The change is so minuscule that she nearly misses it but focusing on the painting, on the newly born yet fully formed Venus; her golden hair curled in her fingers covering her nakedness, the tenderness of her feet resting on the scallop shell that ferries her, the winged wind god Zephyr and the light breeze of Aura blowing her toward the shore, the cloak offered by the attending goddess, the folds of fabric, the floating flowers. All of this is the highest order of beauty, but it's Venus's face that is the key to the opening within Delphi. Her expression is infused with tranquil understanding, her eye line falls directly into Delphi. And what is transmitted is the gift of life. That Delphi must choose to be fully alive. Did she actually hear the words? Is this delirium or grace? Either way, something sublime has kissed her.

Her moorings dislodge and Delphi is swept back from the painting by the crowd.

Reluctantly she turns away and finds a guard to ask him where she will find Da Vinci's *Annunciation*. He explains and she wends her way towards it. Vivian loved this painting and standing before it Delphi can see why. An angel is telling Mary she is to conceive the son of God. Both of them express themselves through serious eyes and eloquent hands. Delphi wants to reach up and touch the canvas. 'I love you Mama,' she whispers.

A fresh impulse strikes and Delphi seeks out *The Madonna with the Long Neck*. Locating it, she stands transfixed before its stillness and grace. There is resplendent Mary looking down at her strangely adult infant with unadulterated love.

Arthur.

The great and protracted numbness that has encased Delphi recedes and the full flush of feeling returns. Her humanity rises. All parts of her are in the light. Delphi staggers and finds a bench. She sits present with herself as this turning takes place. It is terrifying yet ebullient. The blood is pumping in her veins. She has no idea how she will survive but she turns to Madonna of the wonderfully long neck and she makes a solemn vow that she will no matter what.

CHAPTER 23

Delphi is in Fiesole, the hill town above Florence. A panoramic view of the ancient city and the rolling green hills of the Arno Valley sprawl before her. This breathtaking elevation is said to have inspired Da Vinci to build his flying machine. Delphi imagines him sitting where she stands studying the birds, his revelations about to change the course of the world. A small black bird dances and swoops past Delphi. She watches it for a long time.

She twists her hair up on the top of her head and stretches her back. She's thirsty. Delphi has spent the afternoon asking for work in the little village but with no luck. She must find a job and buy another phone. She wants to call her people and tell them she loves them. She also must see a doctor to find out what is happening inside her. Delphi is still hit by waves of nausea and wonders if that means she should be hopeful. She remembers being told about a friend of a friend who miscarried and it took time for her pregnancy hormones to fade, keeping her body thinking that it was still pregnant. A frightful trick where the trusting body is the last to know.

A black dog with white markings trots up the road and puts its wet nose on Delphi's calf. She jumps and the dog bolts sideways. Delphi squats down and calls him back, her arms outstretched towards him. Soon they're buddies and she's patting and talking to him about his lovely velvet ears.

'You speak Italian well.' Delphi looks up to see a small woman in late middle age walking towards her.

'*Grazie*,' Delphi answers and they talk together in Italian.

'You like my dog? He's a very naughty boy. Forever zigzagging over the road. He was hit by a Vespa once and broke his leg. I worry the next time it will be his head.' The woman's teeth tilt inwards like a shark, but there is nothing sinister about her.

Both of them are looking at the dog.

'What's his name?' Delphi asks.

'Berlusconi.' The woman chortles. 'So, are you the one who's been looking for a waitressing job?' She readjusts the dog leash that is hanging about her neck. Hard working bra straps digging welts into her shoulders.

Delphi stops patting the dog and stands up. '*Si*, I am.'

'I own Vallata Vista.' She points back down the road. 'I hear you have experience?' In small towns news travels fast.

'*Si*. I do, lots.'

'Tell me, then?'

'I'm a hard worker, I'm honest and I'm good at it.' Delphi hates talking herself up but needs must.

The woman looks her up and down.

'You seem sick,' she says, not dispassionately.

'I'm okay, I just need a bath.'

The woman nods. 'Where are you living?'

This may be where this falls apart.

'I'm looking for a home too.' Delphi hopes in Italian that sounds less literal.

'Ah...' the woman bends down and calls Berlusconi over and attaches the leash.

'*Va bene*. I will give you a trial. You won't be paid for it. If you are competent you can have the job. We are understaffed, and I am too stressed to go on.' She makes a wonderfully wild operatic gesture with her arms. 'If you break anything it comes out of your salary. If you're late or you steal you get the sack. You can have one meal each shift, and you look like you need it. Do you understand?'

'*Si*,' Delphi answers.

The woman starts to walk away but turns back. 'Are you coming?'

Delphi shifts her weight from one sore foot to the other foot. 'To your restaurant? Now?'

'*Si*, but we will go via my villa first. It is nothing special. My father is in the downstairs apartment but upstairs is empty. He can't manage the steps as his knees are very bad. It's very regrettable. If I give you the job you can stay in the villa. You will be responsible for keeping it clean and I will deduct the rent from your wages.'

Delphi feels the boulder in her stomach dislodge. She picks up her suitcase. '*Grazie mille.*' The woman gives her an endearing sharky smile and the three of them walk down the road, careful to stick to the side to avoid the crazy Italian drivers.

*

The restaurant is beautiful. Delphi likes the solidity of it. The dining area is traditional and dark as a cave when Delphi navigates her way back to the kitchen with orders or empty plates from the garden. This outdoor section is where most of the diners sit, even in this cool weather. It has gorgeous views and is protected beneath a leafy canopy. The history is tangible in the worn tread of the sandstone stairs and you can feel that many people have worked, eaten and gathered here. Delphi is just one of the countless people moving through. Something about this notion makes her personal struggles feel less important.

Only locals come for dinner as it is winter and not tourist season. Delphi works hard and listens attentively to the directions given to her as she works. Roberto, the chef, with his receding hairline is married to Lucia the owner. He doesn't talk much, but he offers her half a cake and a loaf of bread to tuck into her bag at the end of her first shift. He slings a tea towel over his shoulder and says in broken English, 'Seez you tomorrow.' Delphi catches a glimpse of the mischievous boy he once was in his ageing face.

She is exhausted as she pushes out through the front doors and descends the worn stairs. Further up the hill, above the restaurant, there is an ice-cream parlour where, Lucia told her, throngs of young people meet. As Delphi walks towards it, she can hear music and laughter pumping into the night air. They sound so free and joyful. What a juxtaposition to her seemingly a hundred years old waddling home, an underground creature reefed out into the open plains. Her sense of exposure is compounded when an approaching car's headlights illuminate her. She squints, blinded. The car passes and she returns to darkness. She sees herself as the car's occupants must have; floodlit, wincing, cold, alone, worn out.

She reaches a turn-off and takes a left down the dirt track as she was instructed. It becomes even colder and she shivers. Lucia had given Delphi a torch, she charged her four Euro for it, but the beam of milky light is showing up the uneven ground before her. The trees on either side look Brothers Grimm ominous, but Delphi refuses to give into thoughts of witches' fingers and bewitched creatures. It is so very dark. Like the bottom of the ocean. Like death. Lucia had described this shortcut through the fields, only accessible by foot. Delphi wonders if she should have gone the longer way by road.

After a few minutes of walking, the path rises and Delphi crosses through an olive grove, coming to the perimeter of the villa garden. Lucia left the porch light on when they'd dropped off Delphi's bag making it easier to see where she's going. There is an empty pool clogged with leaves and a huge stone shed. The door of which stands open with some sort of threshing machine long abandoned inside. The shadows are like spilt ink. Delphi moves under the stone arch, turning off her torch, past a Fiat 500 with a flat tyre, then up the narrow flight of stairs. She gets the big key out of her coat pocket and puts it into the lock. It turns stiffly. Once inside she shuts the door and locks herself in. Re-potted. She stands still listening to the darkness. She must not fall asleep on her feet. Horses can do that, and flamingos by shutting down one side of their brains. Delphi feels herself sway, which prompts her to paw the walls looking for a light switch. Finding it, the kitchen jumps into retina-punching life. She shields her eyes with her hand. A small 1970s kitchen, green and white floor tiles, a table with two chairs, decorative plates erratically dotting the walls. Her suitcase sits waiting for her. Delphi drops her handbag beside it and goes into the bathroom, turns on the lights and blinks at the musk-pink amenities. She likes it. The only other room is the bedroom. A double bed in the middle, a chest of drawers, one side table, a lamp and a window with wooden shutters. The place smells musty. She opens the shutters and the view stretches down the valley to a twinkling Florence below. There's a cypress tree that is so large and solitary that it calls special attention to itself. Delphi says, 'Hello tree.' She trusts the tree has heard her.

She turns to look back at the room. Here she is. Alone. Tonight, she will shower and sleep in that bed. For a moment she imagines Orlo waiting beneath the sheets for her. She knocks the thought away. No more rescuers, she tells herself and returns soberly to what is. She has food in her belly and a job to go to tomorrow. She is alone, but that isn't a death in and of itself. She has known far worse.

Delphi is too worn down to carry on being frightened. This is her reality. She will accept it for what it is. Nothing more and nothing less. Silence. Delphi is grateful to be hidden from drama, away from anyone else's needs and disappointments. The shift is, she's no longer interested in escaping herself. A golden leaf has turned over.

Delphi showers then tucks herself into bed with her mother's ashes and her gnome.

*

'You do well here,' Lucia says to her in Italian.

'Thank you. I am grateful to be working for you.'

'Is the villa okay? Can you hear my father snoring below you at night?'

All the diners have left so Berlusconi has been let out of the back room and runs through the restaurant cavorting.

'No, not at all, I've not seen him nor heard him,' Delphi answers. She's gearing herself up to do something unusual, something that makes her feel horribly uncomfortable – to ask for help.

'Lucia, I am sorry to ask this of you, but may I use your phone to call my grandfather? He's not well.'

'*Si si*, just don't take too long as it charges by time.'

'Of course, thank you, and another thing, I need to see a doctor.'

Lucia stops flipping through the reservation book and studies Delphi. 'Are you sick?'

Delphi makes the last wipe of the table she's cleaning and turns to face her boss. 'No. I'm not ill.' Delphi is embarrassed to be worrying Lucia.

'My problem, Lucia, is I can't go to the hospital as I'm not a resident and the local doctor won't see me without proof of address.'

Lucia puts the pen in her hand into the pot on the reception table.

'You leave this with me. My brother-in-law is a doctor. I will arrange for him to call you here tomorrow and set up an appointment.'

Delphi looks at this olive woman with her warm, matronly, curvacious body and, in another life, she would have wanted to cuddle her, but she sticks to her plan to stay separate, to stay contained as she heals and offers a thank you and goes back to wiping down the tables.

*

Three days later, walking the goat track home between the lunch and dinner shift Delphi is quiet. As if the sediment within her is settling into her feet. She has found a rhythm these past few days. She's not stupid enough to think she's even begun to integrate the last months of her life, also numbness masquerades as calmness in certain unexamined light. She encourages herself to be silent, not to ask, not to think – occasionally though, her inner voice whispers a defiant question.

Is this freefall or suspension?

Is shock a buffer or a deadening agent?

Is this dormancy or withering?

Or maybe, just maybe, this isn't actually reactivity at all – it's that her soul has been decimated and this mono-level is all she's capable of now. The highs and lows burnt away. Connection, expression, need, all too dangerous to risk.

She doesn't really talk to anyone.

The old lady in the grocery store has no teeth and no interest. Each day she hands Delphi her few staples with a milky gaze set to the middle distance. Delphi wonders if the old lady is wistful or disappointed, but she decides that thinking more on it might dislodge a precious scab and she lets her thoughts float away.

She can disappear in plain sight.

Lucia and Roberto are polite but busy with their own lives. Delphi suspects they're suffering financial strain as Lucia is often poring over the books, punching at her calculator with a great deal of huffing. The other waiters aren't interested in Delphi. One of the young men needed a day or two of deep freeze to get the message, but he leaves her alone, too. Beyond manners they extend nothing, which suits her. The back and forth with the diners is purely transactional also. It's easier to feel safe when you keep separate. Her grieving requires intense privacy. She knows she's not meant to want this forever as the cost would be great, a half-life, a shrivelled heart, but right now it seems the only way possible. This liminal space is all she can manage.

She spoke to her grandfather and he reassured her his health is okay, he's just getting old. He cried about Vivian and that made Delphi cry too. A parent having their child die before them is impossible to reconcile. She thinks about her mother suffering through her life without Arthur and how that most eloquent of women was rendered mute, unable to even approach the outer perimeter of her grief with words. So she carried the cruel burden of that agony alone. While with the phone Delphi had also called Jack, he'd not answered so she'd left a message updating him as to where she is and promising to write soon.

Delphi stops walking when she arrives at the threshold of the villa garden and looks around. This is okay. The two buildings. The absent man downstairs. The neglected garden. The quiet. Her washing looks orderly hanging on the rope suspended between trees. Vivian's nightie pegged from the shoulders is vertical, encasing a ghost. This is okay, she tells herself again. Delphi can just be here. Quietly, modestly, privately, moving through her existence.

Lucia's brother-in-law was helpful and tomorrow morning before work Delphi is off to see a doctor to have a scan. Delphi worries when Catholic Lucia finds out what this is all about, she will get the sack. If that's the case so be it.

Delphi looks at her hand and opens her fingers. Loose grip, she tells herself. Loose grip.

*

The doctor's name is Scuderi. He has grey hair curling at his temples, is short and has the condensed power of someone who is pleased with himself. Delphi lies on an examination table as instructed. Scuderi puts cold jelly on her stomach and is moving the ultrasound's camera around to find the best view of her womb. His aftershave is so strong Delphi switches to mouth breathing.

'You have been bleeding for how many days?' he asks, fiddling with buttons on the keyboard and looking at the screen. His English is excellent. Delphi doesn't understand why she is so nervous, sad would make sense, but to fear the inevitable, the already lost, seems childish. Delphi envisages herself as a five-year-old, hair in pigtails, eyes huge, swimming.

'Um, nearly a week,' Delphi says, flooded with guilt because surely this is all her fault. 'Five, six days.' Each one a slice of hell.

'And you were how pregnant?' His attention is entirely on the screen.

'When I started to bleed? Um… I was, ah… twelve maybe, no, thirteen weeks.' Delphi crosses her ankles but it's just as uncomfortable so uncrosses them again.

'I think you were more than that.' He leans closer to the image. He needs glasses but vanity prevents him. Delphi looks at the screen. There is her baby and there is its heart, still beating.

Delphi's entire self is activated with astonishment. Tears of honey rather than salt fall, wetting the pillow beneath her head.

'It's alive?' she asks. Her voice is unrecognisable.

'Yes,' the doctor nods. 'Your baby is fourteen weeks. I will do the measurements, but yes, I think a bit over fourteen weeks.' Delphi can see her baby's silhouette, it's forehead, nose and chin. A leg flexes. A femur. The longest bone in the body. A hand raises.

'Ah look,' says the doctor. 'Baby sucking its thumb.'

Delphi begins to sob, her shoulders shuddering. Dr Scuderi is unable to hold the camera against her belly so he stands back fascinated and waits for the tempest within his patient to pass.

*

The doctor takes her blood for testing as he lectures Delphi about getting as much bed rest as possible. He holds her hand several beats too long, but Delphi is too overjoyed to be resentful. She taps his wedding ring, thanks him and leaves the room.

On the road, cars and motorbikes zoom past her, horns blaring, carbon monoxide pluming, but the cacophony is all overshadowed by Delphi's joy. Her baby is alive. She shakes her head trying to roll the information to another part of her brain for fresh assessment. So Orlo is the father. Delphi's initial intuition and calculations had been correct and the dating scan done in England that suggested conception had been later was wrong. Orlo Orlo Orlo. That news needs digesting and celebrating. An unfurling in her chest happens as she thinks of him. She sends her blessings out to him wherever he is in the world. What a miracle. What a gift. She can't help but smile. Delphi cups her belly with her hands and projects all her love into her womb. This is utterly surreal. A baby. She is going to have a baby. 'Hold on. Please hold on little person.'

Delphi knows she is going to have to sort herself out. She thinks about all the awfulness her parents have bequeathed her – the damage handed down, adulthoods never truly claimed. What a poisoned inheritance. Delphi decides it won't happen this time. She will do whatever it takes to be as healthy and integrated as possible for this child. She owes her child that. She owes herself that too.

Delphi looks up at the buildings on either side of her. The weak blue sky beyond and she slows to watch a cloud drifting overhead. She wonders if somewhere her mother knows about the baby. She doubts it works like that but she wishes that it did.

She needs to buy paper, envelopes and stamps. She wants to write to Jack as she promised. And to Hugh and Ada to tell them where she is but also about the baby. She wants to buy a gift for Romy, maybe a Florentine notepad. Romy loves little pads and collects them. And something for dear Art. She wonders what would make him happy and sets off towards the Duomo and its surrounding shops. Delphi wants to share her jubilation with the ones she loves.

CHAPTER 24

Delphi wakes in her little room as the light pushes in between the shutters. She turns over to let herself surface gently. Today is her day off. Delphi smiles. The expanse of time and quiet is luxurious. She registers her happiness. It is unusual as it has been gone so long. As the weeks have passed Delphi has stopped assessing the progress of her grief. As when lost in a desert – calculating how much ground is covered is of no consequence unless one survives.

This morning is a miracle of sorts, as if she has woken up in an oasis. She hears a bird singing outside, the cheerfulness permeates her. She's returning to the land of the living.

She has started painting again and several canvases rest propped up against her walls. One that she did of Vivian means the most to her and today she will buy a hammer and nails so she can hang it above her bed. She loves the idea of her mama looking over her and her baby as they sleep. She wonders if any are good enough to send to Art and decides to start a new canvas today especially for him. She looks at his most recent letter sticking out of the book she's reading and she reaches out and runs her finger along its edge.

Delphi looks at the small, framed photograph of her mother and another of baby Arthur on her bedside table. She wonders where they are now but that thinking doesn't hurt as it did before. It strikes Delphi that it was a gift that she had those two people in her life at all.

She pulls the sheets back and looks at her naked body. Her breasts and belly swollen. Her baby kicking within her. Thirty weeks. Three-quarters of the way there. Delphi strokes her tummy. She has never felt awe for her body before. To be a woman is to be powerful. The creator of life.

She wishes someone would open the shutters so she could see the view of the valley, and then that someone could bring her a cup of tea in her one china teacup. But Delphi lives alone. Alone – not such a bad word really. Grateful, she gets up as her baby dances inside her.

*

Delphi drops the letter to Orlo into the slot in the post office wall. She recomposed it many times and then let this final version sit for days on the kitchen table. She was hurt that he never returned her call from months ago in Art's office, nor her email, but this letter, is the right thing to do. It says that he is going to be a father and is free of any obligation. A rush of feelings for him surface and she kisses the postbox. It is done.

She turns and walks out into the piazza. Summer is soon to arrive and the heat is thickening up. Delphi wants to get a milkshake before her appointment. She will have time if she rushes. She runs across the piazza to her favourite café. She is wearing a new sundress that she bought in a crammed, mothballed op-shop. Delphi regards the bright blue fabric encasing her round belly, the long skirt swishing around her legs. She looks up when she hears hollering. Three older Italian men, sitting together playing chess and drinking espresso, are rising to their feet. They are calling out to her and clapping. Their hands raised high, their faces crinkled with smiles. She hears a chorus of *bella donna* and one says, *'Tu sei madre terra'*, 'You are Mother Earth'. Another sings out, *'Benedetto'*, 'Blessed'. She has felt cursed for so long that the power of this word makes her giddy. Language can build up but also destroy. It gives and it takes. And this word, *blessed,* anoints her.

Delphi rubs a hand over her tummy and impulsively she twirls around. Her sundress kicking up around her legs, her hair catching the light and the men delighting in her youth, beauty and fertility clap on.

*

Giulia is dressed in three different patterns: a check, a stripe and a swirl, yet somehow manages to look chic. Delphi knows if she were to try such a radical combination she would look as if she had been attacked by a curtain shop. Giulia has narrow shoulders, her twig-like legs are crossed at the ankle and tilted modestly to one side. Her tortoiseshell glasses slip down her nose and she continually pokes them back with a manicured finger.

Delphi doesn't pay for these therapy sessions in cash, she can't afford to. Instead, she babysits Giulia's son Alessandro in exchange. He has Down's Syndrome and Delphi loves to paint with him and take him to the park. They hold hands and play together. He likes to talk and Delphi likes to listen. Lucia made the original introduction but didn't suggest the contra deal, Giulia did. Delphi knows she's the one benefiting more and suspects Giulia is generous because she also gave birth to a child alone. Once a week, Delphi sits in therapy here, clawing mud from her eyes.

'You wrote to Orlo, Delphi. How did it feel?' Her voice is husky after a lifetime worshipping the cigarette.

'My predominant feeling was one of relief.' As Delphi readjusts herself in the chair she wonders, not for the first time, if there is something to be said for feeling less. The office, which is a room at the front of Giulia's apartment, is a neutral and calm space. Delphi has been coming here for a month, shovelling her way through her memories and traumas, cleaning herself up in anticipation for the clarity that will be required of her as a mother. Giulia is fond of saying, 'Inner work is the most powerful work to be done. You benefit by leading an examined life, but all those around you also gain. It is brave, important work.' Delphi believes her.

'Your father? Did you email him?' The therapist's pen is poised ready to take notes.

'Yes. I wrote and told him about the baby. He'll be appalled.'

'Did you tell him where you're living?'

Delphi wobbles her head. 'Sort of. He knows which country I'm in. If he wanted to know more he could ask Jack or Hugh. You know, what I've realised is that I've always tried to find myself in them. In my family. To catch my reflection in their eyes. My worth only found through their love.'

'Enmeshment and lack of boundaries, Delphi.'

'Yup. I've been shit at boundaries that's for sure.' She says and moves her hand on her stomach to try to feel the baby kick again.

Giulia carefully observes Delphi, then drops her head to write. After a moment she looks up and says, 'Children that have lived through trauma sometimes learn to override danger signals so they can stay in connection. In your case, neither one of your parents offered you safety but you were, quite naturally, so desperate to be in relationship with them you had to ignore the danger. Do you think you did that?'

A car horn makes its way into their space from three floors below, drawing Delphi's attention to the open window.

'Yes, I am not good at knowing how to protect myself. I will hold on when the lights are flashing red.' She thinks of Christoph and her cheeks burn. She flicks her fingers in the way Giulia taught her to move pain out of her body.

When the moment has eased Giulia offers, 'It is progress for you to be clear about what you want and what you don't want. You can't say a proper *yes* without understanding how to say a proper *no*.'

Delphi sees her belly move pushed up by a foot or an elbow.

'Where will you live when the baby comes, when you can no longer work at the restaurant?'

'Lucia and Roberto, they're good people. Some days she's still furious that I'm pregnant and not married.'

Giulia releases a clicking sound from her mouth.

'But on Monday, I think... yes Monday, she said I can stay on at the villa. It's been sitting empty for such a long time and her father downstairs likes the proximity of company. He's a sweet old guy. I hardly see him though. I guess by company she means the sound of my footsteps above him.' Delphi often picks wildflowers on her walk back from the restaurant and leaves them in a jar by his front door. The posy vanishes, then a few days later the cleaned jar sits bearing a gift tucked inside. A smooth pebble, an interesting packet of matches or, best of all, a little drawing.

'So, for the immediate future I am safe.'

'Good, Delphi. I am happy for you. And you have your next scan when?'

'I had my final scan last week. The baby is very healthy. And I decided to find out, the baby is a girl. I'm going to have a daughter.'

The women loop back to their separate thoughts. Giulia's private, Delphi's euphoric.

'Oh, and Romy and I talked for ages the other day. Her band is going really well. I emailed her a copy of the baby's scan and she had it made into a t-shirt that she's wearing. She's going to come for the baby's birth if it works with her gig schedule.'

Giulia flips back through her notes finding the name she's after. 'Will Adarsha come too?'

'I was hoping but she's still in India in an ashram.'

'*Allora*. And how are you sleeping?'

'Not much, but I do as you suggest and stay in bed resting.'

'And your nightmares?'

'Um... better I think. I'm not afraid to go to sleep now.'

'And your grief?'

'Lessening.'

'Are you making friends here in Florence?'

'No, but I've not made the effort. The only people here I talk to, other than at the restaurant, is you and Alessandro, your sweet boy, which really suits me. It's time I stopped jabbering and started listening. Also listening to myself. I like to listen to the trees. What's that quote? "We have two ears and one mouth, use them accordingly."'

Giulia writes this down.

'Delphi, what if I were to suggest to you that your relationships are here to make you conscious rather than happy?'

Delphi turns this over and laughs.

'If that's the case, my relationships, I mean with my family and some of the people I've fallen in love with, they would be extraordinary tools of self-mastery.' She sits still, allowing herself to fully drop into the thought. 'And maybe, looking at it in that light, even though it's been painful, what they've taught me has helped me.'

'That's right, realigning you, directing you towards your higher purpose for living.'

'Well if that's true, that's actually pretty beautiful.'

Giulia settles back an inch in her chair. Now they are getting somewhere.

*

Delphi sits on the floor of the Academia Galleria looking up at Michelangelo's David. The sculpture gleams, all seventeen feet of him, an ode to bravery and masculinity. Delphi comes here so often that the guards no longer charge her. The tenderness of the marble flesh captivates her. The expression on his eloquent face, the flare of his nostrils, the set of his jaw, the furrowed brow, all focus before he goes to war with Goliath. Delphi is reminded that without vulnerability courage cannot exist.

She loves this David. He has a living place inside her heart. Their relationship changes hue each time she visits. Today his nakedness fills her with longing. She yearns to run her hands over his body and imbue the stone with warmth. A noxious vapor trail of her loneliness wafts past her but she doesn't breathe it in. Instead she rifles around for self-compassion and then applies it to her abrasions.

Michelangelo said that in every block of marble he plainly saw a statue fully formed. His only job was to chip away the rough imprisoning walls to reveal the loveliness within.

Delphi knows this as a powerful metaphor for life. Isn't that what we humans all do? Chip away at our own sorrows, angers and shames, exposing imperfections and mortal fears in the hope that this exertion will reveal our most radiant selves? For Delphi this is the meaning of daring greatly. It is the basis of her work with Giulia.

Michelangelo knew this massive block of marble was filled with imperfections but he loved it anyway. Don't we all have cracks inside us? Isn't it through our imperfections that we reveal our humanity? Doesn't that vulnerability allow us to hew more away, revealing our deeper, truer and less defended selves?

Michelangelo carved the pupils of David's eyes in the shape of a heart. Why? Does it suggest that David sees with his heart? Or is it through his heart he is able to face Goliath? Delphi is learning that her own heart is her pure core, the tumbling source of wisdom and power within her. She is going to honour it and trust it to be her guiding star in the black of night. Which will, of course, come again. This thinking makes her fearless.

Delphi is oblivious to the other people around her. She walks around David slowly. Her eyes reverentially moving over the curves of him. This hero, this colossus, this giant killer. The battle cry has been called. He does not falter. Alone he fights the hegemony and wins.

This gives Delphi hope and faith. She knows she's not out of the woods. To survive, to thrive she will need to choose to step back in, to stop holding herself apart.

CHAPTER 25

DELPHI FINISHES TAKING AN order and turns to deliver it to the kitchen when she sees him. Her father is standing watching her. He looks huge and dark. As if he's been coloured in more somberly than everything else. Delphi notices her armour thwack into place, like Iron Man, body moulded protection, solid steel over her skewerable flesh. She is shocked to see him, but on another level, she suspects her subconscious was expecting him. The set of his face pre-warns her that he's come to tell, level and demand.

She holds the docket up indicating she's seen him and will return after delivering it. She moves across the room, conscious of her rounded belly. He is seeing her pregnant for the first time. She wonders if it will soften his heart at all. Delphi chastises herself for her sentimentality, defaulting to old modes again. She reminds herself, soft front, strong back, wild heart.

She wipes her hands on her apron as she approaches him. 'Hello Edward,' she says. Her voice is clear. 'How did you find me?'

He is peering directly into her face as one would a specimen in a jar. He looks tired. Delphi wonders if that was a flicker of concern. Why she has always found him so confusing is because she suspects deep down he loves her, just as she loves him.

'Jack, he told me. He's here too.' Delighted, Delphi looks over her father's shoulder for her brother.

'He's not here now. He's down in Florence. I thought it best if I saw you alone.'

Divide and conquer, Delphi thinks.

Father and daughter stand awkwardly together. The literal space between them indicating the figurative. Delphi's hands begin to tremble so she clasps them together.

He breaks eye contact and looks around, his mouth tight as if everything lacking about the restaurant is her fault.

'So, Delphi, I see you've made a mess of things.' He flicks his eyes towards her stomach. 'Who is the father?'

Delphi concentrates on staying calm. 'An artist. He lives in London. But he's not involved.'

Edward nods, confirming something for himself.

'You need to come home. I can get you a job as a secretary for one of the local doctors. You can have the baby and it can be raised English.'

She shuts her eyes for a second too long and he pounces on her resistance. Edward will not be shut out. His mode of warfare is to unleash the cavalry.

'You cannot possibly have that baby here on your own with no money, no prospects, waitressing for Christ's sake. What a waste. Delphi, it is time to grow up. Come home and I will bail you out of this. I will financially support you until you get back on your feet after the–' He can't locate the word. 'Jack told me you both didn't get very much from your mother's estate. She was never good with money.'

'Edward, I'm okay here,' Delphi says quietly. He's never respected her, never believed her capable of independence. Always trying to hook her with the power of his money but his choice of bait is all wrong. Money holds no interest to her, but the promise of love is a different matter. The tragedy is that what he offers and what she needs are incompatible. Father and daughter always feel dejected, like the repellent ends of magnets forever pushing each other away.

'Thank you for the offer but–'

'But what?' He flares and Delphi turns to see if anyone is disturbed. The idea of a scene makes her feel ill. Vivian and Edward used to clear whole restaurants with their rages. Lucia is watching them and Delphi holds up her fingers indicating she needs two minutes. Lucia looks concerned and carries her tray of glasses in the opposite direction.

Edward doesn't march along anyone else's timeline, his irritation increases. 'You need to swallow your pride and acknowledge you need help. Your mother was always proud too.' His face is corrugated with sadness. Delphi has a memory of him hitting her mother. Of Vivian's bruised eye or jaw. Of Edward driving off during a frightful row with Vivian's skirt caught in the car door dragging her to the ground. Edward responding to this violence by saying she provoked him. And later him taking Vivian tenderly by the hand and kissing her cheeks. As if a poison had been expelled from both of them and they were deposited on the shores of love once more. Dysfunction is so difficult for a child to diagnose from within the family, but Delphi knew even then that this was an illness between her parents. Love and hate confused. Violent polarisation then cleaving towards mimicking passion.

'Please don't talk about Mama.' Her voice low in warning. Delphi has to hold herself back. She can feel another self rising within, incandescent, ready to explode, but she refuses to allow provocation to rob her of her dignity.

Edward hands her a card.

'This is where your brother and I are staying. He wants you to call him. Think about this, Delphi. I will be here for two days and then I'm leaving. At that point the offer will be off the table. Do you hear me?'

And she does hear him but not with all of herself. Parts of her are submerged beneath the waves, as if she's been knocked off a dock and is sinking.

He leans forward and in a whisper says, 'Make the right choice. For this baby if not for yourself.'

Then something extraordinary happens. His chin wobbles, just once, but Delphi catches it, and a tear is released down his face. For Delphi, that single droplet has the power of an inter-planetary collision and everything else recedes as she watches it, utterly mystified as to what it means. It calls to her most tender self and she throws her arms around him. He raises his arms around her and they embrace. Then Edward steps away, sniffs hard and walks back through the doors like a matador.

*

Delphi sits on her villa stoop. It is late at night. Her legs ache from the long shift and her soul aches from a complicated choice. She has a blanket around her shoulders and her mother's box of ashes tucked beneath her folded legs. The box no longer fits onto her lap. That space is taken up with another great love.

From this angle the view of the valley is hidden from her. Here she can see the stone shed and some olive trees, the outliers of the grove before the darkness gobbles all definition up.

Delphi is trying to process her father's visit. His power over her is as sure as a leash lashed around her throat. What would Vivian want her to do? Should she accept his offer? Would it be capitulation or sense? What is the best choice for her baby? If Delphi knew she would choose it in an instant. Delphi looks at the dramatic curve of her belly and refolds the blanket around them both. Will she be submitting to his ownership, beholden and dependent? The idea makes her constrict. Or should she carry on as she is, muddling through, backing herself? Delphi wishes a sage would appear to explain the pros of pragmatism. Her disposition, always more of a romantic bent, has the cons covered. Maybe Edward is right. That she's an egoist, a stubborn fool and she's gambling with her child's welfare. So much, so very much is at stake.

Orlo hasn't replied to her letter. Which makes the muscles which hold her vertical atrophy with disappointment. She doesn't want anything from him for herself, but she does feel sad for her daughter who will be fatherless. Delphi wonders if she herself would have been better off fatherless. Sometimes a gift is the door that fails to open.

Surely Delphi can't go back to England? She's exhausted by her own bullshit. She must be brave – it's not foolhardy, it is courageous.

Women have been having babies alone for centuries and Delphi will join their ranks with her head held high.

She looks up and the sky is vast. She breathes in its colossal size and senses collapsed structures within resolidifying. An inexplicable but palpable energy exchange from the heavens. A shooting star would be perfect now and she waits, hopeful. It doesn't come but she sees an equally wonderful illumination in her mind's eye. She sees three generations of women sitting huddled together on that Tuscan stoop. Vivian, Delphi and the baby girl held within her. A sacred umbilical cord connecting them. Delphi is strengthened. She is unschooled in the art of saying no, but she is going to practise it against the most formidable of opponents. Recognising that thought for what it is, Delphi feels more resolute. Her father is not her enemy. Her tendency to cast him as such comes from fear. She tips her face down onto her arms and cuddles into a ball. She will do better. She is doing better. Each and every day is an opportunity to do better.

CHAPTER 26

JACK OPENS HIS HOTEL door looking dishevelled and stressed. Delphi stands, waiting to be invited in as he processes her pregnancy.

'Wow, look at that,' he says dumbfounded.

'I know.' Her voice seems to break the spell and Jack gives her a clumsy, overly tight cuddle.

'Three of us in this hug, huh?' he laughs. He sounds skittery.

'Yep,' Delphi answers, squashed in his arms. She closes her eyes trying to remember when someone last held her. Oh yes, Christoph, months ago.

'Come in, come in,' her brother beckons and she follows him into the room. The contents of her brother's suitcase are scattered everywhere.

Jack has a large whisky on the go, he takes a sip then asks Delphi what she'd like to drink.

'Nothing, thank you.'

They stand suspended for a moment and he offers her a chair. It's as if they're strangers. Delphi wonders if there's a word for that, in German maybe, when someone you love is unknowable. *Fernweh,* she read recently means longing for, feeling homesick for a place you've never been. So surely there must be.

Delphi sits and Jack settles himself on the end of the bed.

'You look really great, Del. How're you doing?'

She drops her bag at her feet and holds her belly. She is big and she loves it.

'I'm well.' She moves her head from side to side. 'The baby is healthy. She's due in six weeks. How's Zenia?'

Bringing up the niece she's never met probably isn't the smoothest option.

'She's great.'

Another uncomfortable silence de-oxygenates the room further.

'Oh hey, let me show you this.' Jack puts down his drink and pulls at the gold chain around his neck, freeing their mother's locket from beneath his t-shirt neckline. He uses his thumb nail to open it. Delphi steps closer and sees a photo of Vivian looking radiant. Jack tilts the locket so she can see the other panel. 'And this side is you.' Delphi reaches out and holds the locket in her hand, she is acutely moved.

'Passion Fruit, I need to tell you something and I wanted to do it face to face.'

'Okay,' she says, bracing herself.

'Grandpa has died.'

This information filters through Delphi. She waits for it to lodge, for emotion to be released, but her insides remain undisturbed. Shock. Here it is again. She recognises it.

'Oh…' she sighs. 'How? Where?'

'In his sleep at home. Lucky really.'

'Yes,' Delphi answers.

Silence.

'Is it terrible that I'm not feeling anything yet, Jack?'

'No, I don't think so. He was old, he was ready to go and, for my part, I think my capacity for grief is still all taken up with Mama.'

That makes sense to her, too. Delphi stares at the nothingness of a midpoint. She swallows and realises she now wants a drink. 'Jack, do you have any wine by any chance?'

'Should you do that with the baby?'

'A glass won't hurt her.'

'Her?'

'Yes, I'm having a little girl.'

Her brother smiles and goes to the bar fridge. He brings out a bottle of white. 'I don't know what it'll be like.'

'Anything's fine.' She watches him find a corkscrew, open the bottle and pour some into a glass.

She stands to accept it and offers a toast.

'To our gentle grandfather.'

Jack picks up his whisky and clinks it against Delphi's glass.

'A sweet man.'

Delphi sits down and Jack starts pacing.

'Jack, are you okay?' She offers him her open face.

'Ah…' he starts, 'I'm… I don't know. Some days are better than others.'

Delphi sits in silence hoping if she holds the space, he will fill it. In time he does, wrestling with himself.

'I miss her. Mum.' He clarifies unnecessarily. 'And…'

'And?' Delphi asks tenderly.

'Since she died something has crossed over in me. I am not the same person.' He looks bereft.

Delphi puts down her drink, goes to Jack and holds him.

'I love you, Jack. You are a good man.' And as if released by her touch he starts to weep. Delphi is shocked but she holds on, she rubs his back.

For a long time he sobs and when the rawness has subsided a little, she guides him to the bed and sits him down. She goes to the bathroom and finds a face cloth and runs it under the hot tap. She can hear her brother weeping behind her. She returns to him, brushes his long hair back from his eyes and softly uses the warm towel to wipe his tear-stained face.

'Darling,' she says gently, 'I know something of how you feel.'

He blinks up at her, ravaged, as a fresh horror blanches Jack's face. He takes her wrists in both his hands and clamps down on them. The cloth drops from her fingers and she looks at Jack confused. His grip is too firm, he's hurting her. The set of his face has become pure anguish. His mouth twists and the flesh tightens around his eyes making him almost unrecognisable.

'Jack?' she tries to rotate her wrists free.

'Delphi,' he starts, but has to clear his throat. 'Delphi, you are not responsible for Arthur.'

She shakes her head. She's heard this argument before.

'No, listen to me,' he is insistent, there is a desperation.

'Delphi, I am the one who let Arthur drown,' he pauses, making sure he has her full attention.

'That day when he died you needed to go to the bathroom. You asked me to watch him for a moment and I told you that I would. He was nowhere near the pool. The phone rang. I ran inside to answer it. I was waiting on a call from Penny, that girl from school, I had a crush on her.'

Delphi's heart stops beating.

'I heard you screaming,' Jack continues. 'I dropped the phone. The receiver bounced off the floor. The spiral cord extending and recoiling.' He releases his grip on her. 'From the window I saw you, you were so little, six years old and you were screaming out for help. The baby was in the pool but I couldn't move. I just stood there, disbelieving, watching as you went mad. You threw yourself in. Then I came back to life. I ran out to the garden. I jumped in and pulled you out. You were hysterical, your clothes sodden, your hair in your mouth. I went back in for Arthur. I pulled him up by the arm. I slipped getting us out. We both went back in.' The words are tumbling out of him like water released from an opened dam.

'I had to find him in all the bubbles. I got him around the waist and heaved him up. He was splayed on the paving stones. Do you remember that? And then Mama, drunk I think, she was there and she was screaming too. All hell breaking loose. You had a bloody nose. The red was pouring down your face. Mama trying to perform CPR on the baby while screaming for me to call an ambulance. I raced back to the kitchen. I was wet. I slipped in the hall. That's how I broke my wrist. I called emergency.' Jack slumps, his chemistry reconfiguring. A long withheld truth finally released.

He carries on more calmly. 'Then I am missing a whole chunk. It's lost, but the ambulance and police are in the house. All the flashing lights. The sirens. All I can clearly remember is Arthur's face. He looked like a doll. His eyes wide open, so blue, so beautiful, but the life, his life, gone.'

The frenzy of the truth-telling simmers down further and Jack begins to shake. This escalates until his whole body convulses, verging on the clattering of a fit.

Delphi is dazed. She wants to comfort him but her body won't do as she commands so she stands there motionless. She forces herself to lean over him, she takes a firm hold and presses her body against his. She rocks him back and forth, supporting him, marshalling all her strength.

With chattering teeth, he continues, 'I do remember something else. I do remember you, Del. You went to another dimension. That blood dripping from your nose. Your huge eyes blinking. A vast stillness about you. As if you had drowned too. I didn't intend not to own up. It just unfolded that way. I'm not trying to make excuses. It's inexcusable, but I do want to try to explain, my God I owe you that. I was twelve. You never told anyone. I think you just forgot or maybe you loved me too much to think me capable of letting you down so terribly… maybe if you'd acknowledged I was responsible you knew you wouldn't be able to love me anymore, that you'd have lost two brothers that day… I don't know, but the longer I held my silence the harder it got, eventually I lost the chance to tell the truth. Then it turned on me and my shame ate me like cancer. I learnt to bury it, but I couldn't do that near you. So, you see, Delphi?' He turns to her, his voice thick, and he cups her face in his shaking hands. 'It was my fault all along. I am the one who destroyed everything. And worse than that, I let you think it was you because I am weak and I am spineless. I'm sorry. I'm so ashamed of myself.'

Delphi pulls her face free, she doesn't want him to touch her and yet she looks on at her tortured brother through her immense confusion, hurt and anger and still she chooses to meet him in his grief. She recognises his nightmare as the very same one she's been living in for twenty years. She can't abide him being there alone. Delphi pulls him back into her arms and strokes his hair. He draws in a ragged breath, then he cries like a little boy.

*

Delphi holds Jack a long time, until eventually he falls asleep and she turns her reeling thoughts to herself. Everything she understood is morphing. She didn't kill Arthur. She isn't that person. But poor destroyed Jack, he is. She has more compassion for him than she ever did for herself. In a way it hardly matters who is responsible now. Everybody suffered. Truth and accountability don't bring Arthur back. But she wants to get away from Jack now, to be on her own, to take the time that is required to sift through this new story.

*

Delphi arrives at her villa door and lets herself in. As soon as the sun is up she will call her father and arrange to see him. She still doesn't know what the right course of action is, but she must see Edward before he leaves in the afternoon.

She strips her clothes off and lets them drop to the ground. She walks into the bathroom and turns the shower on hot. The water takes a long time to heat up, but Delphi stands patiently watching the liquid column fall. Clouds of steam billow up. She is in a fog of warmth. Delphi steps into the small cubical and shuts her eyes as the water falls over her head, face and shoulders. She moves back a little and lets it caress her belly. The baby girl within responds to the heat by pushing out. Delphi opens her eyes and sees a bump protruding from the sphere of her tummy. It must be a fist or a heel. Delphi touches it with her fingers. Her baby pulls away, and then, wonderfully, pushes back. Delphi laughs. It is deliciously freakish. Back and forth they tap each other, communicating in Morse code. Delphi is specific in what she is saying to her daughter. She is saying, I love you. I can't wait to meet you. Stay where you are. Stay safe and grow well. And when it's time I will be waiting for you. My love. My child.

*

Her father orders a cup of coffee and then rearranges the sugar in the bowl on the table. He can't bring himself to look at his daughter.

'So, you saw Jack?' he asks.

Delphi sips at her water. 'Yes.'

'And did he talk sense into you?'

Delphi reminds herself to not draw battle lines, that's the strategy where everyone loses.

'We didn't actually talk about me that much.' She is wary, edging her way around the topic that changed the world. She has no intention of revealing it to her father. To tell him would be to throw Jack to the wolves.

'Christ,' he says, exhaling. 'So, what have you decided?' He looks at her now. His eyes are pointed at her like drill bits.

'Edward, can I ask you, do you ever miss Mama?' She hadn't intended to open with this but her mother's absence, along with her pregnancy, is omnipresent to her.

Edward looks at his watch. A Patek Philippe he bought himself to commemorate his own father's early death. Delphi knows her paternal grandfather's birth and death dates are inscribed on the back. As is her father's birth date with a dash and a blank. The gap sitting ominously, waiting for his death date to be inscribed in due course.

'Miss your mother? No, Delphi. I do not.'

'Did you love her at any point? Can you tell me about the love?'

His mouth is clamped tight.

'Once, I suppose I did, I must have, yes, very much but I can't remember now. It's all so long ago and she was a terrible wife. She was mad.'

Delphi lets the insult drop to her feet. Why is it that some men are forever calling women hysterical and insane? Because they are frightened of us, she thinks. Undermine to control the tactic of choice.

'I don't want to argue,' she treads on gently, eliciting a derisive snort from her father.

'Why was I sent away to boarding school? I wasn't even seven. I was grieving. Do you know how desperately unhappy I was? I just wanted to be at home. I needed to be at home.'

Her father sits back in his chair looking exasperated.

'Please tell me, Edward? I want to make sense of it all and now that Mama has gone, you're the only one I can ask.'

'Because of what happened with Arthur, of course. You were sinking, your mother was unhinged. I thought it would be best for you to be out of all that.'

Delphi looks at his aged face and decides quite simply to forgive him. She's done keeping score. Maybe he couldn't bear her grief? Or perhaps it was because he simply couldn't fix her. Delphi sees that it doesn't really matter. As it doesn't matter that today is her twenty-seventh birthday and he hasn't remembered. Sometimes to be strong we need to be a little smaller. Don't puff up, she thinks to herself. Choose a quiet, fierce strength. Like a tree. An oak.

'Another question,' She knows she's probably squeezing blood out of a stone but everything tells her now is the last time to try. The world seems to have taken on a visual lucidity.

His coffee arrives and her pot of tea. She thanks the waitress. He doesn't.

'Is it true you don't want me to come to your funeral? Are you unwell?'

'Not that I know of. If you don't count old age as a disease.'

'So why did you tell Jack that? Was it to punish me? What for?'

He doesn't respond.

'Edward, I don't understand. It seems cruel.'

He gives her nothing.

'Do you love me, Edward?'

He looks uncomfortable. Weakened and unsure. 'When you were little, I adored you.' He shares this in the same tone one would use to lob an accusation.

'And what happened to that love? Did I do something to break it or to lose it? Was it Arthur's death? Or collateral damage due to your unhappiness with Mama?'

'Delphi,' he leans forward, intense again, 'This is what you do. Twist and turn everything, making yourself the victim. You have not been a good daughter to me. I have come all this way to save you from yourself. If you don't want to be in my life, why should you come to my funeral? And let's not forget you didn't permit me to go to Vivian's.'

And this is what he does – name calls and bullies. Yet connection is what he seeks, he just doesn't have the skills or he's too damaged. Delphi sees a man in pain. She sees his loneliness and under all of that there is a tiny, beautiful flame. His love for her. This theory feels right, like a lock turning true. It makes Delphi sad for him.

'This is the lay of the land, young lady. Either you come home and sort out the train wreck of your life or you are out. You are excommunicated. I can't be chasing you all over the world anymore.'

Delphi massages the hinges in her jaw to steady herself.

'You've never, ever, come looking for me, Edward. Not now. Not ever. I think you're really here looking for yourself.'

Fury catches fire and she braces herself for the full force of it. Recognising the body memory of cowering as a child. This time around the sun, though, she refuses to disintegrate.

'Hello, you two.'

Delphi and Edward turn to see Jack approaching their table. A pigeon flies off, similarly disturbed by his arrival. Her brother looks deathly pale as if he's unearthed himself from a grave.

'Will you sit?' she asks him, stunned.

He is jumpy and his hands are jammed deep into his pockets.

'No, Del, I won't sit, I just wanted to come to tell Dad what we spoke about last night. I think it's well overdue, don't you?' Delphi gets to her feet, shaking her head. She wants to protect her brother.

'You don't need to do that for me, Jack, truly you don't.' She reaches out and takes one of his hands. 'We are okay, we are good.' Dread is making a rushing sound in her ears and she loses her voice inside it. But Jack won't be stopped, a train in motion, twenty years of anguished silence fuelling him forward.

'Dad, Delphi didn't let Arthur drown. It was me. She asked me to watch out for him and I didn't.' He says it simply. As if he's over rehearsed taking all the life out of the lines.

Their father stands up and the paper napkin flutters from his lap. He is slightly stooped, unable to pull into his full frame. It is as if he's been punched. He looks blankly from his son to his daughter. His face reassembles into a thick mask.

'Delphi, did you really think I would believe this?'

And the world is ripped apart. Delphi is whipped by the force.

'I know it was you.' Edward points his finger at her heart. Then he turns back to his son.

'Shame on you letting her twist you around, Jack.' Edward has found his height now and he is formidable.

The blood drains from Delphi and she looks to the ground mystified to see that it isn't flowing red. She is falling backwards yet her body is stationary. She lifts her arms to stop her brother lunging at their father and holding them apart she says with a channelled calmness.

'I don't accept your offer, Edward. I won't be coming back to England but I want you to know this…' She is steady and direct. 'I have always loved you. I am sorry for my share in our pain. We were not made for each other in this life. Or maybe we have been each other's greatest teachers. Whatever the explanation, you are my father. I hope you can forgive me as I forgive you. I won't cause you any more distress. Be free of me. Be free of the mess that has always been us. And when it's your time to die, and I say this without malice, don't have any regrets in relation to me.' The wind has exhausted itself. Delphi has accessed an ocean of tenderness within and she looks at her father, her own face in the masculine. She says gently, 'Dada.' It's the long-ago name she called him before she was old enough to know it didn't make sense.

Edward has nothing to give, concede nor refute in response. He snatches his wallet off the table and puts it in his pocket. He looks at his children appalled. Then he turns and walks away.

CHAPTER 27

It's 6 PM, AND Delphi has been lying on her bed for the last hour listening to her body. Her due date is tomorrow. She looks at her vast belly, awestruck at what a shocking design this all is. How on earth will this baby find its way out?

This morning she had been walking around the Florentine markets after being told by the doctors that her baby probably wouldn't come for days. She'd been lifting herbs to her nose and squeezing nectarines between her fingers. Delphi had felt full of energy and noticed that the bustle, the buildings, and her pregnancy… the moment felt enchanting.

And this afternoon she was compelled to come home via Fiesole. She wanted to sit up there and look at the view. The optical equivalent of taking a great big drink. And there, overlooking Florence, the cramping had begun.

The pain dashes in and retreats every five minutes. Delphi wonders if she should call the hospital but decides against it, long schooled in not making a fuss. She marks an asterisk beside this pattern for later inspection. Delphi forces herself on to her feet to look for something to eat. Vivian's nightie clings to her in the heat. There's some ravioli in the fridge and she puts it in a pot to warm. The tightening in her tummy makes her clutch the back of a chair and grit her teeth. When it passes, like a train leaving a station, she turns on the tiny box TV for distraction. The image is partially distorted on the right side as if it's slipping off the screen. She surfs the channels, wielding the unused remote like a luddite. A weather station with a hostess in a bikini catches her attention. Next is a game show with several women wearing gowns slashed down to their waists or up around their crotches to expose maximum skin. Two channels further on, a mini-skirted woman is changing a lightbulb standing on a desk with her male colleagues jeering like the perverted schoolboys they really are. The sexualising of women usually infuriates Delphi, but now she finds the stupidity a hilarity and she laughs out loud. The sound of her cackle shocks her. Maybe hysteria is part of early labour?

It doesn't actually matter what is on the telly. Anything will provide company. Delphi wishes Romy were here, and she makes a little humming noise and stamps her feet during the next round of contractions. She catches her reflection in the window and suddenly feels frighteningly alone. She pulls herself back from that edge and decides on a police show. It might be from the seventies or from the current day, it's difficult to tell in Italy. She thinks about *The Bill* and sitting watching it with her mother on that fateful night.

Delphi waddles back to the kitchen and lifts the bubbling congealed blob off the stove. She knows she won't eat it. She should but she can't. More tightening bites at her violently. When she's caught her breath, Delphi unplugs her mobile from the charger and calls the hospital. Erring on the side of caution she decides that calling too early is better than calling too late. She doesn't want to give birth on the kitchen floor.

A nurse picks up and Delphi explains she thinks she's in labour. She's told to hold and is put through to the correct department. Outside the villa, Italy is settling into evening. This is the last turn of the planet into shadow before Delphi is to be a mother. Unless, of course, the labour takes days.

Another nurse comes to the phone and says, '*Pronto.*'

Delphi tells the woman her name, due date and how far apart the contractions are. The nurse replies in heavily accented English, 'You don't need to rush. It is your first baby and you will have lots of time if still four minutes apart. Have something to eat because you have a long night ahead of you. And have a gin and tonic. That helps with the nerves. It will relax you. And if you feel like it, make love to your husband. That is good for labour, and good for your man. Having baby can make him feel lonely.'

Delphi laughs. She has no intention of doing any of those things. The last one, never, ever again.

'Relax and come in when you are two minutes apart. Bring socks as your feet will get cold. Ask for Francesca and I will expect you later. *Si? Ciao.*'

'Okay,' she tells herself, 'I need to hold on longer. God knows how but I do.' The pain is becoming sharper, like a hot blade being slashed about inside her.

Delphi carefully takes her Keats-Shelley bag and packs a fresh nightie, some clothes and her toothbrush. She finds the outfit she bought for the baby. A tiny white babygrow with delicate green turtles on it. When Delphi had pre-washed it in the sink, then hung it out, along with the tiny booties and egg-sized hat, she had sat down in awe to watch it all dry.

More contractions ferociously demand her attention. When they leave she takes the box of her mother's ashes from next to her pillow and tucks them into the bag. She gathers the gnome from her bedside table and puts him in as well, making sure his head is exposed so he can breathe.

She looks at the bag and tells herself she can do this. The centre falls out of her conviction and she wonders if she might die. Women have died in childbirth for centuries. The image of her body unclaimed in a Tuscan morgue is grim. A tag tied to her big toe with brown string. What would happen to her baby? Delphi refuses this bleak line of inquiry. She removes Vivian's ashes from her bag. She kisses the box and tucks it lovingly back into her bed.

Now is a time for birth. Not for death.

*

Delphi had been told a taxi would refuse her if she tried to take one when in labour. Amniotic fluid is a special brew of acid. If the waters break during the journey the upholstery can't be cleaned, it has to be replaced. This miraculous nutrient and excrement-dense liquid which forms life kills upholstery.

Delphi thought about pretending not to be pregnant. Just a big girl in a kaftan with a colossal handbag clutched in front of her. Thinking that through it ultimately seemed fanciful. No kaftan nor strategically held bag could disguise the proclamation of Delphi's pregnancy.

Weeks ago, Delphi had arranged for the Fiat in the driveway to be fixed. The flat tyre seemed pointlessly sad and she'd asked the local mechanic to sort it out. The old chap downstairs had been initially confused but ultimately touched by this and had been liberally offering Delphi the use of the car ever since. She would do grocery shopping for him and then open all the car windows and drive far too fast down the laneways feeling herself prickling back to life.

One day she'd plucked up the nerve to ask him if she could borrow the car to get herself to the hospital when the baby came. In the uniting spirit of collegiate eccentrics he had deemed that a permissible idea and promised not to tell Lucia.

Delphi shoves the keys into the ignition and rejoices when it turns on. It growls and the headlights flood the courtyard. She hopes she's not waking Lucia's father whom she now affectionately and officially calls the Downstairs Man and he calls her the Upstairs Woman. Contractions attack her. It feels very wrong to be sitting down. She pants as they ease. Quickly, before the next set, she turns over her shoulder to back along the narrow drive. If she drives off the path, it would be a disaster. She concentrates hard and slowly takes the bend in reverse. The trees are sheltering arms above her. 'Alright,' she says out loud when she reaches the road. It is good to say it so she says it again. The countryside is completely deserted at this time of night. She decides against pulling the belt across herself as the idea of any pressure on her belly is intolerable. Her face is burning hot so she lowers the window. The night is still and she gulps in the thick air.

Delphi checks again for cars; all is silence and darkness bar the rumble and lights of the Fiat. She finishes reversing out, sets the car into first and rolls off down the hill. Bugs jump in her headlights and the air is velvety as it rushes in the window. She tries not to be infuriated having to slow almost to a standstill at the blind corners, and when she accelerates out of them, her lights illuminate the stone buildings, ancient walls and slumbering foliage.

When the contractions come Delphi pulls the car over to the side of the road, gnashes her teeth, cries out and clenches the steering wheel until they are done with her. She sees a cow nearby in a field. Its sleep disturbed and Delphi calls out to it, 'Sorry, I'm having a baby.' And she laughs. 'This is amazing. It's completely extreme, but it is amazing.'

*

Delphi is lying on the examination table as Francesca removes her fingers from inside her.

'*Allora,*' she says, taking her gloves off and putting them in the bin. 'You are two centimetres dilated.'

Delphi wants to voice her disbelief but another round of contractions won't have it. They're much more painful when she's on her back. Francesca indicates she can get up. Delphi uses the other woman's help to pull herself to her feet and she stamps until she's recovered.

'Only two centimetres?'

'*Si*, maybe two and a half, but not three.' Francesca is filling in a form.

Oh God, Delphi thinks. It already feels such a long journey and there's another eight centimetres to go before even trying to push this human out.

'How do you know?' she asks the midwife.

Francesca is in her late fifties, a sun worshipper with close-cropped hair and a kind, loved face. She holds up two fingers. 'Like dis. Two fingers is two centimetres.' She adds another finger to her line up. 'Three is three.' Delphi gets a sharp vision of this woman's fingers filling the widening gap in her cervix. Her body is stretching open as slowly and deliberately as if she were being pulled apart by a torture rack.

'I think you should go home. Your baby is not coming any time soon. You'll be more comfortable there, no? Is your husband parking your car?'

Delphi lifts her hands off the examination table where she'd bent over to catch her breath and repack her blown mind.

'Francesca, there is no husband. I am here on my own and I can't go home. I may have seriously underestimated this labour business, I'm not a wimp, but there is no way it is humanly possible for me to leave this hospital with this baby still inside me.'

Fluid starts running down Delphi's legs and pooling on the ground. 'Oh, I'm sorry.' Delphi says. 'I'll clean that up.'

Francesca laughs good-naturedly and covers the wet ground with paper towels.

'Leave it. I go see if we have a room for you. Stay here and carry on with that very good breathing.'

*

Five hours later Delphi is on all fours in a birthing pool. The pain has been beyond imagining, but now she is about to push. She holds the rim of the bath, determined not to scream so her daughter isn't born to the sound of torment. She channels the wild energy to the centre of her body and pushes down, down, down. The contraction passes and Delphi sees herself collapsing through slab after slab of plate glass. She's been in this dimension before. The ayahuasca ceremony. All that she was shown then, refinds her now, there's a tearing down of emotional barriers, she is plugging into something bigger than herself and the sensation of separateness is torn away. Delphi tastes the euphoria of truth.

Exhausted, clutching on to the bath's rim, breathing through her mouth, resting before the next onslaught. And when it arrives it is so extreme Delphi wants to scream out, 'I can't do this! This is a terrible, terrible mistake!' The doctor reassures her everything looks normal and a second midwife wipes a cloth across her forehead, pushing back her wet hair. 'Not long now,' she encourages her. 'A few more pushes like that and then you get to meet your baby.'

Delphi doesn't know if she has any more reserves and she starts to whimper. Then she hears it. She hears her mother's voice, very clearly, love-infused, spoken directly into her ear.

'Delphi. My spectacular flower.'

She tilts her head up from the side of the bath, longing to hear Vivian's voice again. Her mother is here. A great sob rolls up through her but Delphi catches it before it explodes. She refuses to let it out, fearing it will pull her undone.

Francesca is rubbing her back and telling her to make use of the next contraction. Adrenaline has rendered Delphi a shaking mess, but she digs into the deepest part of herself and as the thunder arrives she harnesses the pain and pushes with all of her might. Stars burst and Delphi's lower half is burning as if doused in petrol and set alight. All three attendants demand she stop pushing and Delphi does as she's commanded. The power of the contraction leaving her empty again.

'The head is out,' says the doctor. 'Don't worry, baby won't take a breath until she is in the air. So as long as you keep low in the water everything is beautiful.'

Delphi cannot speak. The next contraction arrives like the gathering of a biblical storm. 'This is it,' declares Francesca. Delphi pushes as hard as she possibly can. She feels her baby rotate and slither out of her and the relief rolls in like huge breaking waves. Delphi turns over and watches the doctor lifting her daughter out of the water. Just as he said, the baby takes her first breath and opens her dark eyes looking directly at her mother. The baby is placed into Delphi arms – a squashed, dark-haired creature – and they stare at each other, regarding, imprinting. Eventually Delphi must speak, words build worlds, she knows this and she says, 'Welcome, darling, I can't tell you how happy I am that you've arrived.'

Francesca and the other midwife hug each other, the doctor is smiling with his perfect teeth and Delphi asks the room, and the world, 'Is this really my baby?' The women laugh sharing her joy.

'Yes, Delphi. You did so well. And now it all begins for you. Everything will be more. More love. More empathy. More wonder. More pain too, but it's worth it.'

Delphi looks at her child with infinite fascination. The tiny, waterlogged fingernails, the eyelids blinking scalloped by perfect lashes. Her lungs working, in and out, for the first time. The bizarre umbilical cord which connects them floating about in the pool. Delphi picks it up from the water. It feels like rubber and is long and perfectly coiled – *how miraculous,* she thinks. She lets it drift from her fingers and instinctively holds her baby's mouth to her breast. The baby knows what to do too. She accepts her mother's nipple and drinks in the colostrum that is forming just for her.

*

In her hospital room in the middle of a quiet night, the overhead light is off but the bedside lamp bathes mother and child in a gentle glow. They're tucked up together in clean starched sheets. The baby is swaddled in a soft pink blanket and sleeps in Delphi's arms. Delphi can't tear her eyes away from her. Never before, in all her imaginings would this love, this awe, this gratitude be possible. Delphi is reborn, newly made sense of, she is this infant's mother. Seeds earlier planted bloom. She intuits the power of all the women who've given birth before her. The mighty life-creating feminine. She is invincible, vast and ageless. She makes sense to herself for the very first time.

*

Delphi is woken by a nurse she doesn't recognise shaking her shoulder. She offers tea and a little white pill in a paper cup. After some ineffectual back and forth the nurse brusquely disappears and comes back with reinforcements. The matron is straight backed, with an open face and bright smile. Delphi likes her very much on sight.

'Good morning, *la mamma*. I am told your birth was *var bene*. Dr Baronchi says you're a very brave! *Congratulazoni.*' She bends down to inspect the sleeping babe. She nods approval and moves the tea closer to Delphi. *'Molto grande,'* she exclaims, for in this country this baby is a whopper. Italian mothers tend to diet hard right through pregnancy making for smaller newborns.

'I get more pillows then *la mamma* can sit up and have a nice drink and take your pill.'

The sublime miracle of the baby hasn't lessened for Delphi. The child is entirely astonishing. As the pillows are pushed in behind her she shuffles herself up trying to keep the baby undisturbed in her left arm.

'What is the pill for?' Delphi asks, lifting it to her mouth.

The nurse is busy opening the curtains.

'Dis will stop the milk from coming in breasts. Then not sagging, bottle for baby and your husband very happy.'

Delphi's brain does a backflip and she puts the pill back into its little paper cup and takes the tea instead. Even tepid it's beyond delicious.

'May I have some breakfast *per favore*?' Delphi is suddenly struck with a hunger so intense it's like a wild animal is loose inside her.

The nurse turns to look at her patient.

'Che?' She asks, so Delphi repeats herself in Italian.

A look of judgement passes the nurse's face and she says, 'Okay, I will bring you a little something, but please remember time to watch your calories now. You don't want to be a big cow now you're a mama.' Delphi laughs out loud. She would eat a whole cow if given the chance, and she puts the teacup down empty onto its saucer. Food, she must have lots and lots of food.

*

Delphi is standing by the window, rocking her baby back and forth, soothing her after the shock of their first nappy change. The nurse returns to announce a visitor.

'Un signore in un bel vestito e qui per vederti, Mama.' A gentleman in an expensive suit is here to see you, Mama.

Delphi turns with her baby in her arms towards the door. Apprehension is seeping into her like a gas but the moment she sees Hugh in his Panama hat all those feelings are shot through with joy.

'Godfather o' mine,' she calls disbelievingly and stretches out an arm to him. He smiles rakishly, deposits a massive bunch of flowers on the side table, a wicker hamper on to the floor, and swoops in to meet the baby.

'Beloved Fem, look what you've made? A tiny, perfect human! I do hope she's an *enfant terrible* like you.'

'Oh Hugh... You came... I can't believe you came.'

He removes his hat and tosses it on the bed. Always at home wherever he is.

'Of course, of course I came. Now I'm not going to ask you about the birth because frankly that revolts me, but I see you're standing and the baby is perfect so the details are by-the-by really. What can I do for you? What do you two need? I brought champagne. Let's open it. I brought food too as even though we're in Florence I assume it's a global truth that all hospital food is disgusting.'

He sets about opening the hamper, removing champagne flutes and a bottle of Veuve Clicquot.

Delphi hovers watching him, her face alight with happiness.

'When did you arrive in Europe? Why didn't you tell me you were coming? How long are you staying?'

Removing the bottle's foil and muselet he turns towards her. 'I arrived last night and am only here until the end of the week. Then I'm due in London with just enough time for a stiff martini at The Savoy before heading to Cambridge. A Cantabrigian reunion. I've not been back since I graduated it will be fascinating to see who's dead, how many marriages we've all chewed through and how harrowingly old everyone looks.' Neither of them mention the fact that he will see Edward there. Her father loves that sort of thing. It makes him swell with sentimentality, belonging and pride.

'To answer your question, the timing has been perfect. When you wrote to me about your pregnancy I organised my trip a little earlier than already planned and here I am with you. Full of love and astonishment. I also received a charming muti-coloured letter from your friend Romy.'

'Romy?' asks Delphi.

'Yes, that's the one, like Romy Sedgwick. Now she was a great beauty. Tragic story. You know one brother killed himself, another drove into the side of a bus and she, Romy, went out to sea on a perilous raft of barbiturates and alcohol.'

'Yes, but why did my Rom write?'

'I remember meeting her when you graduated from Art School. Impossible to forget her Mohawk. She said how important it would be for me to make it to Italy. I was very touched actually.' And so is Delphi now. He pops the cork from the champagne, hands her a flute and offers a toast.

'To this fresh new human. May she grow strong and rich and take care of all of us in our dotage.'

As they touch their glasses together the door bursts open and standing as if he has travelled across the desert on foot, is Art. He looks quickly but appreciatively at the dapper Hugh and transfers his attention to Delphi.

Delphi hears herself squeal and it takes her a moment to recognise where the sound of unencumbered joy has sprung from.

'Art!' she screams. 'I cannot believe it. You came!' She had so hoped one of them would but to have both is so wonderful she is lost for words.

As he walks toward her tears flood his eyes. He encircles the females and showers them in snatches of poetry interspersed with declarations of love.

'Well, most glorious child. You're a Russian doll now. Duplicated. And I am here. Of course I came. I've come to mother you into submission!' He kisses her hand and then gestures for the baby.

'May I have her, Delphi? Put her in my arms this instant before my heart fails with yearning.'

'Submission?' muses Hugh. 'Good luck getting Delphi Hoffman to submit.'

Art nods. 'Perhaps supplication is the better word?' He winks at Hugh and turns back to Delphi. 'I want to hear every detail of the birth! Wholly fascinating what you women can do.'

Delphi hands the baby across and introduces the men.

'Art Horowitz, please meet my godfather, Hugh Harrison.' Both men have heard about the other already.

Hugh holds out his hand, but Art is having none of it. He steps forward and kisses Hugh firmly on the cheek. Delphi looks at these men through new eyes and she's struck by how compatible they are. Two sides of the same coin or maybe reflections of each other. Delphi observes her understanding of the world expand. She has finally escaped herself and the paradox is that in doing so she has come home.

'So, you're Delphi's famous godfather? You're a lucky man and a devilishly handsome one.'

Art sparkles and Hugh looks uncharacteristically flustered. Delphi laughs so loudly that her baby jumps in Art's arms, her eyes open wide. Art looking momentarily like a little boy himself asks, 'Am I intruding? I know this is a time for family.'

Delphi and Hugh reassure him he is not. Hugh says, 'I've heard from Delphi how kind you've been to her, so it is good to meet you.'

'The pleasure is mine.' Art does a small bow.

'And Art you are my family.' says Delphi.

'Oh child, and you are mine. Hugh, from the moment I met your god-daughter I knew we'd been on this earth together before.' Hugh represses the impulse to roll his eyes, as he has no time for this kind of talk but Art is entirely undeterred. 'My soul recognised hers and I know what it is to be without family. And now this baby. It's wonderfully crackers, but I felt compelled to come, but I don't want to assume nor inveigle myself into this delightful scene so let me know when I should go?'

'Never,' Delphi says cleaving to him, assuring him that his arrival is a gift of solid gold.

CHAPTER 28

THE HIRE CAR IS puttering up the hill to Delphi's villa. She is in the back seat beside her baby daughter in her capsule. Art is at the wheel.

'Child, I am still furious that the gods of theatrical timing delivered me to you late. Bastards of the highest order. Imagine the wondrousness if I'd burst into the labour suite as I intended. I would have declared myself the father. It would have so confused them. A baby. Nothing is more magical. I can't tell you how privileged I feel to be here. I thought firstborns never came on their due date.' His shoulders are shimmying with delight.

Delphi smiles. Art hasn't stopped taking. He is brimming with bonhomie and he's taking them home. Delphi can't remember ever being happier.

'Romy is longing to see you too, Delphi girl. Her flight got in an hour ago.' He looks at his watch. 'Maybe not as much as that. Maybe more. Who knows in Italy? She is going to take a taxi directly to your villa and will be waiting for you and your baby Jesus. For her to come to the hospital was logistically risky with your lack of discharge time. Italy is so disorganised. Wouldn't stand in Britain.'

'Arthur, can you talk of the baby being Jesus when she's a girl?'

'Oh darling, you shock me, so binary. What would Jesus say to you about that?' The car fills with their laughter.

'So, I know we have spoken about this in our letters but I must say it to your seraphic face.' He turns from the road to look earnestly into Delphi's eyes in the backseat. 'I am simply appalled by your experience at The Bodhi Famiglia, child. I desperately regret sending you there. If I had any idea, you do know I'd never have done it.'

'Art, eyes front please.' She makes a note to never let Art and Adarsha into a car together or they'd surely plough off the road.

He redirects his eyes and swerves the car back into lane.

'Art, I have accepted your apology many times over. Truly, I have no bad feelings toward you at all. You didn't know. I chose to go there. I chose to stay, and I chose to run for it, thank God. As upsetting as the whole fiasco was, I learnt a lot.'

'That is deeply gracious, child. If you ever send me off to a cult I'm telling you now, you shall be dead to me, as the young of today say.' Delphi smiles, recognising Romy's term in Art's mouth. She loves their friendship.

'At the very least it will be a splendid chapter in your memoir. This may be inappropriate but I do want to hear more about it if that's not…' he falters looking for the word. Delphi tries to help him, 'triggering?'

'Indeed! Exactly that!'

'My therapist thinks I've processed it all pretty well. But God, Art, it was full on. When I left I thought they were all insane but now, I don't know. I think Christoph is…' her voice becomes soft. 'What I felt for him was like a wildfire, it was mad, breathless… I did a lot of projecting onto him, maybe it was actually one hundred per cent desire, or worse, unadulterated neediness,' she grimaces, 'But whatever it was, I don't want it in my life. I want peace. He's a fanatic. A charismatic, brilliant, saucy as hell, special breed of narcissus. And such good hair. Really ten out of ten for his hair situation.'

Art slaps the steering wheel. 'Oh Delphi, he sounds like my perfect cup of tea! I do adore my men mad, dominating and saucy. Maybe we should drop in for a visit?'

'Art, I ran for it in the pitch dark being chased by Christoph's lackey and a terrifying cackling woman. Although my phone and computer are still there, unless Gita has incinerated them to keep the place pure.'

'Sorry Delphi, my joke was in poor taste. I wasn't really suggesting we go.'

Delphi lets his words fade as she brushes the back of her baby's hand with her lips, and glows with a deep-rooted sense of serenity, contemplating her sleeping infant, each hairpin bend taking them closer to home. She can't wait to see Romy, and to be shepherded to her by this exuberant, caring man. Delphi is suffused with hope.

'It's left here, that driveway.' Delphi leans forward between the front seats so she can direct him. Art swears loudly. 'Jesus, Mary and Joseph.'

As he reverses erratically, he declares, 'Listen to me, obviously feeling exceedingly religious today. I did mention I don't have my licence?'

Delphi is happy he's only telling her that at the end of their journey.

'But how did you hire a car without a licence?'

'Oh, these Italians love to break the rules if you charm them a little and pay them a lot.'

As soon as they are parked in the driveway, Romy bounds around the car in a technicolored rah-rah skirt to pull open the door. Delphi steps out and the women hold each other tightly.

'Perfect timing! I just arrived. Minx, you're a mummy!'

'I am, Romy. Who'd have thought it?'

Art retrieves the luggage and heads off with it singing something from Verde at the top of his lungs.

'It's the absolute best! Can I get her out?' Romy's hair is a bright pink mullet, lending her the guise of a fairy with a proclivity for naughtiness. She has plastic rings that look like boiled sweets on every finger.

'Yes, of course. Careful though, her neck is like asparagus.'

'Oh God, what does that mean?'

'Just support her neck or her head flops about.'

Delphi turns her face to the sun and blinks into the dappled light. Was the world really this beautiful before?

Romy fiddles with the buckles. 'Welcome to our family, little dude. I'm your auntie Rom. Balls, these capsule clips are insanely complicated. Seriously these are fully sponsored by Bastard Incorporated.' She finally lifts the baby free and walks as if holding a bomb back around the car to Delphi.

'Oh, I like her, Del. Let's keep her. What's her name? Mini Minx?'

Delphi leans in, smelling her child's tiny head.

'Grace. I've named her Grace.'

'That's awesome. So perfect.'

'And her middle name is Romy.' Delphi reaches out for her friend. 'You want to be her God-mummy?'

Romy looks as if she's won all the prizes. 'Oh Delph, I'd seriously love too.'

'Rom, thank you for coming to Italy and I'm sorry I disappeared on you for a bit there. I'm sorry about the bloody cult. You were right and I should've listened. I couldn't see it and then when I did I wanted to protect you from how lost I was.'

Romy's face is clear and open. 'Minx, you had some serious grieving to do.'

'Yep, I did, as well as some growing up, but you, you're an all-out guardian angel.'

The women rest their heads against each other's.

'Minx, you've held me up plenty of times, this was just my turn.'

The baby starts squirming and Romy freaks out.

'Will you take her; I don't want to drop her on her coconut.' Romy puts the baby into Delphi's arms. 'Surreal, Minx, you're a natural, looks like you've been her mother forever.' They walk into the courtyard where Romy's backpack is propped up against the stairs.

Art calls out to them from above. He has a bottle of Dom Perignon in one hand and a filled coupe in the other. 'I have arranged a brunch banquet for mother and child. Come in and prepare to be adored. The Indians believe in the Red Tent. Well, I Arthur, King of the Britons, believe in the tent of cheese, olives and bubbles.' He gulps at his drink and brings down the empty glass like a sword.

*

Romy and Art have gone to collect supplies for dinner. Delphi sits, blissed out, under the shade of a tree in the garden feeding Grace. She hears the car return and half listens for their chattering voices. Art and Romy often talk at once, but still seem to understand each other perfectly.

She sees a lone man walking into the courtyard. Hugh is not due for hours and she doesn't recognise this figure so she watches him looking about. He turns around surveying. He looks displaced, hesitant, then he freezes when he sees her. After a solid moment he lifts a hand in salutation. The sun is directly behind him and Delphi waves back lazily.

The man walks toward her and a dawning takes place. Delphi recognises his gait. He steps up the small terrace and comes to a stop a few metres from her. Grace suckles, oblivious to what is about to unfold.

'Hello Orlo,' Delphi says softly.

'Hello Delphi,' he answers. They regard each other.

The silence begins to set itself into stone, but Delphi is not going to take responsibility to soften it. She doesn't do that anymore. Orlo looks to the baby and lifts a hand to his chest.

'Delphi, I hope I'm not encroaching.'

She is listening, her head tilted to the side.

He runs a hand through his hair. 'Romy contacted me to tell me…' he waves an arm in the direction of the baby.

'How?' Delphi asks.

'Ah, she hunted me down online. I have been living in Berlin and just had an exhibition.'

'Congratulations,' she says.

'No, I don't mean… I tell you that because there was some press and a new gallery, that's how she reached me.'

Sweet Romy, Delphi thinks. Disconnection causes her as much unrest as it does Delphi. Love is always a verb for both of them. She thinks back to that evening in Art's apartment when she cried in Romy's lap about Orlo and the love she couldn't shut down.

'Delphi, why didn't you tell me?' he asks gently.

'I did try Orlo. I rang, I sent a letter, I emailed Horizon Art. When you didn't respond I assumed you didn't want to know.'

'Oh, that's terrible. Was the letter addressed to the studio?'

'Yes.'

'I don't rent that space anymore. I don't know why the gallery didn't forward me your email, they knew where I was. I hoped you'd get in touch. And you called?'

Delphi nods. 'The gallery, not your mobile. I lost your number.' 'You lost my number?' Incredulity furrows his brow.

'Yes, my phone was stolen.'

They look at each other, he goes to speak and falters. He clenches his jaw and then tries again. 'I can't properly express how sorry I am that I missed you. If I knew you were pregnant… When Romy told me… and that your mother died…'

She looks down at her baby.

'Delphi, I was really confused when we last saw each other. You just vanished after we… after we met. I called and texted. You ghosted me. You broke my heart.'

Delphi swallows, and without bitterness, explains. 'I went back to your studio to tell you I was going to my mother and I saw you on the street with your arms around your lover. So I guess we're even. You broke my heart, too.'

Orlo looks confused. 'What? When? I didn't have a lover. I've not had a lover since you.'

Delphi directs his memory. 'The tall woman with the long black hair. She looked like Russian nobility.'

Orlo squints as if attempting to solve an impenetrable equation.

'Martha? Oh, Delphi, do you mean Martha?' He smiles.

Delphi prickles with indignation.

'Martha is my little sister.'

Delphi returns to the image of the two of them on the street. She tried so hard to wipe it from her memory but has no problem calling it up. Betrayal burns its imagery sharp. So, the reason they looked so compatible is that they are drawn from the same pool of DNA. Now she understands and it seems rash to have thought otherwise. She was paranoid and skittish. She hardly recognises that version of herself anymore.

'Oh,' Delphi says.

'Yes,' Orlo confirms.

The pair of them allow the other to reconfigure and what remains are two people, virtual strangers yet irrevocably interconnected.

Grace has dozed off. Delphi stretches out a hand to Orlo. 'Come, meet her,' she says.

Orlo steps forward and he takes Delphi's hand. He looks at the bundle in her arms. He quietly and slowly bends to his knees.

'My God,' he utters disbelievingly.

'She is four days old. Her name is Grace. She is 52 centimetres long. Tall like both of us. She was born on my brother Arthur's birthday. Which is a crazy sort of perfect.' Delphi studies Orlo's transfixed face. 'You are not trapped by this. By her nor by me. I don't need anything from you. Don't feel afraid.'

He lifts his face that is filled with tenderness and says, 'I'm not afraid.' Delphi laughs and Orlo blanches. 'What?'

'Oh, it's just… that's good and it makes me realise that I'm not either. I have been for so long, since I was six, and it's extraordinary to be finally free.'

Orlo nods and returns to Grace. 'She's the loveliest thing I've ever seen.'

He reaches out to gently touch their baby's head and on his forearm is a gorgeous, old-school tattoo of an anchor.

'Did you have that when we met?' Delphi asks, resisting the urge to touch it.

'Yes. I've had it for years.'

'How strange…'

'What?'

'I don't remember it.' Delphi wonders about seeing new things in old things and all the times she just mustn't have been ready to see.

Grace opens her eyes and then closes them again.

'*La maison est ton ancre*,' Delphi says quietly.

'You speak French?' They look at each other.

'No. Not at all. It's something my mother used to say.'

'Home is your anchor?' Orlo translates asking her.

'Yes,' Delphi answers, and smiles at him.

*

Delphi is standing at the window holding Grace. Below in the liquid amber dusk, her people are laughing and celebrating. Hugh, Romy, Orlo, Art, Lucia, Roberto and the Downstairs Man. They sit scattered about in chairs dragged into the last of the sun. Art insisted on music, scandalised it wasn't available, Roberto went away and came back with portable speakers. Now Iron and Wine melts all the edges and Art is dancing, twirling slow circles with a champagne glass held aloft and a smile on his face. Lucia is giggling and flirty, uncharacteristically giddy around Orlo. Roberto still eating is nodding and listening to Romy talk passionately about fermenting kimchi. Hugh is off in the olive grove looking at the ancient plants. The Downstairs Man is reading the paper through his milk bottle glasses. Romy, not faltering in her food talk, readjusts a blanket around his shoulders. She performs this intimacy with such an ease, as if they've known each other forever. Downstairs Man has not seen so much social action for years and he looks up at Romy as if she were sunshine after weeks of rain. Berlusconi is sleeping in the centre of the circle. His dear furry head resting on his paws.

And Orlo. Today the truth is that he has been deeply gracious. Empathising with him, feeling her way into his position Delphi is lit with quiet admiration. He has delivered kindness and walked with great sensitivity. His presence has a gentleness and a goodness that simply feels right.

These lovely people, all of them, they are her tribe, her chosen family. She looks at her baby. 'We found them, darling. Just in the nick of time.'

Behind her on the kitchen table are flowers from Adarsha and another bunch from Jack waiting to be put into a vase. His card is warm, celebrating Grace's birth, promising he will visit in nine days with Maria and Zenia. He also shares that their grandfather had squirrelled away a small inheritance for them both. 'Not enough to buy a house but certainly enough to keep the wolves from the door.'

Noise from the revellers makes Grace stir. Delphi walks her into their bedroom. The shutters are wide open and Florence glitters below. Delphi looks over at her mother's ashes on the chest of drawers and says to Grace, 'Tomorrow, let's go and scatter your grandmother's ashes. I think it's time, what about you?' The baby mewls contentedly, Delphi talks on. 'Sleep, my darling. Sleep and I will be here when you wake. Don't ever feel you need to save me, Grace, because something I know for sure is that the only person who can save you, is yourself. My story isn't about fear or loss anymore, baby girl. It's a love story.'

Delphi gently rocks back and forth. Hopeful. Peaceful. Open. 'Let's go and join them shall we, darling?'

ACKNOWLEDGEMENTS

THANK YOU JAMES KELLOW, debonair gatekeeper who took a risk on me. I hope this novel is a success primarily so you will be happy, and so you don't rescind the advance for book two. I am indebted to you and so grateful and thrilled to be a part of Ultimo's stable and vision.

Alex Craig and the full glorious team at Ultimo Press, Brigid Mullane, Katherine Rajwar, Robert Watkins, Emily Cook, Alisa Ahmed, thank you. You made my literary dreams come true. A double helping of gratitude to Alex of the enormous brain, and Jody Lee for editing me through snowstorms and valleys of briars. Who on earth could have imagined one writer to use the words *beauty* or *fold* so many times? Thank you also to Sandy Grant and the good people of Hardie Grant. And Amy Daoud for your elegant cover design. I'm proud to have my words nestled inside it.

Sometimes in life we are lucky enough to meet a guardian angel, like Delphi does in Art, and as I did with Lou Johnson. Lou, you are a golden light and I can't thank you enough for shining your radiance on me. You are all things wonderful and generous. You made me lucky.

Jeanne Ryckmans. Queen. Cameron Creswell Agency. I want to take up smoking ciggies so I can be more like you. Thank you for being in my corner and being so passionate and fantastically cool, irreverent, and smart about everything.

I want to buy each and every one of you a pony.

To my astute first readers and beloved friends; top of the list, Polly McGee my soul sibster, you are a one person cheerleading squad on roller-skates. Your ferocious support, endless generosity, love, wisdom and delicious humour have kept me dancing. Brigid Delaney for reading a few early pages and saying, 'Keep going, it's good.' I put those encouraging words into my heart like rouns and kept on writing. Thank you for your testimonial and celebrating my wins with champagne fizzing joy. Jen Peedom, master of story arc and talking me down off ledges, Mark Rogers photographer (and headshot) extraordinaire, thank you both for always asking, and always loving.

Jemma Birrell, soothsayer and dispeller of dragons. You read the manuscript when your toddler had just been ill and you were fending off the same virus. Such an abundance of kindness surely has a wonderful German word? Your encouragement kept me together when I was in danger of shattering. Thank you Lauren Pearson, I feel badly that I asked your expert eyes to read the first draft. The fact that you still want to be my friend speaks volumes about your generosity. To Roland and Kathleen from The Writers' Studio for giving me the structure to finally get this story out.

Also Jason Burrows for that handshake on a Bondi balcony committing to our pact to create.

My cousin Ed and Alex, whose daughter is the original Delphi, thank you for letting me borrow her mighty name.

And the crowd goes wild!

To my brothers, and our parents. Thank you, I love you.

To Solace, my wirehaired dachshund and constant writing companion. I put a version of you in this novel as Pilot. In the next book you'll be the romantic lead.

It's nearly drop the mic time…

My children, Luna, Viva, Truman and Lorenzo (our Zen Zen). Being your mother is the greatest privilege and deepest joy of my life.

And Martin, you are the best thing to ever happen to me. I always longed for home, I never found it in any one place, but I found it with you.

Zoë Coyle is the founder and CEO of the leadership training company Pilot Light Consulting. She has four children and a wirehaired dachshund named Solace. *Where the Light Gets In* is her first novel.